DECEPTION'S SWEET KISS

GINA ROBINS

ZEBRA BOOKS
KENSINGTON PUBLISHING CORP.

ZEBRA BOOKS

are published by

Kensington Publishing Corp.
475 Park Avenue South
New York, NY 10016

First printing: April, 1990

Printed in the United States of America

This book is dedicated to my husband, Ed, and my children Christie, Jill, and Kurt. With much love . . .

Part I

If one *sees* only what one *thinks* one sees, one had better look again. . . .

Chapter 1

St. Louis, Missouri
February 1867

Holt Cantrell surveyed the group of men who had joined him in the private conference room in the back of Molly's Tavern. The flickering lantern light skipped over the faces of the judge, marshal, and three of the city's most influential potentates—a merchant, hotel owner, and lawyer.

Restlessly, Holt brushed his gloved hand over the itchy gray beard that lined his jaws. With a flick of his wrist he rearranged a lock of silver hair that toppled from under his plug hat. Stealing a glance at the door that led into the alley, he reached down to pat the huge shaggy black-haired dog that sat beside him. The mongrel's broad, dome-shaped head was raised to his master. With an impatient whine the mutt pulled himself up onto his long legs and wagged his tail. His round black eyes focused on the gray-haired aristocrat.

"Did you bring the money?" the sober-faced judge demanded. "We haven't got all night, and I don't want to be seen leaving this meeting. I have an image to uphold."

9

Holt puffed on his cigar and sent several swirls of smoke drifting in lopsided halos around his head. He gestured toward his vest pocket and forced a reassuring smile. "It's all here, Judge. I just want to make certain my investment pays off. When I'm appointed mayor, I want to reap the same benefits as the rest of you have received at the taxpayers' expense."

"You will," Marshal Jacobs grunted. "You'll get all the considerations the rest of these men do. For a price, I'll turn my head the other way when necessity dictates."

Holt's emerald-green eyes darted toward the door, and then he focused his attention on his associates. Ever so slowly, he reached inside his black waistcoat to produce the roll of cash that was to be paid in initial fees to join the judge, marshal, and lawyer, who had formed a secret committee and who had cleverly devised underhanded means to make themselves wealthy by draining municipal funds.

Just as Holt began to dole out the cash the back door slammed against the wall, sending a dribble of dust trickling from the woodwork. Garret Robertson's gigantic form filled the entrance. With a menacing snarl he pointed his Colt .45 at the astounded group of dignitaries.

"Sit easy, gentlemen," Garret demanded as three other Pinkerton detectives filed into the room to hold the astounded group at gunpoint.

With a muted growl Holt Cantrell bolted to his feet, causing his chair to crash against the wall. While the dignitaries sat frozen to their seats, their jaws hanging open, Holt whipped the pistol from his belt and aimed it at Garret Robertson's gorilla-size chest. Before Holt could squeeze the trigger, Garret's Colt barked in the stilted silence. With a groan Holt pitched across the table to land in a lifeless heap. His gray head and arms dangled over the edge of the table and two long legs sprawled out behind him. Dead. The victim of the Pinkerton detective's accurate aim.

The stunned congregation stared at their departed associate and decided not to move a muscle for fear they would wind up in the same state of eternal sleep. They had come to collect their shares of bribe money and had wound up witnessing a daring escape attempt and the consequent murder of their newest committeeman.

Like a lumbering elephant Garret tromped across the room to throw Holt's motionless body over his shoulder. His ominous gaze focused on the men, who sat like marble statues. "If you resist arrest, gentlemen, you'll wind up just like this idiotic fool," he guaranteed in a foreboding tone. His penetrating black eyes swung back to the other three detectives. "Put them in jail. The marshal is going to discover what it's like to stare at the world from *inside* the bars for a change. This is the last time this city is going to be under the thumb of these swindling politicians and supposedly honest officials."

When Garret stalked out the door with Holt's limp body draped over one huge shoulder, the oversize mutt, who was Holt's constant shadow, trotted behind his lifeless master, expelling a mournful whine.

At the threat of being shot down for attempting escape, the other potentates stood with hands high above their heads while the detectives gathered the bribe money. After the procession was trotted off to jail like a column of ants, Garret strode deeper into the alley. There he paused to set the "corpse" on his feet.

"What took you so damned long?" Holt demanded as he peeled off his stage mustache and beard and wiry gray wig. With one fluid motion he shrugged off the padded waistcoat that made him appear twenty

11

pounds heavier than he actually was. "I was afraid those swindlers would have the money stashed in their pockets before you showed up to catch them red-handed."

Garret caught the heavy waistcoat Holt tossed at him. It still amazed him that Holt had so easily assumed the identity of the eastern aristocrat he had apprehended the previous month and then infiltrated the moneymongers of St. Louis. Holt had set those arrogant officials up for the biggest fall of their lives. They had been skimming money from the city's operating expenses and running a scam of protective surveillance that earned them payoffs from business-men who were forced to contribute to the protection agency headed by the crooked marshal. They didn't have the faintest notion how the Pinkerton detectives had managed to sniff them out. They were so cautious with their schemes. Holt had a special talent for espionage, and his imaginative investigations had become legendary during the war. Although Holt's name was never flaunted around the Pinkerton Detective Agency, he was the secret agent who was most in demand—by reputation, never by name. . . .

When Holt repeated his question, Garret gave himself a mental shake and shrugged off his musings. "We were running late," he murmured in explanation, and then handed Holt the telegram from Allan Pinkerton.

"It's about time," Holt grunted after he read the message.

Holt shucked the breeches that he wore over his own clothes and hurriedly stuffed his disguise in the saddlebag. A wry smile pursed Garret's lips as he assessed the handsome rake who looked his old self again—six-foot-two inches and two hundred pounds of steel-honed muscles and lightning-quick reflexes. If

12

the men Holt had just sent off to jail could see him now, they wouldn't believe it was the same man. But, of course, they assumed that Holt, alias Jason Marsh, had been shot to death. They had seen it with their own eyes and had no reason to believe that a corpse could get up and swagger around on his own accord.

Garret grinned broadly as Holt swung onto his horse with graceful ease. "You've died so many times the past few years, you ought to be accustomed to near brushes with disaster," he teased his longtime friend.

Holt raked his fingers through his thick black hair and settled himself in the saddle, prepared for the tiresome ride that lay ahead. "I don't mind having you shoot blanks at me, but Marshal Jacobs knows how to handle a pistol too damned well. If he thought for a minute that I was the one who set up this raid, he would have shot me himself. He was suspicious of me since the beginning of this assignment."

With a nod of farewell Holt nudged his bay gelding through the alley. When Holt and his devoted mongrel disappeared into the darkness, Garret heaved a heavy sigh. After the sound of hooves evaported into silence, Garret pivoted on his heel to send off a telegram to the United States marshal and to Allan Pinkerton, who was the chief of the detective agency that had been established in Chicago seventeen years earlier.

While Garret wrapped up this assignment and filed criminal charges against the swindlers who had been stealing the taxpayers blind, Holt was setting up his scheme to infiltrate another band of criminals who plagued Missouri. And this was one job Holt was eager to take. He had a personal score to settle in southwestern Missouri. He was always determined to see justice served, but particularly so in this case. . . .

Chapter 2

Carthage, Missouri
June 1867

The sun peeked above the jagged horizon of trees, announcing the birth of another blustery day. The warble of birds in the overhanging trees mingled with the steady clop of hooves as the procession of outlaws paraded toward the still-sleeping town of Carthage. Holt's keen green eyes darted to the maze of trees that skirted the rutted road before he focused on the wooden bridge that lay a stone's throw ahead of them. With purposeful nonchalance he glanced back at the desperadoes with whom he had been cavorting for the past three months. Holt's long, shaggy mane, mustache, and beard gave him a most formidable appearance. He was dressed in worn buckskins and armed to the teeth, like the rest of the brigands. He looked as rough, tough, rugged, and unkempt as the men whose company he was keeping. Any unsuspecting passerby would certainly have assumed he was cut from the same rotten scrap of wood as his ruthless companions. And that was exactly what Holt wanted them to think.

At that moment none of the other banditos

15

anticipated trouble. They were filled with confidence as they rode toward the Carthage bank they intended to rob the instant the doors were opened to the local patrons.

The moment Holt's steed clomped across the bridge, Garret Robertson sprang from the underbrush with a Winchester poised in his arms. Emitting a mutinous roar, Holt latched on to his pistol. When Garret's weapon discharged, Holt teetered precariously in the saddle. With a pained groan he tumbled from his steed and plunged off the side of the bridge into the creek. Not to be left behind, the shaggy mongrel who followed Holt everywhere dove off the bridge into the water beside his master.

The desperadoes, unprepared to be bushwhacked by a posse of Pinkerton detectives who had appeard out of nowhere at just the right moment, wheeled about to dash off in the direction they had come. A volley of bullets whizzed through the air and the buscaderos answered with blazing pistols.

While the other dozen detectives surrounded the survivors of the ambush, Garret scurried down the embankment to locate the man he had pretended to shoot for the sixth time in two years.

Looking like a drowned rat, Holt pulled himself onto the bank and raked the wet strands of raven hair from his eyes. As Garret sidestepped down the slope, Holt rolled to his feet to fish into his pocket. When he extracted the damp map he laid it in Garret's oversize hand.

"This will lead you to the money the Henson gang buried last month after they robbed the train," he explained. His anxious gaze fastened on his brawny friend. "Is Bob Henson still alive?"

Garret shrugged noncommittally as he surveyed Holt's map. "I told the men you wanted Bob to live

16

long enough to interrogate him, but I'm not sure how bad he was hit. The last time I saw that murdering son of a bitch he was firing from both hips at our men."

"Get the rest of the gang away from Bob," Holt commanded. "I want him all to myself."

"But you're supposed to be dead," Garret croaked as he followed Holt up the steep embankment. "If one of the survivors of the gang spreads the news that you are actually an undercover agent for Pinkerton, your life won't be worth a red cent!"

Holt wasn't listening, and he was long gone before Garret could claw his way up the hill. "He always takes too damned many reckless chances," Garret muttered to the dripping mutt.

Garret knew why Holt wanted to interrogate Bob Henson, but if any of the banditos saw him, Holt would find himself followed by a vengeful death wish. Shaking his head, he grumbled at the reckless daredevil who had constantly laid his life on the line. Holt's devil-may-care attitude scared the living daylights out of Garret.

While Garret rounded up the gang of buscaderos that had terrorized southwestern Missouri during and after the war, Holt crouched in the brush, waiting to get his hands on Bob Henson. When the detectives led their captives away, Holt strode toward the scraggly renegade who lay faceup in the grass, bleeding all over himself.

Surprise registered in Bob's pained gaze when he realized the man he had known as Tom Morris had been responsible for the disaster that would inevitably cost him his life. "Damn, you miserable bastard," Bob spat viciously. "You set us up!"

Bob's mutinous voice caused the shaggy mutt to pounce at him. Holt snapped his fingers and the mongrel sat back down, but he curled his lips to display

17

the deadly set of fangs, just in case Bob foolishly thought his bark was worse than his bite. The dog had never liked the scraggly renegade, and he had no qualms about taking a few bites out of the outlaw leader's hide.

"Where's Kirby Thorn?" Holt questioned in a harsh growl.

Bob grimaced in pain. "I'll never tell you, you sneaky son of a bitch. You're one of Pinkerton's men, aren't you?"

With a wordless snarl Holt gave the outlaw leader a fierce shake that sent his head snapping backward. "Tell me, damn you," he demanded in a whiplash voice. "If you don't, I'll cut you up in bite-size pieces and feed your carcass to Dog. He'd love that. He's wanted to make a meal of you since the first day we infiltrated your gang."

"Why should I care what happens if I'm dead?" Bob sneered in defiance.

Dog growled at the haughty outlaw and Holt trembled with raw fury. He had tolerated this vile vermin for three months when he would have preferred to slit his throat at first sight. When Bob refused to talk, Holt twisted his arm up his back, converting his pain into agony.

"Why do you want to know?" Bob queried, sucking in a ragged breath.

"Anna . . ." Holt gritted out between clenched teeth.

The last speck of color ebbed from Bob's ashen face. The name triggered a flood of memories. During the war Bob Henson and Kirby Thorn had thrown in together to form a Confederate guerrilla band and had staged hit-and-run raids on Union troops along the Missouri-Kansas border. At one time there had been fourteen men in the band. With commando precision the renegades had struck against Union troops and

Northern sympathizers. They had spawned a wave of terror with their raiding, plundering, and murdering campaigns. They had become addicted to blood, lust, and booty, and they had never batted an eye at murdering at random. It had become their way of life.

Bob and his one-time partner, Kirby Thorn, had raided a farm in southwest Missouri. After plundering the home for food and supplies, they had murdered the old man and kidnapped the spirited young woman to satisfy their lusts. It was Bob and Kirby's hungry desire to possess the pretty spitfire that had inevitably caused conflict between the two men. They had battled for sole possession over who would keep Anna for his private pleasure. Kirby, being the more brutal and ruthless of the two, had come away from the fisticuffs with the spoils of battle in tow. If not for the interference of Bob's brother, Kirby would have riddled Bob with bullets.

While Bob was left to recover from his wounds, Kirby took half the gang and Anna and rode off into parts unknown. Later Bob had learned from one of the men who left to rejoin the Henson gang that Kirby had cruelly disposed of Anna when she attempted to escape him for the third time.

If Bob Henson weren't the kind of man who held a grudge, he never would have answered Holt's demanding question with his last dying breath. But he had his own personal vendetta against Kirby Thorn, one he wouldn't live to satisfy. He ached to see Kirby as deep in hell as a buzzard could fly in a week. And if this cunning undercover agent could see to it that Kirby was roasting over the hottest fire in Hades, more power to him. Mustering his last bit of energy, Bob stared up into the icy green eyes that drilled into him.

"Texas . . ." he breathed before he collapsed, never to rise again.

With considerable effort Holt attempted to compose himself. It had been almost two years since the bloodthirsty outlaw gang had raided and plundered the sprawling farm that was nestled in the Ozark Mountains. And for two tormenting years Holt had waited to satisfy his thirst for revenge. One of the two men who had molested Anna and murdered his father was dead. But while Kirby Thorn was running around loose, leaving a bloodbath in the wake of his trail of terror, Holt could never rest.

It was premeditation and forethought that had allowed Holt to infiltrate Henson's gang, hoping to learn about Kirby's activities as well as destroy this band of desperadoes. Cautiously, Holt had laid the groundwork, building a formidable reputation for himself through posters and hearsay that would gain him the trust of these renegades. Employing the alias of Tom Morris, Holt had contacted law officials in St. Louis and ordered a warrant posted for Tom's arrest. With a long list of concocted crimes that would appeal to these scalawags to his credit, and a sketch of his face, Holt had set about to lure Bob Henson to him.

After a month of making a nuisance of himself in Carthage and other nearby towns, one of Henson's men had approached him with a proposition. And for two months Holt had licked his lips in anticipation of serving these bastards their just desserts. They had left a path of blood and destruction in Missouri before scampering back to their hideout in Indian territory, where state and federal marshals had one helluva time locating them. But at long last the trap had been sprung. Bob Henson was dead and the survivors of the gang were on their way to the gallows.

Even though most of the men who were responsible for his father's and Anna's death were either dead or waiting the hangman's noose, Holt wanted Kirby

Thorn with a passion that overshadowed all other thought. Holt had never forgiven himself for not being there when Anna needed him most. He should at least have left Dog with her for protection. But Holt had taken the invaluable mongrel when he was sent on a reconnaissance mission in the South. Too late he learned of the tragedy that still haunted his thoughts. He was a man hounded by guilt and remorse. When Holt finally caught up with Kirby and extracted his vengeance, maybe he could put his life back in perspective. . . .

Shaking off the gruesome thoughts of what Anna had endured, Holt stalked over to retrieve his gelding. Someday, somehow, he was going to catch up with Kirby Thorn and his recently formed outlaw gang that was lying low in Texas. At least now Holt knew where to begin his search. He felt certain Pinkerton would give him authority to track the deadly killer. This was one assignment Holt would gladly accept. He couldn't get on with his life until he had avenged Anna's violent death.

Anna. . . . Holt squeezed back the tender memories of flaming chestnut hair, sparkling hazel eyes, and a dazzling smile. God, he bled every time he imagined the hell Anna had lived through while Kirby and Bob used her to satisfy their animal lusts. The last few months of her life must have been a nightmare that made dying a blessing.

Swearing vehemently, Holt stuffed his foot in the stirrup and trotted off through the trees, leaving Garret to wrap up the loose ends and take all the glory for apprehending another swarm of criminals. But Holt didn't give a damn about the publicity. He preferred to remain the unsung hero who infiltrated hoodlum gangs and risked his life to serve as the invisible arm of the law. He wasn't in the detective business for the praise, but for the satisfaction of a job well done. Holt agreed to take only the most dangerous assignments, to challenge his abilities and sharpen his wits for the task that lay ahead of him—confronting Kirby Thorn. As long as Kirby Thorn was alive, Holt could never be content. He had just one purpose, even if he was forced to bide his time and take the other assignments Pinkerton requested of him. But one day, Holt swore, he'd send Kirby Thorn on a one-way trip to hell!

Chapter 3

Rolla, Missouri
June 1867

Allan Pinkerton stared at the swarthy but undeniably handsome man who had served him long and well during and after the war. Holt, his valuable guard dog, and Garret Robertson made a remarkable team that could tackle the impossible. Holt Cantrell was the most inventive spymaster and detective in the country. He played by his own rules and made them up as he went along. His uncanny knack with disguises, his shrewd perceptiveness, and deadly calm made his accomplishments phenomenal. Holt had a gambler's daring, a limitless imagination, and breathtaking boldness. His incredible powers of observation, cold nerve, unshakable composure, and accuracy with all sorts of weapons allowed him to excel where other men would have failed.

Through the years Allan had given Holt several impossible tasks, and this daredevil never met with defeat. It was Holt's partner, the giant of a man by the name of Garret Robertson, who was credited with the feats. But Holt was the mastermind behind every accomplishment, the silent force that got things done when less competent men would have met with disaster.

Holt had worked in espionage behind Confederate lines and infiltrated guerrilla bands. He had played the role of the village idiot, the rough-edged renegade, and the dignified gentleman all with fascinating ease. At age thirty there was very little Holt Cantrell hadn't done and done exceptionally well. He was the most sought-after detective in the agency. When a desperate client requested the best man on Pinkerton's staff and offered to pay a bonus for the privilege of buying the services of Pinkerton's "special agent," Holt was offered the assignment and he named his own price. The raven-haired, green-eyed rake always found inventive ways to get his foot in doors that remained closed to other agents.

But for the past two years Holt had become even more daring in his manhunts and secret missions. He seemed to defy death, and Garret had privately asked Allan to give Holt an assignment that would overpower his obsession with the task of hunting down the Thorn gang.

Allan knew what Holt was about to ask him because Garret had briefed the detective chief the moment he stepped out of the southwest branch of the Pacific Railroad depot in Rolla. But Allan had another assignment in mind for Holt anyway. Garret needn't have warned Allan about the task Holt wanted to assume in Texas. Holt wasn't going, not yet, and that was that.

Patiently, Allan listened to Holt explain his suggestions of drifting into Texas to locate and infiltrate the Thorn gang. When Holt laid out his detailed plan, Allan gave his head a shake and fastened his somber gaze on his indispensable agent.

"I have received an urgent request from J. W. Baxter, who is president of the railroad line that intends to extend its tracks through Kansas into Indian territory and on to Texas," he announced while Holt muttered under his breath.

"I have no desire to ride up and down the rails like unclaimed baggage, keeping an eye out for suspicious characters who are contemplating robbing trains," Holt snorted disdainfully. "Give the job to somebody else."

"Just hear me out, Holt," Allan insisted as he accepted the drink Garret offered him. "Baxter suspects that the rival company based in Springfield has been utilizing underhanded tactics to lay rails across southern Missouri to reach the border of the Badlands. Baxter is certain there is corruption in the company and that the president himself is the ringleader who is cheating stockholders out of their money. We have been asked to investigate Colonel Victor McBride's railroad company. J. W. Baxter is certain McBride has overstretched the government guidelines to gain federal funds and win the race to Texas. McBride has been accused of getting his contracts from the government by bribing officials and luring in politicians and eastern tycoons. McBride's company, to whom public domain and rights-of-way have been lavishly granted, offers him unlimited opportunity for plunder and fraud."

Disinterestedly, Holt reached down to pat Dog's broad head. The answer was no. He had already made up his mind, even if he was courteous enough to let Allan have his say.

"McBride received a thirty-year loan of government bonds to value twenty-five million dollars and has graciously been allowed to mortgage the company's properties to that same sum of twenty-five million,"

Allan went on to say. "At present he is working to get the government to allocate Indian lands in the territory to his railroad company so he can mortgage those rights-of-way for another eight million. J. W. Baxter contends that McBride has stooped to bribery, dirty dealing, and only God knows what else to gain investors and real estate for his railroad."

Still brooding over Allan's rejection of his plans to take the Thorn case, Holt puffed on his cigar and stroked Dog's muscular neck. Allan peered soberly at the man who had surrounded himself in a cloud of smoke.

"You do remember the name Colonel Victor McBride, don't you, Holt?" Allan smirked when his agent never changed expression. That was another of Holt's multiple talents. His handsome face was a mask that revealed none of his emotions unless it was his wont. He could be consumed with murdering fury or utter boredom, and no one would ever know it until it was too late.

"I remember," Holt acknowledged. "But I also remember what Kirby Thorn did to Anna and I want that son of a bitch's head on a platter," he added in a bitter tone.

Discreetly, Allan shot Garret a sideways glance. Both men exchanged a silent message before Allan focused his full attention on the tall man who had unfolded himself from his chair to pace his elaborate hotel suite.

"I know you want your own personal revenge on Thorn," Allan said in a patronizing manner. "I want him out of action as much as you do. But he has gone into hiding and it could take six months to locate him. He'll be back in Missouri one day. This is his stomping ground, and he always returns to prey on familiar territory. I'll send some of my men to Texas to look around while you're investigating the feud between Baxter and McBride. They are both eager to place the first railroad through Indian territory and tap the riches of Texas and Mexico. I ask it as a personal favor, Holt."

Holt stopped short. With unexpected grace he ambled back to peer down at the detective chief. His piercing gaze swept from the plug hat that sat perched on Allan's thinning hair, past the deepset eyes and long, straight nose. Silently he assessed the close-trimmed beard that rimmed Allan's face. Allan was a Scottish-born immigrant who had settled in Illinois in 1843. He had been the first detective on the Chicago police force and had decided to form his own agency in 1850. For years he had worked with the Illinois Central Railroad, supplying them with guards to prevent robberies.

When the war broke out, Lincoln had asked Pinkerton to set up a secret service for the Union Army. Using the alias of Major E. J. Allen, Pinkerton had sniffed out a plot to assassinate Lincoln on the train from Baltimore to Washington and had sent out a corps of agents to infiltrate enemy lines. Holt had been in constant contact with Allan and greatly admired his tireless efforts during and after the war. Allan was always conscientious and dedicated. He made certain his clients were satisfied and that justice was served. But there were times when a man had to reject requests for personal favors from his friends. This was one of those times.

"I don't want the case. I want Thorn and I don't want anyone but me to tangle with that bloodthirsty maniac," he growled irritably. "Kirby Thorn is all mine."

"I wasn't suggesting that someone else flush him out," Allan hastily informed Holt. "I only suggest letting some of our experienced trackers do the legwork for you. It would save you several months of chasing down possible leads. When you go after Thorn, you'll know exactly where to find him."

Pensively, Holt puffed on his cheroot. After a moment he sank deeply into his chair and stretched his long, muscular legs out in front of him. "Garret has been bending your ear since he picked you up at the depot, hasn't he?" he questioned point-blank.

Both Garret's and Allan's eyes flew wide open. Neither of them had mentioned their private conference, so how the devil did Holt know what they were discussing behind his back? Mental telepathy? Allan wouldn't have been surprised. That would certainly explain how this brawny detective could outguess his quarry nine times out of ten.

"Garret did suggest that you were pushing yourself too hard," Allan murmured tactfully. "But he has your best interest at heart. Why, I'll wager that in two months you can offer J. W. Baxter a report on the workings of the McBride Railroad Company. By then there will be several strong leads on Kirby Thorn awaiting you and you can go after him with my blessing."

"Are you guaranteeing that?" Holt scoffed. "Thorn has eluded detectives and law officials for more than ten months."

Allan's deepset eyes drilled into those well-disciplined green pools that disguised all emotion. "I'll take the assignment myself if I have to," Allan promised. "Now, are you going to listen to the information I've gathered about the railroad rivalry and their race to the border, or aren't you?"

Long black lashes swept up to survey the Goliath of a man who towered beside the smaller Allan Pinkerton. Garret Robertson resembled a granite mountain. He stood six feet six inches in his stocking feet and weighed two hundred sixty-five pounds if he weighed an ounce. Every sinewy inch of this massive gorilla was unbreakable bone and iron-hard muscle. Garret was bigger than your average lumberjack. He had shoulders like a buffalo and huge hands that could squeeze the life out of any foe. He looked as if he were considering applying brute force to convince Holt to accept this assignment.

Holt and Garret had wound up in only one or two fights through the years they had worked together—fisticuffs that had been staged for a group of men who were convinced Holt was a Yankee spy. He was, of course, but the Confederates certainly didn't need to know that!

Holt, strong as he was, was barely an equal for Garret's beefy fists. It was only Holt's lightning-fast reflexes and quick reactions that would save him from being pulverized if he and Garret ever fought in earnest.

"Take the damned job," Garret growled, his muscled arms flexing in silent threat.

"You aren't my mother, for God's sake," Holt grumbled at his burly friend. "It shouldn't make a bit of difference to you whether I investigate McBride's company or track down Kirby Thorn."

"It matters," Garret snapped gruffly. "You saved my life once and I haven't forgotten. And in my opinion, you've been pushing way too hard. You want Thorn, but he isn't ripe for the picking just yet. If you go after him now, you'll get yourself killed, and I'm not sure I can prevent it." He exhaled in a rush. "Let some of the other agents do your footwork for you in Texas while you enjoy the luxuries of fancy railroad cars and mingle with high society in Springfield."

Holt took a long draw on his cigarillo and stared meditatively at the towering giant. "And just what is

Allan going to have you do while I'm tripping the light fantastic in Springfield, pretending to be an investor interested in McBride's company?"

A wide grin spread across Garret's leathery features. With his flair for the ridiculous, he flexed his already bulging muscles and struck a pose. "I'm hiring on the road gang that's laying tracks near Primrose," Garret announced with a chuckle. "Pinkerton wasn't certain whether the scandal of unauthorized money that is changing hands is McBride's doing or if one of his associates down the line is turning his own tidy profit. I'll be sniffing out information at the bottom of the totem pole while you are perched on the top."

Holt grinned despite himself. Garret reminded him of Atlas poised with the world on his broad shoulders. Maybe Holt did need to set aside his fierce preoccupation with Thorn for a few months and reevaluate this obsessive hatred. He had to keep his wits about him when he confronted Thorn. Holt could not allow his personal vendetta to overrule caution and logic. One careless mistake, and he could follow Anna to her grave before he had avenged her senseless death.

"All right, dammit," Holt muttered begrudgingly. "I'll take the assignment." When Garret and Allan beamed triumphantly, Holt punished them with a frown. "But I'm holding you to your promise, Allan. I expect an informative report when I ride off after Thorn at the end of this assignment."

"You can have the Thorn case and the report," Allan obliged. Setting his glass aside, he extended his hand to shake on the compromise. "I'll explain the situation in the McBride Railroad Company over dinner."

"Good, I'm so hungry I could eat a horse," Garret inserted, snatching up his hat and leading the way to the door.

"It looks as if you already did," Holt teased as he

30

moseyed across the room.

"I can't help it if it takes a ton of nourishment to keep me operating at top efficiency," Garret mumbled as he lumbered down the hall. He stared accusingly at Dog. "I don't eat as much as your mutt, and you don't complain about him."

"Don't sulk," Holt snickered, patting his friend on the shoulder. "I'll buy you a whole pie for dessert."

"I couldn't eat the whole thing!" Garret objected. But the way he licked his lips indicated he could and would with the least bit of encouragement.

"Of course you can," Holt insisted.

"Well, maybe I could at that," Garret concurred with a hungry grin.

"I thought so," Holt countered as he strode down the corridor, flanked by Garret and Allan and followed by his constant shadow—Dog.

While Garret was swallowing his food like a python, Allan offered detailed information about the workings of McBride and his company. By the time Allan completed his soliloquy, Holt had decided on his method of infiltration.

Pushing back in his chair, Holt lit his cheroot. "It seems Victor McBride's daughter is my avenue. All I have to do is pretend to be an eager investor and charm Miss McBride into inviting me into her home."

Allan shook his head in response to the suggestion. "That won't work," he told Holt flatly.

One thick brow climbed to a challenging angle. "Are you implying I don't have the ability to charm a woman?"

Allan knew perfectly well that was one of the many things this suave, charismatic rogue did best, even better perhaps than his endless talents of apprehending criminals. "I'm forewarning you that Shiloh McBride, lovely and witty though she is, is also a dreadful cynic who views the male population as a colony of lepers. She has been courted by both aristocrats and adventurers, and they've slinked away with their tails between their legs after she broke their hearts. She has a low tolerance for fortune hunters and overzealous rakes. According to reports, Shiloh was jilted by a debonair adventurer who had designs on her fortune. She and her father were living in St. Louis at the time. Victor was commanding Union troops and the fortune hunter moved in to work his wiles on Shiloh, who was a naive seventeen-year-old debutante. She fell hopelessly in love with the rake and he cast her aside when a wealthy young widow caught his roving eye."

"And so Shiloh McBride hates all men on general principle," Holt concluded. "If I cast her an interested glance, will she automatically despise me?"

"In a word—yes," Allan remarked with a sigh. "Shiloh accepts dates to social functions that her father requests she attend. She fraternizes with his clients and keeps company with Victor's potential investors, but they receive no more than her token courtesy. Since her ill-fated romance four years ago, she has become a bit of a shrew, and when she loses her temper"—he shook his head dismally—"well, a man doesn't want to be within ten feet of her when she becomes doubled-up fists and flying fur. The more suave and charismatic her suitors are, the less attention she grants them. And when one of them dares to overstep his bounds, he comes away sporting the scars of battle."

Allan touched the napkin to his lips and chuckled. "I am one of the first to boast your legendary talents with women, Holt. But utilizing Miss McBride as a gambit is a dead-end street. She has become extremely cautious and very perceptive since her heart was broken. I myself have seen and heard her physically and verbally unman one overeager beau who took liberties with her. Why, the poor dandy only tried to steal a harmless kiss and she brought him to his knees with a well-aimed blow that caused his voice to become two octaves higher than normal—permanently.

"And after she raked the man over the coals with insults that cut his dented male pride to the quick, her suitor literally crawled out the door! To say that Shiloh is the ice maiden of Springfield and a terrorist in expensive silk doesn't do that lovely lady justice. She is a fire-breathing hellion whom her father has spoiled terribly. She has become so fiercely independent and wary of men that she is practically unmanageable. I would have to say Shiloh is uncourtable, even to a man like you. Her only weakness, as near as I can tell, is that she loves her father dearly. He is the only man she will tolerate for extended periods of time. . . ."

Allan's voice trailed off when he noticed the wry smile on Holt's full lips. "Have you suddenly concocted a way to get your foot in the door?" he questioned, cocking a curious brow.

Holt blew a ring of smoke and gave his raven head a nod. "I do believe I have."

When Holt didn't bother to elaborate, Allan peered impatiently at him. "Well? How are you going to go about worming your way into the organization without drawing suspicion on yourself?" he wanted to know that very second.

Holt grinned devilishly while he watched Garret attack his steak with a vengeance. "It's simple. I'll defeat Shiloh McBride at her own game," he explained in an optimistic tone.

"And just exactly what is that supposed to mean?" Allan frowned puzzledly.

Holt plucked up a chunk of steak from his plate and

33

tossed it to Dog. "You see to it that my credentials are in order and that I come highly recommended from the East," Holt requested.

Allan began a mental list of information required to certify Holt as a man with King Midas's touch when it came to making money. His reputation would precede him to Springfield. By the time Holt arrived, using another of his aliases, he would be the most sought-after investment potential in the state of Missouri. Allan would see to that.

"What name will you be using this time?" Allan queried.

Holt gave the matter a moment's consideration. "Reuben Gilcrest," he decided. "Reuben was raised by his spinster aunt Mildred, educated in a private male seminary in . . . let's say Chicago, since I'm familiar with the city. Reuben was born with a silver spoon in his mouth and a legacy of millions at his fingertips. Every investment he has made has earned him another fortune. He knows nothing about the railroad industry, but he envisions a direct route to Texas and Mexico which would be as beneficial as the transcontinental rails to California."

"Is that all?" Allan questioned as he hurriedly jotted down notes.

"No." Holt stared Allan squarely in the eye, and with a straight face he added, "Reuben is painfully shy and awkward around women. He is a wealthy, eligible bachelor who lacks nerve around the female of the species, and he becomes so nervous that he turns into a bungling oaf around women. If Shiloh is the ice maiden of Springfield, she wouldn't be the least bit intimidated by a clumsy millionaire whose self-confidence wouldn't fill a thimble when he comes within two feet of the fair sex."

Garret and Allan stared at the clean-shaven man

34

who was grinning roguishly. Holt Cantrell, shy and awkward around women? That would be the day! Women flocked to him like kittens on the trail of fresh milk. He could never pull off such a difficult charade. The aura of virile masculinity that clung to him would never permit it.

"Your mind has finally snapped," Garret snorted sarcastically. "You've played a helluva lot of masquerades over the years, but none as out of character as this! You can't do it! Shiloh would see through you in a minute."

Two black brows jackknifed. "Are you willing to bet I can't convince Miss McBride that she doesn't have to fear for her virtues when Reuben Gilcrest is underfoot?"

"Damned right I am," Garret challenged between bites.

When he had licked his platter clean, the waitress set an entire pie beneath his nose. When Holt cast the wench an appreciative glance, Garret knew he would win this wager hands down. Women were naturally drawn to Holt. They always had been and they always would be. That was a simple fact of life. Shiloh McBride would take one look at this swarthy rake and know in a minute that Holt was more man than his supposed reputation with women suggested. She would feel threatened and Holt would be kicked out the door on his backside.

Very sure of himself, Garret dug into his pocket to fish out a twenty-dollar gold piece. "If you last three days in Miss McBride's company without her realizing your role is a sham, this coin is yours. If not, you owe me twenty dollars, friend," Garret wagered.

Holt smiled wryly. "And if I win the bet, you have to be nice to Dog for the rest of his life."

Garret slanted the ugly mutt a distasteful glance. He had tolerated Dog's presence because Holt kept the animal with him constantly. Garret couldn't say for certain why he didn't like the mongrel, he just didn't. It surely couldn't be because he was jealous of all the consideration Holt gave the oversize creature. Hell, Holt treated Dog as if he were a human, and he carried on conversations with Dog as if he possessed more than simple canine intelligence.

"Oh, all right," Garret muttered resentfully. "It's a bet. Thank God I know I'll win. But in the event I don't, I draw the line at sharing my meals with that fleabag mutt the way you do."

Holt snickered as he stroked Dog's broad black head. "You wouldn't share a meal with a starved orphan," he mocked playfully. "Not the way you lust after food."

"I wouldn't deprive a . . ." Garret started to protest.

"I was only kidding, and you damned well know it," Holt interjected, and then gestured toward the meringue pie. "Eat your dessert. I have a few matters to attend to this evening, and none of them involves debating with you whether you eat more than an entire cavalry troop."

Grumbling at Holt's taunts, Garret gobbled his pie while Allan jotted down a few ideas to lend credence to Holt's latest charade. Allan wasn't confident that Holt could hoodwink the young woman in question. The saucy blonde was no man's fool, to be sure. Allan thought it wiser to make friends with one of McBride's close associates than tangle with that sassy little minx. Although Allan admired Shiloh's spunk, he wouldn't have wanted to pit himself against that sharp-tongued, quick-witted sprite. If she became suspicious, the entire ploy would split wide open and the Pinkerton Detective Agency would wind up with a black eye.

"If you foul up this assignment, we'll never be able to infiltrate McBride's company again," Allan warned with a stern glance. "You better know what you're doing."

The reckless smile slid off Holt's lips when the trickery of his thoughts led him back through time to the one unpleasant memory that haunted him. As much as he thrived on challenges in his job and derived satisfaction from seeing justice served, it still stabbed his soul when he thought of Anna and his decision to once again postpone tracking Kirby Thorn.

"The only reason I'm taking this case at all is because you promised to locate Thorn for me," Holt countered as he climbed to his feet. "Now, if you two gentlemen will excuse me, I have things to do."

Garret smirked as Holt sashayed across the restaurant with Dog plodding behind him. *"Things to do* with that flirtatious wench who was giving him the eye in the hotel lobby, he means," Garret chuckled.

Allan pursed his lips to prevent a smile from bursting free. "He does have an incredible way with women, doesn't he?"

Garret expelled a heavy sigh. "Yeah, but since Anna died, he goes from one female to another without feeling much of anything. It nearly killed him when he discovered what horrors she had suffered. I wonder if Holt will ever let himself care about anyone as strongly as he cared about Anna. It's as if he's afraid to experience any kind of attachment, especially to women. Hell, Dog receives more genuine affection from Holt than most people do."

"Maybe when he finally locates Kirby Thorn, he can lay the ghosts to rest," Allan murmured sympathetically. "Holt is too good a man to walk around with open wounds tormenting him. It has made him a little too daring and reckless lately."

"Amen to that," Garret chimed in. "It seems the only reason he has stayed alive is so he can repay that murdering bastard for what he did to Anna. Until Holt gets his hands on that scoundrel, he seems determined to take on all the Kirby Thorns in the world."

While Garret finished off his pie, he mulled over Holt's attitude of late. Lord, he would be glad when Holt satisfied his vengeance. But now was not the time. Holt had met himself coming and going, refusing to take time off between assignments. Hopefully, the McBride investigation would be less difficult than the other jobs Holt had tackled the past year. He definitely needed to take a breather.

A sly smile hovered on Garret's lips. Maybe Shiloh would provide a challenging distraction for Holt. He could certainly use one! The man was working himself to death.

Chapter 4

A look of boredom etched Shiloh McBride's delicate features. Absently, she listened to her father boast about the prospective investor he had met at the company meeting the previous day. Her attention was focused more on Victor himself than on what he was saying while he restlessly paced the spacious study.

Victor was a fine figure of a man in Shiloh's opinion. His chestnut-brown hair and deep blue eyes gave him a striking appearance. At the age of forty-four her father was a powerhouse of energy, six feet and one hundred eighty pounds of finely tuned muscle. Since his wife Marjorie's death, Victor immersed himself in his work to compensate for the loneliness. He was ambitious, wealthy, and yet not content to sit back and count the money he had made in his business ventures. Victor was a doer—always on the go, always striving for excellence. During the war he had accepted a command in the Union Army and was quickly promoted to the rank of colonel. He and his regiment had seen action not only in war-torn Missouri, but also in the

Deep South.

There was very little about her father that Shiloh would have changed if she could. Her father had many saving graces, although there were some who would argue the point. In her estimation, his only fault was that he was a mite overprotective of her. Shiloh had grown up very quickly while her father was involved in battle. When he returned, he still treated her like a child. But he had made progress of late, she reminded herself as she watched Victor attempt to wear a path in the carpet. More and more, he was becoming aware that Shiloh had a mind of her own and that she knew how to take care of herself. There had been a time when he rushed in to fight her battles for her. But day by day he was beginning to realize that Shiloh was a very capable young woman whose free spirit refused to be stifled.

"I have invited Reuben Gilcrest to dine with us this afternoon and to join our company conference," Victor was saying when Shiloh finally got around to listening. "He will be our house guest for the next week."

Shiloh was not at all pleased to learn her father had invited the newcomer to stay at their home. As always, she was expected to be cordial and polite to her father's associates—a duty she would have preferred not to have delegated to her. But considering all her father had done for her, Shiloh decided she owed him that much and more. But in her cynical opinion, men were as annoying as a swarm of mosquitoes and she didn't give a flying fig about any of them. Since Lance Draper taught her the meaning of heartache and wounded pride, Shiloh had vowed never to let another man that close, never to allow her heart to be broken and her pride to be crushed again. She tolerated Victor's associates out of respect for him and for no other reason.

40

Distracted, Shiloh toyed with the renegade strand of silver-blond hair that had formed a ringlet at her temple. Lord, she would love to forgo lunch and exercise the palomino mare her father had presented to her for her twenty-first birthday. . . .

"Shiloh, did you hear what I said?" Victor demanded when Shiloh did not immediately respond to his comment.

Long, thick lashes fluttered up, and luminous silver-blue eyes glistened in the sunlight that splattered through the bay window. "I'm afraid not. My mind must have wandered."

"Now, blast it, Shiloh," Victor grumbled. "Pay attention. Reuben Gilcrest is a very important prospect. We need his money if we are to win this race with Baxter to the border. I want you to make Reuben feel welcome, and for God's sake don't badger him!"

A teasing smile pursed her heart-shaped lips. Primly, she settled the folds of her pale blue silk gown about her. "Shall I meet Reuben at the door with a shower of adoring kisses, Papa?"

Victor's winged brows arched over his intense blue eyes. "What I *don't* want is that you cut his pride to shreds and send him slinking off the way you did my last prospect's young son!" he replied with a volcanic snort. "Reuben is nothing like the other men I have asked you to politely entertain while they are guests in our home."

One delicate brow rose acutely. "No? Does he walk on all fours, then?" she mocked playfully.

Victor cast his mischievous daughter a withering glance. "I didn't say Reuben was a freak from a circus sideshow, only that he is . . . different from the men you know. He's"—Victor paused to formulate a tactful way to describe Reuben—"he's socially and physically clumsy and very shy and unsure of himself around women. Females make him extremely nervous, and he

41

has little confidence in handling the simplest of associations with them. I ask that you not ridicule him. He requires patience, sympathy, and understanding, and I need his investment."

Shiloh could not begin to picture the man her father described to her. The suitors who hounded her door never lacked arrogance or long lines of flattery that were designed to win her favor. Because of her skepticism of men and her mistrust of their underlying intentions, men were left to handle *her* with kid gloves, not the other way around.

"Please keep your snide remarks to yourself for once," Victor requested. "And spare Reuben your rapier wit. . . ."

The timid rap at the door interrupted Victor's last-minute instructions to his vivacious daughter. Spinning around, Victor strode into the foyer to greet his guest. Curiously, Shiloh bounded to her feet to have a look at the wealthy but painfully shy millionaire.

When the elaborately carved door swung open, Shiloh took one look at Reuben and burst out laughing. Quickly, she composed herself. Her scrutinizing gaze swept over Reuben's broad frame to peer at the powder-blue bowler that sat on his raven head. It was all Shiloh could do to prevent bursting into giggles as she assessed the six-foot-two-inch dandy who towered in the doorway. Reuben's ill-fitting hat sank so low on his forehead that it forced his ears to stick outward as if they had been glued onto the sides of his head. His darkly tanned face appeared small in comparison to his oversize hat. Large wire-rimmed spectacles sat on the bridge of his nose, giving him a froglike appearance. With one shaky finger Reuben reached up to poke his contrary glasses back into place while he removed his bowler.

The hat toppled from his head and, mumbling to

42

himself, Reuben bent over stiff-legged to snatch it up. Another amused smile pursed Shiloh's lips when she spied the midnight-dark hair that was crookedly parted in the middle and plastered down with enough beeswax to fill a hive. The man's expensive clothes hung off his tall, lean frame like garments on a clothes rack. The cravat that had been knotted around the starched collar of his white linen shirt looked as if it were strangling him. His attire did nothing to compliment his physique, and it was difficult to tell what lay beneath the sloppy garb. The black frock coat was at least two inches too short in the sleeves, and his sagging black breeches were so short they revealed the tops of his pointed boots. The embroidered handkerchief that protruded from the pocket of his blue checkered vest had not been neatly folded, but rather hastily stuffed inside to flop over like a wilted flower.

Muffling a snicker, Shiloh surveyed the thin mustache on his upper lip—one that looked noticeably unsymmetrical. The goatee that cupped his chin was just as uneven, and it made his face appear oddly lopsided. Her first impression of Reuben Gilcrest was that he didn't have the vaguest notion how to dress. He reminded Shiloh of the fairy tale in which it had taken a kiss to transform the pitiful frog into a charming prince. This unsightly toad would need a score of kisses if he were going to become anybody's Prince Charming!

Behind the round glasses, a pair of emerald-green eyes darted from side to side. Holt's uneasy gaze flicked past Victor to settle on Shiloh. The instant their eyes met, Holt's gaze dropped to his own boots as if they had suddenly demanded his rapt attention.

To his credit, though, Shiloh noticed, he had a straight nose, a strong jawline, carved features, and prominent cheekbones. His face was deeply tanned, and he had a full, sensuous mouth. But his barber and

43

tailor, if indeed he had visited such, had not done the man justice. His garments and hairstyle detracted from his assets, making him appear pitifully ridiculous. Even his poor posture indicated that he didn't find himself handsome and that he had absolutely no self-confidence.

Although Shiloh had never been able to muster a smidgen of sympathy for any man, she immediately put her guard down when Reuben was unable to return her smile. He did seem terribly self-conscious and unsure of himself in her presence. He resembled a gunshy rabbit who expected to be attacked from all directions at once. Even when Shiloh voiced a greeting, Reuben dodged her stare, unable to pay her the courtesy of looking at her for more than a tenth of a second. Uneasily, he studied his feet and toyed with the bowler hat that was clamped in his fists.

While Reuben murmured to Victor in a meek, melodic voice, he nervously began to twirl the hat on his forefinger. When his fumbling hand lost its grip, the hat plummeted to the floor a second time. Biting back a giggle, Shiloh watched as he made a bungling attempt to retrieve the hat before his shifting feet squished it flat.

Once Holt had jerked back to full stature to apologize all over himself for Reuben's clumsiness, Victor motioned for Shiloh to approach. Holt automatically retreated a step and ducked his head, showing Shiloh little more than the ridiculous part in his waxed hair.

Shiloh's attention shifted to the huge shaggy black dog that stood at Reuben's heels. When the mongrel spotted her, his tail slammed against the wall in an enthusiastic wag. To her disbelief, the creature reared up on his hind legs to place his gigantic paws on her shoulders. A startled shriek burst from Shiloh's lips when the mutt greeted her with a slobbery lick on

44

the cheek.

"Good God, Dog!" Holt croaked, aghast. "Sit down!"

Obediently, Dog hunkered down on his haunches and wagged his monstrous tail which pounded against the open door like a drumstick.

"I'm so sorry," Holt apologized all over the place. Nervously, he shoved his droopy spectacles back to the bridge of his nose for the umpteenth time. "I don't know what got into Dog. He must have taken an immediate liking to you, ma'am."

"Dog?" Shiloh scoffed as she dusted the pawprints from her puffed sleeves. "What an unimaginative name."

In silent reprisal, Victor gouged her from behind, but the gibe had already struck. Holt's face fell like a rockslide. Meekly, he reached down to pat Dog's broad head. "Perhaps so, ma'am," he murmured in a dejected tone. "I am a dull, unimaginative man, I suppose. But the name Dog seemed appropriate for him. He just sort of walked up to me one day and adopted me. It does not seem quite so important what is in a name, but rather the tone in which you convey it." For a scant second Holt's gaze flitted to Shiloh. "The tone of one's voice can cut quickly and deep, more so than simply stating a name. . . ."

His deflated voice and woebegone expression made Shiloh feel like a heel. Reuben had managed to put her in her place. "Forgive me," she murmured. "I should not have made such a rude remark."

She was apologizing to a man, even over an insignificant matter? She hadn't meant to, but something about this man had dragged the apology from her lips.

"Reuben Gilcrest, I would like to present my daughter, Shiloh," Victor said formally while Holt

45

shifted nervously from one foot to the other.

With exaggerated politeness Holt doubled over in an ungraceful bow. "It is a pleasure to make your acquaintance, ma'am." Rising, he pushed his spectacles back in place, extending an arm as if he meant to shake her hand. Then, in afterthought, he self-consciously dropped his arm at his side. "I'm really sorry about Dog. I haven't succeeded in teaching him his manners. When he meets someone he likes, he gets a mite carried away."

"Don't fret over your dog. Just fetch your luggage, Reuben," Victor insisted as he pivoted on his heels. "I'll show you to your room before our other dinner guests arrive."

With a nod of compliance Holt latched onto his satchels, clanking them against the door as he fumbled his way inside. Turning, he glanced back at the mutt, whose tail still banged against the doorjamb in a permanent wag. "You will have to stay outside, Dog," he cooed affectionately. "These nice people don't want you in their home."

"Poppycock," Victor sniffed in contradiction. "Bring Dog along."

Shiloh rolled her eyes as the overgrown mutt leapt onto all fours and charged off after his master. Sweet mercy, her father was right about Reuben Gilcrest, she mused as she watched him flounder up the spiral staircase. Shiloh could never recall meeting such a bashful man in all her life. His apparent wealth and expensive clothes hadn't given him one iota of confidence or arrogance. He had taken one look at Shiloh and all his fingers had turned to thumbs. He had been so nervous in her presence that he danced around as if he had ants in his drawers.

And those ill-fitting clothes! Shiloh burst into unrestrained giggles. He could use the advice of a good tailor. The man had possibilities with his handsome face and tall, lean physique. But his garments detracted from his strong attributes and called far too much attention to the weaker ones. What he needed was someone to take him under wing and teach him a thing or two about sophistication. Well, at least she wouldn't spend her time defending her virtue. Reuben was as harmless as a fly, Shiloh assured herself.

While Shiloh was wasting sympathy on the house guest, Holt Cantrell was silently chuckling to himself. He had given a most convincing performance, he thought. He had received not one wary glance from the ice maiden of Springfield. But it had taken incredible self-control on his part not to feast on that saucy little sprite in blue silk. He could have stood there the rest of the day paying homage to her femininity and sexuality if he hadn't had a role to play.

Allan Pinkerton's modest description of Shiloh did not do the lady justice. She wasn't lovely, she was downright breathtaking! She was five feet one inches and one hundred pounds of the prettiest package of femininity Holt had seen in a while. Her oval face was surrounded by silky tendrils of silver-blond hair that had been meticulously pinned in curls that accented her perfect features and the swanlike column of her neck. Her form-fitting gown called attention to her voluptuous figure, and the décolleté assured him that the young lady was exceptionally well endowed.

Some men were attracted to a shapely set of legs and others to a hypnotic sway of curvy hips. Then there were those, like Holt, who had a particular fascination with the upper portions of a woman's anatomy. It had taken incredible willpower not to stare at the creamy swells that rose and fell with each breath Shiloh inhaled. Good God, how was he to appear unaffected by that curvaceous blonde when the mere sight of her caused his capillaries to spring a leak?

Holt quickly decided Shiloh's pale-colored dress was as inappropriate to her as his clothing was to him. There were some individuals whose drab garments matched their dull personalities. Other folks selected vivid colors to call attention to their assets and dark ones to downplay their physical flaws. But Shiloh had no flaws that Holt could see, and the pale colors contradicted her vitality and strength of character. What she should have worn was startling colors that warned the world of her approach—bold red, sunny yellow, or bright green.

Holt sighed, remembering the delightful blush of sunshine that caressed Shiloh's satiny cheeks. It was certain that rambunctious beauty hadn't spent all her time under a parasol, shielding herself from the sun. Her face carried the natural blush of the whole outdoors. There was a bouncing spring in her walk—a strong inner driving force that oozed out of that decidedly feminine bundle of beauty.

And those eyes! Holt's face took on a dreamy expression. He had never seen such unusual eyes. They were such a light shade of blue that they almost appeared silver in the light. They sparkled with inner fire and untamed spirit, and Holt could have been mesmerized by them if he hadn't been so determined to portray the role of the bungling fop.

It was no wonder that tempting minx had to fend off overzealous beaus with a stick. Her tantalizing good looks invited admiring stares. Her scintillating figure provoked a man's caress, whether she welcomed a man's touch or not. It had been a long time since Holt had met a woman who had such an electrifying impression on him. He silently thanked Allan Pinkerton for insisting he take this assignment. It was going to be an amusing distraction and an intriguing challenge.

48

And by the time he was finished with the saucy firebrand, he would have her eating out of the palm of his hand instead of *biting* it.

While Victor was settling his visitor into the guest room, Shiloh breezed into her father's office to pour three glasses of Madeira wine. From all indication Reuben could use a drink, Shiloh mused . . . or three . . . to settle his nerves. He behaved as if women carried some terminal disease he might catch if he ventured too close. The poor man, Shiloh thought sympathetically, he was so inhibited that he couldn't meet her gaze or bear her touch in a harmless handshake.

Still tittering to herself, Shiloh swept into the richly decorated parlor to set the drinks on the coffee table and await the fumbling tycoon from Chicago. Shiloh's wandering thoughts conjured up Reuben's handsome face, wondering how he would look without those circular spectacles, lopsided mustache and goatee, and slicked-down hair that was haphazardly parted in the middle. He might well be a dashing prince if he could shed his uncomplimentary garb. Perhaps if she quelled Reuben's fears, he might turn out to be a prospective suitor whose company she'd enjoy rather than loathe. . . .

Shiloh gave herself a mental slap for visualizing Reuben as a possible beau. She didn't need a man in her life other than her father, not even a safe, harmless one like Reuben. . . .

Her head swiveled toward the door when Holt caught the toe of his boot on the edge of the carpet. Stumbling, he struggled to regain his balance before he sprawled on the floor. But the man's coordination was practically nonexistent. He flapped his arms like a windmill, teetering one way and then the other. Before he could upright himself with some degree of dignity,

Dog bounded forward and "Reuben" tripped over his mutt.

Swallowing a grin, Shiloh watched him untangle his long legs from Dog's. As if nothing out of the ordinary had happened, she patted the empty space beside her on the sofa. Holt stared at the spot as if a three-day-old fish were lying there. His expression suggested that sitting so close to a female was hazardous to his health.

"Come sit down, Reuben. I won't bite," she teased gently.

Ducking his head, Holt sidestepped around the coffee table to plunk down a safe distance away from Shiloh. Slumping forward, he laced and unlaced his fingers and swallowed with several noticeable gulps. When he spied the glass of wine, his hand shot out to it. But the abrupt movement caused his arm to collide with Shiloh's elbow just as she drew her glass to her lips.

The result was disastrous. Wine dribbled down her chin, slid down her throat, and trickled between the exposed swells of her breasts. With an embarrassed groan, Holt snatched up his handkerchief to dab at the spilled wine on Shiloh's clothes. His hand brushed across the creamy swells of her breasts and Shiloh flinched at the unfamiliar feel of a man's fingertips trespassing on private territory. Her involuntary reaction to being touched caused her to spill another drip of wine. This time Holt's sleeve was the recipient of splotches of liquor.

"Good God!" Seemingly horrified by touching the feminine parts of Shiloh's anatomy, Holt jerked back as if he had been bitten by a snake. Nervously, he patted the spills on his own sleeve. "I've made a bungling fool of myself again," he mumbled to himself. "It happens every blessed time I get too close to a woman." His well-guarded gaze darted to the petite blonde who was struggling to her feet. "Please don't take this personally, ma'am. This has nothing to do with you. I just have this unreasonable fear of women. I always seem to do the wrong thing when I'm near them!"

If any other man had made such a fumbling mistake and laid a hand on her bosom, Shiloh would have chewed him up one side and down the other and then pounded him into the floor. But Reuben looked so pitifully apologetic to her that she couldn't remain angry with him.

Her dainty hand folded around his, urging him to his feet. "Come along, Reuben. We had both better change before Papa's associates arrive." When Holt refused to be uprooted from his spot, Shiloh smiled disarmingly. "All will be forgiven if you escort me up the steps so I don't trip over my feet."

That wasn't likely, of course. Shiloh was as graceful as a gazelle and as surefooted as a mule. If there was any tripping to be done, chances were Reuben would be doing it, she mused.

Reluctantly, Holt rose to full stature and offered Victor a murmured apology before he fell into step behind Shiloh. Like a lanky puppy, he followed Shiloh up the steps, muffling his amusement behind an artificial cough. This curvaceous minx didn't have the foggiest notion that she had participated in his staged performance.

Garret Robertson was going to lose his bet, Holt assured himself confidently. He not only had his foot in the door, he had Shiloh's sympathy. He had skillfully burrowed through her barriers of defense. Instead of shying away from him like a skittish colt, she was leading *him* up the staircase by the hand!

Chapter 5

In the twinkling of an eye Holt shucked his stained jacket and shrugged on another one that was just as uncomplimentary to his muscular physique. Hurriedly, he whizzed down the hall to barge into Shiloh's room without announcing himself—on purpose, of course. To his delight, Shiloh was standing in her chemise and petticoats and he was allowed a delicious view of her arresting figure. And she was gorgeous! Silky arms and legs protruded from her skimpy undergarments. The rose-tipped crests of her breasts peeked back at him through the sheer fabric, and Holt felt the stirring of arousal in his loins.

"I wanted to apologize again for . . ."

A sharp gasp erupted from Shiloh's lips when Holt burst in to see her in a state of undress. Her face flushed seven shades of red. Awkwardly, she clutched her discarded gown in front of her.

Seemingly horrified by his bunder, Holt spun around to stare at the wall. But Shiloh's shapely figure was shadowed on the tapestry that decorated her elaborately furnished boudoir. "I'm so embarrassed I could die!" Holt wailed. "I thought you would have been dressed by now, and I felt the need to apologize once again for spilling wine on your lovely gown. I must apologize for barging in on you. I don't know what has happened to my manners." Holt smiled wickedly at the wall. "You are so extremely beautiful, ma'am, that I am more uncomfortable and nervous around you than I am around most women."

Shiloh stared at Holt's stooped shoulders and wide back. He was truly afraid of her, she realized with a start. He did not have enough self-confidence when he was near a female to fill a thimble. And he appeared more upset by the incident than she was, even though he was the first man to see her in her unmentionables.

"I . . . a . . . that is . . . a, should I . . . a," Holt faltered as he leaned his weight on one foot and then the other. "Should I offer a marriage proposal after I burst in to see you in such an indecent manner? I had no intention of soiling your reputation or causing you distress. Or perhaps it is proper for me to offer to pay for your soiled gown and dented dignity." His breath came out in a rush. "Good God, I'm not sure what is the gentlemanly thing to do when a man humiliates a properly bred young lady in such a scandalous manner. This has never happened before!"

A sympathetic smile widened Shiloh's lips as she tossed her soiled dress aside and wiggled into another. She had no fear that he would turn around to gape at her. Reuben Gilcrest posed no threat, and she felt oddly at ease with him, even in this awkward situation.

"There was no harm done," Shiloh insisted as she pulled on her pale yellow gown that was adorned with row upon row of dainty ruffles.

Just listen to her! *She* was comforting *Reuben*. That was a switch. If any other man had caught her with her dress down, she would have seen to it that he was stabbed, shot, and hanged. But Reuben had made an honest mistake and it was obvious that he was chagrined by his blunder.

"I expect no retribution or compensation," Shiloh assured him. "And you certainly don't have to propose to salvage my dignity. You don't seem all that eager to take a wife, and I wouldn't saddle you with one just because of this minor incident. Don't give the matter another thought."

Holt expelled a deep sigh. "It isn't that I wouldn't like to have a wife," he said ruefully. "But the truth is, ma'am, I'm not sure what to do with one if I had one. I . . . a . . . I'm not experienced with women, and it would be my wife who would wind up at the short end of the bargain."

Shiloh smiled to herself. It was the first time she had met a man who had as little experience in passion as she did. If she knew that Holt Cantrell, alias Reuben Gilcrest, had probably forgotten more about love-making and seduction than she could possibly hope to learn in her lifetime, she would have snatched up the figurine from the nightstand and beat him black and blue.

"Reuben, could I impose upon you to help me with these lacings," she requested after struggling in vain to fasten the garment into place. "Marcella is downstairs seeing to the last-minute preparations for lunch."

Reuben wheeled about to gape at her through his spectacles and his jaw dropped. "I'm not sure I should or could, ma'am!" he chirped, even though he was licking his lips in anticipation of touching her again. "I've already soiled your garments, intruded on your privacy, and I have seen far more of you than a gentleman should see of a lady who is not his wife! I have offended you in every possible way, and I am deeply ashamed of myself."

"Just fasten the lacings, Reuben," she insisted as she moved gracefully toward him and watched him cower in the corner. "I give you my word that you will not be poisoned if you touch me."

When Shiloh pirouetted in front of him, Holt smiled roguishly. In all the years of working for Pinkerton's agency, Holt had never enjoyed a charade quite as much as this one. Purposely fumbling, he struggled with the lacings, delighting in the feel of Shiloh's silky flesh beneath his fingertips.

And for the first time in a long time, thoughts of Anna didn't distract him. Shiloh totally preoccupied him, and he had to fight down the maddening urge to spread a few dozen kisses along the alabaster column of her neck and shoulder. She aroused him without trying. And if this cynical beauty could have read his mind at this moment, she would have had him dragged to the gallows and hanged within the hour! Lord, he was already addicted to touching her and fantasizing about how it would feel to have her luscious body lying intimately against his.

After Holt had fastened her gown, Shiloh turned to face him. His gaze immediately dropped to the floor, and he refused to meet her eyes. "This is a painfully uncomfortable situation, ma'am," he murmured awkwardly. "In less than an hour I have made an ass of myself twice . . ." Holt groaned miserably as he danced around on one foot and then the other. "Forgive me, ma'am. You have me so rattled that now my tongue has outdistanced my brain. I hope my language didn't offend you. What I meant to say was that I have made a *mule* of myself again."

For the life of her, Shiloh didn't know why she reached out to lift his chin, forcing him to meet her gaze. Furthermore, she had not a clue why she made the brash request that leapt from her lips. It wasn't at all like her to invite a man's attention. But Reuben needed to bolster his self-confidence, she thought, and she intended to see that he did.

"Reuben, I want you to kiss me," she requested point-blank.

Holt's green eyes popped behind his spectacles, ones that would steam up if this desirable imp didn't watch her step. And he would give himself away if he buckled beneath the lusty passion this curvaceous beauty aroused in him. Never in his wildest dreams did he expect this cynical sprite to verbalize such a bold invitation!

"I—I don't think that is such a good idea," Holt croaked. "I might hurt you, and I have done that several times already."

"I happen to think it is a very good idea," Shiloh contradicted him, staring into his fascinating green eyes. "You need to know that a woman is not a creature to be avoided as if she carried some deadly disease. And I would very much like you to kiss me."

Holt's painful expression was not all make-believe. What he wanted from this tantalizing minx had nothing to do with strengthening his self-esteem and everything to do with appeasing needs she instilled in him. He wanted to kiss her senseless, to caress what his eyes had devoured, to feel her shapely body molded to his masculine contours. But that would have been out of character for the bashful Reuben Gilcrest.

When Shiloh reached up on tiptoe and wrapped her arms around his neck, Holt shuddered in barely restrained desire. He was not accustomed to having a woman in his arms without appeasing his basic needs. And if he didn't tread carefully, he would melt to the consistency of strawberry jam and give himself away by doing what came naturally.

Shiloh, inexperienced though she was, placed a passionate kiss on Holt's full, sensuous lips. He barely responded to her amorous assault, and Shiloh found herself challenged in a way she had never been before. It was the first time she had invited a man's kiss and was allowed to instigate it. But he gave nothing in return. That stung her feminine pride more than she ever thought it would.

Gracefully, she withdrew to peer into those fathomless green lakes that were surrounded by a fan of long black lashes—ones that were magnified by his rounded glasses. "Don't you find me desirable or attractive?" she questioned huskily, tracing his lips with her forefinger.

Hell, yes, he did! He wanted to gobble this appetizing morsel alive. "Of course I think you're pretty, ma'am," he insisted in a strained voice.

"And desirable?" she prodded him, trekking a tapered finger along the lapel of his navy blue frock coat.

Holt removed her straying hand. "Of course I do. What man wouldn't?" he squeaked nervously. "But I would have to have a good deal more practice in kissing before I could ever hope to pleasure a sophisticated woman like you."

Sophisticated? Shiloh would have laughed out loud if she didn't fear treading on his sensitive emotions. What she knew about passion and desire couldn't fill the first page of a sex manual!

With no fear of attack, she laid her arms over his broad shoulders. "To be honest, Reuben, I haven't had much experience myself. Mostly, I find myself fending off unwanted advances. But it's different with you—a refreshing change that I would like to enjoy . . . if only you will let me. . . ."

Jeez*us!* Holt thought with a strangulated gulp. He had been patting himself on the back for his successful ruse, but he had waded in over his head. Lately he hadn't given a thought to the females who found their way into his arms. He simply took what they had to offer and then went on his merry way when his needs were satisfied.

"I don't think . . ."

Shiloh refused to permit Holt to finish his sentence. Her fingers slid around his neck, drawing his face to hers. Timidly, he kissed her, using only a scant few of the zillion techniques he had perfected. Shiloh responded, unafraid that this man would take unfair advantage of her. For once she merely enjoyed the feel of a man's lips playing tenderly upon hers. She became vividly aware of the man who had hesitantly slid his arms around her to cradle her against him. Beneath the sloppy garments was warm, solid flesh, a man who had great potential in pleasing a woman if he could ever overcome the hurdle of self-consciousness. . . .

To Shiloh's amazement, she felt an unfamiliar tingle of excitement trickling through her. It astounded her that she was physically attracted to this mild-mannered millionaire who had an unreasonable fear of women. But his gentle, inquiring kiss had stirred something deep and unexpected inside her. And it wasn't she who pulled away from their embrace. It was Reuben, and Shiloh wasn't quite ready to let him go.

Dragging in a ragged breath, Holt tugged at his cravat to relieve the pressure of having his heart thump against his ribs like a boxer pounding a punching bag. "Colonel McBride is probably wondering what is keeping us, ma'am," he murmured hoarsely. "It will take me a moment to compose myself." His green eyes darted to her momentarily before he looked away. "I feel a mite woozy after our kiss. . . ."

So did Shiloh. The kiss had worked like a magic potion. It didn't matter so much how ridiculous Reuben looked in his baggy clothes or that his waxed hair, mustache, and spectacles detracted from his stunning looks, she mused. It was the man inside who moved her to tender emotion. Reuben was huggable and kissable and he didn't intimidate Shiloh in the least. She could lower her guard and be herself with Reuben without fearing repercussions.

A muddled frown knit her brows when Reuben backed farther away and dropped his head. "I think I know why you are being nice to me, ma'am," he murmured flatly. "Your father asked you to be polite because I am a potential investor. But you really don't want anything to do with a man who doesn't know beans about courting a beautiful woman. And before I find myself falling hopelessly in love with you, I must know if Colonel McBride put you up to this."

Shiloh felt terribly ashamed, but she was an honest individual. She usually said what was on her mind so there would be no mistake about what she thought and felt. "Papa did ask me to make you feel welcome and at ease, but—"

Holt held up his hand to forestall her. "You needn't say any more, ma'am," he interrupted. With a pitiful smile he added, "I am letting you off the hook. I have no wish to force you to tolerate my company when you risk having me drip food and drink all over you. And I cannot allow you to kiss me because you feel sorry for me."

His comment was like signaling a charge on a trumpet. Shiloh headed straight for him. Without ado she looped her arms around his neck and planted a sizzling kiss on his lips—a kiss that caused Holt's blood to boil. What Shiloh didn't have in the way of experience she compensated for with feminine inventiveness. Her motive was to reassure this timid gentleman that she was not forced to kiss him or even tolerate his presence.

"Now, did that feel as if I were doing the colonel a

favor?" she whispered before pressing her lips to his in one last kiss.

A smile spread across his bronzed face, causing the dimples that bracketed his mouth to dive into his cheeks. "You are a very special young lady, ma'am. You are the first woman who didn't make me break out in a cold sweat when I came this close."

"I would prefer that you call me Shiloh," she requested as she took his arm and walked with him into the hall.

But Holt refused to stir. "I meant it, ma'am . . . Shiloh," he corrected himself. "If there is another gentleman at the dinner table with whom you wish to converse, do not feel obligated to give me another thought. I promise not to allow your lack of attention to influence my decision about investing in the McBride Railroad Company. I know full well that no woman would pay me the slightest attention if not for the fact that I am wealthy, and I bear no grudge against you."

"Reuben, we must do something about this inferiority complex of yours," she chortled as she tugged him into the hall. "Don't you understand? I like you. I only wish you would crawl out of that defensive shell and like me a little bit too."

While Holt permitted Shiloh to shepherd him down the hall, he grinned rakishly. Things were going splendidly, he congratulated himself. His shy, meek charade had touched this ice maiden and had melted her heart. She had accepted him and now he could go about his business of investigating without expecting to be kicked out of the house on his backside. Now, if only he could have a look at the company ledgers to determine how money was being siphoned . . .

When Shiloh's tempting body brushed against his, Holt felt the warm flood of desire surge through his

61

loins. He wasn't sure if the challenge of uncovering the greedy swindlers motivated him as much as this silver-blue-eyed blonde who aroused his male instincts. It was for damned sure that he was wanting more than Shiloh's trust and friendship. Suddenly he found himself wanting a helluva lot more than her kisses. In fact, having her in his bed, arousing her slumbering passions, was quickly becoming his ultimate purpose of infiltrating the McBride Railroad Company. He was obsessed with having her, but he was trapped in the prison of his charade and that torment was one he swore would hound him all the rest of his days!

Chapter 6

In Holt's estimation, the dinner party was a huge success. He had been introduced to the other investors and the company associates who handled the finances. Of the seven men who joined the McBrides for the noon meal, there were three men whom Holt's suspicious mind had singled out as possible suspects besides the colonel himself, whom J. W. Baxter had blatantly accused of misconduct.

Max Fletcher was a pompous old goat who had bought real estate near two proposed railroad stations before the tracks progressed southwestward. He seemed greedy for every penny he could get his hands on. Max was a stout man in his mid-forties. His face was round and his cheeks shone like polished apples. He had sloping brows, a bald head, and deepset gray eyes. He was partial to bright, flashy clothes and chewed incessantly on a thick cigar. His dramatic hand gestures left Holt wondering if the man could speak without waving his arms and flashing his jeweled rings. Max was a self-made man, but Holt doubted the entrepreneur had made his millions without bending and breaking a few dozen rules. Being a betting man, Holt wagered Max would do whatever needed to be done to add more wealth to his already sizable fortune.

Elijah Conners also drew Holt's suspicion in the very way he handled himself in interactions with the other associates of the company. He was fiftyish with a crop of silver-black hair and a peppered beard that hugged his sagging jowls. Freckles and moles splattered his face as if he had been slopped with mud. Elijah was also fond of flamboyant clothes, and he possessed a nasal voice that reminded Holt of some ornery student scraping his fingernails over a slate. The arrogant easterner had inherited old money and spent most of his time in New York when he wasn't overseeing his latest investment in Missouri. He seemed to be a shrewd miser who never intended a cent to escape his hands unless he could triple his investment.

Holt's third suspect was the energetic twenty-eight-year-old promoter who did most of the colonel's legwork for him. Walter Jameson had enough enthusiasm to move mountains, almost too much to suit Holt's tastes. The fact that Walter spent every spare minute courting Shiloh with roguish smiles left Holt wondering if his dislike of the handsome rake was because Walter was just the sort of dynamic individual who could invent ways to cheat the company, or if it was his blatant attempt to woo Shiloh that made him suspicious. Walter's hazel eyes, surrounded with long, thick lashes, his sandy blond hair, and fair features gave him a wholesome appearance. He walked as if he had springs in his shoes. He dressed superbly and he was very sure of himself.

From a woman's point of view he was probably attractive, Holt mused as he studied Walter over the rim of his glass. Walter always seemed to know the right thing to say at the right moment, and he could undoubtedly charm most women out of their slippers if it were his wont.

But as attractive and personable as Walter seemed to be, Shiloh showered him with no special attention. She was a cordial hostess who shared her views on the westward movement of the railroad, proving she was not only lovely but extremely knowledgeable about her father's business endeavors.

Last but not least was Colonel McBride himself. Victor was a tireless entrepreneur of above average intelligence. He was a bundle of energy with a dream and a cause. The question was—to what extent would the colonel go to see his railroad line stretched across Missouri to channel trade and passengers in and out of Texas?

Holt speculated on his suspects, studying each one astutely until the meal ended. At Victor's request, his associates filed into his study for a stockholders' meeting. Holt took advantage of the opportunity by glancing at the ledgers, making a quick mental tabulation of the funds required to lay track west of Springfield to the corner of Indian territory. He calculated the projected expenses of reaching Dallas, Texas, and compared his speculations to that of the company files.

According to the tallies, the company's projected expenses were a good deal higher than average railroad costs. He knew McBride had received government right-of-way grants that could be sold to other investors or citizens who wished to establish business sites in the towns that would be created en route. The staggering expenses certainly left room for discreet skimmings of profit by a clever scoundrel—whoever he may be.

Without being obvious in his intentions, Holt jotted down notes and posed questions about the workings of the company. Later, he would scrutinize the ledgers. Later, when no one was there to glance over his shoulder and offer the kind of answers a prospective investor wanted to hear, he would delve into the accounts.

The moment the meeting adjourned, Holt found his gaze sweeping the hall in search of the striking blonde who could make a room light up the instant she breezed into it. But Shiloh was nowhere to be seen. While he and Victor were lounging in the parlor, the front door burst open and then slammed shut with such force that the entire mansion shook. The instant Victor bounded to his feet to investigate, Holt followed in his wake.

With extreme effort Holt swallowed the amused grin that tugged at his lips. Shiloh was dressed in a pale green riding habit that was snagged with dry leaves and clinging twigs. The neatly pinned curls that once sat atop her head were now in a tangled mass that cascaded down her back. Her breasts heaved with indignation, and her cheeks burned with color. Holt didn't have the faintest notion what had put her in a snit, but he knew she was fuming. Flames flew from her silver-blue eyes, and she was so furious she couldn't stand still.

"Did you take a spill from your mare, honey?" Victor questioned with fatherly concern.

Light blue eyes flashed like mercury. "No, I did not!" she spumed, stamping her foot in irritation. Shiloh was a foot stamper. When she was angry she stomped to vent her emotions. "Your Mr. Jameson tried to . . ." Shiloh clamped her mouth shut and counted to ten twice. It didn't help. When she noticed Holt leaning against the doorjamb, she attempted to compose herself. "Your Mr. Jameson's enthusiasm spilled over from his business interests into his personal interests."

Victor was distressed by Shiloh's insinuation. He wasn't blind. He could see that Walter found Shiloh fascinating. Most men did. She was so vibrant and vivacious that men were irresistibly drawn to her. Shiloh had her mother's southern grace, beauty, and poise and Victor's inexhaustible vitality. The combination had earned her a score of eager beaus and a cynicism toward men that nothing could crack.

In the past Victor would have stormed outside to hurl several venomous threats at Shiloh's overeager suitor. But he was trying to be less protective of her these days. For too many years he had hovered over his only daughter, and Shiloh had come to resent his interference. She considered herself capable of fending for herself. The fact that Walter Jameson was second in command made the situation touchy. Victor didn't want to lose Walter. When something needed to be done, Walter saw to the matter. And this wasn't the first time one of his associates had become so enamored with Shiloh that he forgot his place. Shiloh attracted trouble because of her stunning good looks, wealth, and feisty spirit. If Victor fired every man who made eyes at his daughter, he would have been a one-man company.

"Your Mr. Jameson now has a noticeable limp," Shiloh continued when she had regained control of her volatile temper. "I warned him, but like a stubborn mule he had to be hit first before I could get his attention. Then I explained what the word *no* meant."

Victor squared his shoulders and strode out the door.

"I do not need you to come to my defense, Papa," Shiloh called after him.

The colonel paused and pivoted to face his annoyed daughter. "I know that. I had only hoped to smooth over the rough edges with my second in command and remind him that he has forgotten his manners," he assured Shiloh somberly.

Stuffing his hands deep into the pockets of his trousers, Holt rocked back on his heels. For a moment he floundered for something appropriate to say in hopes of soothing Shiloh's ruffled feathers. But he found himself comparing her attack to Anna's, and raw fury flooded over him. Apparently, Walter Jameson was almost as pushy as Kirby Thorn when it came to women. Although Holt had a bad habit of taking females for granted, he had never been rough or abusive with a single one. There was a vast difference between seducing a woman and thrusting himself on one. His skin crawled at the thought of any man forcing this saucy blonde to experience the horrors Anna had suffered.

"I would challenge your Mr. Jameson to a duel to avenge his unwanted attack," Holt announced, drawing himself up to full stature, a gesture quite out of character for Reuben.

Shiloh gaped at the seemingly uncoordinated gentleman who towered over her. She could envision Reuben fumbling with his pistol and shooting himself in the foot long before he managed to fell the muscular and very agile Walter Jameson.

"If there is any shooting to be done, I'll do it," Shiloh declared, raising a proud chin. "This was his first offense. If Walter makes a fool of himself again, I will chop his octopus arms off at the shoulders."

Holt scrutinized the determined flicker in Shiloh's eyes. "I do believe you would," he chuckled as he slouched back against the edge of the door. "But perhaps you would enjoy seeing Dog take a bite out of his hide, just for good measure."

Shiloh glanced down at the huge, muscular mutt who sat at Holt's heels, panting and simultaneously licking his lips. She couldn't envision this mutt posing a threat other than demolishing furniture with his incessantly wagging tail.

The first hint of a smile bordered her lips, making her extraordinary eyes dance like diamonds. "Perhaps I should find myself a monstrous dog like yours to serve as my bodyguard," she mused aloud.

"Dog is yours for the asking since he has taken such a fancy to you," Holt generously offered. "Feed him and pet him and he will be your friend for life."

"Ah, if only it were that easy with men!" Shiloh sighed whimsically.

Holt would have crossed the hall to offer her a comforting hug, but it would have been so unlike the bashful gentleman who had appeared to work up only enough courage to converse with Shiloh and occasionally meet her gaze.

"I'm very sorry that your exquisite beauty and bubbly personality have been such a curse to you," he murmured softly.

"My worst curse is my abundance of wealth," she clarified in a bitter tone.

The vision of Lance Draper sprang to mind. Wherever that serpent was, she hoped he was miserable. He had certaintly ruined a naive young girl's dreams with his broken promises and tempting kisses from lying lips.

Pushing away from the door, Holt moseyed through the foyer, taking a wide berth around Shiloh. "Tell your father I won't be joining you for supper. I would like to take a look around Springfield."

"Would you like some company?" Shiloh offered, unsure she wanted to be left alone with her frustration.

What he needed to do needed to be done alone, Holt thought, but he couldn't tell that to Shiloh. He had to reject the offer of her companionship without offending her.

A humble smile curved the corners of Holt's lips as he glanced down at the floor. "I doubt you would want to be seen with me, ma'am," he said with a sigh. "I am not exactly what women call a 'catch.' If not for *my* money, I wouldn't be given the slightest consideration by the female of the species."

"Dammit all, Reuben, you are much too hard on yourself," she blustered.

Characteristically, Holt blanched. "Proper ladies shouldn't curse," he chided her gently.

"And proper gentlemen shouldn't say things to provoke a proper lady to curse," she parried. "There is nothing wrong with you that couldn't be repaired. If you would purchase clothes that accentuated your physique instead of—" Shiloh clamped her mouth shut so quickly she nearly bit off the tip of her tongue.

Holt assessed his torso with a hasty glance and then tossed the embarrassed beauty a melancholy smile. "Another reason why women do not find me attractive, I suppose," he mumbled before he and his four-legged shadow strolled toward the door. "I do the best I can with what I have to work with. . . ." He dropped into an exaggerated bow. "And now, if you will excuse me, I will remove your source of irritation so you won't have to resort to unladylike curses."

"Reuben, I didn't mean to . . ." Shiloh's voice drifted off when Holt ambled around the corner. Dammit all, she had stuck both feet in her mouth and cut another gash in his deflated self-confidence.

"Holy saints! What happened to you, child?" Marcella Pearson crowed from the top of the steps. The aging housekeeper waddled down the staircase to survey Shiloh at close range.

"I had an unfortunate encounter with one of Papa's

business associates," Shiloh muttered crankily. "Men! What disgusting creatures they are."

"I've told you and told you that these things wouldn't happen if you would get yourself a husband," Marcella scolded as she towed Shiloh up the steps. "You need a man to take care of you. If you had a husband to accompany you on your outings, men would keep a respectable distance. A wedding ring would work like repellent. If you ask me, your papa is doing you a disservice by not finding you a suitable mate and . . ."

Shiloh rolled her eyes ceilingward. Marcella, bless her heart, was as good as gold. The rotund widow had become the mother Shiloh had lost during the birth of an infant son sixteen years earlier. Both mother and son had perished and Marcella decided it was her duty to raise Shiloh as only a woman knew how.

In Marcella's opinion, Victor had coddled and spoiled Shiloh terribly to compensate for the loss of his beloved wife. Marcella had found herself losing ground when she tried to discipline this high-strung sprite. Now Victor was paying for sparing the rod on his only child. Shiloh was fiercely independent and highly skeptical of men. Victor should have insisted she take a mate long before now. The male population of Springfield lusted after this rambunctious heiress, and Shiloh had suffered several near-brushes with catastrophe because she was so pretty, unattached, and fabulously rich. She definitely needed a husband to watch over her, to control her! But wild horses couldn't drag Shiloh to the altar. She was destined to become a spinster. And in Marcella's opinion, that was a pitiful waste. Shiloh had a great deal of love bottled up inside her and no one with whom to share it. If Shiloh stayed single much longer, there would be no controlling her. She was already as unmanageable as one woman could get!

Mad as a hornet, Kirby Thorn stormed into the farmhouse near Dallas that he and his men had claimed as their hideout. The unsuspecting couple who had once owned the out-of-the-way farm had become victims of Kirby's ruthless takeover and were hastily buried in their family's cemetery.

Kirby was in a foul temper—worse than usual. He had gone into town to stake out the bank he intended to rob to replace the cash he and his men had squandered the past few months. While he was there he had overheard two strangers interrogating one of the barmaids in his favorite haunt. That was not the sort of thing Kirby had wanted to hear when he was planning a strike.

When Kirby sneaked around to the back of the saloon to confront the loose-lipped calico queen, he had taken his frustrations out on her. The lady, if one could call her that, was repaid for divulging information about Kirby, and it would be a long time before local patrons of the saloon would take a second look at the barfly.

Kirby Thorn's true medium was profanity. He was in rare voice while he stamped around the perimeters of the cottage, expelling one string of curses after another.

"What's eatin' you, Kirby?" one of his men had the bravura to ask in between swigs of whiskey.

"Pinkerton's men know where we are, goddammit," Kirby snarled.

Seven pairs of startled eyes focused on the man who was pacing like a caged predator. "How the hell did they find us?"

"How do I know how those son of a bitches go about tracking us? Those bastards got noses like bloodhounds," he growled before snatching a bottle away from one of his cohorts and taking a gulp. Recklessly, he wiped the drips from his lips with his shirt-sleeve. "We're headin' back to Missouri. Grab yer gear. . . ."

In fifteen minutes Kirby and his men had picked up everything they had brought with them, plus a few items they had stolen along the way. Like a misdirected cyclone, the brigands rode off with a cloud of dust at their heels.

Chapter 7

The clanking noise in the hall roused Shiloh from her restless sleep. Straining her ears, she listened for the sound that had disturbed her. A thump followed by a muffled groan caught her attention. Flipping back the sheet, Shiloh padded barefoot into the hall to see a shapeless specter hopping up and down on one leg while clutching the other foot in both hands.

The lantern in the hall revealed the long nightshirt that formed a tent around Holt's tall frame. He looked utterly comical in his night clothes, and Shiloh had to pinch herself to prevent bursting into snickers.

"What are you doing up at this late hour?" she inquired.

Holt carefully set his injured foot to the floor and hobbled around to peer at the shapely goddess whose gossamer gown displayed her alluring assets. The flickering lantern speared through the sheer fabric to outline the provocative curves and swells that lay beneath it. Holt's temperature rose a quick ten degrees.

"Dog and I needed a midnight snack," Holt explained through a grimace, one caused by the tingle in his loins rather than by the pain in his foot. "But I forgot to grab my spectacles and I don't see all that well

75

without them. I smashed into the wall." A hopeful smile dangled on the corner of his mouth. "Do you suppose Marcella would mind if I stole off with the leftover tarts?"

"Help yourself," Shiloh invited him, struggling to keep a straight face. With sylphlike grace she floated toward him, unaware that Holt was about to suffer heart seizure when more of her luscious figure was revealed to him. "But on second thought, perhaps I should lead the way. If you tumble down the steps in the dark, the whole house will know you are robbing the pantry."

In an erotic trance Holt limped down the steps, mesmerized by the hypnotic sway of Shiloh's hips. He had to force his hands to remain by his sides while they ached to clamp on to her, to measure her tantalizing figure with exploring caresses. Holt gave himself a mental shake and struggled to instigate some form of conversation that would distract him from his erotic contemplations.

"I didn't mean to disturb your sleep," he apologized in a whisper. "I turned a short corner and ran smack dab into the corner of the door."

In actuality, Holt had just returned from a thorough examination of the company ledgers in Victor's study. He had jotted down a few figures that seemed highly suspicious—ones that he predicted were being utilized to skim cash for the railroad's shrewd extortioner. While he was hurrying back to his room he had misjudged the corner in the shadows and slammed into it. Fumbling for an excuse, Holt invented a reason for Reuben's nocturnal prowling, and apparently Shiloh had accepted it as truth.

When Shiloh had led him into the kitchen, Holt plunked down in a chair and gobbled the tart, oddly content to be in Shiloh's company, even if he were restricted to no more than harmless conversation. She was the one bright spot that shone in his life after two tormenting years of darkness. But, of course, nothing could come of this peculiar relationship between them, even if he wanted one, he reminded himself sensibly. Garret Robertson would shoot him, just as he always did when an assignment was concluded. And Reuben Gilcrest would be laid to rest beside Holt's other departed aliases.

"I haven't robbed the pantry since I was a child," Shiloh mused between bites. "I think I would have been much better off if I hadn't grown up. Life was simpler then."

Holt expelled a deep sigh. "Indeed it was. . . . Well, most of the time," he amended. "Even at a tender age I was scared speechless around girls. I think I must have missed my calling by not becoming a monk. Then I would have had an excuse to shy away from women."

Shiloh found herself rising from her own chair to curl up on Holt's lap. She had never been so forward with a man. Maybe that was because she usually had to keep on her toes and remain on the defensive. But with this man she could respond to impulse without fearing that he would pounce on her when she displayed even a smidgen of affection for him.

"Good God, Shiloh! What would your father say if he caught us like this?" Holt gasped, more disturbed by the scintillating feel of her shapely bottom planted in his lap than any apprehension of having the colonel catch them in the clench.

"This is nice," she said with a contented sigh. "I have never been able to do this with a man." Shiloh laid her head on his shoulder and leaned back in his arms as if she belonged there.

"And we shouldn't be doing this now," Holt squeaked, his voice one octave higher than normal. "If we keep this up, we will have to marry to put a halt to scandalous gossip!"

Shiloh leaned back. Her long blond hair tumbled over his elbow like a shining river of sun and moonbeams. Impulsively, she raked her fingers through his thick raven hair, mussing that silly part in the middle of his head. Only shafts of moonlight splintered through the window, illuminating his handsome, angular features. He was strikingly attractive with his hair ruffled and without those monstrous glasses perched on the bridge of his nose. Shiloh speculated that without his lopsided mustache and goatee, Reuben would turn many a woman's head.

"I thought you said you found me attractive, Reuben," she murmured, distracted by the dashing picture he presented in the moonlight.

"I do," Holt groaned uncomfortably. "Much too attractive, I fear."

The feel of her supple body half reclined against his had his heart pounding like a tracklayer driving railroad spikes. Good God, what was it with this sprite? She ventured close to him while she avoided other men like the plague. She touched him as if they were the best of friends and he felt like a blazing torch. Was she so naive that she didn't know how easily a man could become aroused by a beautiful woman?

"I am beginning to understand why Walter Jameson lost his head," Holt mumbled. "You are making me want things I've never wanted from a woman before. Perhaps you had better return to your own chair before I forget I'm a gentleman."

Silver-blue eyes blinked up at him, and an impish grin settled on her exquisite features. Her adventurous hand migrated over his gaping nightshirt to investigate the dark mat of hair on his chest. "And to be truthful, you tempt me to experiment with desire—something I

78

have cautiously avoided for twenty-one years."

"You shouldn't say such things," Holt croaked. Lord, if she knew what was rushing through his mind, she would have leapt over the table to avoid him.

"You shouldn't tempt me so," she countered with a playful wink. With more bravura than she had ever displayed in the company of a man, Shiloh slid her hand inside his shirt to monitor the thundering beat of his heart, to explore the sleek muscular planes that were concealed by his baggy garment. "I find you very sexy in your own modest, reserved way, Reuben. You don't flaunt your masculinity and virility, but it's there, waiting to blossom. You shouldn't stifle it."

Her finger curled beneath his chin, lifting his downcast face to hers. "If I am willing to risk my pride and heart with a man again, I don't know why you can't comply. I wouldn't hurt you or trifle with you because I know how it feels and I wouldn't wish that embarrassment on anyone." Her fingertips limned the sensuous curve of his lips, suddenly wanting to feel them whispering softly against her own. "I know you are a gentleman and your intentions are as honest and open as mine. . . ."

Holt couldn't breathe normally. He was playing a charade, pretending to be someone he wasn't, using this unsuspecting nymph for his own purposes. Honest and open? He scowled at the thought of deceiving her, of being imprisoned in this role he had designed to suit the situation. He knew he had to tread carefully with Shiloh and yet she started uncontrollable bonfires inside him. She touched him with curious caresses, and fiery desire flooded through his veins. . . .

Shiloh's hand collided with the paper that Holt had stashed in the pocket of his nightshirt. "What's this?"

Before Shiloh extracted the paper and unfolded it, Holt clasped his hand around hers, stilling it. "It's just a few notes I have made about the company. Since I couldn't sleep, I was glancing over them," he replied with a dismissive gesture that cast the topic of conversation aside.

Her hand drifted down his ribs to map the muscles that lay beneath the full garment, and her sparkling eyes focused once again on the tempting curve of his lips. Odd, she had never been so bold in all her life. Touching this virile man who refused to flaunt his masculinity stirred her. Suddenly, she wanted more than to touch him, to be encircled in his arms. It was no longer a matter of wanting to experience his tender kiss, but rather a matter of *needing* to. . . .

Good God, he thought in anguish. She looked as if she were about to kiss him! How the blazes was he going to pretend he didn't want to ravish her right here in the kitchen when that was exactly what he ached to do? And why did he have to be so magnetically attracted to this lovely sprite? Damn, why couldn't Victor McBride have had a homely daughter who was as standoffish as Reuben Gilcrest? Poor ol' clumsy Reuben was going to get himself into trouble, sure as hell!

When her breasts meshed against his chest and she raised parted lips in invitation, Holt clamped down on his iron will, or what was left of it. Before her soft mouth melted against his, he turned his head away and struggled to ignore the tempting picture she presented. It took some doing. Lord, he needed a cold shower and quickly! He was going to burn himself into a frustrated pile of ashes.

A disappointed frown clouded Shiloh's brow. She had never been refused a kiss. In the past, *she* was the one who rejected amorous advances. Suddenly she was the aggressor and Reuben was protecting *his* virtues. What an ironic twist of fate! Now she knew what frustration men experienced when they were denied what they wanted. And Shiloh wanted very much to kiss Reuben, to inhale the delightful fragrance of his cologne, to feel his muscular body pressed familiarly against hers. He stirred her in a quiet, subtle way that compelled her to him. She enjoyed the opportunity of responding to her own desires without being threatened by the man who held her so tentatively in his arms.

Holt's chest swelled as he sucked in a steadying breath. "It isn't that I don't want to kiss you, Shiloh, for I surely do," he said in a tone that barely concealed his raging desire. "It's just that I'm afraid I might want more than you are offering. I feel your body against mine and I want to touch you as inquisitively as you have touched me. Having never been so bold before, I'm not sure I will want to stop once I get started. . . ."

What a relief it was to know he was as curious about this phenomenal reaction that set sparks between them as she was. Reuben was holding back because of his respect for her feelings. No man had ever been so considerate, so polite. What a wonderful man Reuben was! He would never hurt her or do anything to destroy her trust in him. He was nothing like Lance Draper or Walter Jameson.

"Touch me, Reuben," she offered in a throaty whisper. "I want you to. I will let you know when you have dared too much. As of yet, you haven't dared enough. . . ."

A groan of unholy torment rattled in his chest, and he found himself buckling to impossible temptation as her petal-soft lips merged with his, her tongue tracing and exploring the inner recesses of his mouth. A shudder rocked through him as his hand glided gently over the curve of her hips and tracked across her ribs, counting them one by one. His caress receded to follow the same languid path, aching to push away the sheer garment and feel the soft texture of her skin beneath his inquiring hand.

As he explored the smooth flesh beneath the sheer gown, his hand brushed the side of her breast. Holt felt Shiloh tremble uncontrollably and he cursed under his breath. Good God, she *was* terribly inexperienced, he realized. In fact, he was probably safe in speculating that he was the first man to caress her without having his hand slapped away. But what really rattled Holt was that she didn't protest the feel of his fingertips grazing on previously uncharted territory. He didn't want to stop what he was doing and yet he didn't dare frighten or offend her.

This was Shiloh's first experiment with passion, he knew. She bore enough invisible scars because of overzealous men who tried to take what she didn't know how to give and wouldn't have wanted to even if she did. But, Lord . . . touching this naive beauty was exquisite torture, and Holt could have continued what he was doing all night! And if he did, he knew he would be digging his own grave and burying himself in it. Caressing and kissing Shiloh was going to leave him with a fever for which there was only one cure—one that was off limits to him. He would be left to burn alive.

A riptide of emotions went against all Shiloh had ever known when Holt touched her. The most wondrous sensations spilled through her when his feather-light touches mapped the fullness of her breasts and encircled the taut peaks. His tender touch left her craving more. A flame flickered in the core of her being and spread through her loins. She felt warmed from the inside out. Each place he touched tingled and Shiloh felt herself involuntarily arching toward his hand while she deepened their kiss.

Good God, what a gentleman he was turning out to

be! Holt realized that some of Reuben's cautious, reserved characteristics were beginning to rub off on him. He was no longer interested in simply satisfying himself, but he yearned to please Shiloh without frightening her. He wanted her first taste of passion to linger in fond memories, not humiliating nightmares.

With patience he didn't know he had, Holt caressed the rigid peaks and then slid his fingertips down her belly to trace lazy circles on her inner thigh. And still Shiloh didn't pull away. Ever so gently, his hand tunneled beneath her negligee to touch—flesh to flesh. The texture of her skin was like silk. It was warm and firm and utterly exquisite.

The vision of every other woman he had touched faded into a blur as he learned the feel of this angel's tantalizing body. The throb of desire pulsating through him urged him to explore every delicious inch of her. His willpower buckled. While he kissed her with more expertise than he had yet to display, his hand glided downward. His fingertips delved and teased, arousing her in ways Shiloh was unaware existed.

Sensations sizzled through her, leaving a burning ache that demanded satisfaction. What kind of satisfaction? Shiloh wasn't sure. She didn't know where these feelings would lead, but she suddenly wanted to find out, and she wanted to experience them with Reuben.

It astonished Shiloh that there was a wildly sensual man lurking inside Reuben's reserve. Yet, instinctively he knew how to stir her without frightening her, to pleasure her with gentle caresses and warm, addicting kisses. For certain, Reuben could be a lady-killer if he freed that potential sensuality that was encased beneath his ill-fitting clothes and unstylish hair. Now, more than ever, Reuben Gilcrest was becoming the shining example of the adage that stated that it wasn't the clothes that made the man. It was what was on the inside that counted. And inside those expensive but sloppy garments was a man who held a mystical power over her. . . .

Mmmm . . . Reuben had the most phenomenal knack of making her feel feminine, she thought with a ragged sigh. He wasn't taking from her the way most men tried to take. He was giving pleasure, the kind Shiloh had never experienced when she was in a man's arms. He made her naive body long to join with his, made her yearn to learn his masculine body as well as he now knew her feminine curves. . . .

Like a tide rolling out to sea, the sensations gradually faded away, leaving a gnawing ache in its wake. Shiloh's thick lashes fluttered up to see Reuben peering down at her in a way that was totally unfamiliar. Even the shadows couldn't hide the taut lines in his face, the tightness that thinned his lips, the indecipherable flicker in his emerald-green eyes.

Her fingertips traced his handsome features like an artist committing a masterpiece to canvas. Gently, she smoothed away the tense expression and then blessed him with the lightest of kisses. "What's wrong, Reuben?" she queried, her voice rattling with disturbed desire.

What's wrong? For chrissake! Didn't she know what she was doing to him by allowing him unprecedented privileges? Didn't she know the conflicting emotions that were hounding him while he touched her and pretended to be the personification of gentlemanly behavior?

Holt ached to do more than kiss and caress this tempting package, and yet Shiloh had him hating himself for daring to do as much as he had done. This innocent pixie didn't understand men. She had spent her time warding off bold advances, nursing her broken heart, and vowing never to be hurt again. But Holt was going to hurt her, even if he hadn't meant to. If he didn't stop this instant, this midnight rendezvous was going to get totally out of hand! Lord, he deserved a medal for calling a halt to his intimate caresses when he did. And before this night was out, there was a good chance that he was going to disintegrate into a pile of smoldering coals.

"If we don't stop now, I won't be able to in another minute," Holt declared in Reuben's strangled voice. "You are too much temptation for your own good. And I'm not sure how much longer I can remain a gentleman in your presence."

As if she were as light as a feather, Holt set her to the floor and clambered to his feet. Nervously, he tugged at his blousy nightshirt to disguise the evidence of his desire for her. Hesitantly, Holt lowered his raven head to press a parting kiss to her lips. "I don't think it's a good idea for us to see too much of each other for the next few days," he advised her, his voice husky with barely contained passion. "And it will take twice that long for me to forget what I'm feeling just now. I thought I was immune to women, but you have made me realize I have all the instincts that prevail when a man . . ." An embarrassed smile grazed his lips. "I want you a little too much for my own good, as well as yours. You might not be as safe with me as you first thought."

Holt backed away, bumping against his chair. With head downcast, he scooped up a tart for Dog and felt his way out of the kitchen.

Shiloh stood like a statue. Her naive body still tingled from the aftereffects of her first taste of passion. Reuben left her with a warm glow of desire that demanded more than he had permitted himself to give. Shiloh was hounded by a burning curiosity about all the intimacies between a man and a woman. It had been almost four years since Lance Draper's skillful kisses had prompted her to speculate on romantic fantasies. But now those forbidden dreams rose like ghosts from her past. Lance had wanted only her fortune, but Reuben didn't need her money. He was truthful and sincere and considerate. . . .

Shiloh inhaled a deep breath and willed her runaway heart to slow its frantic pace. What a fine man Reuben Gilcrest was. He was a magnificent butterfly who hid inside his restrictive cocoon. For the first time ever, Shiloh found herself doing the *chasing* while her suitor was doing the *running*. No one but Shiloh knew what possibilities Reuben had. Apart, she was a cynical shrew and Reuben was a bashful moth. But together . . .

Wearing an impish smile, Shiloh sashayed through the dark house, listening to Reuben collide with unfamiliar sticks of furniture. Drawing Reuben from his protective shell was an intriguing challenge. Given a little time, he would spread his wings and prove to all the world that he was a very desirable man whom every woman would want. Maybe even Shiloh McBride . . .

That thought caused Shiloh to miss a step and plow into the edge of the banister. She could not believe that she, who had sworn off men forever, was suddenly entertaining thoughts of wooing the reluctant Reuben Gilcrest and grooming him to become her loving husband. He fascinated her and left her hungering to discover every facet of his personality. His gentle touch made her yearn for more than he had given. Reuben wasn't quite as shy with her as he had been at first. When they kissed he lost the initial nervousness that had plagued him. Shiloh found herself wondering how Reuben would respond if they made love, speculating on whether he would be as tender as he had been with his caresses and kisses.

Shiloh flinched at the sordid direction her thoughts

had taken. What a difference Reuben had made in her life! Suddenly she found herself in a reversed role. She was pursuing a man who was doing his best to run from the unexpected magic between them. It was comforting to know that Reuben was aroused by her, even if she wasn't an experienced lover. And she was content with his gentle touch even if he hadn't practiced his techniques on a score of women. Perhaps that was what warmed her, Shiloh mused. She and Reuben were learning the ways of passion with each other. It made their encounter special, and Shiloh was deeply touched to think she had met a man whose greatest aspiration in life was *not* seducing as many women as it was humanly possible to in a lifetime.

Victor was right, Shiloh realized. Reuben was different from all the other men she had met. And believe it or not, she liked him!

While Shiloh was in the kitchen mulling over her tantalizing tête-à-tête, Holt was flopping on his bed like a fish out of water. He was a tormented man whose conscience was stabbing him from every direction at once. He was a prisoner of his unappeased desires. He had been around enough to know where passion led, and he had purposely deprived himself of the heady pleasure of making wild sweet love to that lovely vixen. But at what tremendous cost to his composure! Having and having not was blasting holes in his sanity. Holt swore he would have to strap himself in bed to prevent sneaking into Shiloh's room to finish what she had innocently started. Good God, he was aching for her in places he didn't realize he had!

Each time Holt rolled over to find a new position to ease the gnawing in the pit of his belly, he became entangled in his cotton nightshirt. Usually, he slept in the buff and it was damned difficult to maneuver around all this fabric. If thoughts of that tempting blonde weren't enough to torment him, his nightshirt tried to strangle him. Lord, he had to put a safe distance between himself and that shapely sprite before he lost the good sense he had been born with. She made him forget his purpose for being here. If he knew what was good for him, he would hurriedly expose the culprit in McBride's company before he found himself in so deep with Shiloh that he couldn't get out.

Shiloh. He waited, wondering ... if they would make a scene or if ...

Chapter 8

In frustrated disappointment Shiloh watched as Holt scrunched down in his chair at the breakfast table and hid behind his newspaper for the third day in a row. When she glanced in his direction, all she could see was the crooked part in his waxed hair and the top of his wire-rimmed spectacles.

Reuben refused to look her squarely in the eye these days, she realized. In fact, he spent more time staring at the floorboards. It was as if he were ashamed at the intimacy between them. He was polite to her but extremely remote. He had erected an invisible wall between them that nothing could crack. He fumbled with his silverware, assuring her that her mere presence in the room was causing him considerable distress. If he spoke at all, he directed his conversation at Victor, asking questions that pertained only to the workings of the railroad.

Shiloh longed to draw him aside and apologize for making him so uncomfortable. How strange it felt to be the one who needed to be begging forgiveness for an amorous advance! Shiloh would never have imagined herself capable of encouraging a man to kiss her or touch her. And never in her wildest imagination would she have expected a man to be the one to call a halt to a midnight rendezvous. The tables had suddenly turned, and Shiloh was left to doubt her ability to arouse the one man who constantly piqued her interest.

The mere thought of their encounter in the kitchen burned through Shiloh's mind and body. She peered at the oversize garments and bright red vest and remembered the muscular man whose body she had explored. He was shying away from her, withdrawing into his protective shell. She felt as if she had lost a friend, one who knew her better than any other man on the planet.

As had become Reuben's custom, Holt excused himself from the table immediately after breakfast. When he loped toward the door in uncoordinated strides, Shiloh scuttled along behind him. Today his excuse for making himself scarce was his interest in inspecting the trainload of lumber and rails that was to be delivered to the road gangs that were laying track near Primrose. The previous day his reason for leaving was to interview some of the small-time investors who had bought land from the railroad along their right-of-way.

Shiloh had no idea what Reuben would dream up to take himself out from underfoot the following day. But if the past few days were any indication, he would concoct another believable reason to avoid her. Raising a determined chin, Shiloh breezed onto the porch.

"Reuben, I would like you to go riding with me today," Shiloh declared before he could scamper away.

"I don't ride very well," Holt mumbled as he paused by the side of the house. That was an outright lie, of course. He was an excellent equestrian who could ride all over a horse and shoot from both hips when need be. But Shiloh didn't know that, and he needed to invent another excuse to keep his distance from her.

"Then it's high time you did learn to ride," she contended as she bounded down the steps to catch up with him.

Hesitantly, Holt lifted his gaze to study the vivacious pixie who constantly preyed on his mind. "And if we go riding and I wind up attacking you the way Walter Jameson did, what then? I warned you that I am more human than I first thought when it comes to women . . . especially you."

A radiant smile blossomed on her face when Holt finally met her gaze. "You are not Walter, thank the Lord," she assured him in a saucy tone. "And dammit all, Reuben, sometimes I wonder if you aren't more concerned about *your* virtue than I am with *mine.*"

Holt bit back a roguish grin. He had lost his innocence so long ago that he barely remembered when, where, and with whom. And this sassy minx was wrong if she thought he wasn't worried about *her* virginity. She was in more danger of losing it than she thought! And wasn't it ironic that the man who was trying very hard to protect her was protecting her from *himself!* Shiloh was correct when she declared there was another man lurking underneath his baggy clothes. But it wasn't the man she assumed him to be.

"Please, Reuben, come ride with me," Shiloh murmured as she pushed up on tiptoe to press a tempting kiss on his lips. "I've missed you the past few days."

Heaving a defeated sigh, Holt looked everywhere except at her, and then nodded compliance. "Very well, I'll come, but you had better not take advantage of me," he added with a teasing smile.

Muffling a giggle, Shiloh looped her arm through Holt's and led him down the stone path to the stables. She watched him fumble with the saddle and bridle, but she refused to poke fun at him for being so inexperienced with horses.

Holt could have saddled a horse blindfolded, but he had a role to portray and his bungling performance should have won him an award for his superb acting ability.

Once he had fastened the girth and pulled into the saddle, he cast Shiloh a hasty glance. And sure enough, she was having difficulty swallowing her amusement. He had her believing he didn't know the first thing about horses. Rocking back and forth, Holt encouraged his gentle mare to plod across the meadow. Taking care to appear ill at ease in the saddle, he bobbed up and down from the instant he urged the steed to a trot. With his coattails flapping behind him and Dog at his heels, Holt followed Shiloh across the clearing and into the clump of trees that lined the creek.

After riding for a quarter of an hour, Shiloh bounded from the saddle to allow her steed to drink from the stream. When Holt followed suit, Shiloh clutched his hand and led him along the grassy bank. But they had walked only a hundred yards when Holt set his feet and refused to budge from his spot.

"I don't think it's a good idea for us to be alone . . . and on foot," he mumbled awkwardly.

Shiloh had maintained her good disposition as long as it was possible, considering her explosive temper. She had been patient, but Reuben was still dragging his feet. His remark set her teeth on edge and put words on her tongue that shouldn't have been there at all.

"Dammit all, Reuben!" she spumed, stamping her foot. "Why are you always so suspicious of me? You're as jumpy as a grasshopper and I have given you no reason to be. You seem to think I purposely brought you out here to attack you." Silver-blue eyes flashed, making him the brunt of her frustration. "It is not the least bit flattering that I always have to be the one who instigates something as harmless as a kiss. I am not accustomed to chasing men. And the one man I long to get to know avoids me. It is very exasperating when I want very much for him to kiss me!"

There, she had said it. At least she was honest with him. If he wanted to scurry away, he could. But he knew that she felt something for him, something that could blossom and grow if only he would permit it.

"Why?" Holt questioned somberly.

"Why what?" Shiloh spluttered in exasperation.

"Why do you want to get to know me better than you already do and why do you want me to kiss you?" he asked in a much calmer tone than she employed. "I'm sure there are scores of men hereabout who would leap at the chance of kissing you if it is extra practice you want."

"That's the point," Shiloh bit off in annoyance. "I don't want a man to *leap* at me. And yes, I want to practice kissing you. You and not anyone else. In case you aren't aware of it, you happen to be a very good kisser." When he finally braved a glance at her, she stared him straight in the eye. "I like you, Reuben. I really do. Is that so difficult to understand?"

"Yes, as a matter of fact, it is," he croaked, more uncomfortable than he had ever been in his life.

Holt had thought this assignment was going to be a piece of cake. But there was nothing simple about pretending he didn't want to scoop this curvaceous nymph into his arms and ravish her. For days he had been hounded by fantasies that had everything to do with seducing Shiloh and nothing to do with investigating the McBride Railroad Company. And furthermore, it was killing him to know Shiloh was being honest and sincere with him and he was being cunning and deceitful with her. Although he had defeated this cynical minx at her own game, he had certainly wound up the loser. He was trapped in a charade of his own making, unable to enjoy the intimate pleasures of seducing this lively and extremely lovely sprite. Double damn. . . .

Shiloh stared at him for a long, meditative moment. "Maybe I did bring you out here to kiss you," she admitted.

Casting aside all feminine reserve, she moved toward him. She yearned to explore the realm of delicious sensations she had discovered three days earlier. She needed to test her reaction to Reuben, to assure him that it had been the man himself who stirred her, that she was not merely satisfying womanly curiosity. With Reuben, she felt so at ease, so responsive. He had such a gentle touch and yet his caresses could make her burn with a hunger only he could appease. . . .

Shamelessly, Shiloh looped her arms around his broad shoulders and pressed full-length against him. She needed his kiss more than she needed air to breathe. And kiss him she did, with all the pent-up emotion that had hounded her while he avoided her and shut her out of his thoughts.

Well, he wasn't going to forget this afternoon, Shiloh promised herself as she yielded to the bubbling sensations that erupted when she molded herself to his masculine contours. She wanted to explore his body, to delve beneath those uncomplimentary clothes, to touch his muscular flesh. She yearned to unlock the virile, sensual man who loomed behind this restrictive shell.

She had become addicted to Reuben's timid kisses so quickly, Shiloh mused as their breath merged as one. He hadn't wanted to return her embrace, but she could feel the sparks flying. Suddenly they were both desperately clinging to each other, their lips slanting and twisting, their breath coming in ragged, irregular spurts.

He did feel something for her, Shiloh realized when Reuben's arms fastened about her as if the world were about to come to an end. This wasn't just a one-sided fascination. He felt the same needs that bombarded her.

There were undoubtedly those who would question her interest in this long-legged, uncoordinated gentleman who had led a sheltered life under his aunt's thumb. But Shiloh was intrigued by the untapped well of potential strength and character in Reuben Gilcrest. There was something unique about him, something that lured her like a moth to a flame. She wanted to be the one to bring him to life, and she longed for him to be the man who healed the wounds of first love's bitter rejection.

When Shiloh melted in his arms, Holt's knees very nearly folded beneath him. Her kiss was like a torch set to dry kindling. Even while he reminded himself not to step out of character, his traitorous body was responding, demanding more delicious pleasure. Holt felt like a man strung out on a torture rack. He was damned if he yielded to the fiery sensations Shiloh so easily aroused in him, and he was damned if he didn't. Either way he was going to hate himself. This shapely beauty was tearing him apart bit by agonizing bit.

All thought scattered when Shiloh's inquisitive hand slid beneath his shirt to explore the taut tendons of his back and ribs. Holt closed his eyes and repeated his vow to treat Shiloh with the respect she deserved.

To hell with respect, his instincts screamed at him. Enough of this noble honor! A man could be tempted for just so long before he buckled to a beautiful, desirable woman.

Good God, her fingertips were doing incredible things to his self-control. Her hands roamed to and fro, investigating each vertebra of his spine, measuring each muscle. Her touch was light and inquisitive, and it left him trembling with needs that mushroomed with each passing moment.

Holt sucked in his breath when her straying hand drifted over his hip and then retraced its tantalizing path along his backbone. His pulse leapfrogged through his blood, and he cursed himself for allowing his desire for this saucy sprite to swell completely out of control.

Despite the constant warning signals that flashed in his head, his hands glided up her sides to trace the fullness of her breasts. Holt was so absorbed in their steamy kiss that he forgot to monitor the activity of his contrary hands. He was as shocked as Shiloh was to find that he had loosed the buttons on the bodice of her riding habit to expose her lacy chemise. The tempting swells begged for his touch, and Holt surrendered to the overpowering urge to spread a row of greedy kisses along her throat to the valley between her breasts.

Shiloh's breath stuck in her chest when she felt Holt's sensuous lips whispering over her quaking flesh. And when his tongue flicked at the throbbing buds he had exposed, Shiloh's heart stalled. A steady flame billowed in the core of her being, and she surrendered to the intimacy and the tenderness Reuben displayed. Never once did he paw or grope at her the way other men did. He worshiped her as if she were a special gift, as if she were the most important person in his life. His warm draft of breath drifted from one taut peak to the other while his hands freed the buttons to bare her well-sculptured body to his all-consuming gaze.

It was difficult to tell whose idea it was to sink down onto the plush carpet of grass. It was as if the thought

96

struck them simultaneously. But they were there, touching each other, kissing, shuddering at the pleasures they aroused in each other. The newness of having a man's exploring fingertips migrating over her sensitive skin left Shiloh drifting in wild abandon. Her hands moved of their own free will to peel away the vest and shirt that prevented her from seeing the magnificent man beneath his distracting garb.

He was swarthy and powerful, not at all the weakling he appeared to be in his loose garments. Beneath the baggy clothes was bottled vitality, a sinewy, awesome specimen of masculinity that put all strutting rakes to shame. Adoringly, Shiloh's caresses skimmed over each nipple and skitted through the thick mat of hair that covered his chest. When his wandering hands trailed lower, hers did likewise.

Holt groaned huskily when tapered fingertips traced the band of his breeches. He could feel the maddening sensations sizzling through him like the striking of lightning bolts. And even while he told himself to stop, his betraying hands continued to explore every exposed inch of her alabaster skin. Mesmerized, Holt surveyed the firm swells that he had kissed and caressed. Lord, Shiloh was so incredibly lovely, so perfectly formed. If there was another woman on the planet who was so delicately structured, he had yet to meet her. He stared at Shiloh and he wanted her—all of her. He touched her and his mind went blank. . . .

Suddenly Holt was suffering severe oxygen deprivation. Shiloh's adventurous hand delved beneath the band of his breeches to track along his hip. He went hot all over. Shaken by the hungry sensations she instilled in him, Holt sought out her heart-shaped lips and lost himself in a kiss sweeter than cherry wine. Engulfed in passion's mindless spell, his hand moved along the curve of her hip to rediscover the soft flesh of her inner thigh. Gently, he guided her legs apart. When Shiloh gasped at the intimacy of his hands, his mouth rolled upon hers. And while he teased and aroused her with masterful techniques, her caresses glided over his bold manhood, returning each familiar touch, learning what excited him to the point of frustrated frenzy.

"Shiloh . . ." Holt growled as his body half covered her.

Long lashes swept up to meet his hungry stare. Shiloh trembled, hovering on the threshold of forbidden pleasure, aching to discover where these feelings would lead, knowing she was at fault for tempting fate. But the glow in Reuben's emerald eyes melted her thoughts into puddles. She had never felt this way with a man before, had never wanted more than a kiss. But Reuben made her eager to investigate the mysterious dimension of passion. If she could choose who would accompany her into this dark, sensuous realm of rapture, it would be Reuben—the man who knew how to arouse her past the point of resistance, the man who had never shared such intimacies with another woman.

"Make love to me, Reuben. I want you," she whispered as her hand flowed over his back in an inviting caress.

Reason came rushing back when Dog lifted his head and emitted a bark that could have been translated as a fierce scolding. Right then and there Holt swore the shaggy mongrel had more sense than he did. Frustrated to no end, Holt stared down into that innocent face that was poised only a few inches from his. What the sweet loving hell did he think he was doing. Jeezus, he needed his head examined! This wasn't some tavern maid who pleasured men for the money she could earn on her back. This was Victor's pride and joy! How could he face Shiloh again if he robbed her of her virginity? She trusted him, but she didn't really know him at all. She saw in Reuben what Holt allowed her to see. And as much as he ached to bury himself within her, to revel in the pleasures he knew she could provide, he was living a lie.

He was complicating an assignment from which he would walk away, never to return. What could he offer Shiloh? A few weeks of stolen pleasure? In time she would come to her senses and regret this day. There was something special between them now, but he would spoil it if he dared to take more than Shiloh should give without expecting anything in return. Never in his life had Holt been more ashamed of himself. This charade was quickly mashing his conscience flat. As much as he wanted this lovely goddess who was the stuff masculine dreams were made of, he couldn't have her, not if he hoped to live with himself.

Gathering what was left of his crumbled willpower, Holt sat up in the grass to fasten Shiloh's gaping blouse. With trembling hands he smoothed her hiked-up hem into place. Tenderly, he bent to kiss away the astounded expression that claimed her exquisite features. Then he stood up to tuck his shirt into his breeches.

Like a startled owl Shiloh levered up on one elbow and blinked at him. Shame flushed her cheeks when she realized what an idiotic fool she was. Reuben probably thought she had been a harlot in another lifetime. And she may very well have been, judging by the way she had thrown herself at him. What had come over her? Never in all her life had she been so bold with a man. But she had touched Reuben intimately and reveled in the pleasures she derived from his caresses, his breathtaking kisses. If not for his gentlemanly reserve, she would have lost her innocence. Dammit all, he probably hated her for forcing him into such an uncompromising situation. If he never spoke to her again, she wouldn't be surprised.

"I'm sorry," Shiloh choked out, humiliated beyond words.

"You don't want me," Holt muttered more harshly than he intended. "I am your experiment with passion for passion's sake. And if we had overstepped the bounds of propriety to become lovers, what then?"

Again Shiloh found herself on the wrong end of the conversation that usually transpired after one of her eager suitors had attempted to take more than she wanted to give. In the past *she* did the reprimanding and now it was *Reuben* who was reminding her of her sagging morals. Her, the woman who had sworn off men!

"Today only confirms my belief that we tempt each other far too much," Holt grumbled as he bent over to retrieve his hat. "When you come to your senses you will realize that it isn't me you want, Shiloh. And if I truly thought it was, things might have turned out differently. I don't want to be the time you're killing at the colonel's request. I'm not a toy to be used and discarded when recess is over."

As Holt strode off, stiff-legged, Shiloh cursed herself for thrusting another obstacle between herself and this shy, reserved man who could arouse her slumbering passions when he shed his confining shell. If she understood this phenomenal attraction to Reuben, it would certainly help matters! But she didn't. She was instinctively drawn to him, curious about the intimacies that she was tempted to explore after they shared their first kiss.

Feeling like a blundering fool, Shiloh ambled back to fetch her steed. Although Reuben waited her return like the gentleman he was, he spoke not a word as he bounced in his saddle during their return trip. An invisible partition separated them—one Shiloh knew she was responsible for erecting. My, what Reuben must think of her! She had wanted only to assure him that she found him desirable, and he refused to believe that she was interested in him as a man, not merely an object of physical pleasure.

The moment they reached the stable, Holt clambered down from the horse and requested the groom to fetch the buggy Victor had offered him earlier in the morning. With a parting nod and a quick glance in Shiloh's direction, Holt aimed himself toward Springfield, silently kicking himself as he went. Damnation, this tug-of-war between his brain and body was wearing him out. How much longer could he deny himself? And worse, what was he going to do if he did buckle to his lusty desires for Shiloh? A man could stop himself only once or twice before he yielded to such great temptation. Holt had depleted his noble reserve. If that silver-blue-eyed nymph made one more reckless advance, his willpower would crack wide open.

Muttering to himself, Holt resolved never to let Shiloh get that close again. He had wanted her wildly, maddeningly. Distance was all that would prevent him from breaking his vow, he lectured himself sternly. Shiloh was a dozen kinds of passions seeking release with a man she didn't know as well as she thought she did. Blast it, he should have taken Allan's suggestion to fraternize with one of Victor's associates. When he had taken on the challenge of Shiloh McBride, Holt had bitten off more than he could chew. There was no triumph in defeating that proud beauty at her own game. He was forced to deprive himself of something rare and special and unique. Taking that silver-blue-eyed blonde was every man's dream—and one man's nightmare. Talk about torment, Holt mused dispiritedly. Reuben was the one man Shiloh had offered herself to and the one man who had to turn her down. Holt would have laughed at the bitter irony of his predicament if he weren't so busy cursing himself.

Victor took one look at the melancholy expression on Shiloh's face and frowned in concern. "What's troubling you, honey?"

"Reuben," Shiloh said with a sigh.

Victor's winged brows rose in surprise. "Has he done something to upset you?" he wanted to know.

Shiloh was too ashamed to tell her father she had made advances toward Reuben and he had backed away . . . permanently. Victor would have snickered if he knew his daughter—the very same daughter who rejected suitors left and right—had been jilted because she was too forward for the reluctant gentleman who had been plagued with an unreasonable fear of women.

"No," she responded after a moment. "I tried to befriend him and he behaves as if I have offended him. I honestly like him and he refuses to accept that as truth."

A muffled chuckle bubbled from Victor's lips. "I warned you that Reuben was nothing like the other men you've known." A wry twinkle lit his bright blue eyes as he regarded his rambunctious daughter. "I find it difficult to believe you have taken a liking to our guest."

Shiloh's gaze dropped to watch her hands knot and flex in the folds of her brown riding habit. "As odd as it sounds, I do find him fascinating. There is more to Reuben than meets the eye, Papa," she hedged.

Victor masked his amusement behind the brandy glass that hovered at his lips. "Oh, really? You're the only one who thinks so. Shiloh, I'm surprised at you," he teased gently. "I thought you had decided the male of the species, me excluded, should be condemned to the fiery pits of hell for all eternity."

A sudden thought leapt to mind. "And speaking of men, Walter dropped by a while ago. He is sporting a black eye and a split lip. He refused to disclose how he had acquired them. The two of you haven't gone another round, have you?"

Shiloh was delighted to hear Walter had been bruised and battered, and she wished she had been responsible. "I only punched him in the jaw and kicked him in the shins," she reported bitterly. "But I applaud whoever left his or her mark on that human octopus."

"Walter did ask me to convey his sincere apologies for his overzealous reaction to you," Victor announced. "He seemed very ashamed of himself."

"Then he should have offered his apology to me, not to you. After all, I was the one he offended," she spewed in annoyance.

"I think Walter is afraid to approach you until I have laid the groundwork." He flicked Shiloh a speculative glance. "Walter fears you will come after him with claws bared again."

Shiloh's snapping eyes narrowed on her father's wrinkled face. "If you had my best interest at heart, you would fire Walter for attempting to take liberties with me."

"You informed me two years ago that I was not to meddle in your private affairs," Victor reminded her with a mocking smile. "And if Walter wasn't such a capable promoter, I might have fired him even if you do begrudge my interference. Unfortunately for both of us, if I had every man arrested who actively courted you, there would be no males left in Springfield." His chest fell in a heavy sigh. "Maybe Marcella is right. Perhaps you do need a husband to watch over you."

Shiloh glanced at her father, aggravated by his seeming lack of concern over the incident. Sometimes she swore he silently hoped one of her suitors would overstep his bounds to the point that she would be forced into marriage. Victor wanted a son-in-law to follow in his footsteps. Shiloh had refused to give him a man he could train in his own image.

"Perhaps I should ask Reuben to marry me," she suggested flippantly. "At least with him, *I* could do the choosing."

Victor tried to control his burst of laughter, but it bubbled forth like a geyser. "Reuben is so leery of you that he won't even meet your gaze at the dinner table," he chuckled. "And besides, you would have to drag him to the altar in shackles."

It was the first time Shiloh could recall hearing her father shrug a man off as a prospective husband. For two years Victor had shoved eligible bachelors at her under the pretense of entertaining them for business purposes, secretly hoping one would pique her interest. But Shiloh was wise to his schemes. And this time it was Victor who didn't think she had a snowball's chance in hell of luring Reuben to the altar, even if it was her wont.

"Don't waste your time with Reuben," Victor advised. "I have asked you to be polite and courteous to him while we are discussing a business investment and you complied. But Reuben is a lost cause as far as women are concerned. You couldn't win his affection even if you honestly wanted it, sweetheart. You see him as an intriguing challenge, but don't set your sights on him, even to spite me."

That certainly sounded like a dare to Shiloh! Victor seemed confident that she could attract the type of man for whom she had no interest, but not the ones who fascinated her.

"Thank you very much for the insult, Papa," Shiloh snapped.

An undecipherable expression passed across Victor's face. He reached out a hand to give Shiloh's forearm an affectionate squeeze. "I am not trying to insult you. I just don't want to see you hurt again. Don't waste your time and efforts on Reuben, baby. You don't have to prove me wrong. Despite his unorthodox dress and awkward mannerisms, I like Reuben, too. But he isn't the right man for you. You are captivated simply because he is the first man who hasn't groveled at your feet in search of whatever scraps of affection you might toss at him. Leave well enough alone."

When Victor exited through the front door, Shiloh stared meditatively at Marjorie's portrait that hung above the mantel in Victor's study. She wondered at the type of relationship her parents had shared. Shiloh didn't know what went on between husband and wife because her mother had died before she was old enough to observe them together. Her father must have loved her mother deeply, Shiloh mused as she compared herself to the portrait. Would she and Reuben enjoy that same bond of mutual friendship as well as physical affection, she wondered. How would they resolve their differences of opinion?

Shiloh jerked straight up when she realized she was envisioning herself married to that shy, uncoordinated man. She was viewing him in elegant clothes that enhanced his muscular physique instead of detracting from it. Without his mustache, goatee, and that crooked part in the middle of his hair, he would be a strikingly attractive man. He had so much to offer and yet he was afraid to trust in Shiloh, to believe she cared about him.

A long sigh gushed from her lips as she ambled up the steps to her room. Victor was probably right. She shouldn't give Reuben another thought. What did she know about attracting a man who ran away from her instead of after her? Nothing, obviously. She certainly had botched up her afternoon with Reuben.

But her father was wrong about one thing, Shiloh thought to herself. Reuben was not a hopeless case. Shiloh had simply employed the wrong approach and had frightened him away. She wanted to attract a tender, caring man like Reuben, not the endless rabble of fortune hunters and adventurers who lusted after her body and her money. For once she would like to be a willing participant in a courtship instead of always defending herself from men.

Reuben might come to care for her if he realized that she did like him for what he was. It was time he stopped being so concerned about her reputation, she decided. If there was ever a man to whom she wouldn't mind losing her virginity, it would be Reuben. She had learned that this afternoon, and he refused to believe that she really wanted him. He was gentle and responsive to her feelings and she reveled in his touch, inexperienced though they both were. He was a very imaginative lover who proved that it wasn't necessary to have years of experience to satisfy a woman. So what if he didn't look overly masculine in those godawful clothes? What difference did it make when a strong, virile man like Reuben was lying naked . . .

Shiloh blushed to the roots of her silver-blond hair. Her mind had deteriorated! Now she was not only longing for the tenderness she had discovered in Reuben's arms, she was visualizing him in her bed . . . in the altogether. That man had stirred uncontrollable feelings inside her and he wasn't even trying to! In fact, he discouraged any further intimacy between them. Maybe this was her punishment for rejecting so many suitors. She had invited Reuben's touch and he had climbed back into his shell like a confounded turtle!

Well, maybe it was time Reuben overcame his apprehension of women. Maybe he was harboring a fear that he would be inadequate in a woman's bed. Well, he was wrong! He had proved himself capable enough this afternoon.

Mulling over their encounter, Shiloh dashed up the steps two at a time to change into her gown. She had to devise a way to reassure Reuben of his virility without scaring the living daylights out of him. But how? Shiloh wasn't very good at inflating a man's pride since she had spent the past few years deflating pride in men every chance she got. But one way or another Shiloh vowed to prove to Reuben that he was every bit a man—a desirable, exciting man. And she was going to convince him that he had no reason to avoid women if it was the last thing she ever did, even if she wasn't the woman he really wanted!

Chapter 9

Holt threw his long leg over the pommel of the
saddle. Impatiently, he waited for Garret Robertson to
appear in the secluded clearing that was located five
miles from the road gang crews that were grading and
laying track. Holt had stashed his disguise in his
saddlebag and donned attire that would draw less
attention to himself. He couldn't do much about the
lopsided mustache and goatee, but his pale green shirt
and brown breeches blended into the scenery better
than his bright frock coat would have.

The last two days and nights had been hell, Holt
mused as he puffed on his cigarillo. He had kept his
distance from the saucy blonde, but he could tell she
was hurt by his standoffishness. Blast it, sometimes a
man had to be cruel to be kind. If he had encouraged
Shiloh one little bit, there was no telling where they
would have ended up.

Every time her bewitching face popped to mind he
burned on a hot flame. He could see her sinking into
his lap, her skin glowing like honey in the dim light,
her eyes sparkling like diamonds. He could feel her
responsive body lying familiarly against his, feel her
silky skin beneath his exploring fingertips while they

lay by the stream in the shadows and sunlight. She had been so at ease, so damned trusting with him!

Lord, he had wanted Shiloh in the worst way. But a reckless affair with that saucy beauty would only complicate matters. He needed to complete this assignment in record time and concentrate his efforts on Kirby Thorn. For over two years he had been driven by his personal vendetta to locate Thorn, and now that blond-haired hellion had distracted him to the point where he would waken each morning in a cold sweat. . . .

The crackling of twigs jostled Holt from his deliberations. He glanced up to see the giant of a man striding toward him, sporting a grin that silently poked fun at Holt's ridiculous mustache and goatee. Before Garret made a wisecrack, Holt flashed him a glare that warned him against directing comments to the telltale signs of his disguise.

"How's the investigation progressing?" Garret inquired, still staring at the silly mustache that dangled on Holt's upper lip.

Holt blew a smoke ring into the air. "I've narrowed it down to four probable suspects," he announced blandly.

"How many were there to begin with?" Garret queried as he flicked a leaf from his shirt-sleeve.

"Four," Holt replied dryly.

A deep skirl of laughter echoed in Garret's massive chest. "That doesn't sound like progress to me. You must be losing your touch for investigative work. What's the matter, are you having trouble with the colonel's daughter?" he teased. "She won't have anything to do with you, will she?"

Holt declined comment. Boasting of his success in combating Shiloh's cynical defenses had little appeal to him. He had found her to be an exceptional young woman who deserved more than lies and charades.

110

Unfortunately, Holt could offer her nothing else.

Leisurely, Holt dipped into his pocket to flip Garret a twenty-dollar gold piece. He pretended to concede the bet, even though he had won.

"So Shiloh McBride turned out to be more woman than even you could handle, did she?" Garret taunted unmercifully. "Good for her. I didn't relish the thought of fawning over that big mutt the way you do." His brown eyes swung to Dog, who, as always, was one step behind Holt.

"Have you come up with any possible leads?" Holt asked, purposely changing the subject.

Garret nodded. "The track foreman had a list of supplies and equipment needed to lay rails to the border of Indian territory. I caught a glimpse of it and jotted down the figures as best as I could remember." He produced the paper so Holt could compare the tallies he had seen in the company ledger. "Walter Jameson, Max Fletcher, and Elijah Conners came by yesterday on their way to survey the terrain ahead of us and to plot out the next town site for the railroad." His thick brows arched curiously. "They wouldn't happen to be three of your suspects, would they?"

Holt nodded, but he didn't have much to say. Thoughts of Shiloh still preoccupied him.

"Walter was sporting a black eye," Garret continued. "He didn't say how he came by it when some of the employees razzed him about it. Any ideas?"

The faintest hint of a smile quirked Holt's lips before he took a long draw on his cigar. "I have a better idea how Walter acquired his black eye than he does," he admitted wryly. "He walked into a doubled-up fist on his way out of a local tavern. I didn't hang around to watch him wake up."

Garret's brows jackknifed. "Why the hell did you hit him?"

111

Holt's broad shoulders lifted in a noncommittal shrug. "Because he deserved it," he replied cryptically.

After the incident between Shiloh and Walter, Holt had looked the man up. He didn't know why he felt the impulse to bury his fist in Walter's face. Shiloh hadn't asked for anyone to give Walter a well-deserved punch. Indeed, she had reminded her father that she could fight her own battles. But Holt had discreetly gone about settling the score for Shiloh without taking the credit. The blow to Walter's eye was satisfaction in itself.

A ponderous frown plowed Garret's forehead. For a long moment he stared up at the imposing figure of the man who lounged in the saddle. Wasn't it just like Holt to retaliate in his own private way? He followed the same procedure in his investigations. Holt took all the risks while he tended his difficult tasks. Garret was the one who received all the glowing accolades and commendations. But Holt was the silent, ominous force who got things done. He didn't give a fig about the praise. He wanted only the challenge of sniffing out offenders of justice.

Whatever Holt's beef with Walter Jameson, the taciturn detective was keeping his own counsel. If Holt thought Walter deserved an unexpected punch in the jaw, he probably did. But Garret was dying to know why Holt had stuffed a meaty fist in Walter's face.

"Would you mind explaining why you did what you did?" Garret prodded.

"Yes, I would," Holt replied without changing expression. Before his burly friend could give him the third degree, Holt tossed out his own question. "Do you think the track foreman might be involved in embezzlement?"

"Brian King could be skimming the top off the expense funds and splitting the profit with McBride or

112

one of his men," he speculated. "Walter and Max have been by here a couple of other times to talk to the adventurers, immigrants, and the riffraff that are pitching tents and waiting to populate new towns along the route. I'm not exactly sure what those two are up to. But Brian King strikes me as an individual who wouldn't turn down extra payments if he were asked to join some sort of conspiracy. But he damned sure isn't smart enough to devise a scheme. Brian knows his business of laying track and constructing sound bridges, but he isn't what I would call a swindler. The instant word reached our crews that J. W. Baxter's gangs were pushing south toward the border, Brian put us on double shifts to compensate. He has pride in his work and he's a fierce competitor. But if he is on the scam, he isn't the ringleader."

"Well, somebody along the way has been reaping the profits by buying up real estate and stock that was sold to small-time investors," Holt snorted disdainfully. "It seems the company has complied with the government regulations of selling stock to at least two hundred different stockholders. But three of the investors I interrogated yesterday begrudgingly admitted they had been encouraged to buy the stock for only one dollar and the company paid the rest of the share. In turn, the investors took bribes of small tracts of real estate at projected town sites to keep their mouths shut."

Garret thoughtfully chewed on a twig and stared at some distant point. Apparently, Holt had employed very persuasive tactics to drag information out of the three investors he had contacted. Garret didn't bother to ask Holt how he achieved his goal. That Holt had gained the information he required was all Garret wanted to know about the matter.

"Any man who wanted to buy up the McBride stock in hopes of acquiring the majority of shares in the company will have his hands on a tidy sum of money when the shares begin to pay off," Garret mused aloud.

"Money could also be siphoned from federal funds that were granted to pay part of the expenses of laying track and by buying up previously owned land that lies on the route," Holt added. "It would be a simple matter to estimate the costs of laying rails and then add a few thousand dollars to that total. When the company offers money to pay those expenses, our swindler could be padding his own pocket and then turning around to buy up the stock he sold to smaller investors for a dollar a share."

"Now all you have to do is figure out who did it," Garret said with a tired sigh. His gaze shifted to Holt. "Do you think J. W. Baxter was right in accusing Victor McBride of being the culprit?"

Holt stuffed the paper Garret had given him into his pocket. "Time will determine who has been swindling from whom. But things don't look good for the colonel. He has initialed every entry and transaction in the company ledgers, and that makes him responsible for what's been going on. But when I determine who the mastermind is behind this scheme, you'll be the first to know."

"If I come across any information I think you could use, I'll send you a letter from your dear aunt Mildred," Garret informed him with a toothy grin.

"Thanks, Aunt Mildred," Holt snickered as he trotted off into the trees with Dog following obediently behind him.

Muttering to himself, Holt paced the confines of his room like a caged tiger. He had intended to spend the evening at the McBride home, scrutinizing the ledgers to seek out discrepancies in the expense accounts, employing the information Garret had given him. But the colonel had adamantly insisted that Reuben join the McBrides. They were attending a ball hosted by Max Fletcher—the highfalutin merchant who was eager to push the railroad southwest to the town sites where he had purchased land that would soon be sold for double and triple its original cost.

Victor insisted that Max had arranged the party for the sole purpose of acquainting Reuben with the other pillars of society. Holt was in no position to have Reuben refuse the invitation since he had supposedly ventured from Illinois to Missouri to inspect the railroad company for possible investment. It wasn't attending the grand ball that worried Holt. It was the inevitable time he would be forced to spend with Shiloh that disturbed him. He didn't want to cope with the crosscurrents of emotion that tormented him when he was near that enchantress.

Playing this masquerade was wearing on Holt's disposition. Now that he had come to know the ice maiden of Springfield, he no longer wanted to cut her down to size as he had planned to at the onset of this assignment. But what baffled him most was that Reuben's enigma and his bashfulness appealed to a vivacious sprite like Shiloh. It wasn't Holt Cantrell she wanted. It was that cloddish dandy who stumbled over his own feet. What on earth could a rambunctious, vivacious young woman like Shiloh possibly see in a man like Reuben? Holt asked himself bemusedly.

"Good God," Holt scowled as he purposely knotted his cravat at the left side of his throat. This ill-fated attraction to Shiloh was frustrating him to no end. Driving him crazy was nearer the mark, Holt amended as he plastered beeswax on his head and put a crook in the straight part in his hair. He wanted Shiloh, not because she was vulnerable to Reuben, but because

115

Holt was irresistibly drawn to her. And to further exasperate him, the character of Reuben Gilcrest was constantly voicing comments that Holt didn't want to have to make. He had fed her a crock of lies and they stuck in his craw. The conflict of logic versus desire was wearing Holt's nerves to a frazzle.

Holt wasn't sure who he was these days. In all his vast and varied assignments he had never suffered such twinges of guilt and inner turmoil. Certainly, there had been other women he had used to gain information when he infiltrated organizations and secret cults in the South. But his conscience had never hounded him quite so much as it did now. Nor had his basic instincts warred so fiercely against his crusades for justice.

Oh, what the hell, Holt finally told himself as he stuffed his arms into his oversize jacket. There was nothing he could do about this situation with Shiloh. He would enjoy her company this evening, but he would be very careful not to overstep the guidelines he had set for himself. He wouldn't have to fret over being tempted by that sassy beauty, not when they were surrounded by a houseful of guests and men vying for Shiloh's attention. He would simply admire her from a distance and attempt to pry information from Victor and his associates. It was only for one night. How much trouble could a man get into in one evening? he asked himself.

After delivering that pep talk to himself, Holt set his spectacles on the bridge of his nose and stared at his reflection in the mirror. He resembled an exotic bird with his emerald-green frock coat, gold brocade vest, and black breeches. He would stand out like a sore thumb and again become the object of ridicule at the party. Not that Holt gave a hoot. After all, he was playing a charade that suited his purpose. After he completed this assignment he would never see the citizens of Springfield again. What did he care if they laughed at Reuben behind his back?

Anticipating the McBrides' reaction to his outrageous attire, Holt clomped down the hall like a giraffe. The moment he caught sight of Holt, Victor's eyes widened in astonishment. The colonel watched in mute amazement as Holt clambered down the steps with so little coordination that it looked as if he might fall flat on his face.

Victor refrained from commenting on his house guest's outlandish garb, restricting himself to no more than a cordial greeting. When Victor caught a glimpse of his daughter on the landing above them, he awaited her reaction to Reuben's extraordinary clothes. To his disbelief, Shiloh hardly bothered to inspect Reuben's garments. When Holt glanced over his shoulder, her spellbinding eyes focused on his bronzed face before she graced him with a smile that would have melted a normal man. Holt, however, immediately stared at his own feet—not because he was shy, as everyone assumed, but because staring overly long at the bewitching beauty who was poised on the steps could start fires that refused to burn themselves out.

What a glorious sight she was, Holt mused with an appreciative sigh. He had dared to take only a quick peek as she breezed down the hall behind him, but her image was branded on his mind in a matter of seconds. Shiloh was garbed in a flowing gown of pink silk. The dress matched the rosy color in her cheeks and accentuated the creamy texture of her skin. The scoop-necked garment exposed a generous display of bosom, reminding Holt that he had caressed those luscious swells when he never should have touched her at all. He could still feel her soft flesh beneath his fingertips, inhale the fresh fragrance that clung to her, taste kisses that had only whetted his appetite. It may as well have

117

been minutes instead of days since he had held Shiloh in his arms. He recalled every sweet tormenting moment all too vividly. . . .

Yards of delicate lace ruffles rippled along the hem of the gown as Shiloh gracefully floated down the steps. Shiny silver-blond curls danced around her forehead and temples as she approached Holt and her father. Shiloh reminded Holt of an angel descending from heaven. He had to force himself not to take more than a hasty glance before staring in the opposite direction. Lord, she looked gorgeous! Men would trample each other to beg a dance with her, Holt predicted.

Shiloh was one of those rare, unique women whose natural beauty could not be disguised or downgraded, even when she looked her worst. And when she looked her best . . . well, there wasn't a man in the galaxy who wouldn't succumb to her mystical charms. This vision of unrivaled beauty would knock the props out from under any man.

Masking her disappointment behind a sunny smile, Shiloh murmured a greeting to Holt, who was doing his damnedest not to glance at her. She had fussed over her appearance all afternoon, hoping to present a picture this shy gentleman couldn't ignore. But Reuben had reverted to his old ways again, she mused. He looked terribly uncomfortable and he constantly pushed up his glasses while he stood staring at the rug beneath his pointed boots.

The I-told-you-so glance Victor flung at Shiloh didn't help matters one whit. Victor was silently taunting Shiloh into admitting defeat. She could have primped the entire day and it still wouldn't have fazed Reuben. He had no intention of emerging from his shell unless Shiloh split it wide open with a sledge-hammer.

118

He would never forgive her for throwing herself at him that night in the kitchen and that day on the creek bank, she realized. He was ashamed of what had transpired between them, while Shiloh longed for the warm, tender lover who had introduced her to the initial pleasures of passion.

When Victor offered his daughter his arm, Shiloh accepted. And to her chagrin, Reuben chose to give last-minute instructions to his shaggy mongrel before he plodded along behind his host. When the threesome sank down into the phaeton, Reuben strategically slouched into the seat across from Shiloh instead of beside her. Dispiritedly, Shiloh endured the silent ride to Max Fletcher's grand home on the outskirts of Springfield. Reuben said not one word the whole way. He merely sat on his seat, nervously flicking imaginary specks of lint from his breeches. A few minutes before they reached their destination, Victor began rattling off the names of important guests who would be attending the party, but Reuben wasn't listening. He was lost in his own world—a prison of self-inflicted torment.

To Holt's relief, Shiloh was met at the door by a half dozen young men who immediately begged for a dance. Briefly, Shiloh glanced at Holt, hoping he would announce that he would be sharing her company for the majority of the evening. No such luck. Holt merely looked the other way.

When one eager beau grasped Shiloh's hand, insisting she dance the first waltz with him, Holt frowned disconcertedly. He could see the wall of cynical defense rising between the curvaceous blonde and her drooling admirers. She had let her guard down with Holt, but he alone was allowed to know the warm, responsive woman whose protective instincts did not permit her to reveal her true nature to other men. Although Shiloh accepted the offers to dance, Holt was quick to note the respectable distance she kept between herself and her partners. Her polite but remote manner shouted instructions to her beaus—things like don't venture too close, don't linger too long, and don't expect anything in return.

While Shiloh was twirling around the ballroom and being shifted from one pair of arms to the next, Holt was dragged through the receiving line to meet the potentates Victor had mentioned. Once the formal greetings had been made, Holt grabbed a glass of brandy, sought a secluded corner, and stood in it. There were dozens of attractive females in attendance, and any one of them would have caught Holt Cantrell's eye if he hadn't been comparing them to that shapely bundle of femininity in pink satin. But Shiloh stood out like a glittering diamond in a roomful of pebbles.

Good God, Holt would have given most anything to invite one of the other females onto the terrace to ease his frustrated cravings. But he was a hopeless captive of his charade. He couldn't ease his insatiable hunger for Shiloh by substituting another chit in her place. And if he did dally with another woman, it would blow holes in his masquerade of a meek, mild-mannered gentleman who broke out in hives when he came within two feet of the female of the species. A man who was rumored to be awkward around women couldn't very well step out of character without drawing suspicion. Damn, Holt was trapped like a rat, wanting a woman he couldn't have, wanting *any* woman who could appease his gnawing desires.

And so Holt sipped his brandy and paid his penance in gloomy resignation. The only satisfaction he enjoyed was the sight of Walter Jameson, who still bore the telltale signs of the black eye the "unknown assailant" had delivered.

Holt's keen gaze narrowed when Walter approached

Shiloh. He waited, wondering if the feisty beauty would make a scene or if she would discreetly reject Walter's dance invitation. When Shiloh darted her father a glance, he countered with a warning look. It was apparent that Victor expected Shiloh to bury the hatchet somewhere besides in Walter's chest. And out of respect for her father, Shiloh complied with the silent command.

With cool politeness Shiloh accepted Walter's hand and joined him on the dance floor. But the instant his arm stole around her waist, Shiloh was reminded of the day in the meadow when he had attempted to wrestle her to the ground to steal a kiss. Involuntarily, she flinched in response to the unpleasant memory.

Walter expelled a regretful sigh. "I don't expect you to forgive me for behaving like a lecher," he began, flashing her an apologetic smile. "But I ask you to put the past behind you and forget our unfortunate conflict. You must realize how difficult it is for a man to control himself when he is near you. You are a very lovely woman, Shiloh."

It wasn't difficult for Reuben to control himself when she was underfoot, Shiloh mused dismally. She wished Reuben could be a little less of a gentleman and Walter could be more of one. And the only reason she was dancing with this blond-haired Don Juan in the first place was that her father had silently demanded that she call a truce with his second in command. But there was no rule that stated Shiloh had to like Walter, only that she tolerate his presence and his touch until the dance ended.

"I am willing to let bygones be bygones," she replied stiffly. "But if you ever again overstep the bounds of propriety, you will sorely wish you hadn't."

Walter sorted through his repertoire of disarming smiles and selected one of highest quality. "I promise to behave myself from this day forward."

That remained to be seen, Shiloh mused, but she refrained from voicing her skepticism. Walter had many likable qualities, ones that had earned him a high position in the McBride Railroad Company. But his worst flaw was assuming that he was God's gift to women. Shiloh saw no particular reason for his colossal male arrogance. As far as she was concerned, Walter was just one of the endless rabble of men whose presence she was forced to endure. The best she and Walter could hope for was peaceful coexistence. If Walter tried to crowd into her space, and if he didn't focus his amorous attentions elsewhere, they were bound to clash a second time.

Although Shiloh much preferred to be swaying in Reuben's arms, she endured Walter's company while he was on his best behavior. But it was difficult to keep her eyes and thoughts from straying to the man who ambled around the perimeters of the ballroom, ducking away from curious glances cast by the female guests. If only that handsome prince would emerge from his shell and show the rest of the world what great promise he had, Shiloh thought with a wistful sigh. Poor Reuben. He was as afraid to be himself in the company of women as she was in the presence of all other men. But nothing was going to change her or Reuben, she reckoned. They were both doomed to hide behind their protective fortresses of reserve for their own private reasons.

Shiloh was deluding herself if she thought Reuben would ever work up enough nerve to ask her to dance even once this evening. She was doomed to remain in the company of other men, longing for the companionship of the one man who rejected her friendship and affection.

It seemed Victor was right after all, Shiloh thought

defeatedly. She didn't know how to attract a man who wasn't chasing her. She appealed to men in whom she had very little interest and not to the one man who did appeal to her in his own unique way. What bitter irony, Shiloh mused with a rueful smile. All these years she had envisioned exactly what she wanted in a man, and now she was getting what she deserved for being so particular. The man she might possibly have loved for all the right reasons didn't want anything to do with her!

Chapter 10

While Shiloh was passed to another set of waiting arms, Holt discreetly worked his way around the room, eavesdropping on conversations as he went. He overheard a variety of comments, ranging from several men's secret desires to get the stunning blonde alone in the moonlight to speculations on the railroad company's chances of winning the race to Indian territory.

Holt posed a few well-aimed questions to Max Fletcher and the eastern tycoon, Elijah Conners. Their conflicting estimates of projected costs of reaching the border before Baxter's crews did left Holt to reevaluate his speculations. He was quick to accuse Walter Jameson of guilt, but he had the feeling his suspicions were influenced by the man's blatant interest in Shiloh. Holt couldn't be objective about Walter.

If he looked a little deeper he would probably learn that Elijah Conners was far more familiar with bribing government officials to pass legislation that would benefit the railroad company in which he had invested. Holt had dealt with Elijah's type before. Elijah knew all the right people in the right places. It took money to make money—whether it was made above or below the table. And Holt certainly couldn't rule out Max

Fletcher either. The bald-headed, rotund gentleman who garbed himself in flashy but stylish clothes and incessantly chewed on his unlit cigar had a scheming mind. Holt could see Max's beady little eyes shifting and his mind cranking while he spoke. Max hadn't gotten where he was without several shrewd maneuvers. He was a self-made millionaire who had known just where to purchase land before the railroad reached Springfield. No one could be so lucky as to acquire several sections of land that just so happened to lie on the railroad's right-of-way. He had inside connections, Holt predicted. Whether they came directly from Victor McBride or from one of his confidants was anybody's guess. Holt still didn't know for certain. . . .

The swish of petticoats dragged Holt from his silent reverie. Glancing up, he spied the attractive copper-haired beauty he had been introduced to in the receiving line. Employing her drumroll walk, Felicia Fletcher sashayed toward Holt. Her pale green eyes flooded over his gaudy attire and then bubbles of giggles erupted from her full lips. With a discerning gaze Felicia assessed the tall, midnight-haired gentleman a second time. Another round of giggles erupted from her lips as she struck a seductive pose in front of her father's guest.

"Rumor has it that you are terribly bashful around women," Felicia purred, and then burst into another gurgle of laughter that could grate on a man's nerves.

Good God, just what he needed, Holt thought disgustedly. He would be forced to tolerate this incessant giggler whose coquettish manner instantly nauseated him. The chit was pretty enough, but her personality detracted from her visible beauty. There was a paradoxical air about Felicia that outwardly suggested she was striving for sainthood. But in Holt's opinion there was no way in hell she could acquire it.

126

He kept receiving contradicting vibrations from this buxom one.

Although Felicia seemed about the same age as Shiloh, she wasn't nearly as mature of mind as she was of body. Her cut of clothes testified that she had blossomed fully. Holt wasn't an expert on women's undergarments by any means. But he was curious to know how Felicia had invented the most remarkable technique of pushing up her generous bosom as far as it could go without shoving it out the top of her low-cut gown. There was no need to speculate on how well Felicia was built because it was all there for the world to see. If a man wasn't overly particular, Holt supposed Felicia would make an interesting bed partner. But as for himself, he wasn't eager to find out. Felicia's annoying snickers would be impossible to tolerate for extended periods of time. No wonder this chit wasn't married. Who could stand to listen for years on end to a giggle that was reminiscent of a cackling witch? As seductive as she appeared to be in her own mock-innocent way, her cackle killed the effect like cold water on glowing coals.

Felicia tossed her head in a carefree manner and glanced over her shoulder at the congregation of young ladies who had gathered around the refreshment table. Then she singled out Shiloh, who had lines forming behind her on the dance floor. It was obvious that Felicia wanted Reuben to know where Shiloh's attention had shifted. She might as well have gestured with a dainty hand.

"Rumor also has it that our dear friend Shiloh has a crush on you," she remarked with pretentious nonchalance and a voice that dripped molasses.

Holt stifled a grin. The wench was so obvious in her tactics that he felt the urge to laugh her out of her own home. "Does she?" Holt commented before focusing on Felicia's slippers, picturing himself tripping this spiteful chit and watching her sprawl all over the floor. It was a most gratifying picture.

"According to Walter Jameson, the two of you went riding together without a chaperone this week," Felicia replied airily. "Wouldn't it be the icing on the cake if our little ice maiden fell in love with you, Reuben?"

It was with great difficulty that Holt kept hold of his brandy glass instead of wrapping his fingers around this ornery minx's neck. She was a troublemaker, he decided. Felicia was probably jealous of Shiloh's effect on men, and this little witch would like nothing better than to make Shiloh the laughingstock of Springfield.

"My host's daughter has been charming company the scant few times we have been together," Holt countered in a bland tone.

"But you are not in love with her?" Felicia had the audacity to ask. "My heavens, Reuben, you are one of the few men in Springfield who isn't. Shiloh attracts men like mosquitoes."

This conversation was headed nowhere. If Holt as Reuben admitted to disliking or liking Shiloh, Felicia's tongue would be wagging all night. This pesky wench was waiting for him to make a careless slip so she could tattle to her gawking friends.

Holt raised his head momentarily to glance at the persnickety young woman. "I am a very private man, Miss Fletcher," he informed her in a tone that disguised his irritation. "I have been taught to mind my own business and I prefer others do likewise. It seems the honorable thing to do in most instances. Don't you agree?"

Reuben Gilcrest was a tough case to crack. Felicia had given him every opportunity to divulge information. But Reuben was as closed as a clam. She had bet her friends that she could get a rise out of the fumbling dandy. And if not a rise, at least a juicy tidbit of gossip to pass behind Shiloh's back. In Springfield, Shiloh had scores of male admirers and twice as many female rivals, but very few close friends. That was the way it was for a woman of Shiloh's beauty, spirit, and wealth. She was lusted after and envied and rarely befriended. Felicia was one of the many women who envied Shiloh's sex appeal. She did keep a stable of studs at her beck and call, but it was Shiloh whom men lusted after, not Felicia.

"Then if you have an aversion to someone prying into your private life, perhaps you would prefer to dance," Felicia suggested in a tone that could have been poured over a stack of pancakes. Maybe she could pry information out of Reuben under the pretense of dancing. But she was not going away empty-handed, not when her friends were waiting to determine if she had the slightest effect on this shy, reserved bachelor.

A mutinous glare flashed in Shiloh's eyes when she spied Felicia flaunting herself under Reuben's nose. There was no telling what that vamp was up to. Felicia always brewed trouble. She wasn't happy unless her vicious gossip was making someone miserable. Now she was taking unfair advantage of Reuben, who preferred to be left alone.

Excusing herself from her dance partner, Shiloh cut her way through the crowd. It was ridiculous for her to be protective and possessive of a man who barely offered her the time of day since she had openly invited him to seduce her. But possessive she was, and she had every intention of delivering Reuben from Felicia's clutches. That witch had a tongue like a poison arrow, and Shiloh had no wish to have Reuben demoralized by Felicia's insulting remarks.

When Shiloh strode up beside the copper-haired sorceress who had obviously discarded her broom and decided to walk instead of riding on it, Holt frowned disconcertedly. Shiloh was not a shrinking southern violet, not by any stretch of the imagination. She had that daring look about her, one that indicated she wasn't above making a spectacle of herself to prevent Felicia from poking fun at him. If he took Felicia's offer to dance, he would hurt Shiloh's feelings more than he already had and he would give the spiteful Felicia a weapon to use against her female rival. And if he asked Shiloh to dance, he could expect Felicia to dig up some slander to fling at Shiloh. Felicia couldn't have been more obvious.

"It seems my glass has run dry," Holt observed for lack of much else to say. "Excuse me, ladies . . ."

As he zigzagged his way through the crowd to disappear into the hall, Felicia flung Shiloh a flippant smile. "It seems even your legendary charm has cast no spell on your bashful beau," she mocked.

There had been many times in the past when Shiloh had itched to smear Felicia's goading grins all over her face. This was another of those times. Felicia was a pest—a conceited, gossiping pest who tried to move up in the world by stepping on as many toes as possible during her ascent.

"You disappoint me, Felicia," Shiloh taunted with her own sarcastic smile. "I thought you had learned to pick on people your own size—thumb-sucking toddlers, for instance."

The barb struck like a hurled dagger. Felicia's back stiffened and her painted lips curled in a sneer that did her delicate features no justice. "At least I don't have a futile crush on that awkward goose," Felicia sniped. "Walter saw you and that fumbling dunderhead riding off into the thicket. What did you do, decide to spread yourself beneath the shy Reuben Gilcrest to teach him a thing or two about women? What a

130

comical scene that must have been. You have been so stingy with your charms that you don't know the first thing about pleasing men. And why any man lusts after you is beyond me." Her glittering green eyes flitted over Shiloh's shapely figure with mocking disdain. "If men knew what they were missing, they would probably wonder why on earth they ever fantasized about sleeping with you."

A sharp gasp erupted from Shiloh's throat. She shouldn't have been surprised that Felicia would transform into the vicious witch she was, right in the middle of her father's party. But she most certainly had, and Shiloh refused to be intimidated by the spiteful twit.

"And by that same theory, the men of Springfield wished they had taken a wide berth around you, Felicia," she parried through clenched teeth. "You give out free samples of your *charms* . . . and I use the term loosely. A man has but to look interested and you are flat on your back, ready to accommodate him. But no man bothers to come back for a second helping of your favors. You would have to buy a husband with your father's money. No one seems to want baggage that has been claimed by half the male population in town."

Felicia looked so sour it turned Shiloh's stomach. "You little bitch!" Felicia spluttered maliciously. "I ought to have my father throw you . . ."

It was at that crucial moment, before fur began to fly, that Holt returned to the scene. Even from a distance he had noticed the sparks flaring from Shiloh's silver-blue eyes. He couldn't overhear the ridiculing remarks they had flung at each other, but he could tell that Shiloh's temper was about to explode when she stamped her dainty foot. Whatever these two young ladies had said had put them at each other's throats. Although Holt knew Shiloh could take this

131

copper-haired twit apart at the seams, this was neither the time nor the place. It seemed he would be forced to give Felicia food for gossip or allow Shiloh to wring the woman's skinny neck with a houseful of guests as witnesses.

"May I beg a dance with you, Shiloh," Holt requested, shoving his contrary glasses into place as he wedged his way between the two fuming women.

Sporting a sardonic smile, Felicia ran her gaze down Holt's outlandish attire and then bounced off Shiloh's mutinous glare. "Do, by all means, grant the gentleman a dance, dear Shiloh," Felicia purred caustically. "The two of you deserve each other."

When Felicia pirouetted to make her theatrical departure, Shiloh prepared to pounce. Holt slid his hand around Shiloh's waist before she could launch herself at the spiteful redhead.

"She isn't worth it," Holt murmured, holding Shiloh's rigid body at bay.

Shiloh inhaled a furious breath and struggled to grasp the trailing reins of her temper. Reuben was right about Felicia, but she would have felt infinitely better if she could have pounded Felicia flat and stuffed her in a box, and mailed her to Australia.

"You invited me to dance, so let's dance," Shiloh muttered.

When Shiloh had calmed down, Holt dropped his hand from her waist, afraid the harmless touch would become the caress he couldn't allow himself to enjoy. "The truth is, I don't dance very well. But I thought it was best for me to intervene before you and Miss Fletcher came to blows."

Now that Reuben had finally asked her to dance, Shiloh was not about to allow him to weasel out of it. "I will be happy to teach you the steps," she volunteered, managing a smile for the benefit of Felicia and her clan of gossips.

Holt ducked his head, as was Reuben's custom. "I doubt that it would do any good. Although you don't mind walking on your own feet, I don't think you will enjoy having me trounce on the top of them."

"Nonsense." Shiloh dismissed his comment as she grabbed his hand. "All you lack is confidence. For once I wish you would live up to your potential."

The moment her small hand slid over his, Holt groaned inwardly. It took so little to remind him of their forbidden moments together. He didn't want to remember how he ached for her. He wanted to keep his relationship with this feisty blonde in proper perspective. But Shiloh refused to allow him to retract his invitation. She was tempting fate and she was too naive to know it.

Damnation, he had spent more than a week trying to forget how wondrous it was to hold this curvaceous beauty in his arms. He had tried to erase the picture of her lying in the grass with her body partially exposed to his hungry gaze, her eyes glistening with unappeased passion. They might be doing nothing more than dancing in each other's arms in a crowded ballroom, but Holt had the sinking feeling he would be fantasizing about far more arousing activities.

Wouldn't it have been nice if Holt could simply have requested that the swindler in the McBride Railroad Company step forward and admit his guilt? Then Holt could get the hell out of there! He needed to wrap up this assignment for Pinkerton and retreat before he found himself so involved with this innocent beauty that he . . .

Holt's thoughts evaporated when he was forced to concentrate on dancing as if he didn't know beans about it. He purposely moved like a stiff-legged stork, hoping Shiloh would give him up as a lost cause. But

133

she didn't complain when his toe collided with hers or when he rammed his knee into her thigh.

"I'm just no good at this," Holt finally muttered.

Long lashes swept up to peer into the vivid green pools behind the unflattering glasses. "You don't want to be good at it because you don't want to be near me," Shiloh said in a deflated tone.

Begrudgingly, her gaze darted to Felicia, who was having a laugh at Shiloh's expense. She and her partner must have looked like two logs bumping into each other as they floated downriver, and Felicia was erupting in those grating giggles of hers.

What was the use? Shiloh thought gloomily. She had employed every tactic imaginable to draw Reuben from his cocoon. He didn't want to become a graceful swan. He preferred to be the ugly duckling, the clumsy toad. Well, fine, she decided. She was through trying to befriend a man who wanted nothing to do with her. Victor had told her not to waste her time, but being the stubborn individual she was, Shiloh refused to give up on Reuben. But she was giving up now! Let him spend the rest of his life avoiding women. What did she care? she tried to reassure herself. She had resolved to become a spinster anyway.

Gracefully, Shiloh stepped away and propelled herself across the ballroom. In swift strides she sailed out onto the terrace to inhale a breath of air and regain control of her temper, one that had been sorely put upon once too often this evening.

Damn that Reuben! He had thwarted every attempt to recapture the pleasure they had twice enjoyed. He was still afraid she would throw herself at him. But she had tried only to dance with him tonight. How intimate could two people get while they were twirling around the dance floor in the midst of a crowd? It wasn't as if she had asked him to make love to her again. Dammit all, what was the matter with her that Reuben found her so offensive?

Maybe Felicia was right about her. Maybe she didn't have anything to offer a man. Reuben's constant refusals had her questioning her femininity and the flaws in her personality. Obviously she wasn't woman enough to tempt any man, especially one as cautious and reluctant as Reuben . . .

"I don't want your pity, Shiloh." Holt's voice wafted its way through the shadows to jolt her from her contemplative deliberations. "And if you will look past your bruised pride, I think you will realize that is the reason you have bestowed any type of attention on me. You want to make me over, to draw something out of me that isn't there."

She spun around, her eyes flashing like lightning. "Is that what you think, you dim-witted fool?" she snapped, stamping her foot in a fit of temper. "Can't you accept a woman's friendship and affection without being so cynical and mistrusting of her intentions?"

"Why should I?" he countered, his tone far more controlled than hers, even though he was every bit as exasperated with the situation. "I saw the way you held your interested suitors at bay. You don't trust them as far as you can throw them. But you expect me to put my guard down and believe you are harboring honest affection for me. I know you were instructed to make my stay in Springfield pleasant. You admitted it."

"For heaven's sake, do you still think I am acting under orders from my father?" she asked in a blistering tone. Her breasts heaved with indignation while she let him have it with both barrels. "In case you are too damned blind to notice, I happen to like you the way you are. It certainly isn't because of your dashing appearance and stylish clothes. If you want the truth, you look ridiculous in those sloppy, wild-colored

135

garments. And if you wouldn't part your hair down the middle and plaster it against your head, you would be a lot more handsome. You have a magnificent body . . . at least as much as I have viewed of it . . . and you cover it up with the most unflattering attire I have seen in all my life!"

Shiloh hadn't meant to be so blunt and intimidating, but she was angry and her tongue was outracing her brain. "You are so all-fired concerned about treating a lady like a lady that you won't allow her to be a woman. I should be the one to decide if I wish to be kissed or not, if I wish to be touched. You don't even give me the satisfaction of saying no when I am damned good and ready to say it . . . which I wasn't while we were kissing in the kitchen or under the canopy of trees. You are trying so hard to be a gentleman that I find it insulting! And to top off this strained relationship between us, Felicia is having a field day with her wagging tongue. She has spread it all over town that I have a crush on you and you won't have anything to do with me."

Pausing, Shiloh inhaled a quick breath and plunged on, spurred by her unchecked temper. *"I* feel sorry for *you?"* she repeated sarcastically. "Ha! I feel sorry for myself for caring more about you than you care about yourself! I'm the one who will be left to counter the gossip when you depart from Springfield!"

Holt battled down a chuckle. Shiloh was a bona fide spitfire when she was in a snit. "I hope you have been listening to what you have been saying, ma'am," he replied in a tone that was meant to be a tactful reprimand. The formal address was a strategic attempt to remind Shiloh that they were to remain respectful acquaintances, not intimate lovers, even if he did ache for her up to his eyebrows.

"Oh, shut up and don't call me ma'am," she bit off

136

testily. "I am not a madam; I'm a miss. And I'll tell you exactly what I *miss* most—your companionship, your kisses. I even wanted you to make l—"

Shiloh slammed her mouth shut and blushed beet-red. Thank God the darkness concealed her embarrassment. It was bad enough that she had begged Reuben to seduce her that day beside the creek. Now she had blurted it out at a party! Sweet mercy, she would have to bob her tongue if it didn't quit running away with itself.

"You wanted me to make love to you," he finished for her, and then stared off in the opposite direction. "And if I had, I fear we both would have regretted it. I have no intention of repaying my gracious host by seducing his daughter. Then Felicia really would have a field day."

Too flustered by her flapping tongue and the outright rejection of her whimsical desires, Shiloh whizzed toward the terrace doors. First she had insulted Reuben and then she had confessed her forbidden fantasy. She had made a fool of herself in front of a man who looked to all the world like an unsophisticated bumpkin, a man whose stroke of good luck had placed a fortune in his lap—money that would have been well spent on a decent wardrobe of clothes and a knowledgeable barber!

Well, if Reuben wanted to look like a frump and reject her invitation, so be it. She wasn't going to go out of her way to be near him ever again. He could curl up in a corner and mildew for all she cared! Whatever, this illogical attraction she felt for him was over and done. She was never going to give Reuben another thought. The powerful package of masculinity that was confined inside his ill-fitting cocoon could stay there and rot. If Reuben never wanted to be more than a shy, awkward dolt, that was his business. Shiloh didn't give a whit anymore!

"Shiloh, wait a minute," Holt requested as she buzzed through the door, madder than a hornet.

But Shiloh was long gone. She was leaving the festivities to return home. And never again would she give any man the time of day. And no man would ever hear the shameless invitation she had offered Reuben twice! Dammit all, she needed to have her head examined. She sounded like a trollop flinging propositions to the first man who breezed past her. She didn't want to make love to that clumsy oaf, she wanted to punch him in the nose and break those damned spectacles.

When Shiloh elbowed her way through the ballroom and fled out the door, Victor peered curiously after her. The moment he spied his house guest dodging dancers to follow in Shiloh's wake, his brows puckered in a bumfuzzled frown. Now, what the blazes was going on?

Since Reuben appeared to be in pursuit to resolve whatever differences of opinion had put him and Shiloh at odds, Victor remained where he was. He had business to discuss with Max, Elijah, and Walter. While he exchanged ideas with the other board members, Shiloh would have time to cool down. When she was rational again, Victor would approach her without appearing the overprotective father.

Confound that girl, Victor mused. He had warned her to let Reuben alone. But would Shiloh listen? Hell, no, she was stubborn and headstrong. With all the men who courted her, why did she have to turn her attention to an awkward, self-reserved man who was immune to her charms? Wasn't that just like a woman to want what she couldn't have? If Reuben had chased her or shown the slightest interest, Shiloh would have shrugged him off the way she did all other men. Reuben Gilcrest was her exact opposite and yet . . .

Victor scolded himself for analyzing his rambunctious daughter and her unexplainable fascination with Reuben. For the past two years Victor had thrust men at Shiloh every chance he got. And what did she do? Turn to a man who wanted nothing to do with her. Women! Victor had learned long ago that a man could never hope to understand the workings of the feminine mind. He only had to shower her with love. And love Shiloh he did. But sometimes loving her meant letting her sulk.

He had spoiled his daughter because she was all he had. He had sheltered her for too long and he had promised himself he would let her spread her wings and fly, that he would allow her to confront her problems and resolve them as she saw fit. It was difficult for a father not to trail after his daughter when she was upset, but Victor reminded himself that sometimes letting go was better than clinging too tightly. When Shiloh finished telling Reuben to get lost, she would adjourn to her room. She would storm about the confines of her boudoir, stamp her foot, and throw a few things. Then she would regain control of her temper all by herself. When the storm blew over, Victor would go to console her. Shiloh didn't want her father to resolve every crisis in her life.

And so Victor let Shiloh sail off like a flying carpet, knowing she didn't expect or want him to come trailing after her. Damn, being a father wasn't easy. It killed him to see Shiloh hurting, no matter how insignificant the pain. Victor had told himself through the trying years that things would get better with time. They didn't. Daughters were difficult to raise. One would think he would have gotten good at it after twenty-one years!

Chapter 11

By the time Shiloh stamped into the brick mansion on her father's spacious estate, Marcella and the other servants had retired to their quarters. Muttering to herself, Shiloh undressed on her way up the steps. When she reached her bedchamber she stood only in her short chemise. In a burst of fury she hurled her expensive gown and petticoats into the corner, her satin slippers following shortly after.

This was the last time she was ever going to let a man interrupt her life, she vowed bitterly. She had discovered a tender, caring man beneath Reuben's frumpy garb and she had tried to reach out to him. But he didn't want her affection, and neither had Lance Draper. It was clear to Shiloh now that all that attracted men to her were her elegant clothes and her fortune. No man gave a tinker's damn about the personality attached to her wealth. In Reuben's case it wasn't even her wealth or her reasonably good looks that attracted him. He wasn't attracted to her period! In a way, Shiloh had tested herself with Reuben for her own curiosity. And the painful truth was that the woman who hid behind her protective shell wasn't memorable enough to stir a man who hid behind his protective shell. There was nothing special about her, Shiloh realized dejectedly. . . .

"You are making things very difficult for me."

Shiloh wheeled around to find Reuben poised in the doorway, his hands stuffed deep in his pockets, his shoulder propped negligently against the wall. He stared somberly at her through the dancing shadows and dim light cast by the lantern. Shiloh forgot her modesty when her temper flared up at the sight of the slouched intruder who had put her in a huff in the first place.

"Go to hell, Reuben," she spumed before she pivoted to present her back to him.

Astute green eyes measured her shapely derriere and the smooth contours of her bare legs. She was incredibly well sculptured, Holt thought. In his experience with women, he had discovered there were very few "perfect" figures. However, Shiloh McBride possessed one of them. She had all the well-proportioned curves and swells in just the right places. And to add to her unforgettable physique was a lustrous mass of silver-blond hair and a pair of glistening blue eyes that could captivate a man and hold him spellbound.

Although Shiloh was undoubtedly thinking she had little appeal, she had too much of it for her own good. Holt could pretend he wasn't affected by her unrivaled beauty and untamed spirit, but he was vividly aware of it. His forbidden desire for Shiloh had been his cross to bear since the moment he laid eyes on her.

Shiloh was the devil's own temptation, and Holt was having one helluva time keeping his distance. He longed to touch what his eyes beheld, to succumb to the lusty cravings he had cautiously held in check for

142

almost two tormenting weeks. Dammit, no other assignment had been this difficult, Holt thought in frustration. When Garret walked up and shot him in the past, all fascination for the women he encountered died with his charade. Lord, where was Garret when Holt really needed him?

Even as Holt turned the thoughts over in his mind, he found his footsteps taking him across the room. For God's sake, don't touch her, Holt warned himself. Just talk to her, just smooth her ruffled feathers and get the hell out of there!

But his body was paying not one tittle of attention to the good advice his brain was sending to all parts of his anatomy. His hands, as if they possessed a mind of their own, slid up Shiloh's silky arms. And once he dared to touch her he became like the little boy who tried to hold back floodwaters by stuffing his forefinger in a crumbling dam. A maelstrom of sensations rushed over him like a tidal wave. His senses immediately came to life. Holt inhaled the subtle fragrance of her hair, the compelling aroma of jasmine. The feel of her creamy skin aroused him. The sight of her barely clad body sent tingles down his spine.

"Shiloh, if you are thinking I don't want you, that you don't appeal to me, you are very wrong," he murmured as his hands scaled and then descended her taut arms in a gentle massage. "But the last thing I want to do is hurt you. In my own way, I'm trying to protect you."

Turning, she peered up at him through moist lashes and silver-blue eyes that filled with tears that she refused to permit to spill down her flushed cheeks. "You have hurt me more by rejecting me when I reached out to you," she muttered defensively. "I know I'm not very good at displaying my affection because

143

I've been afraid to be open with my feelings. I've had so little practice. But you won't even let me try!"

Hesitantly, as if he resented the fierce attraction between them, Holt lowered his head. His unblinking gaze focused on her quivering lips—lips that he remembered could melt like summer rain, quenching his thirst. God, he wanted to crush her to him, to mold her luscious contours into his. He longed to take full possession, but he valiantly fought to restrain himself. Holt settled for a kiss even though he was starved for more than the merging of his lips with hers.

The moment his arms slid around her to lift her to his kiss, Shiloh buckled to the turmoil of sensations that swirled inside her. She wanted his kiss, wanted to block out her frustration. And she couldn't accuse Reuben of being overzealous. Indeed, he showed more constraint than she did!

The instant their lips met, her senses were saturated with the scent, taste, and feel of him. All inhibition fled. Her arms curled around his neck and she arched toward him, longing to absorb his hidden strength, to feel his rock-hard flesh pressed familiarly against hers.

Reuben had kissed her before, but never quite like this. His lips rolled over hers, savoring her for a long, breathless moment. His tongue probed into the dark recesses, and Shiloh's racing heart catapulted to her throat. The world shrank to fill the space no larger than this enigmatic man occupied. A sweet, compelling flame burst inside her, and she returned the uncontrollable pleasure he instilled in her with a hot, explosive kiss. Longings unfurled deep within her as his hands wandered over her hips to guide her to him, allowing her to feel the full extent of his arousal.

He did feel something, even if it was simple male lust, Shiloh encouraged herself. Eagerly, she gave herself up

144

to the tantalizing body so intimately close to hers, to the devouring kiss that caused her pulse to leap into triple time. Perhaps she wasn't woman enough to draw upon Reuben's carefully protected emotions, but he was experiencing physical desire for her. That was a start. Maybe in time he would let his guard down and realize that she wanted his friendship as well as his affection, that she wanted to get to know him as she had known no other man.

As his hands drifted up her spine in a most arousing technique, she wondered if Reuben knew he possessed the power to excite and tempt a woman to the limits of her sanity. Usually, Reuben seemed so unsure of himself, but tonight the invisible wall he kept between them had come down and he gave in to his masculine desires. How she longed to understand this secretive, standoffish man! He had so much to give and he gave incredibly well. Even though he admitted to little experience, he had the most masterful touch imaginable. He was bestowing kisses and caresses on her that melted her into bubbly puddles. . . .

Her thoughts scattered when Reuben's exploring hands slid beneath her chemise to make titillating contact with her trembling skin. She felt that same unexplainable need begin to consume her as it had that night in the kitchen and that afternoon beside the creek. As he drew the flimsy chemise away, he greeted each inch of bare flesh with reverent kisses, making Shiloh feel cherished and special. It was as if he had saved this extraordinary passion that had been bottled up inside him for her alone. And she accepted his precious gift, coveting each wondrous sensation that his magical touch aroused.

It must be true that passion is its own instructor, Shiloh decided as she surrendered to his wandering

145

caresses. Reuben instinctively knew where and how to touch her to awaken her slumbering desires—ones no other man had ever aroused. The erotic path of his hands was wildly exciting as it extended over her breasts and down her ribs, driving her to distraction. Her knees were weak, and if Reuben hadn't clutched her to him, Shiloh swore she would have collapsed at his feet.

Sweet mercy! How could this man have known what pleasured her so? How could he make her beg for a dozen more whispering kisses and butterfly caresses? She adored the feel of his hands and lips skimming her flesh, learning the exact location of each ultrasensitive point. He made her feel so feminine . . . so out of control. . . .

A tiny moan tripped from her lips as he effortlessly scooped her up in his arms and carried her to her bed. Ever so gently he laid her upon the satin sheets and then stepped back to marvel at the tantalizing picture she presented.

Try as he may, Holt couldn't take his eyes off the silky goddess who peered up at him with those spellbinding silver-blue eyes so alive with passion. He hadn't meant this to happen. But this luscious beauty had challenged the raw, driving force that he had honorably restrained . . . until now. Wild horses couldn't have dragged him away from Shiloh. She looked so vulnerable and receptive lying there with her blond hair spilling over the pillow like a waterfall sparkling in the light. Her heart-shaped lips were swollen from his greedy kisses, and they were parted in an invitation he couldn't refuse. He wanted to discover all the delights of loving her.

She was so magnificently formed—the epitome of perfection—and Holt wanted her the way a starved man craved a long-awaited feast. For too long Holt had deprived himself, but the weeks of denial had taken their toll. Now there was no will to fight the ardent desires that he had valiantly tried to subdue.

When he peeled off his vest and shirt, he watched her appreciative gaze roam unhindered over his chest. God, why did she have to look at him that way? It drove him over the brink. She made him feel so cherished, so desirable, so wanted. Shiloh made him glad he was a man—the man she wanted in her bed when no others had been there before. . . .

That thought caused Holt to still his hands, ones that hovered on the band of his breeches. She was a virgin. What the hell did he think he was doing? He couldn't take what he wanted the way he had with the women in his past. This was different, this was . . .

The moment he hesitated in doffing his breeches he detected the apprehension in Shiloh's exquisite features. She was afraid he was going to turn and walk away, leaving her to cope with another round of rejection. For an instant Holt debated which would be worse—humiliating her or forcing her to deal with this reckless affair after she had time to analyze it.

It was no contest. His body was all too willing and his nagging conscience was no match for the raging passion that riveted through him. Later, he would probably regret making wild, sweet love to Shiloh. But not now, not when she looked so incredibly desirable lying there. Not when she had silently assured him that he was the man she wanted to have teach her the pleasures of passion. That in itself was enough to drive him mad with longing.

Never taking his eyes off the bewitching beauty who was offering him what she had given to no other man, Holt pushed his baggy breeches from his hips, letting them fall into a rumpled pool around his feet. When Shiloh's wide, luminous eyes ventured down his naked torso, he felt his legs turn limp. Lord, did she have any idea how masculine she made him feel when she peered at him as if he were the most magnificent creature to walk the face of the earth? She openly admired him, caressing him with her gaze, silently beckoning him into her waiting arms. Shiloh played no coy games. Her heart was in her eyes—innocent eyes that roved over him with undisguised appreciation and feminine curiosity.

Shiloh was mesmerized by the man who towered over her. She had felt Reuben's warm, hard strength against her before, but she never imagined him to be such an incredible monument to masculinity. Even her embarrassment of observing a man in the buff for the first time couldn't stifle her marveling admiration.

There was an aura of primitive maleness about him that set off sparks as ancient as time itself. She was enthralled by his virility. His shoulders were broad, tanned, and bulging with whipcord muscle. There wasn't an inch of flab on him anywhere. He looked like a bronzed mountain standing in the golden lantern light. Her all-consuming gaze flooded over the taut tendons and long columns of rippling muscle, wondering at the scar on his shoulder. But it was the only thing that marred his steel-honed body. The rest of him was perfection.

"You are so very handsome, Reuben," she whispered with wide-eyed innocence.

That really did it! Noble reserve and common decency packed up and abandoned him. Her compliment and the husky tone in which she conveyed it was Holt's undoing. Like the victim of a trance, he stretched out beside her, allowing her to brazenly touch what

148

she had caressed with her awestruck gaze.

Oh, how delightful it was to brush her hands over his hair-matted flesh. It was like caressing a living fire. Shiloh mapped each muscled plane and steel-hard contour like a blind woman seeing by touch. She examined and investigated every masculine inch of him, learning his body far better than she knew her own.

Holt allowed her to explore him as long as he could stand without ravishing her. She had instilled such gnawing hungers in him that he swore he would devour her any second. He had to return the splendorous pleasure that her innocent and yet imaginative touch aroused in him or he would surely go mad. He ached to press his hands and lips to her satiny flesh, to shatter her composure as thoroughly as she had shattered his.

When they satisfied their need to explore and arouse, the flame between them flared up and burned like wildfire. Holt could feel the sparks leaping from his body to hers and back again. As his eager caresses traced an erotic path across the star-shaped birthmark that was located just above her right kneecap, passion rose like a floodtide. Restlessly, his hands glided upward to cup her breasts and his lips skimmed down her swanlike throat to suck at the taut peaks. Over and over again his hands and lips moved on their own accord, hungry for the taste and feel of her creamy skin. He was drugged by the fragrance that fogged his senses, entranced by this vision of exceptional loveliness, totally and completely aware of her.

Lord, this enchantress was the personification of beauty. Touching her left him quaking with unappeased desire. He had intimately caressed her and she responded in wild abandon. But it wasn't enough that he had touched and beheld what no other man had possessed, much less gazed upon. Holt needed to feel her pliant body beneath his, to lose himself in the sweet, compelling fog of passion. He wanted her as he had wanted nothing else in more years than he cared to count. . . .

When Shiloh's fingertips brushed against his bold manhood, Holt forgot how to breathe. He felt like an overinflated balloon that was about to burst. And yet, amid the violent onrush of unrestrained passion, one thread of thought managed to keep him in touch with sanity. If he rushed Shiloh over the hurdle of initiation, he would leave her with invisible scars. His experiences with virgins numbered *none*. The women who had lain in his arms were seasoned lovers. But this silver-blue-eyed blonde was an innocent maid who didn't know what to expect or where the stepping-stones of desire led. And she was so tiny, so petite, he reminded himself as his masculine body half covered hers. He didn't want to hurt or frighten Shiloh. He wanted her to revel in the pleasure of intimacy, to give and share in passion until it consumed both of them.

As if he were touching fragile crystal, Holt levered himself above her, gently guiding her thighs apart with his knees. When he peered down into her elegant face he was overwhelmed by the trust and fascination mirrored in her unique eyes. Holt felt guilty as sin all over again. She was making love to Reuben—a man she presumed to have no previous experience with women, a man she supposed knew, by pure instinct, what he was doing. Holt felt that he was betraying her trust in him, and yet he couldn't stop himself from wanting all of her. He wasn't going to be satisfied until they were as close as two people could get, until this ungovernable passion that strained against its captive chains was allowed to run free.

150

"Shiloh, I—"

Her tapered forefinger brushed his sensuous lips to shush him. She wanted no apologies, and this was not the time for conversation. Reuben had kissed and caressed her senseless, and she ached to know where these wild tremors of desire would lead. Her naive body quivered in expectation, in wonderment. She had never wanted a man the way she wanted Reuben. No man had ever made her crave him in such phenomenal ways. Her body needed his touch. She ached to be one with his flesh. She was a prisoner of breathless curiosity, a slave to staggering pleasures that channeled through every part of her being.

"I want you," she murmured raggedly. "Make the ache go away. . . ."

With a groan of unholy torment Holt settled exactly upon her. His mouth took possession of her lips as his hips glided over hers. He felt her stiffen at the unfamiliar intimacy and he willfully restrained himself from seeking his own selfish pleasure. In a deliberate caress his hand slid down her ribs to reassure her that he offered tenderness, not ravishment.

Shiloh forced herself to ignore the sharp stab of pain. She reminded herself that Reuben was not a man who would purposely hurt her in any way. She closed her eyes and remembered the wonderfully gentle man who had kissed and caressed her until she cried out for him to satisfy these fervent needs that overwhelmed her.

Ever so slowly, Holt withdrew, his chest brushing provocatively against the throbbing peaks of her breasts his knees gliding seductively against the sensitive flesh of her thighs. And this time, when his muscular body uncoiled upon hers, Shiloh gave herself to the pulsating flame that burned her inside and out. He hypnotized her with the slow, sweet cadence of love.

151

Bubbling sensations crested upon her, ones that swept her farther from reality's shore. The voyage from maidenhood to womanhood was a languid, sensuous journey that held Shiloh suspended in time and space.

Holt had absorbed her strength and stripped the breath from her lungs. Boundless energy flowed between them as the magical crescendo built and expanded into an explosive melody that vibrated through every fiber of her being. Her name was on his lips, whispering to her like a magician murmuring incantations. Her nerves screamed for release, and Shiloh feared the simmering caldron of passion that boiled through her was about to erupt.

When his sleek, muscular body drove into hers, Shiloh gasped for air before she was lifted by a fierce draft of wind. Suddenly she was spiraling through puffy clouds and gliding over pastel rainbows. Instinctively, she arched to meet his demanding thrusts. She matched his ardent passion, moving in perfect rhythm with the love song that strummed on her soul. They were heart to heart, flesh to flesh. They were one beating, breathing essence that transcended the physical limitations of passion to skyrocket through a universe that Shiloh never dreamed existed.

Shiloh was deliriously dizzy. The world evaporated into shades of black. She could feel herself drawn into that dark realm of desire that defied rhyme or reason. Her brain broke down when a multitude of devastating sensations swamped and buffeted her. She was living and dying, soaring through space without leaving the sinewy circle of Reuben's arms. One ineffable feeling after another riveted her until she feared she couldn't endure another moment of such sublime pleasure without shattering into a thousand pieces.

She was going to die in Reuben's arms, she

prophesied as her body shuddered convulsively against his. No one could enjoy the quintessence of ecstasy without sacrificing her life. But Shiloh didn't care if she surrendered her last breath as long as Reuben satisfied this monstrous craving that lured her into the foggy mist of passion.

And then, suddenly, a cloudburst of emotions pelleted her, thoroughly devastating her. Shiloh hung on for dear life. She feared she would split apart when the dark, sensual universe swirled over her like a collapsing thunderstorm. She was towed through turbulent clouds and plunged back to reality with the speed of a meteor that blazed across the heavens. An astonished gasp burst from her bone-dry lips when another shudder rocked her very soul. Shiloh couldn't begin to describe the unparalleled pleasure that splattered over her. She lay limp in Reuben's arms, trying to sort fantasy from reality and swearing they had just become one and the same.

Tangled lashes fluttered up to find a pair of emerald-green eyes peering back at her. A tender smile hovered on Holt's lips as he bent to offer her the softest whisper of a kiss. He had found sweet, satisfying release in this siren's arms, and she had discovered the meaning of passion in its purest form. He gazed down into Shiloh's flushed face, watching the disheveled mass of silver-blond curls stream out in all directions. This had to be heaven, he decided. He was in the arms of an angel.

For more than two years Holt had gone through the paces of passion for the sole purpose of satisfying his sexual appetite. But tonight he had discovered the vast difference between appeasement and ardent love-making. Shiloh touched him emotionally as well as physically. Instinctively, she knew how to please a man. She had given of herself, holding nothing back.

153

Her innocent responses made lovemaking a rare, unique journey into ecstasy.

Whatever Holt had been doing in the past wasn't remotely close to the sensations and emotions he and Shiloh had aroused in each other. Their responses defied explanation. They fed off each other's passions. Holt had found himself reveling in each moment until all emotion erupted like a volcano and currents of molten lava poured through him, taking forever to cool.

Even in the aftermath of love, the sensations were slow to ebb, lingering like a warm flame that could flicker anew when stirred by the slighest breath of wind. Holt still felt as if his composure were held together by one fragile strand of thread. He could look at Shiloh, and the fire threatened to blaze out of control again.

A contented smile bordered Shiloh's lips as she reached up to comb the raven strands across his forehead, ridding Reuben of the comical part that usually zigzagged over the top of his head. Her fingertips limned the crow's feet that sprayed from the corners of his bright green eyes and the smile lines that bracketed his sensuous lips. Gently, her index finger traced his full mouth, remembering with vivid clarity how she cherished the feel of his lips upon her skin.

"I didn't know lovemaking could be anything like this," she whispered in a marveling voice that wobbled with the side effects of passion. "I'm so glad no other woman knows what a fantastic lover you are. . . ."

Holt felt as if she had pulled a knife and buried it between his shoulder blades. Shiloh assumed, just as he had intended she would, that he was a stranger to women's beds. And before this lovely pixie forced him to verbalize a lie, he took her lips under his to savor her

154

honeyed taste.

"Do you suppose it's always like this, Reuben? Or do you think we might be the lucky ones?" she asked when he allowed her to come up for air. "Surely all other lovers don't experience these same—"

This time it was his turn to press his index finger to her lips to shush her. The fact that it had never been like this before rattled Holt more than he wanted to admit. Shiloh hadn't been around enough to know the difference between lust and lovemaking, and he hoped to God she never found out. They had created something rare and special while they were in each other's arms. It was *she* who made all the difference.

Shiloh was living proof that passion was something that had to be experienced with an open heart and blind trust or it was nothing more than the nourishing of a basic hunger. Animals bred because instinct demanded it. But Shiloh made love a precious gift of giving, the generous art of sharing every human emotion. Springfield's notorious ice maiden was, in actuality, a dozen kinds of volatile passions that could explode like fireworks. Beneath the bitterness and cynicism caused by love's first betrayal was a heart as wide and untamed as the ocean.

And the question was—how the hell was Holt going to allow this delightful nymph to keep her perspective of love without crushing the delicate blossom of newly discovered womanhood? She had been hurt once. If he destroyed her belief in love, she would never be receptive to it.

Yes, Holt could lie to her and she would believe him because he had been so deceptively cunning in his masquerade. He had gained her trust. But if he were honest with her and admitted that this wasn't the first time he had been with a woman, she would crawl back into her cynical shell and go on hating all men forevermore.

Damn, he was frying in his own grease! He couldn't bring himself to lie and say she was his first time, and yet he couldn't confess the truth without destroying his charade and jeopardizing his reason for being in Springfield. And so Holt chose to distract Shiloh instead of responding to her question. If he procrastinated long enough, chances were Shiloh would forget the topic of conversation.

Not that he minded distracting her. It was a delightfully appealing prospect. Holt had expected to feel compelled to dress and leave after they had shared the intimacies of lovemaking, just as he had the past two years. But Shiloh's magical inventiveness had only whetted his appetite. Surely, after he made love to this passionate beauty a second time, he wouldn't be consumed by such soul-shattering emotions. When they had explored all the mysteries of desire, he could let her go and amble back to his own room to kick himself for daring to tamper with this innocent goddess in the first place.

But when Shiloh eagerly responded to his kiss and returned each arousing caress, Holt began to wonder if he would ever tire of making love to this vivacious nymph. The first time was only a prelude to fully blossoming passion. He had foolishly thought love couldn't get better than this and he would lose his mindless craving for Shiloh the second time around. . . .

Now that Shiloh had been introduced to the sensual world of desire, she utilized her newly discovered skills to drive Reuben over the edge. So quickly had she learned what aroused and pleased him. She knew where to locate his most sensitive points, how to intensify the cravings that mushroomed inside him.

This time it was the silver-blue-eyed enchantress who took the initiative to practice her innovative techniques. She kissed him without one smidgen of feminine reserve and his mind turned to mush. And when she caressed him . . .

Holt gasped, and it took forever to inhale a breath. His overworked heart was hammering against his ribs with such violent force that he swore the bones would eventually crack under the pressure. Shiloh displayed such mystical finesse that Holt was astounded by her ability to arouse him by astonishing degrees. She satisfied one wild hunger and created another to take its place. She employed her shapely body to caress him, inventing such unique ways to excite him that he moaned in sweet agony, wondering if he could survive this devastating assault on his body and his senses.

Holt felt as if he were flying into the sun. He was burning in a holocaust of flames that were fanned by kisses whispering enticingly over his hair-rough flesh. When Shiloh moved evocatively above him, he swore he would go mad before she eased the mindless cravings that consumed him. This time she took possession of him, and his body moved upon command. Frothy waves undulated through him like the turbulent sea eroding the sandy shore. Each grain of self-control tumbled away as she taught him things he didn't know about passion, even when he arrogantly supposed he knew it all.

The tantalizing feel of her silky body gliding over his dragged a groan from his lips. Passion reared its unruly head, taking control of his body. Holt felt his pulse leapfrog like migrating toads as the intense pleasure swelled out of proportion. He clutched Shiloh to him, lost to the heady ecstasy that whirled over him. Fierce shudders destroyed the last shred of composure, and Holt clung to Shiloh as if the world were about to disintegrate. And indeed it did. The universe shattered, flinging him in a thousand different directions at once.

Holt was so numb with rapture that he felt as if he had been struck deaf, dumb, and blind. It was several breathless minutes before the cloudy haze faded from his vision and he was able to pry open his eyes to survey the bewitching face that hovered a scant few inches above his.

Was this the same skeptical hellion he had met the first day he stumbled into the McBride mansion? Hardly! This curvaceous blonde made love with as much panache as she displayed in everyday living. She did nothing halfway, and when she shared the wild splendor of passion, she exceeded his wildest imaginings. They had made love twice already, and he wasn't any closer to wanting to let her go. Good God, how many times would it take before enough was enough, he wondered dazedly.

Shiloh had it exactly backward, Holt mused as he stared into those mystical eyes that twinkled like diamonds. He was the one who was thankful no other man knew what an innovating and responsive lover Shiloh was. The rest of the male population *thought* they knew what they were missing when they pursued this rambunctious sprite. But they would be beating down her door if they had experienced the ineffable pleasures Holt had discovered in her arms.

"I don't want this night to end, Reuben," Shiloh murmured as she cuddled up beside his powerful frame like a contented kitten nestling beside a cozy fire.

Holt's arm slid beneath her to press her even closer. His full lips brushed over hers in a kiss that conveyed his own contentment. Holt knew he should tiptoe back to his own room, but he couldn't drag himself away from this tempting minx. He still wanted her. Like an eternal spring, the cravings bubbled forth to lure him to Shiloh again.

"I can't seem to get enough of you," he breathed hoarsely. "When you're here beside me I . . ."

Victor McBride had given his daughter a reasonable amount of time to cool off before he moseyed upstairs to check on her. He knew she had been upset with Reuben, and Victor felt compelled to console her. He had tried to warn Shiloh that she saw something in Reuben that no woman could ever touch, but Shiloh had taken his advice as a direct challenge to prove her father wrong. Victor didn't want to see Shiloh hurt by the shy, awkward man who had somehow piqued her fascination.

Mentally rehearsing his soliloquy, Victor moved silently down the hall to Shiloh's room. After listing all the comforting platitudes the way a good father should, Victor would kiss his daughter good night and reassure her that somewhere out in the wide world there was a man who deserved her affection, one who knew how to cherish her.

When he noticed the shaft of lantern light spraying around the edges of the door, he wondered if Shiloh was lying awake, grappling with whatever Reuben had done to annoy her. Quietly, he turned the doorknob to let himself in.

Bare shoulders protruded from the sheet and two pairs of startled eyes gaped at him. Victor had expected to find his daughter abed, but never in his worst nightmare had he dreamed Reuben Gilcrest would be there with her!

159

Victor blinked incredulously at the scene before him. "What in the hell . . . ?" he croaked, his voice shattering like fragile crystal.

"Son of a bitch . . ." Holt muttered into his pillow. Although the most common expression to float from his lips was *good God,* he was known to utter this particular oath during times of crisis. This crisis was so severe that Holt muttered the curse again.

Shiloh, however, was too dumbstruck to speak. After swallowing with an embarrassed gulp, she pulled the sheet over her head like a turtle ducking into its shell and then she proceeded to turn seven shades of red.

When Victor recovered his powers of speech he hopped up and down in indignation and ranted and raved in fluent profanity for fifteen minutes. His voice grew wilder and higher with each passing second. With a lightning tongue and thundering voice, he pelleted the man in his daughter's bed with a furious tirade of ultimatums. Since he wasn't wearing a stitch and he couldn't rise and take his leave without exposing more of himself than he already had, he was forced to lie there and endure the verbal crucifixion. He had been caught in the wrong bed with Victor McBride's pride and joy. The irate father of the compromised young lady was muttering about shotguns and wedding rings and "the honorable thing to do."

Good God, of all the assignments in all the world, why did this tempting beauty have to wind up in this one? And why had he wound up in her bed? Nothing had turned out as Holt anticipated when he followed Shiloh home to apologize for wounding her pride. Now Victor was on the rampage. Holt had the inescapable feeling that if he didn't comply with Victor's demands, he would be walking to the gallows to confront the hangman's noose.

Glancing heavenward, Holt sent up a prayer that Garret Robertson would appear from thin air and shoot him out of this uncomfortable predicament.

But Garret didn't come and Holt was in one helluva mess!

Part II

Even a reluctant groom goes eagerly to the altar with a shotgun at his back. . . .

Chapter 12

It was a quiet, simple wedding attended by only the McBride family, Marcella the housekeeper, and the members of the railroad company. Holt, garbed in the now-familiar ill-fitting clothes and spectacles, was joined in the parlor by his faithful mutt. Colonel McBride, although he had threatened to use his Union army rifle as incentive to see his daughter wed to the man who had deflowered her while he was a guest in the McBride home, gave the bride away.

Victor was appalled and outraged by the uncompromising predicament he had walked into two nights earlier. But in all honesty, he couldn't say he was chagrined by the subsequent marriage between his daughter and Reuben Gilcrest. Surprised, yes. Chagrined, no. He had hoped Shiloh would wed, if only to put a stop to the endless rabble of suitors that congregated on his doorstep. The fact that Shiloh had been intrigued by this mild-mannered gentleman still baffled Victor. Reuben and Shiloh appeared a hopeless mismatch, but the man had gotten exactly what he deserved. That rascal was full of unexpected surprises!

The decision to become an integral part of the McBride Railroad Company was made for Reuben

Gilcrest. As Shiloh's husband, he would take his place on the board of directors alongside Walter, Max, and Elijah. In Victor's opinion, Reuben had made his bed and now that he had slept in it with Shiloh, he was destined to become a member of the family and the company—complete with wedding vows and gold bands.

While Holt stood beside Shiloh, cursing himself for letting his hunger for this tempting beauty overshadow logic, he speculated on Garret Robertson's reaction to the news. This had not been part of his scheme. But Reuben Gilcrest was obliged to fulfill his duty now that he had projected the image of a man of honor and propriety. He couldn't very well step out of character and tell Victor where he could stuff his demand for this hasty wedding. Holt supposed he would have reacted the same way if he had a daughter who had wound up in bed with a man. But confound it, Victor didn't have to look so damned smug. He was delighting in this ironic twist of fate.

And Shiloh . . . Holt squeezed his eyes shut and murmured "I do" when Victor gouged him in the ribs. Shiloh hadn't protested her father's demands, but neither had she appeared enthused about having the ceremony two days after her premature wedding night. Holt had the feeling she held herself personally responsible for the unfortunate incident. But Holt had accepted full blame for his actions. Of course, there hadn't been time to discuss the matter. Victor had kept them up all night, returning every hour on the hour to spout another degrading insult. At the crack of dawn he had hustled them to their respective rooms to bathe and change and then accompanied them to the preacher's home to make arrangements for the wedding. The following day was a bustle of activity that involved inviting guests that Holt would have preferred stayed home.

After feeding his prisoners their last meal, Victor had marched them into the parlor to await the pastor and guests. Flashing his new son-in-law a warning glance, Victor had stalked into the hall to usher in the guests.

The ceremony itself was painless, but the reception was an exercise in self-restraint. The men in attendance cast Holt teasing grins, and Walter Jameson had the gall to offer to take his place in the bridal suite. And to top off a completely miserable afternoon, Felicia Fletcher was there to needle Shiloh as if she were a human pincushion.

Of course, Victor hadn't humiliated himself or his daughter by confessing he had found Shiloh and Reuben in bed—in the clench. He had merely explained to his guests that after the party at the Fletchers', Reuben had proposed and Shiloh had accepted. Aware of Reuben's phobia of women, Walter had asssumed the match to be a marriage of convenience—the merging of one fortune with another. But he was no less jealous that Reuben had legal rights to the saucy blonde Walter lusted after.

Holt had been overcome by a fierce wave of possessiveness when Walter suggested the groom needed a stand-in on his wedding night. Apparently Walter assumed Reuben had been born without the standard equipment that made a man a man. Holt had certainly played a convincing role in his charade, he begrudgingly admitted to himself. But tolerating Walter's vile remarks during the reception had Holt gnashing his teeth, wishing he could beat the tar out of his antagonist. Walter sorely needed another black eye and Holt was yearning to give him one!

Confound it, what a mess he had made of things, Holt mused disgustedly. Because of his uncontrollable desire for this curvaceous beauty he had wound up married to her. Well, at least he didn't have to pretend he didn't want her in the worst way. The lure Shiloh held over him was like a gravitational pull. It wasn't something a man could walk away from, at least not on this planet.

Holt had forced a cheerful smile when Max and Elijah congratulated him. Married? Holt Cantrell? To Shiloh McBride? Good God, he still couldn't believe he had been rushed through this whirlwind ceremony. He had promised himself after Anna's tragedy that he . . .

"It seems you are more enamored with Shiloh than you would have had me believe," Felicia purred mockingly. Her pale green eyes worked their way down Reuben's unflattering attire. "I hope you won't be too disappointed." Her tone was nowhere near sympathetic. It bordered on spiteful. "We haven't been calling your new bride the frigid female of Springfield for nothing, you know."

It was with tremendous effort that Holt refrained from knocking Felicia flat. She and Walter were cut from the same scrap of thorn bush, he thought sourly. What one of them didn't think to fling as insult the other one did. But Holt refused to get mad. He simply concentrated his energies on devising ways to get even with Walter and Felicia when the time was right.

Shiloh's dainty hand slid into Holt's. When she peered up at him with those mystical silver-blue eyes that glittered like sunlight, his brain malfunctioned. He didn't give a damn that he had to endure Walter's and Felicia's snide remarks, but he wished he could protect Shiloh from them. A tender smile grazed his lips as he gave her hand an affectionate squeeze—a gesture that had Felicia grinding her teeth. She had hoped Shiloh and Reuben would be miserable with each other, but from the look of things there was a mutual admiration between them. What Shiloh saw in this meek bumpkin

168

was anybody's guess. And why the shy gentleman had asked for her hand was a bumfuzzling puzzle. It made Felicia wonder.

Clamping a hold on her temper, Shiloh glanced first at Felicia and then at Walter. Her body stiffened and her face grew red with suppressed anger when Walter's gaze bounced back and forth between her and her comical groom. She knew that varmint was going to make some intimidating remark, Felicia would chime in with him, and Shiloh would be overcome by the urge to claw out both of their eyes.

"I must admit I am baffled by your taste in men, Shiloh," Walter declared with a ridiculing smirk.

Silver-blue eyes shot sparks. "My husband is far more of a man than you could ever hope to be," she sniped.

Walter's insulting glance flicked over the baggy garments. His chuckle mingled with Felicia's annoying snicker. "Just in case you have overestimated your new husband, you know where to find me, Mrs. Gilcrest. I'm not sure if you wed a man or a two-legged mouse."

When Walter pivoted on his heel and sauntered away, Felicia giggled in wicked delight. "And in case you overestimated your new wife, you know where to find me, Mr. Gilcrest," she teased unmercifully. "I think both of you need to practice elsewhere before your wedding night."

And sure enough Shiloh couldn't contain her anger. Suffering both Walter's and Felicia's goading remarks was simply too much. In a burst of fury she launched herself at Felicia, but Holt towed her back to his side before she could sink her claws into the spiteful witch's ridiculing smile.

"You need not rush to my defense," Holt insisted in a tone that barely disguised his own agitation.

Since Reuben's impression on all who knew him was

such that he wouldn't harm a fly, he couldn't level a blow to the two vicious individuals who were so richly deserving of retaliation.

"They insulted us," Shiloh hissed furiously.

Gently, Holt reached up to tip her animated face to his and graced her with a smile. "Yes, they did," he acknowledged. "But my hide is tough." He studied her flushed features for a thoughtful moment. "Are you angry because they dented your pride by suggesting you married out of your species?"

Shiloh glanced away, feeling guilty for forcing Reuben to marry her and salvage her dignity. If that wasn't bad enough, he was now being subjected to harsh ridicule and the risk of gossip, thanks to Felicia's wagging tongue.

A frustrated sigh escaped Shiloh's lips. This whole affair was all her fault. Twice she had practically invited Reuben to make love to her. And when he yielded to his physical needs, he was caught red-handed. She wouldn't blame Reuben one bit if he held her personally accountable for his misfortune. He was probably wishing he were back in Chicago with his spinster aunt.

All Shiloh wanted to do was make the situation easier for Reuben to bear. And that meant defending him against rude, intimidating remarks from Walter, who didn't know the first thing about making a woman feel whole and alive. And let's not forget Felicia Fletcher, Shiloh tacked on bitterly. That woman had a tongue and the venom of a deadly viper. She probably knew nothing about love, only about satisfying her voracious sexual appetite. Walter and Felicia would make a perfect match. They were both selfish barracudas who had no sincere feelings for anyone but themselves.

"I'm annoyed that Walter doesn't know the better man when he stares him in the face," Shiloh said in belated response. "If I would have had the chance to choose a husband, I would have picked you even if you didn't ask me." Her gaze lanced off his. "I'm sorry, Reuben. I never meant you to find yourself obligated to me. And I will understand if you prefer to lead a separate life in separate quarters."

When she breezed across the room, Holt expelled a frustrated breath. He was still a captive of his charade, shackled by the role he was forced to portray and laden with excessive guilt. He was a deceitful cad and Shiloh would heartily agree if she knew the truth. Thank God she would never find out.

Blast it, if Holt could have contorted his body to become the donor and recipient of a swift kick in the seat of the pants, he would have. What the hell was he going to do with that tempting sprite? She felt responsible for his plight and he had to let her think it was so. If he didn't, he would expose himself for what he truly was and Shiloh would despise him for deceiving her. Good God, what a narrow corner Holt had backed himself into! He had wound up hurting the one person who had come to mean more to him than she should have. He cared too much about Shiloh, and it was beginning to influence his judgment. Hell's bells, he couldn't even concentrate on his assignment while he was entangled in this web of his own making!

Holt found numerous excuses to venture from the house during the days that followed. But the nights were by far the worst of his torments. As if he felt the need to test his resistance to his bride, Holt eased onto his side of the bed while Shiloh remained on hers. The

171

time would come when he'd be removed from her life and he feared he would become so fond of this intriguing blonde that he wouldn't be able to give her up. He had concluded that abstaining was practice for living without her when he completed this assignment. The more attached he became to his new wife, the more difficult it would be to forget her. And following that sensible philosophy, Holt retired each night, forcing himself not to enjoy his husbandly rights.

Each night Shiloh lay on her back, staring into the darkness, wishing just once that Reuben would become the aggressor. What a bitter twist of fate, she thought disappointedly. She had come to know the warm, virile man beneath the loose-fitting clothes and thick spectacles, and she desired him the way she desired no other man. But Reuben had never once offered her more than a fleeting good-night kiss since their wedding.

Did he view her as an overeager lover who had purposely sought to entrap him? He had said she pleasured him, but when he found himself bound to her in marriage, he never came to her to recapture that night of splendor. Maybe he had said those things only because he thought she wanted to hear them. Maybe he was one of those men who preferred . . .

Shiloh squelched the depressing thought. She wasn't going to allow Walter's crude insinuations to distort her thinking. Reuben had scores of admirable qualities. Just because he didn't flaunt his masculinity and devour his wife each night didn't make him less a man. He simply had no need to prove himself to the rest of the world. Reuben was compassionate and kind and he treated her with the utmost respect. Wasn't that what she had always wanted from a man? His courtesy, his respect? Hadn't she harshly criticized rogues who

172

wanted no more than sexual favors from women?

Well, now she had what she always claimed she wanted—a man who was more interested in her mind than in her body. It served her right, Shiloh lectured herself. Her relationship with her new husband was a direct contrast to every encounter she had with other men. Reuben never groped, never treated her as if she were an object of lust. And if this was all she had ever wanted from a man, why was she so miserable? Shiloh cautioned herself against wishing for things she wanted again—for fear she would get them. This was one whim that hadn't turned out anywhere near the way she had anticipated.

Was she destined to plod through life, aching to reexperience the magic she had discovered the one night Reuben had given in to his desires? He had wanted her then, she knew. So why didn't he want her now? Was it because he felt strangled by matrimony, trapped into a business arrangement with her father? Or had his mild fascination for her ended after one night of lovemaking? Maybe her lack of experience had left Reuben disappointed in passion. Perhaps he was wishing he could explore the realm of desire with a woman who was worldly and experienced in pleasuring men.

Lord, Reuben probably despised her, but he was simply too much the gentleman to admit it. In anguish, Shiloh wiggled onto her side and blinked back the tears. As strange as it would seem to the rest of the world, she truly had fallen in love with this majestic lion in lamb's wool. Despite his ridiculous clothes and meek disposition, he came to life in moments of passion. Shiloh had viewed his striking physique and observed his potential. When Reuben let his guard down, Shiloh was attracted to him like metal to a

173

magnet. She longed to draw out the sensual, vital man who possessed such incredible control of mind over body.

"Reuben?" Shiloh whispered, wondering if he was asleep or only pretending to be, as she was.

"Hmmm?" His voice was so quiet she had to strain her ears to hear him.

"For what it's worth . . . I think I love you," she murmured sincerely.

Holt gnashed his teeth and cursed himself for the umpteenth time. Him and his bright ideas! He would show Little Miss Cynic, he had boasted. He would defeat her at her own game, he had arrogantly declared. Well, he didn't feel so damned proud of himself for pulling off this charade. In fact, he felt as tall as a table leg.

The silence that stretched between them was deafening. Shiloh waited, hoping Reuben would say something . . . anything. But he didn't return her quiet confession. He simply lay there like a slug, mentally beating himself black and blue.

After what seemed forever, Reuben levered up on the side of the bed. "I'm going downstairs for a midnight snack," he announced as he untangled himself from his hindering nightshirt.

When Reuben clomped out of the room with Dog one step behind him, Shiloh died a slow, painful death. What was the use? They would never enjoy a true marriage. Reuben was too inhibited. He obviously viewed love and passion as evils he should avoid religiously.

For an eternity Shiloh awaited Reuben's return, unable to sleep. Frustrated, she flipped back the sheet and padded down the hall. A muddled frown knit her brow when she spied the light seeping around the partially closed door to her father's office. Curiously,

174

Shiloh tiptoed across the foyer to peer into the room. There she spied Reuben laboring over the company ledgers, jotting down a page of notes. What the blazes was he doing?

Shiloh was suddenly reminded of the notes she had felt in the pocket of his nightshirt the evening they had sneaked to the kitchen for a midnight snack. When she had questioned him, he had shrugged noncommittally and replied that he had only been jotting down a few thoughts concerning the prospect of buying into the company. But now he was a stockholder, so why was he thumbing through her father's accounts in the middle of the night instead of in broad daylight? It made no sense.

"Reuben? What on earth are you doing?" Shiloh inquired as she eased open the door.

Holt nearly leapt out of his nightshirt. Annoyed at being caught snooping, he swiveled in the chair to glare at the shapely beauty who constantly tormented his thoughts.

A dark shade of vexation clouded his brow. "Is a man allowed no privacy around here?" he snapped more brusquely than he intended. "Just because you're my wife does not give you the right to spy on me."

Shiloh was unaccustomed to having this mild-mannered man bite her head off. When he did, her temper automatically flared up. "And just because you married into my father's company does not give you the right to pry into his books in the middle of the night!" she hurled nastily.

"I didn't marry into the company," Holt growled at her. "I was *dragged* into it. And being a betting man, I'd wager you and your father planned that seduction just to get your hands on the money needed to keep this dream of his afloat." It was a rotten thing for Holt to say, but bad temper had a hold on his tongue.

175

He couldn't have hurt her more if he had backhanded her across the cheek. With eyes flashing, Shiloh proudly drew herself up after being slapped with his insult. "And maybe I should take Walter up on his offer of allowing him to stand in your stead," came her blistering reply. "You don't want me in your bed, but there are plenty of men hereabout who do." With that cutting remark voiced, Shiloh pivoted on her heel and shot through the hall and out the front door.

"Damn," Reuben swore at himself. Hurriedly, he folded his notes and stuffed them into his pocket. After replacing the ledgers exactly where he had found them, he followed after Shiloh. But she had become one of the skipping shadows.

"Dog," he commanded abruptly.

The shaggy mutt snapped to attention.

"Go find Shiloh and don't come back until she does," he ordered.

As if the mongrel understood English perfectly, he bounded off the porch with his tail wagging. Determined of purpose, Dog trotted down the path that led to the meadow. The sound of thundering hooves reached Holt's ears, and he muttered under his breath. His keen gaze narrowed on the fleeting apparition who flew across the rolling hills on her winged steed. In frustration, Holt watched Shiloh's glistening mane of hair trail wildly behind her as she chased the wind.

How was he going to smooth over their unfortunate encounter in the study? Blast it, he couldn't tell her why he was laboring over her father's accounts. And he couldn't let himself fall in love with that hellion either. That wasn't part of the plan. But, dammit, it was difficult not to be intrigued by Shiloh. It seemed the harder he tried to ignore her, the more difficult the task. Trying *not* to think about her was exhausting.

Well, maybe it was better if they were at odds, Holt

mused as he ambled back into the house. In a few more weeks he would be gone, and it was best if Shiloh was happy to see him go. When Garret conveniently removed Holt from his present assignment with another staged showdown, Shiloh wouldn't grieve Reuben's passing. The young widow could tell him good riddance and be glad to be done with him. She would go her merry way and he would go his. In Holt's line of work, he didn't have room in his life for lasting relationships.

Yes, he had become a little too involved and much too possessive of that saucy sprite. And yes, he lusted after her to the point that denying himself the pleasure he had discovered in her arms was preying on him. And yes, he had worn his nerves ragged trying to maintain this charade. But, blast it, he had a job to do!

Let Shiloh run to Walter or anyone else for consolation, he grumbled as he flounced on the bed and wrestled with his restricting nightshirt. What did he care? That fickle vixen claimed to love him one minute and threatened to find herself another man the next. She was too unpredictable and she preoccupied him too much as it was.

All the while that Holt was assuring himself that he didn't give a flying fig where Shiloh went on her late-night ride, he couldn't beg, borrow, or steal a moment of sleep. He knew Dog would take care of Shiloh if she ran into trouble, but, nonetheless, he was as edgy as an expectant father while Shiloh was doing her midnight prowling.

Although Holt pretended not to notice when Shiloh finally eased into the bed two hours later, he knew she had been gone long enough to do exactly as she had threatened, and that turned his disposition black as pitch. And even though Dog understood Holt's command, he couldn't speak a word to offer a detailed

177

report of what Shiloh had been doing for exactly two hours and seven minutes! Holt was suffering nine kinds of hell, wishing he hadn't snapped at Shiloh in the first place and kicking himself for caring where she had been and with whom!

"You got the money?" Kirby Thorn demanded, staring straight through his edgy companion.

A purse of coins clanked on the table in the dark corner of the saloon. A gloved hand shoved the pouch across the table. "The supply train is due in Primrose this week. I don't want anything left of the equipment. Demolish it all."

A wicked smile dangled on one corner of Kirby's mouth before he inhaled another drink of whiskey. "I did my share of sabotaging trains durin' the war," he snorted haughtily. "There won't be nothin' left to build a track when I git finished with that boxcar." He leaned across the table, his small gray eyes hard and cold as the polar ice cap. "I'll do you this favor, but I want that payroll car. When does McBride make his monthly payments along this route?"

The man squirmed uneasily in his chair under Kirby's unnerving gaze. "First of the month. You'll have all the information you need to seize it."

"You better, goddammit." From beneath the table the click of his pistol punctuated his remark. "Nobody tangles with me and lives to tell about it. If me and my boys don't get all the gold in the pay car, you're a dead man. . . ."

A satanic grin curved Kirby's lips as he watched his cloaked companion slink back in his chair. With a nod of his head Kirby silently demanded the man make his exit with his tail tucked between his legs. Kirby had struck fear in his accomplice's heart. He would cooperate, Kirby assured himself confidently. And if by some unlikely chance the man thought of betraying him, Kirby would exact his revenge just as he had intended to do the first night he had held up that arrogant stuffed shirt who had pleaded for his life in exchange for information about McBride's railroad and its lavish payroll car.

Chapter 13

Things became progressively worse instead of better. For two days Holt went about his business, suffering all the tortures of the damned. When in the presence of others, Shiloh was the epitome of politeness, but in private she refused to acknowledge that Reuben existed. Holt had endured a score of Walter's snide remarks and Felicia's taunting smiles. Although the mild-mannered Reuben bore the criticisms, the ridicule, and Shiloh's cold shoulders, Holt Cantrell was frustrated to no end. He felt terrible about the night he had jumped down Shiloh's throat, making her the brunt of his irritation as if she were solely responsible. But he knew he had made Shiloh his scapegoat that night, and she hadn't deserved the hell he had put her through— not the strained marriage, not Felicia's vicious gossip, and certainly not Walter's cruel innuendos.

The more Holt thought about it, the more he felt obliged to make compensation in the only avenue open to him. When he announced to Victor and Shiloh that he was not attending the evening conference at Max Fletcher's home and that he was going out alone, his father-in-law frowned in disappointment. Victor, who was becoming increasingly aware of the tension between husband and wife, volunteered to take Reuben and Shiloh out to dinner before the company conference he invited Reuben to attend. But Reuben graciously declined.

What Holt wanted to do had to be done alone. He could see the pain of rejection in Shiloh's expressive silver-blue eyes when he demurred. But he had his own way of alleviating part of the anguish she was suffering. Holt could do nothing about the personal conflicts between them, but there were some wrongs he could right. In his quiet, discreet way he wanted to spare Shiloh some of the mortification she had been forced to endure.

Holt had anticipated that he would be made the brunt of many a joke while he played his clever charade. But he had never meant to drag Shiloh down with him. A little compensation was definitely in order, Holt reminded himself as he and Dog clomped down the front steps.

With a heavy heart Shiloh watched him become one of the swaying shadows. Although his exit relieved the tension, she was still plagued with mixed emotions. She wondered how Reuben intended to fill the hours of the evening. He wasn't the kind of man who ambled off in search of feminine affection. Indeed, he could have had more than enough affection at home if he wanted it! Shiloh, although she was so frustrated with her rocky marriage and with Reuben that she couldn't think straight, was dying of curiosity about his mysterious evening plans. . . .

"I made a mistake, didn't I?" Victor questioned as he peered sensitively at his daughter, who stared out the window like a posted sentinel.

Shiloh winced. Was she so transparent that her father had realized she was miserable? With tremendous effort Shiloh pivoted to grace her father with a smile of feigned innocence. "Whatever do you mean, Papa?"

Victor's winged brows flattened over his penetrating blue eyes. "Don't play naive with me," he demanded. "You know exactly what I mean. I'm referring to the shotgun wedding I hustled you through. I thought I was doing both of you a favor, but it seems I have committed a great disservice."

Inhaling a tremulous sigh, Shiloh ambled around the perimeters of the parlor. "My reputation with men before matrimony should have indicated to you what kind of wife I would make—a lousy one," she admitted in a self-deprecating tone.

A volcanic snort passed Victor's lips. "I rather think the fault lies with Reuben, not with you, daughter!"

Condemning Reuben was a privilege Shiloh permitted no one but herself. It was one thing for her to criticize Reuben's lack of interest in her and quite another for Victor to point an accusing finger.

"How can you blame Reuben when he was marched to the altar with an invisible rifle at his back?" she sniffed defensively.

"Well, he asked for it," Victor grumbled in a resentful tone. "If I had found the two of you in *his* room instead of *yours,* I might have read the situation differently."

Shiloh blushed profusely at the intimate topic of conversation. It was not an incident she could openly discuss, even with her father. She and Victor had never withheld secrets from each other, but Shiloh had never confronted such a delicate matter before. Discussing what had happened and why was unnerving.

"Nevertheless, Papa, you did misinterpret the situation," Shiloh protested, unable to meet her father's

183

probing stare. "I was more to blame than Reuben was."

Victor couldn't contain the gurgle of laughter that erupted in his chest. "You expect me to believe you were responsible?" he crowed incredulously. "I can't imagine why you feel inclined to protect Reuben from guilt." He took a sip of brandy and then glanced pensively at his fidgety daughter. "Men have flocked to our doorstep since the day we moved to Springfield, and you have turned each and every one of them away, even the ones I hand-picked. You have been exceptionally particular and selective of the invitations you accept. Judging by the precedent you have set the past few years, it seems incredible that a fumbling easterner could have such a dramatic effect on you and that you encouraged him when you rejected everyone else."

Shiloh's silver-blue eyes threw sparks. "If memory serves, you were the one who cautioned me not to waste my time on Reuben because of his noticeable fear of females," she flung at Victor. "You knew perfectly well that one of my worst downfalls is accepting challenges. Why should this be any different? You practically dared me to pique the interest of our shy house guest, and I rose to the challenge. In the past I have risen to the challenges of defending myself against men who thought to become more amorous than I permitted. And I also accepted the challenge of overseeing our home and personal finances while you were battling the Confederates. I set a precedent of meeting every challenge, great or small. Why would daring to win Reuben's love be any different . . . ?"

Annoyed that she had said more than she should have, Shiloh swore under her breath. Stiffly, she presented her back to her father and stared out the window into the darkness.

Silence stretched between them.

"You really do care about Reuben, don't you, honey?" Victor said after a long moment.

More silence.

"Yes, Papa, I do," she admitted so quietly that Victor could barely decipher her words. "But I fear Reuben feels strangled after you ordered him to do the honorable thing by marrying me."

When Shiloh was hurting, Victor bled. He felt handcuffed, just as he had when Shiloh had suffered the bitter rejection of first love. Lance Draper had devastated the young woman's romantic dreams four years earlier, and Shiloh had fiercely protected her heart thereafter. She had been wary and cynical until Reuben came along to stir her sympathy and emotions that she had kept locked behind a wall. Victor sorely wished the right words would form on his lips to comfort Shiloh. How he wished he could magically wave his arms and make everything right again.

"Life is full of disappointments," Victor murmured with a sigh. "I have never gotten over losing your mother and our infant son. And to compensate for my losses I have doted over you and thrust myself into this dream of a railroad that joins this war-torn country like a new lifeline. When troubles confront us, we have to make the best of what we have. Sometimes we simply have to get on with our lives without dwelling on what was or what might have been. I had hoped you and Reuben could have . . ."

His voice trailed off while he attempted to formulate his thoughts, but he was frustrated and tact escaped him. "I know you have never been long on patience, and you are quick to temper, but you have to bite your tongue occasionally and make the best of things. Hopefully, in time, the wrinkles in this marriage will iron themselves out. And if that muleheaded Reuben doesn't know what a lucky man he is to have you, then he is a bigger fool than I first thought!"

Shiloh broke into a smile when her father burst out with his last remark. "It is nice to know that someone around here loves me."

Victor set his brandy glass aside and closed the distance between them. His arms went around her as he dropped an affectionate kiss to her brow. "I do love you, Shiloh, too much I fear. And if I had more control over the situation, I would shake some sense into that husband of yours."

"There are times when I have to handle my problems my own way," she reminded him gently.

"So I have been told on numerous occasions," Victor replied, giving her another heartfelt squeeze. "I'm trying to let you live your own life. But being a parent isn't that easy, believe me. Luckily for you, you won't ever have to be one."

On that light note Victor strolled into the foyer to fetch his hat and then summoned Shiloh to him. "Join me for dinner," he insisted. "While Reuben is away, you can sit in on my meeting with the board members."

Shiloh frowned distastefully. "I don't think I'm in the mood for more of Felicia's intimidating smirks."

Victor cocked a teasing brow. "No? I thought you held your own with Felicia. But if she is there tonight, I can draw her aside and give her a good talking to if you like."

As expected, Shiloh declined to let her father slay the female dragon. "And then again, maybe I am in the right frame of mind to clash with that gossipy twit," she announced. "It will take my mind off other matters."

A triumphant smile quirked Victor's lips as he and his daughter strolled out the door. He didn't relish the idea of Shiloh spending the evening at home alone, brooding over her crumbling marriage. He rather suspected she would have stood as a lookout until Reuben's return and then trotted off to bed before he knew she was awaiting him. Distraction was important in times of turmoil, Victor reminded himself. He had been operating under that philosophy for years.

A fog of smoke curled around the broad-brimmed Stetson and the heavily bearded face of the man who lounged in the dark corner of the saloon that was a favorite haunt of Walter Jameson's. Vivid green eyes measured the smartly dressed Walter, who sat at a distant table, enjoying a drink and a game of cards. Walter was unaware that he was being watched like a hawk from afar. He was too busy spreading gossip about Shiloh and her clumsy husband and boasting of his talents in promoting investments in the railroad.

But Walter was definitely under surveillance. Pinkerton's best detective had Walter in his sights and he was growing increasingly annoyed with the braggart with every second that ticked by. Brooding, Holt Cantrell poured another drink from the bottle that sat before him and downed it in one swallow. Discreetly, he reached down to fetch his timepiece from the pocket of his buckskin jacket that rippled with long fringe. It was seven-thirty and Walter was due at Max Fletcher's at eight. Sooner or later the cocky rake would have to toss in his cards and make his exit. And when Walter walked outside . . .

"Excuse me, gentlemen," Walter announced as he unfolded himself from the table to tower arrogantly over his companions. "Business awaits me." He displayed one of his charming smiles. "And don't forget what I said. If you decide to invest your money in McBride's company, you can double your profit in a year."

As Walter swaggered away, Holt rose from his chair with pantherlike grace and stalked his prey. While Walter strolled down the boardwalk, whistling a light tune, Holt was lurking a few feet behind him, waiting the perfect moment to strike. The instant Walter stepped down to cross the alley, Holt pounced with lightning quickness. A startled squawk burst from Walter's lips when he was attacked from behind and his face was slammed against the outer wall of the telegraph office. He didn't have the foggiest notion who had grabbed him, but whoever it was was no hundred-pound weakling. The bone-crushing grasp on Walter's arm indicated he was tangling with a man who knew how to fight in hand-to-hand combat and had lost very few bouts . . . if any.

At any moment Walter expected to have his wallet ripped from his pocket, knowing full well he would never be able to identify the thief while his face was squished into the rough-hewn lumber. And sure enough, he was relieved of his wallet—vest pocket and all. Holt had reached around with one hand while mashing Walter against the wall with the other. Tearing the wallet loose, he left the expensive vest in shreds.

While his heart pounded like a sledgehammer, Walter was roughly wheeled about to have his backside shoved to the wall. He still couldn't identify his assailant in the darkness. Only the image of a wide-brimmed hat, long hair, and grisly beard formed the picture that was immediately imprinted on Walter's brain. The hat was set so low on Holt's forehead that it concealed his glittering green eyes. But flashbacks of another time not so long ago skipped across Walter's mind. He recalled the night he had walked out of the tavern and directly into a blow that had knocked him silly. . . .

"If I ever hear you spread another vicious lie about Shiloh McBride, I'll cut out your tongue," Holt sneered in such an ominous tone that Walter flinched as if he had been stabbed in the back.

"Who are you?" Walter croaked, wondering why he had dared to pose such a stupid question. After all, what were the chances of this swarthy villain stating his name after committing his crime and issuing threats?

A skirl of devilish laughter vibrated through Holt's chest as he doubled a fist and rammed it into Walter's ribs. "Don't you recognize me?" he taunted. "I'm Shiloh's guardian angel."

A pained grunt gushed from Walter's lips. Instinctively, he doubled over to protect his bruised innards from another punishing blow. But Holt clenched his fist in the collar of Walter's shirt and jerked him upright. Frantic, Walter struggled for freedom before he became the recipient of another devastating punch in the midsection. But quick as Walter was, he was much too slow and sorely outmatched in strength and agility. He swore he heard his teeth rattle when hard knuckles pelleted his cheek with two consecutive blows that were delivered with the astonishing quickness of a striking snake and the devastating force of an enraged grizzly bear.

Like syrup, Walter dribbled down the wall to plop on his backside. His arms dangled loosely at his sides and his legs sprawled limply before him. His right eye immediately swelled shut and his dazed brain floundered to correct his fuzzy vision. Sweet mercy! He hadn't encountered Shiloh's guardian angel, Walter mused sickly. He had confronted one of her secret admirers who possessed Satan's brand of vengeance.

While Walter sat like an anesthetized snail, Holt grabbed the lapels of his jacket and hoisted him onto legs that were as sturdy as wet noodles. Walter blinked the only eye that still functioned—the one that was still recovering from similar blows the previous week. The tongue he had practically swallowed flicked out to lick the blood from his puffy lip, and he peered up with one droopy eye to survey the faceless avenger who had pounded him into the ground without Walter being able to get off even one answering blow.

"You're been duly warned, Jameson," Holt snarled menacingly. His scare tactics had worked. Walter looked terrified. "From now on, you speak of Shiloh McBride with the utmost respect or don't speak at all. If I hear you degrading her to your prissy friends, you'll wish you had heeded my advice. . . ."

He let the threat hang in the air, allowing Walter to draw his own conclusions as to what consequences he would suffer for wagging his tongue. While Walter's mushy brain was grappling with the fierce warning, Holt reared back to deliver a punch that compensated for all the times the past week when he had itched to knock the living daylights out of this arrogant weasel and couldn't.

A ring of stars swirled around Walter's head immediately after he found himself on the receiving end of a mind-scrambling blow. Like a delicate flower wilting beneath the scorching summer sun, he folded up at the knees and kerplopped facedown in the dirt.

Dusting off his hands, Holt strode deep into the alley to fetch the horse he had borrowed from Victor's stable. "One down and one to go," Holt murmured to Dog, who patiently held the reins in his mouth.

A victorious smile bordered Holt's lips as he trotted

down the dark passageway to reappear on the street adjacent to one of Springfield's more unseemly hotels. The sound of a woman giggling reached his ears, and Holt glanced at the two silhouettes that scampered from the buggy to scurry into the hotel lobby. Holt would have recognized that cackling snicker anywhere. It was Felicia Fletcher's all right. It seemed luck was riding with him while he went about town settling scores. He had expected to have to trail that promiscuous witch for an hour or two before he caught up with her to give her a taste of her own medicine. But here she was with her latest indiscretion and Holt didn't have to bother sniffing her out.

A flirtatious smile hovered on Felicia's lips as she wiggled from her form-fitting gown. Her companion's hungry gaze flicked down her shapely torso and he licked his lips in anticipation. Felicia had learned long ago that her body was the object of male attention. She thrived on the compliments and appreciative stares she received from her various beaus. Her greatest aspiration in life was to acquire as many lovers as time allowed, and she used her feminine wiles to get whatever she wanted. It wasn't just sex that appealed to Felicia. It was the power it gave her over men. And there was an endless rabble of men, married and single alike, who had buckled to her charms and found themselves obliged to her in ways they had never imagined until it was too late. If they refused her demands, they became the subject of slanderous gossip that had ruined more than one man's reputation and business in the community.

Even Felicia's father was unaware that some of the favors he had gained during his rise to wealth should have been attributed to Felicia's devious schemes.

Tonight it was the owner of a piece of valuable property that Max wanted who had stumbled into this black widow's web. The victim would sell out to Max at Felicia's request or he would risk scandal and family humiliation. Felicia would see to it that this man's prim little wife knew all about his rendezvous if he didn't cooperate.

Using a provocative form of striptease, Felicia peeled off her lacy undergarments and playfully tossed the perfumed petticoats at her eager lover. It was to her advantage that the man was starved for physical affection. His stuffy wife found sex to be too offensive to suit her delicate tastes, and the child she had borne him was enough for her. Although the frigid wife refused to share her husband's bed, she expected him to remain loyal to her. Felicia had done her homework well, and she knew this man would be all too willing to take a tumble with her in the sheets. She wasn't disappointed.

While Felicia was playing cat-and-mouse, dodging eager arms and building anticipation, Holt was creeping along the upper balcony to locate the source of the snickers. Patiently, he crouched beside the open window, waiting for Felicia to complete her mating dance.

Watching and listening to Felicia's antics made Holt appreciate the open affection he had come to expect from the curvaceous blonde enchantress he had wound up marrying. To the rest of the males in Springfield, Shiloh was stingy with her charms. Although Shiloh did have a temper and she definitely knew how to use it, she was straightforward in her dealings with men. She never played taunting games when it came to passion. She unselfishly shared what she felt, and she returned the pleasures in such devastating ways that a man could not help but be stirred by her.

God, how he wished he could accept Shiloh's heartfelt invitations without complicating their relationship more. Shiloh was so generous in her giving, so honest with her affection. While Felicia played the coy seductress—the same role she had played dozens of times before—Shiloh offered a priceless gift with no underlying purpose but responding to what she felt in her heart. Holt hated it that he couldn't be as generous in return when he was trapped in a web of his own making. If he let himself, and it would have been so easy to do, he could fall hopelessly in love with that spirited sprite whose affections were the whimsical desires of every man who pursued her. But love was out of the question for a man like Holt, who was chained to his past and entangled in a deceitful charade. If Shiloh knew who he was and how he had schemed to win her trust, she wouldn't have let him near her.

It was lucky that Shiloh would never discover the truth, Holt mused as he listened to the last phase of Felicia's disgusting ritual. Holt would never have come to know the warm, sensitive woman who hid behind her cynical barriers of defense. Holt would then become one of the nameless number of admirers who stared at her from the outside, wishing he were the one who could tame her wild, free heart. . . .

The instant the lantern light evaporated, Holt shoved his thoughts aside and unfolded his muscular frame. While Felicia and her unsuspecting lover were tripping the light fantastic in their darkened room, Holt drew back the curtain and eased a hip over the windowsill. Positioning himself in the scant light that slanted into the room, Holt cocked the trigger of his Colt to make his presence known. A shocked gasp burst from Felicia's lips when she spied the shadowed figure who loomed behind the silver-barreled pistol that glistened in the moonlight.

While Felicia and her lover lay frozen to the spot, Holt strode over to gather the chit's strewn garments, leaving nothing behind. When Felicia left her love nest in this shady hotel she would return home in whatever improvised clothes she could find. This time *she* was going to become the brunt of gossip—the very kind she spread. As for the man in question, Holt was a mite more forgiving.

In the same low, gruff tone he had employed when confronting Walter, Holt ordered Felicia's lover to collect his clothes and hastily shrug them on. While Felicia clutched the sheet under her chin and emitted humiliated gasps in irregular spasms, Holt nudged her beau toward the door.

"If you know what's good for you, friend, you'll keep your distance from this female shark. She has a nasty bite."

Outraged but frightened half to death, Felicia refrained from contesting the harsh insult. She was forced to lie and take it, wondering if she was to be raped and victimized after her cowardly lover slinked out the door with his hide intact.

Seeing nothing more than an ominous shadow poised with the gleaming barrel of the Colt, Felicia waited to learn her fate. If she could keep her wits about her, she could turn the situation to her advantage and emerge from this crisis unscathed. . . .

A peal of mirthless laughter reverberated in Holt's chest as he peered at the girl wrapped in the sheet. "Aren't you going to offer me the same treat your boyfriend was about to be served?" he mocked sarcastically.

The comment prompted Felicia to utilize her wiles on the unidentified intruder just as Holt anticipated she would. Felicia was not particular or discriminatory. She would attempt to seduce anything in breeches.

Tossing her mane of copper-red hair, Felicia pushed up to strike an inviting pose against the headboard.

Holt's skin crawled at the thought of touching such well-used merchandise. Felicia was not only cheap but she was free, and Holt wouldn't lower himself to partake of her. "It's a shame there isn't time for us to get to know each other," Holt taunted with an unpleasant laugh. As if he wanted anything to do with this crafty witch! "By now your father will have formed a posse of servants to round you up. He received a message stating that you were seen in the company of a married man and that scandal was inevitable if you persisted in giving away free samples again."

Felicia's mouth opened wide enough for a family of sparrows to nest. Her vocal cords collapsed in her throat. She sat like a marble statue while the mysterious intruder silently exited the same way he entered. The instant she was alone Felicia rewrapped the sheet around her in a makeshift toga and dashed toward the door. Her only recourse was to rush home as fast as she could, sneak to her room to change, and insist someone had played a spiteful trick.

Amusement danced in Holt's eyes as he watched Felicia bound into her carriage. "And that takes care of that," he chortled as he climbed down from the balcony.

Muffling an ornery snicker, Holt wound his way through the alley to where Dog waited with reins in his mouth. Within a few minutes Holt had jerked off the fuzzy wig and wiry beard that disguised his identity. Quick as a wink, he shed his frontiersman garb and stepped into Reuben's baggy clothes. After stuffing the worn garments into the feed sack that was strapped to the saddle, Holt trotted on his way.

"This calls for a celebration," Holt declared to Dog as they aimed themselves toward one of the many saloons in Springfield.

Holt was well satisfied, having doled out just punishment for deeds that had been long left unanswered. Retaliating against those two annoying pests was Holt's reward. It made no difference to him that neither Walter nor Felicia knew who had dished out retribution. Holt knew, and that was all that mattered. And now that he had settled the score, he intended to get rip-roaring drunk so he wouldn't return to the McBride mansion and tempt himself with Shiloh.

It would have been so easy to fly into her arms, he thought, especially after he compared Felicia's disgusting rituals to Shiloh's exquisite brand of passion. What he had seen and heard made him appreciate Shiloh's innocent responses. She put the *love* in lovemaking, and no one could equal her. She was in a class by herself. But she was also off limits—the forbidden fruit in the garden of paradise.

"To you, little nymph," Holt murmured as he raised his glass to toast the bewitching vision that hovered above him.

He inhaled his drink in one swallow and eased back in his chair to take a long draw on his cigarillo. By the time he drank several toasts to Walter's new black eye and Felicia's humiliating return home, he was feeling the full effects of the whiskey. But it still wasn't enough to curb his thirst for Shiloh's explosive kisses.

And so Holt helped himself to a few dozen more drinks, substituting liquor and cigars for what he really wanted. In Holt's pickled mind, his vices were his compensation, meager compensation at best, for the splendor he had discovered in Shiloh's silky arms. He had sent her two gifts tonight, knowing she would be at Max Fletcher's home for the conference. He hoped Shiloh enjoyed his offerings even if she didn't know from whence they came. But it was of little consequence that Shiloh didn't know he was responsible for bringing Walter and Felicia down a notch. He knew she preferred to slay her own dragons, but this was one time Holt deputized himself as the silent force who avenged her humiliations—ones for which he felt responsible in the first place.

Chapter 14

Long after Victor had retired for the night, Shiloh was still lingering at the window, wondering what could be keeping Reuben. After the amusing events of the evening, Shiloh was eager to relate the episode to Reuben, even if he wasn't anxious to see her.

An anonymous note had arrived during the evening meeting, accusing Felicia of dallying with a married man. While the servants scurried out into the night to locate her, Walter had arrived upon the scene. Someone had punched him so thoroughly and repeatedly that his once-handsome face reminded Shiloh of risen bread dough.

Shiloh supposed Walter's new black eye and swollen lips were the reasons he didn't bother to fling out some nasty remark about her marriage. She didn't have the foggiest notion that her guardian angel had been hard at work that evening, and Walter wasn't about to tell her. His lips were sealed—literally! The painful incident was a mite too fresh on his mind, and Holt's gruff words still echoed in his ears.

Before the stirring household could recover from the startling note and Walter's rumpled appearance, Felicia arrived in her sheet. She had attempted to sneak to her room undetected, but people were swarming everywhere and she was caught in an even more embarrassing predicament than she had been when the mysterious intruder made off with her clothes.

Felicia had turned every color of the rainbow when one of the servants, who had little use for the spiteful chit anyway, raised her voice like a sounding bugle to summon Max. When the congregation gathered around the back exit, there stood Felicia, clutching her sheet to her bosom and silently cursing in mortification.

Max would have gone through the ceiling if he had been standing under one. His daughter had humiliated him in front of his distinguished guests and his servants and had besmirched the family's reputation. Max was in a towering rage. At first he confined his promiscuous daughter to the house for the duration of her life. But when he had calmed down he relented enough to limit her seclusion to the day he found an agreeable man to marry her and make a respectable woman of her—if that was possible.

Blubbering, Felicia ran into the house. Her loud wailing could still be heard as the guests filed outside. The conference was over on account of the family's disgrace and Walter limped home to nurse his cuts and bruises.

All in all it had turned out to be a gratifying evening that Shiloh wished Reuben could have enjoyed as thoroughly as she had. Even though she and Reuben were having difficulties, Shiloh wanted to share the juicy incident with him. But the clock had chimed midnight and she hadn't seen hide nor hair of Reuben.

Since this seemed to be a night for disasters, Shiloh became apprehensive about Reuben's lengthy absence. Her imagination was running away with itself, and she envisioned him lying somewhere in the night, the victim of assault. She would never have believed

Reuben was the one who had gone around assaulting victims!

Concerned, Shiloh ambled into the stables without changing from her nightgown and robe. She fully intended to become a one-woman search party. Shiloh had just retrieved her palomino mare from her stall when she heard a peal of reckless laughter ringing in the muggy air.

A bemused frown puckered her brow when she surveyed the shadowy figure on horseback. Dumbstruck, she watched the rider teeter precariously on his perch. A gasp escaped her lips when the rider very nearly toppled to the ground. When he drew closer, Shiloh had the sinking feeling it was Reuben who was floundering all over the back of his horse.

Holt had gotten a little carried away during his drinking spree. If not for the steed who knew his way home and Dog's built-in compass, Holt would have been roaming around the darkness like a lost soul.

"Reuben?" Shiloh blinked owlishly when the horse paused in front of the stable door.

Sure enough, it was Reuben. My, but he looked a sight! His plug hat sank low on his head, pressing his ears outward. His spectacles hung on the end of his nose and his sloppy clothes were twisted around him. And he had the silliest smile imaginable on his mouth. If he had one ounce of dignity left, he had surely sat down upon it and squashed it flat.

Holt tried to jerk himself to attention, but his sluggish movements very nearly sent him sliding off the saddle. Lord, he was drunk! The world was a fuzzy shade of gray, and it had been spinning furiously around him since he navigated his way around the tables of the saloon to retrieve his horse. The last person he wanted or expected to see in his inebriated condition was Shiloh. Good God, part of the reason he had drunk himself half blind was to forget what he wanted from this gorgeous minx. And here she was to remind him of what he had drunk to forget.

For several seconds Holt wrestled with his droopy facial muscles, attempting to muster a dignified expression. But his features felt as if they were slipping off his face. The thought provoked him to burst out laughing. His mirthful spasms caused him to tilt sideways, and he groped in the air to clutch the pommel before he plunked to the ground.

"Reuben Gilcrest, you're drunk!" Shiloh realized, and said so.

"Am I?" he slurred out, and then exploded in a horse laugh.

"Was it because of me that you got yourself soused?" she wanted to know that very second.

Holt was having one helluva time keeping up with the conversation. In his condition, comprehending four-word sentences was his limit. "What?" he mumbled, watching Shiloh's image split apart and then merge in the fuzzy shadows.

"I said, did you get drunk because of me?" she shouted at him.

Holt cringed when her booming voice crashed through his sensitive head like a cymbal. "Good God, woman," he drawled in agony. "I'm drunk, not deaf."

Flinging him a withering glance, Shiloh grasped the reins to lead the steed and Reuben into the barn. "Watch your . . ." Crack! His forehead slammed against the top of the doorway. "Head."

Shiloh couldn't control her giggles when Holt flopped backward on the horse, groaning miserably. He looked so pathetic it was comical.

For the life of him, Holt couldn't determine which way was up. His head throbbed in rhythm with his heart. "God, I really am drunk," he said.

"Did you just notice?" Shiloh asked with an amused grin. Grabbing his flailing arm, she tried to haul him into an upright position in the saddle. "Shall I help you down?"

A shocked yelp burst from her lips when she realized all she had succeeded in doing was knocking Reuben completely off balance. Like a spinning top, he whirled on the saddle and then flipped backward. Shiloh knew a half second too late that she was standing in the wrong spot. But she seemed to be moving in slow motion and she couldn't remove herself from the path of the body that gravity dragged downward.

Holt tumbled off the horse headfirst and backward. Shiloh became his landing mat. If not for the straw that padded the floor, Shiloh was certain she would have been squished flat. As it was, she and Holt were both smashed—he from too much liquor, and she from bearing two hundred pounds of rock-hard muscle.

When they hit the floor Shiloh's breath came out in a whoosh. "Get off me!" she croaked with her last ounce of air.

Like a gigantic overturned beetle Holt struggled to slide off Shiloh. But he had very little coordination left and he gouged her twice with his elbows before he managed to wriggle down beside her in the straw.

"Reuben Gilcrest, you should be ashamed of yourself!" Shiloh railed as she checked for broken bones.

"I already am," he assured her thickly. "You're probably considering shooting me for making such a fool of myself." Holt sucked in a deep breath and levered up on an elbow. "But it's a waste of time. The hangover I'll have in the morning will kill me anyway."

His glazed eyes circled to the streaming mane of hair that sprayed around her shoulders like a silver-blond cape. His hand lifted to smooth the tangled tresses away from her flushed face. The lantern she had lit near her mare's stall cast a faint light that formed a halo around her head. Captivated, Holt stared at the blurry features that faded and then cleared to reveal a face that was absolute perfection.

"Good God, you're lovely," he blurted out. "Why do you have to be the devil's own temptation?"

Shiloh grinned at his ruffled appearance and his uninhibited manner. She rather liked this new facet of his personality—one that obviously remained confined until it was loosened by an overdose of whiskey. Shiloh had never been impressed by men who showered her with lavish compliments, but Reuben's always flattered her. He had never been generous with them. When he voiced a compliment she knew he meant it, and that made all the difference.

His hand tangled in her long hair, twisting it around his fist like a rope, tilting her face to his. Holt was drawn to Shiloh like a moth to a flame. The whole idea of drinking until he couldn't think hadn't eased his obsessive craving for this enchanting minx. One bottle of whiskey had allowed him not to think, but he would have had to consume two bottles to numb himself to these erotic feelings that refused to go away.

His tousled raven head moved slowly toward hers. "You're going to wish you weren't here to greet me, nymph," he mumbled in warning.

Shiloh wished nothing of the kind! She wouldn't have missed this for the world. Even if Reuben didn't know what he was doing, she was delighting in his reckless behavior and the ravishing kiss he bestowed on her. When he pressed her back into the straw, Shiloh went down like a drowning swimmer and her arms lifted to curl around his broad shoulders. He tasted of whiskey and cigars, neither of which she knew he partook of. But she didn't complain, not even when his

204

hands tunneled beneath her robe and nightgown to make inquisitive contact with her quivering flesh.

Wild tingles galloped down her spine, and the familiar ache burned in the pit of her belly. Instinctively, she arched toward his seeking hands, cherishing his touch, drinking deeply of his kiss. The pleasure she had discovered the first night Reuben made love to her unfolded to lure her deeper into the sensuous web of passion. And just as before, Shiloh found the universe shrinking on Reuben's handsome features. His spectacles had fallen by the wayside and his eyes glittered with unmistakable desire.

The liquor had caused the well-disciplined mask to slip from his expression, unveiling the emotions that churned within him. Holt had no room in his hectic life for emotional involvement with Shiloh or any other woman, but he wanted her madly and it showed. He had always wanted her, even if Shiloh wasn't aware of it.

Holt felt himself losing his grasp on his self-control when Shiloh allowed him to caress her at will. The feel of her satiny skin beneath his fingertips ignited his passions which were situated a little too close to the barrel of whiskey he had consumed. One careless spark and he would explode. He had enough difficulty clamping down on his desires when he was sober. And now that he wasn't, there was no subduing the hungry cravings that ran rampant.

Holding this shapely sprite was like lying beside a blazing stove. He could feel the fierce heat waves scorching him inside and out. Holt swore he would have walked over live coals to have her, to recapture the night that had satisfied him and yet tormented him so. His conscience was too numbed by liquor to caution him against taking her here and now, and the voice of reason had drowned in the bubbly brew he had been drinking like a fish. His traitorous body seemed to have only one purpose—to appease the maddening needs that Shiloh so easily aroused.

Murmuring her name over and over again, Holt tugged at the material that prevented him from tasting and touching every exquisite inch of her shapely body. He resented his own baggy clothes for restricting him from lying flesh to flesh with this lovely temptation who had revealed new dimensions of passion to him.

Shiloh didn't protest when Reuben pulled her robe and nightgown from her shoulders to expose the swells of her breasts. She yearned to feel his moist lips whispering over her bare flesh, longed for his gentle, exploring touch that compared to nothing she had ever known.

Even under the influence of alcohol Holt never once resorted to manhandling her. He cherished her and murmured his need for her. He was intimate without intimidating her, and Shiloh responded to his arousing touch. Her fingertips worked the buttons of his shirt, eager to spear her hands into the dark mat of hair that covered his muscular chest. She relished the feel of his strength beneath her palms, reveled in the power to make him tremble with awakened desire.

A tiny gasp tripped from her lips when his hot kisses skied down the slope of her shoulder to hover over the taut peaks of her breasts. His wandering hands glided down her belly, peeling away her garments as he went, baring more flesh to his worshiping caresses. Streams of sweet torment trickled through her, shattering what was left of her self-control. Each place Reuben touched sizzled, and her naive body cried out for more.

It was as if Reuben had suddenly sprouted an extra dozen pair of hands, she mused. They were everywhere at once, driving her mad with wanting, triggering sensations that rippled over her like waves rolling out to sea. His questing fingers spread over her hips and thighs and then receded to encircle the dusky buds of her breasts. Shiloh felt herself sinking into the straw and discarded clothes that formed their makeshift bed. She was clay being molded and formed by a master craftsman. His tantalizing caresses siphoned her strength and absorbed her energy until she was living and breathing only for him. She was a mindless puppet who moved upon Reuben's command, wanting no more than his kisses and caresses, surviving on the wondrous sensations that he instilled in her.

Holt couldn't get enough of her. Each kiss magnified the ravenous craving that gnawed at him. Each caress ignited another living wall of flames that collapsed upon him, frying him alive. He was like a desperate man trying to outrun a wildfire. But he knew he would never escape the blaze of passion. He was about to be consumed by something so fiery, nothing could save him. And he wasn't sure he wanted to be rescued. Dying was small sacrifice to pay for the ineffable pleasure that awaited him in Shiloh's arms.

A rumbling groan vibrated in his chest when her adventurous hands slid over his hips, shoving away the last of his garb. Her caresses were reminiscent of a tender massage that transformed flesh to living desire. Every nerve, every muscle, demanded more of the tantalizing sensations that channeled through them. He adored the touch of her hands and lips on his skin. He reveled in returning the indescribable feelings she aroused.

Shiloh's breath lodged in her throat when his muscular body glided over hers. Her lashes fluttered up to see the shimmering desire in those vivid green eyes. As his raven head swooped downward, his mouth rolled over hers in a kiss that testified to his hunger and promised the intimacy and ecstasy to come. His body merged with hers in rapturous union, and Shiloh was immediately swept up into a fast-moving current that sent her swirling into the dizzying whirlpool of passion. He had become the flame inside her and a flood of fire rushed through her. His body drove into hers and she answered each penetrating thrust, giving in to the turbulent winds of passion that sent tidal waves tumbling across this sea of rolling flames.

Holt feared he would crush Shiloh beneath him. He had so little control over his responses to her. Desire had plunged him into a wild, windswept storm that uprooted logic and flung him in a thousand different directions at once. It was no longer the spell of liquor that drugged his mind and body, but rather passion that had such a fierce hold on him. The taste of her was on his lips. The subtle fragrance of her perfume warped his senses. The feel of her luscious body moving in perfect rhythm with his left a sweet, compelling melody strumming on his soul.

One incredible sensation after another pelleted Holt like hailstones. Ecstasy, like pattering rain, poured over him. Holt groaned in sweet torment when his soul unfurled its wings to escape the storm-tossed sensations that sought to shatter it. And suddenly he was soaring above the cyclonic winds that devastated his body. He was adrift beyond the moon, counting each ineffable sensation that sparkled upon him. He was reaching upward to clutch that one bright shining star that lay beyond his grasp. . . .

And suddenly he was there! He was an integral part of that distant evening star that burned with the heat of a thousand suns. He was the fire, fueled by Shiloh's wild, uninhibited responses. A fierce, vibrating shudder rocked his soul when all the fantastic feelings that rocketed him into the star world beyond the moon converged upon him. His body quivered beneath the intensity of passion's sweet release, and he swore he would never survive this last, soul-shattering sensation. But survive he did, though his flight through time and space left him drained and disoriented.

It was several breathless moments before the darkness parted to allow the golden shards of lantern light to filter across his line of vision. An angel's face appeared to him—a goddess whose mystical powers had taken him on the most incredible journey.

Holt devoured Shiloh's petal-soft lips and then slipped back into the bottomless abyss. But in his hazy dreams there was one delicate face that lured him like a beacon in the night, one sweet memory that inflamed his soul and burned brands on his cautious heart. . . .

"Reuben?" Shiloh whispered tenderly.

When he didn't respond, Shiloh glided her fingertips up and down his back to investigate the sinewy muscles and the broad expanse of his shoulders. A contented smile pursed her lips as she remembered the sweet magic of their lovemaking. She doubted Reuben would recall what they had shared, as the fog of whiskey clouded his brain. But she wouldn't forget even one rapturous moment. He had amused her with his silly antics and then satisfied every yearning that had plagued her since she discovered the meaning of passion.

It still amazed Shiloh that a man who had no previous experience with women could be such a tender lover. He always knew just the right ways to arouse her and satisfy needs that she hadn't known existed. Reuben was both the cause and cure of her tormented longings. The desire they aroused in each other lured her to him even though she knew Reuben would probably be much happier if he could go his own way. . . .

When he stirred enough to inch down beside her,

Shiloh nestled against his swarthy frame. These few brief moments when they were as close as two people could get were worth Felicia's and Walter's mocking taunts. It was worth the torment of loving a man who didn't really want her for his wife. Shiloh cherished each moment of splendor as if it were twenty-four-karat gold. These stolen hours she spent with Reuben were so few and far between. But they rivaled nothing else Shiloh had experienced in all her twenty-one years.

Shiloh couldn't imagine why she had opened her heart to this shy, awkward man. She had vowed never to risk her emotions to love after Lance Draper had betrayed her. But there were so many mysteriously fascinating qualities about Reuben that intrigued her. Shiloh had let her guard down to look beneath the cautious shell. Under that calm reserve was a powerful package of strength and a dynamic character. Reuben hid this aspect of himself from the rest of the world, but these were the things that captivated Shiloh and held her spellbound. And knowing that she and Reuben had discovered and explored the dimensions of passion together brought immense satisfaction.

What she and Reuben shared was special and unique, she mused as she pressed a kiss to his dark brow. They had made their own brand of passion without being influenced by experiences from their pasts. They had come together with innocent, instinctive responses, learning what pleased and aroused each other, creating their own private paradise. They had taught each other all either of them knew about desire. . . . Or so she thought . . .

If Shiloh had known she was so naive that she couldn't recognize an experienced lover and that she had been purposely misled from the very beginning, she would have shot Reuben as he slept in his drugged stupor! But she was an innocent maid who had been cleverly deceived. She presumed Reuben had been born with a special gift of tenderness and a magical instinct for passion.

And Lord have mercy on Holt if Shiloh ever did learn the truth! He would discover that hell knew no fury like the woman deceived—especially this particular woman with a feisty spirit and a legendary temper. Holt, as Reuben, had been allowed to see the facet of her personality that no other man had seen. He alone had been in Shiloh's good graces. She had generously opened her heart to Reuben, exposing her warmth and gentle soul. But if she knew she had been played for a fool, he would be sorry he ever met this fiery hellion who had held every other man in contempt and at arm's length. As warm and generous as Shiloh was now, she could be a force to be reckoned with when she got her hackles up. Making a fool of oneself was one thing. But having someone do it for you was ten times worse, and Shiloh was not the type of individual who allowed a man to humiliate her. Holt had observed her once or twice when her notorious temper got the best of her. But being on the receiving end of her wrath was another matter entirely!

But thus far Holt had said all the right things to insure that she believed the deceptions he had employed in his cunning charade. But how long would his luck hold out?

The warble of barn swallows infiltrated Holt's soggy brain, chasing away the fuzzy cobwebs one by one. Holt woke up feeling half dead. The sun announced the dawning of a new day and the bright light struck like daggers. Pain plowed through his skull as he glanced around, asking himself where the hell he was. Sick, his gaze fell on Shiloh's partially covered body. . . .

211

Good God, what had he done? The implication jolted him awake and panic immediately set in. Frantically, he racked his spongy brain to set the events of the previous night in chronological order. Bits and pieces of incidents pierced his throbbing head like porcupine quills. Moaning miserably, Holt grabbed his breeches and stuffed his muscular legs into them. Remembering the feed sack that contained his disguise, he wobbled over to his horse to retrieve it. After stashing the sack in a corner under the straw, Holt plunked back down beside Shiloh. He mentally kicked himself a few dozen times. Damn, he couldn't keep his distance from that appetizing minx, drunk or sober!

Although he recalled flashbacks of a warm, intoxicating dream, he couldn't swear that Shiloh had been a willing participant. If she had been offended by his inebriated state and he had forced her to . . . The thought nauseated him more than he already was. If he had done one thing to hurt or frighten Shiloh while he was out of control, he would never have forgiven himself as long as he lived.

The moment Shiloh stirred beside him, Holt braced himself for the worst. He didn't have to portray the role of Reuben Gilcrest in this instance. He was truly ashamed of his disgraceful behavior.

"I'm sorry," he croaked in a hoarse voice, refusing to meet Shiloh's gaze.

Sleepy silver-blue eyes blinked up at him. Holt forced himself to glance in her direction and then kicked himself a few times for good measure. "I deeply regret everything I said and did last night. I wish it had never happened."

Ordinarily, Holt knew just the right thing to say to prevent Shiloh's volatile temper from erupting. But Shiloh hadn't regretted one delirious moment, and it stung her pride to hear Reuben wish the splendor of the night away.

Shiloh wasn't a morning person anyway. She was one of those individuals whose disposition improved as the day progressed. She wasn't exactly grumpy, but then, she wasn't the picture of cheerfulness either. His remark hit her the wrong way, and she jerked upright, clutching her robe about her.

"You regret everything that happened?" she snapped in question. "Every single thing?"

Holt twisted to peer into those mystical eyes that were suddenly alive with indignation. Good God, had he done something else he couldn't remember? Is that why Shiloh was glaring at him as if he were a slimy serpent that had slithered out from under a rock? He had offered an apology that was meant to cover every idiotic shenanigan and any rough handling to which he might have resorted when lust got the best of him. What the hell did she want? For him to get down on his knees and plead forgiveness for whatever he did that he couldn't remember doing?

"I said I was sorry," he mumbled in frustration.

"For everything?" she prodded again, growing madder by the minute.

When Reuben nodded, Shiloh vaulted to her feet and rammed her arms into her robe. So he did regret making love to her, did he? Reuben hadn't wanted it to happen, and he hadn't wanted it to happen the first time either! He had successfully destroyed the precious memories and Shiloh didn't feel the least bit sorry for him. She hoped his hellacious hangover blinded him permanently!

Dammit all, why had she fallen in love with such an impossible man? Shiloh didn't know which was worse, being chased by men who didn't appeal to her or being rejected by the one man who did! But one thing was certain, she was going to have to get over this fascination for Reuben. It was painfully apparent that she was wasting her time on a marriage that was made, and was presently residing, in hell!

When Shiloh stamped off in a huff, Holt frowned bemusedly and then groaned. Even his facial muscles ached from his bout with liquor. Hell, even his eyelashes hurt! And if he wasn't feeling bad enough already, he had managed to irritate Shiloh and he didn't even know what he had said to offend her. He had tried to soothe her and beg forgiveness for whatever sins he had committed against her. Lord, if only he could remember exactly what had happened, it would make it easier to deal with that saucy sprite. Holt had the inescapable feeling he was treading on very thin ice. Had he betrayed his charade the previous night by doing something out of character besides getting himself rip-roaring drunk? Was Shiloh wise to him? Good God, he hoped not!

There was only one thing to do, Holt mused as he dragged himself to his feet to fetch the feed sack and Walter's missing wallet. He would simply play out his charade and pretend the night before didn't exist. When Shiloh got over being furious with him, they would revert to the civilized war they had been waging since the night she had caught him laboring over her father's ledgers. Damn, nothing had turned out as he had intended. He had delivered her his offerings of Walter and Felicia, but he hadn't meant to go so far as to physically attack her in his drunken stupor. Damn, Shiloh surely must hate him.

On that tormenting thought Holt trudged to the house to soak in a warm bath and thumb through the wallet to see if there was anything in it that might be of use to him. But all in all, it turned out to be a rotten day. Shiloh didn't even bother to be civil. She simply gave him the silent treatment when he was underfoot and practiced her disappearing acts every chance she got.

Chapter 15

The next few days were torment pure and simple. Holt cursed himself for the way he had behaved with Shiloh. To compensate, he threw himself into his investigation and spent as little time as possible at the mansion.

Hurt by Reuben's obvious avoidance and his rejection of their interlude in the stable, Shiloh made certain she wasn't around to distress him. She was sure she was the reason for his drinking spree and she knew he wanted to forget the incident and her if at all possible. When Reuben entered the mansion, Shiloh exited. When he departed, she returned.

Even Victor became aware that the relationship was quickly deteriorating between his daughter and son-in-law. Reuben was clumsier than ever during those infrequent moments when both he and Shiloh were forced to be together. And if Reuben glanced at Shiloh, it was a rare occasion. To say that Reuben and Shiloh seemed trapped by the arrangement was an understatement.

Meals were barely tolerable in a silence that could have been sliced with a knife. Victor began to wonder if both Reuben and Shiloh were including him in this private war they were waging. Victor became so frustrated that he finally threw up his hands and decided it was time to annul this mock marriage. And he was on the verge of voicing that very suggestion when a messenger arrived to sidetrack him.

The moment Victor read the hastily scrawled letter, he erupted in muffled curses. "Damn, that's all we need right now." He scowled disgustedly.

Holt accepted the note Victor thrust at him. When he had read the message he swore under his breath. The letter from Brian King, the track foreman, stated the trainload of equipment and building material had been raided by a gang of thieves who had burned the lumber and stolen the supplies of food and tools that were intended for the road gang near Primrose.

"J. W. Baxter is undoubtedly responsible for this," Victor accused as he slammed his fist on the table, rattling the dishes and silverware.

"That is a rather rash accusation," Colonel," Holt inserted, studying Victor with a scrutinizing gaze.

"No, it isn't," Victor blustered out. "Baxter is power hungry. That scoundrel probably hired thugs to sabotage my train of supplies so his railroad crews could reach the Indian territory border before we do. They will claim the contracts with the tribal councils and we will be bankrupt." Hoping to walk off his frustration, Victor bounded from his chair and paced like a caged tiger. "Pack your bags, Reuben, we are going to see for ourselves how much damage those raiders have done. The payroll train is scheduled to leave for Primrose late this afternoon, and we are going with it."

Shiloh was offended that her father hadn't extended the invitation to include her. Reuben may have been her husband—one who didn't want her as his wife—but he wasn't taking her place by her father's side! She had always accompanied Victor when he clambered into his private cars to inspect the tracks and the road gang's southwestward progress. She was going along even if Reuben had to tolerate her presence, and that was that!

When Holt hastened to the room to collect his belongings, Shiloh was one step behind him. In mute irritation Holt watched her stuff her clothes into her satchel.

"You aren't going," he informed her flatly. "There may be trouble awaiting us."

Shiloh jerked upright to fling him a heated glare that was meant to fry him to a crisp. "I will go where I please, just as I always have," she informed him in no uncertain terms. Shiloh shoved another dress into her satchel and slammed it shut. "Just because I spoke the vows doesn't mean I will allow you or anyone else to dictate to me."

Day by day Holt discovered what other men already knew about this rebellious spitfire. She was very much her own woman. She no longer viewed Reuben as a friend, but rather as her foe. If she had truly felt anything for him, he had destroyed it with his ridiculous shenanigan in the barn. And although the clever ploy had managed to counteract her usual reaction to men, it had served only to postpone clashes between them.

The fact was no man pushed Shiloh around, not even Reuben, who had attempted to pose not the slightest threat to her. But destiny and fate had joined hands to spoil the charade Holt had so carefully employed. Now that he and Shiloh were at odds, he was having the same difficulties that all other men encountered when attempting to manage this spirited misfit. The fragile bond between them had been severed and Shiloh was making no attempt to be compatible. In her opinion,

Reuben was like the other men who had complicated her life at one time or another. He didn't love her or want her for who she really was. Her bitterness prompted her to spare him not even the smallest consideration.

"I don't want to see you hurt, Shiloh," Holt declared as he unpacked her clothes.

Shiloh jerked her undergarments from his hands and shoved them back into her satchel. "So you have said a dozen times before," she countered, a distinctly unpleasant edge in her voice.

"I meant it," Holt muttered grouchily. "And forgive me for saying so, but you are a mite too stubborn and independent for your own good."

Shiloh scooped up her satchel before Holt could swipe it off the bed. In stiff strides she marched toward the door. "Don't do me any favors, and spare me your free advice," she flung over her shoulder as she buzzed into the hall. "From now on I expect nothing from you. Nor should you expect me to give you another thought. You stay out of my way and I'll stay out of yours."

When her footsteps receded, Holt spewed a flood of unprintable curses. It was a shame that hellion didn't know her place. But even if she did, Holt doubted she would stay in it. Shiloh considered herself a part of the McBride Railroad Company, and she intended to join her father, just as she had in the past. That was all Holt needed with threats of hoodlums ransacking the supply train. If Shiloh didn't watch her step, that belligerent daredevil could wind up just like Anna. . . .

Holt's blood turned to ice at the dismal thought. He had never wanted to feel such a strong emotional attachment to a woman again. He had suffered all the torments known to man when Anna met with disaster. If this spirited blonde endured the same fate at the hands of ruthless renegades, Holt wasn't sure he could cope. As much as he hated to admit it, he cared a great deal about Shiloh. He couldn't bear to see her subjected to the same molestation Anna had experienced.

Damn, he was going to have to do something . . . and quickly. Although he thought he knew who the force behind the shady dealings in the McBride Railroad Company was, he was still operating on theory instead of concrete evidence. Holt had sent a telegram to one of Pinkerton's agents in St. Louis to check on Victor's, Max's, Elijah's, and Walter's ties with government officials. Until Holt had a sworn statement from one of the officials who risked incrimination if he failed to cooperate with Pinkerton's agency, no one would be indicted for embezzlement. And unless Holt had solid evidence that would stand up in court, Reuben's demise would be premature. But in order for Holt to protect Shiloh, Reuben had to perish. Unfortunately, things were moving too quickly to suit Holt, and he had become too attached to that sassy imp. He needed to shed his alias to investigage the gang who demolished the railroad supplies, but he also needed evidence. In short, he needed to be two people at once.

Giving Victor and Shiloh the excuse that he wanted to send a telegram to his aunt Mildred in Chicago, Holt and Dog clambered off. By the time he reached the train depot, the other entrepreneurs of the railroad were ready and waiting to climb aboard.

Good, Holt mused as he reached out a hand to assist Shiloh up the steps. Having all his suspects on the same train was to his advantage. Perhaps some of his unanswered questions could be resolved during this trip. . . .

"I do not need your assistance," Shiloh snapped, slapping the offensive hand away. With her chin tilted to a defiant angle that Holt had come to recognize at a

219

glance, Shiloh struggled up the steps, laden down with her luggage.

Holt heaved a frustrated sigh. He had hoped that he and his new bride could part on a friendly note before his arranged death. For some unexplainable reason Holt wanted this firebrand to cherish a few of the memories she had experienced during wedlock. He shouldn't have cared, he knew. It was better that Shiloh readily give Reuben up. But Holt found that he had acquired a sentimental streak all of a sudden. Of the many women he had seduced and left the past two years, he wasn't sure he wanted Shiloh to forget him. He didn't like deceiving Shiloh, but conveniently disposing of his aliases in past assignments worked too effectively not to utilize.

Shiloh would probably be glad to be rid of him, Holt mused as his gaze swept the cars that were attached to the locomotive. When Reuben staged his death, Shiloh would be relieved. Not that he could blame her. He had given her very little reason to miss him since he had done nothing to enrich her life. . . .

Holt's musings trailed off when he focused on the payroll car that had been coupled in front of Victor's personal coaches. The pay car gleamed and the windows sparkled like crystal. The ornate rear platform shone like pure gold, and the brass work on the sides befitted a Spanish galleon bearing a treasure. A quarter-inch-thick boiler plate protected the gold, and two portholes had been cut into the back wall so the pay teller could shoot thieves from behind his barricade if necessary. The car was equipped with an automatic drop window so the eighty-pound window would crash down on the arm of anyone who was not authorized to reach into the money cage on payday. And although the car was built like a vault, its flashy color was an enticement to thieves. The fact that this elaborate car had been hitched to the train worried Holt considerably.

His thoughts turned elsewhere when he lumbered up the steps to enter the extravagant car that was resplendent with tapestries and brocade upholstery. Double mirrors set in gold frames hung beside the doors at the front and back of the car. Wood panels that had been polished to a shine surrounded the expensively furnished suite. On either side of the room were windows adorned with velvet curtains and plush velvet sofas that provided more comfort than could be found even in a first-class passenger car. In the back corner of the room sitting beneath one of the mirrors was a conference table and tuft chairs.

Holt's gaze swept over the flamboyant furnishings and drapes, marveling at the expense to which Victor had gone to insure that he and his associates traveled in style. And impressed though he was with the private suite, he was curious about the sleeper that had been coupled between the payroll car and this magnificent parlor on rails.

The thought of sharing space with the stockholders and with Shiloh annoyed Holt. But more specifically, it was the thought of Walter Jameson sharing closed spaces with Shiloh that irritated him most. The man lusted after Shiloh. That was obvious. All the snide remarks Holt had endured from Walter were delivered because of the man's obsession and jealousy. If Holt knew Walter's type as well as he thought he did, that blond-haired rake was actually in love with Shiloh. But Walter wasn't good at expressing his love since he had obviously spent most of his life perfecting lust. Not that Holt was an expert on love, for he certainly was not. But he did have a little self-control. Yet, there was no telling what Walter would do when he was closeted in the same sleeping quarters with Shiloh.

Damn.... Keeping Walter a respectable distance away from Shiloh meant that Reuben would have to keep a watchful eye on his wife. And lately Shiloh preferred solitude to Reuben's company. Blast it, between prying valuable information from these railroad entrepreneurs and attempting to make amends with Shiloh for her own protection Holt would be kept on his toes. What a long day lay ahead of him!

With both ears turned to the discussion at the conference table and one eye on Shiloh, Holt slouched in his chair and reached over to give Dog an affectionate pat. Discreetly, Holt listened to the men discuss how they would compensate for the damaged equipment and supplies. Every moment of delay would slow their southwestward progress and give Baxter's company the opportunity to win the race to Indian territory. If misfortune befell the McBride Railroad Company . . .

Holt's gaze bounced back and forth between Max Fletcher and Walter Jameson when he cruised past that particular thought. Pensively, Holt shoved the contrary spectacles back to the bridge of his nose and frowned. Both Max and Walter were tossing out possible solutions to the problem of shipping new equipment from the warehouse to the tracklaying crews. Max was chewing vigorously on his cheroot, Victor was pacing, Elijah was muttering about issuing bonds to collect enough ready cash to pay the unexpected expenses, and Walter was enthusiastically attempting to sell his ideas to the rest of the men. The company was already mortgaged to the limits of government regulations and beyond. McBride desperately needed to win the race to the border or his investors risked heavy losses.

In Holt's estimation, the border raiders who had

preyed on the train carrying rail equipment could not have come at a worse time. It was a little too inconvenient, in fact. It made Holt wonder.

After the guests feasted on rabbit pot pie and pastries prepared by Victor's personal cook, the committee continued to debate the problems facing them. Holt took his leave to wander onto the breezeway that separated the luxurious passenger car from the kitchen and supply car. He digested the information he had learned about the committee's wheeling and dealing. They were all scavengers in their own right—men who scratched and clawed to realize a dream of connecting the East with the riches of the South and West. Holt couldn't condone all their methods, some of which seemed underhanded, but their goal of tying this widespread nation together with rails was commendable. Many citizens would profit because of this adventurous dream, especially the tycoons who would wind up with a good share of the riches. They scrounged to collect other people's money as well as their own in order to finance the huge operation of building track through difficult terrain. They promoted real estate, struck only God knew what type of bargains with the state legislature, and only Satan knew what type of arrangements to meet their objectives. . . .

"You have no taste for railroad business, do you, Reuben?" Shiloh's quiet voice jostled him from his contemplations. "And if that is so, why did you travel to Springfield in the first place?"

Damn, that minx was a little too perceptive for her own good, Holt mused as he pivoted to face Shiloh's probing stare. His breath caught in his throat when he peered at the pert beauty. The breeze lifted the long tendrils of hair that had trailed down her back like an invisible hand toying with strands of silk. The sunlight sparkled in those unique silver-blue eyes, giving them a supernatural quality. Her pale blue gown hugged her curvaceous figure, enhancing what Holt already considered to be perfection. It was a long, fanciful moment before Holt gathered his wandering thoughts and concentrated on her pointed question.

Composing himself, Holt produced a faint smile. "You have misread my thoughts, my dear," he contradicted her in a diplomatic tone. "I am the black sheep of the railroad flock. Our marriage solidified my investment with your father, but I will never really be one of them. If you were paying close attention, you must have noticed that not one of your father's disciples asked my opinion on how to deal with this catastrophe. Even if the money I have agreed to invest had already been deposited in the company funds, I would not be given a vote on how to solve the problems at hand."

Shiloh stared across the plush grasses that rolled toward the Ozark Mountains in the distance. Her emotions were entangled. One moment she detested Reuben—his awkwardness and his standoffish behavior toward her. But while she was listing his faults, the forbidden memories of the passion they had shared filtered through to her. At times she was sure Walter was right. She had married out of her species. And yet the man who remained locked behind those godawful spectacles, sloppy clothes, and that self-imposed reserve fascinated and appealed to her.

What an exasperating man Reuben Gilcrest was! Shiloh had been willing to overlook his bashfulness and his lack of coordination. She had sought to build a relationship with the warm, tender man who emerged from his shell on occasion. But dealing with Reuben was like dealing with two entirely different men—the one who couldn't place one foot in front of the other without tripping himself and the one who instinctively knew how to send her on a journey into the sensual dimensions of passion. He was like a flower waiting to bloom, a potential that had yet to be tapped. Shiloh was stirred by the challenge and so very frustrated by the obstacles she constantly encountered.

She had made progress, she encouraged herself. In the beginning Reuben couldn't even meet her gaze without falling all over himself. At least now he would glance at her occasionally. And he could be a gentle, considerate lover when he forgot his fear of women. But Shiloh still made him uncomfortable in too many ways, and she doubted he would ever come to feel any true affection for her. He just didn't know how to love, and he was afraid to learn. She, on the other hand, didn't know how but she was willing to give love a sporting chance.

Heaving a defeated sigh, Shiloh peered down at her fists which were knotted in her billowing blue gown. "I will not hold you to our wedding vows, Reuben. It was not my intention to entrap you, even though you believe it was. When we return to Springfield, I will file for an annulment. I will also see to it that Papa holds no grudge when you decline to transfer funds from your bank account to the company treasury. You will be free to go your own way."

Reuben should have been relieved that Shiloh was graciously letting him off the hook. That was what he wanted, wasn't it?

"Did you hear me, Reuben?" Shiloh prodded when he didn't respond. "I hold myself accountable for the night my father found us together, not you. I am not an utter fool. I know when a man doesn't want me. I can tell when he feels trapped. You show all the signs of a prisoner held against his will."

"It is for the best," he murmured, pushing the droopy glasses back in place. "You deserve more of a man for a husband."

"You were man enough," Shiloh burst out, and then struggled for hard-won composure. "The problem is that I am not woman enough to attract you."

"Not woman enough?" Holt would have laughed out loud at that ridiculous statement if it wouldn't have been out of character for the personality he projected. Hell's bells, he had fought tooth and nail to smother his fierce attraction to this enchanting sprite. She was what men's dreams were made of, and he had done his fair share of fantasizing. Sliding into bed each night without ravishing Shiloh had been a valiant display of self-restraint. Not woman enough? That was a joke!

Tentatively, Holt reached out to draw Shiloh to him, but he cautiously kept her at a respectable distance. "Again you have misjudged the situation," he countered, his voice husky with unappeased desire—desire that could not be satisfied without giving himself away.

Shiloh had viewed another side of Reuben the two nights they made love. She had discovered how human he was. But that part of Reuben could never gain complete control of the shy, awkward individual Holt portrayed. At this very moment Holt was planning to have Reuben killed. He and Shiloh had no future, and he had to make that important point without arousing her suspicion or hurting her worse than he already had.

"I fear you have it exactly backward," Holt insisted as his hands absently drifted up her arms to cup her exquisite face. "I am not man enough for you, Shiloh. And if I remain here, I will only wind up making you more miserable than you already are. When I'm with you I'm hounded by conflict. You want to make me into something I'm not, something I can never be. What I am is what you see." His chest rose and fell in a heavy sigh. "I was taught never to take advantage of a woman, to display impeccable manners at all times. I feel guilty because of what transpired between us. . . ."

"And I have longed for more of it," Shiloh admitted, and then clamped down on her lip. She was a fool to voice confessions that made Reuben uncomfortable.

That was not the kind of comment Holt needed to hear when he was battling the same voracious hunger that gnawed at him each time he touched this appetizing nymph. Against his will Holt was helplessly lured to those heart-shaped lips that were as soft as rose petals. Despite the warning signals that his conscience was sending him, he took her sweet mouth under his, savoring the intoxicating taste, aching for her in places he tried to forget he had.

When Shiloh's arms wound around his neck, he found himself pulling her full-length against him when he should have set her away. The feel of her ripe body meshed familiarly to his unleashed the forbidden memories of the nights of splendor they should not have shared. Holt could close his eyes and remember the hot, sizzling sparks, feel the wildfire of passion coursing through his veins. This tempting goddess could arouse the lusty beast in any man. It was no wonder she found her suitors stealing kisses and caresses every chance they got.

All the while his hands were roaming over her hips, Holt cursed his lack of willpower. But he was addicted, and all the silent lectures he had delivered himself hadn't worked worth a damn. There were times when his brain and his body refused to agree. This was one of those times. When he dared to take Shiloh in his arms and lose himself in her explosive kisses, he forgot his charade and his purpose. . . .

"Well, well." Walter smirked as he crossed his arms over his chest and arrogantly propped himself against the rail. "I wouldn't have believed it if I hadn't seen it with my own eyes. I didn't think you knew the first thing about romance, Reuben." One blond brow arched over a laughing hazel eye. "Tell me, has this ridiculous marriage of yours progressed past kissing?"

In a flash of temper Shiloh reeled to launch herself at the arrogant varmint whose amorous techniques had done more to repulse her than arouse her. Before she could smear the haughty smirk all over Walter's face, Holt clamped both hands around her waist and towed her back against him.

Although Holt would have delighted in mashing Walter's nose flat as a pancake, he couldn't. Reuben wasn't a violent man. He was one of those meek individuals who turned the other cheek. But Holt couldn't allow Shiloh to make another attempt to come to his defense. There was enough tension between Shiloh and her father's second in command without her tearing him to shreds, even if Walter deserved it. Holt reminded himself that he had discreetly blackened both of Walter's eyes when there was no one else around to witness the belated retaliations. That was his consolation and the only satisfaction he could enjoy at the moment. It was a shame Walter had such a short memory. He had been warned to keep his mouth shut, but his tongue kept running away with itself.

"The intimacies between a man and his wife are sacred and private, Mr. Jameson," Holt replied, assuming Reuben's persona once again. He fought to contain the anger that bubbled just beneath the surface. "And the exact extent of those intimacies are none of your concern. I request that you return to the passenger car. I would like a private word with my wife."

Flinging the coward a taunting grin, Walter pushed away from the rail and sauntered back inside. When the portal eased shut behind him, Holt stared down into Shiloh's flushed face. Her features were so alive with fury that she looked like a live grenade that was about to explode.

"You should have let me tear him limb from limb," she spluttered. "This is the third time he has mocked your virility."

"Walter will be served his just desserts," Reuben's voice assured her as calmly as possible. "Every dog has his day."

"Yes, well, today should have been Walter's day," she grumbled acrimoniously.

Holt gave his head a contradictory shake. "Walter only proved what I have been trying to say. He feels no threat in ridiculing me because he knows I'm not prone to fits of temper, that I will not avenge his insults. But you would do it for me, even though I prefer you wouldn't." A rueful smile curved his lips as he smoothed away Shiloh's aggravated frown. "The incident testified to the fact that I'm not the sort of man you need, Shiloh. You need and deserve a man who can match your fiery spirit and determination. I am not that man, and I never will be. When you attempt to change me, it causes you constant frustration."

Gently, he dropped a kiss to her pouting lips. "Let go, Shiloh. You are holding on to a man who cannot make you happy. Let go, knowing you have made the right decision about an annulment. Someday you will find a man who can be all you expect him to be, a man who can fulfill your dreams."

Shiloh wanted to despise Reuben for rejecting the affection she would have offered him. But he had let her down so easily that it was impossible to remain angry with him. Shiloh reminded herself that there was no rule stating that the man she loved had to love her back. Reuben was sensible and practical and Shiloh was trying very hard to be. But it still crushed her to know that her marriage of two weeks was on the rocks. Walter would rejoice when he learned about the annulment. And when Reuben wasn't around to stop her, Shiloh intended to vent her fury by issuing the punch that arrogant rake so richly deserved. She wasn't as proficient as Reuben was at turning the other cheek. Another of the vast differences between her and Reuben, she realized glumly.

When Shiloh retreated to the passenger car, Holt expelled an exasperated breath. Lord, he was suffering an identity crisis! Shiloh had thoroughly complicated this assignment, and she was tying poor Reuben Gilcrest in Gordian knots. He wanted her. Hell, she was all he thought about! But she was off limits for a dozen logical reasons. Lord, by the time he staged Reuben's death, he would be begging Garret to put him out of his misery.

The next assignment had damned well better be one that demanded his undivided attention, one that didn't prey on his emotions—ones that were presently in turmoil. If Holt didn't forget about that silver-blue-eyed pixie, he would be carrying her portrait in his memory—right alongside Anna's. Holt wasn't sure he could handle a double dose of mental anguish. This conflict of battling his desire for Shiloh was already making him crazy.

Chapter 16

When the passengers retired for the night, Holt prepared himself for another helping of Walter's ridicule. The moment he stepped from the men's dressing room in his long cotton nightshirt, Walter guffawed. Ignoring the intimidating smirks, Holt folded his tall frame into the bottom berth and gestured for Dog to sink down in the walkway beside the enclosed bed.

When all the other men had climbed into their cubicles, Shiloh emerged from the ladies' dressing room in her nightgown and robe. However, Walter— the Peeping Tom of Springfield—drew back his curtain to ogle the shapely blonde. To his disappointment, Shiloh's long robe concealed her tantalizing figure.

The glare Shiloh flung at Walter as she breezed past was meant to maim and mutilate. She had heard him burst into snickers the moment her husband strolled by. The scoundrel delighted in poking fun at Reuben's masculinity and virility and then gawked at women for his own lusty pleasure. Shiloh hated to see Walter enjoy even one iota of amusement at Reuben's expense. Soon he would pay his penance, she promised

231

herself faithfully. When Reuben returned to Chicago, she was going to get even with that cocky blond rake who mistakenly believed himself to be a long-awaited gift to womankind. What a joke that was!

As Shiloh climbed into her berth above Reuben, Walter grinned devilishly. "Tonight it seems the groom has a logical excuse not to sleep with his wife." He flashed Reuben another goading grin. "Lucky for you that I'm the only one who knows you don't know what to do with a woman when you put her to bed."

While Walter peeled off his breeches and swung into his berth on the opposite side of the aisle, Shiloh silently seethed behind her curtain. She couldn't wait to take Walter down a notch . . . or three. He was really asking for it.

Holt couldn't help himself. He had meant to overlook every last insult to which he had been subjected throughout the day. But he just couldn't allow the last snide remark to go unanswered. His hide wasn't as tough as he thought it was. Levering upon his elbow, he glanced across at Walter, who had slipped, bare-chested, into his berth.

"Perhaps it is not so much what a man knows about satisfying a woman, Mr. Jameson," Holt parried with a good-natured smile that disguised the venom in his oncoming gibe. "But the question is, can a gentleman still treat a lady like a lady, even while he makes her feel like a woman who is cherished and adored? It is obvious to me that you have not mastered the technique, since you have been unable to find yourself a wife. It is then reasonable to assume that you have yet to learn the difference between lust and love. Those who are still paying for feminine favors are unable to make the distinction." Holt noticed with wicked delight that Walter's face had turned the most fascinating shade of purple. "When you are mature, Mr. Jameson, you will realize that a husband is greatly rewarded when his wife is assured by both words and deeds that loving is not her duty, but a privilege to be equally shared between man and wife. Now that Shiloh knows the difference, she refuses to settle for less. . . . Which unfortunately is all you know how to give . . ."

Walter's purple face puckered in a mutinous sneer. So adeptly had Holt, in Reuben's soft-spoken manner, pegged Walter as a lusty womanizer who had to resort to whores to find sexual satisfaction. The insinuation also suggested that Walter didn't know beans about pleasing a lady of quality because he was far too concerned about satisfying himself. And Walter could not debate the issue because it was Reuben who had managed to marry the most sought-after heiress in Springfield. For the life of him, Walter didn't know what Shiloh could possibly see in this clumsy dandy. Walter was insanely jealous and his pride was smarting.

For more than a year he had coveted the affection of Victor McBride's lovely daughter. But Shiloh hadn't given him the time of day. And lo and behold, along came this awkward, unsophisticated bumpkin from Chicago. Even if the marriage was a merging of two family names for business purposes, Reuben had walked off with the prize. That really rubbed Walter the wrong way. . . .

"Good night, Mr. Jameson," Reuben murmured as he pulled off his spectacles and drew the curtain around his berth. "I hope one day soon you will discover what you have been missing. Then perhaps you will realize what an ass you have been making of yourself with women."

Shiloh lay in her berth, smiling in satisfaction. She had overheard Reuben's quietly uttered remarks and she mentally applauded how Reuben put Walter in his place. Walter didn't have the knack of tenderness. He knew how to take from a woman but he didn't know how to give of himself. Reuben, on the other hand, had proven himself to be a generous, caring lover, even if he was a mite too cautious about surrendering to passion unless Shiloh pushed him past the point of resistance.

Because Reuben had treated her with kindness, Shiloh had shed her cynicism to blossom into a full-fledged woman. He had brought out the best in her even though she had been unable to return the favor.

After lying there for what seemed hours, mulling over her marriage to Reuben, she heaved a heavy sigh. Perhaps Reuben didn't mean all that he had said to Walter, but he had made several important points. And maybe Victor had made a mistake by forcing a wedding on Reuben. But Shiloh was determined to leave Walter Jameson thinking Reuben held a lure Shiloh was incapable of resisting . . . at least until Reuben went his own way. She was going to give Walter food for thought, she decided. When dawn came she would not be crawling from her berth, but rather from Reuben's. That should really get Walter's goat, she mused with a mischievous smile. When she had the marriage annulled she would allow Walter to think it was Reuben's idea, not hers. For the rest of Walter's rotten life he would assume that Reuben had been every bit the man Shiloh had wanted and needed.

Shiloh was willing to swallow her pride if it meant Walter was left to envy Reuben's hidden charms. For years to come Walter would continue to ask what Reuben had that he himself didn't have. Class, Shiloh mused as she quietly eased from her top bunk. That was something Walter Jameson knew absolutely nothing about. As personable and capable as he was in his business dealings and railroad operations, he was a shallow creature who didn't have enough moral fiber to fill a thimble.

Sometime in the night an unidentified object landed squarely in the middle of Holt's lap. Instinctively, he jerked upright and then groaned when his head slammed into the low ceilng of his berth. When the stars that swam around his head evaporated, he peered incredulously at the silhouette that had employed his groin as a rung of a stepladder.

Good God, Holt had tossed for more than two hours, begging for sleep. Once he finally nodded off, here came temptation in the flesh. What he didn't need while he was battling this ill-fated attraction was the appearance of this delectable siren who had called to him in his dreams.

"Shiloh, what the blazes are you . . . ?"

Her moist lips feathered over his, shushing him.

The instant she dragged her lips from his, Holt peered into her shadowed features. "Are you here because of Walter and his snide remarks?" he whispered.

"Walter is my excuse," she murmured as she sank down beside him. "Wanting you is my reason. . . ."

Before Holt could protest, or muster the will to do so, Shiloh's shapely body half covered his, her knee lying suggestively between his thighs. Holt could feel the tips of her breasts teasing his chest through the sheer fabric of her nightgown and his nightshirt. And when her adventurous hand tunneled beneath his cotton garment to make titillating contact with his hair-matted flesh, Holt's heart catapulted to his throat, depriving him of much-needed oxygen.

Sweet mercy, she could do it every blessed time! Holt thought as he melted into a puddle of liquid desire. Shiloh touched him and he forgot everything except

235

this wild, intense craving that only she could appease. Her light caresess spread over his thighs and belly, and Holt muffled a moan of torment. He wanted to devour her, but there were four men closeted in this sleeping car.

How the hell was a man supposed to control these maddening urges when he had to remind himself every half second not to alert the other passengers as to what was going on?

But Holt forgot to consider the other passengers when Shiloh drew his hand beneath her garment and held it to her full breast. She was inviting him to make love to her, and there was no way to refuse. Propriety and conscience be damned! Holt was on fire, and this seductress provided the flame. He couldn't have denied himself the rapturous pleasures he had discovered in Shiloh's arms if his very life depended on it. His heart was beating ninety miles a minute, running circles around this train, and his breath was coming in rapid spurts. The word *no* suddenly vanished from his vocabulary. He wanted Shiloh, needed her madly. He couldn't have sent her back to her berth because he didn't have enough willpower left to let her go.

His cautious reserve fell like the walls of Jericho. Uncaring who knew what was going on inside his curtained berth, Holt peeled away Shiloh's gown to feast on every soft inch of her flesh. He was starved for her. He tried to remind himself to employ a slow hand and gentle touch, but passion blazed through him, paralyzing his brain. It had been days since he had felt her pliant skin beneath his exploring caresses, agonizing hours since he had lost his head and succumbed to the ecstasy he had discovered in her arms.

The fact that Shiloh was as eager for him as he was for her did nothing to help Holt regain even a smidgen of self-control. Shiloh not only accepted his hungry

236

kisses, she returned them with equal fervor. Her lips opened beneath his ravishing kiss, silently encouraging him to match her own ungovernable passions. As their breath merged, his hands flooded over her luscious curves and swells, reveling in the exquisite texture of her skin. His fingertips trekked across her thigh to tease and arouse her. He could feel her body welcoming him, begging for him to satisfy the burning ache they instilled in each other.

Shuddering in barely controlled desire, Holt braced himself above her. Although their crowded niche was a cobweb of shadows, he could see her bewitching face below his. He distinctly remembered how she looked that first night, when he had made passionate love to her, how she had tumbled with him in the straw when he had gotten drunk to counteract the spell she held over him. The look in her eyes mirrored the same intense need he had noticed twice before. He knew he was seeing the reflection of his own fierce cravings.

Groaning in anticipation of the ecstasy he knew awaited him, Holt bent his head to hers. Like a starved creature he sought her dewy lips and drank deeply of her kiss as his muscular body took complete possession. He could feel her hands gliding up and down his hips and back as she accepted his full weight, as she arched to meet his hard, driving thrusts.

Holt swallowed a groan as best he could when passion burst between them. He wanted to scream in response to the immense pleasure that riveted him. He wanted to crush Shiloh to him and go on holding her until these wild sensations ran their tempestuous course. Silencing himself was practically impossible, but Holt managed not to disturb the other guests while he was being devastated by passion—the likes of which he had never known.

Shiloh hadn't meant to dig her nails into Reuben's

back when desire consumed her. But he stirred such incredible feelings inside her that she clung to him in helpless abandon. When she had crawled from her bunk, she had feared he would reject her shameless advances. But when she touched him she knew instantly that he wouldn't deny her the intimacies they had twice shared. Perhaps Reuben could never love her, but this physical attraction between them was magical and uncontrollable. Nothing could smother these fiery sparks when she melted Reuben's gentlemanly reserve. It gave her great satisfaction to realize that she could arouse him as easily as he aroused her.

When they went their separate ways, she would at least know she had possessed a part of his soul, a part of him that no other woman had ever claimed. And as long as she lived, she would reflect upon these stolen moments of passion, knowing for that short space in time she had discovered what loving was truly all about. . . .

Her breath stuck in her throat when each intense sensation that she had experienced—one by one—recoiled upon her all at once. Reuben muffled her cry of rapture in his kiss and simultaneously shuddered above her. Passion spilled forth like a pitcher of stars streaming across a black velvet sky. Shiloh could feel the twinkling heat penetrating her flesh, feel Reuben's body molded intimately to hers. This was paradise, and she would never forget the wondrous contentment that loving him brought.

As the fog of pleasure dissipated, she heard and felt the rumble of laughter in his broad chest, wondering what prompted it.

"So now you know there is a ravenous lion in this lair," he rasped as his sensuous lips skimmed over hers. "You bring out the beast in me, sweet little witch."

Shiloh stirred beneath him and then raked her nails

over his back. "You didn't hear me complain, did you?" she whispered to him.

"You should have," Holt murmured, attempting to gather the strength to roll away. "I suddenly forgot what it meant to be gentle. It's difficult when you arouse such an upheaval of emotions inside me."

Shiloh linked her fingers behind his back, refusing to let him go. "Love me again, Reuben," she requested in a throaty voice that sent a herd of goose bumps stampeding across his flesh. "Just once more before you go . . ."

Her quiet words ignited the fires Holt swore had completely burned themselves out. He told himself to be gentle with her this time, not to step out of character again. But there was no holding back when Shiloh's lips greeted his with intimate promises, and her supple body moved suggestively against him. She stirred savage needs within him, an unexplainable craving that unfurled and undulated with each kiss and caress. It was a wild, reckless coming together, an intense urgency of flesh melting into flesh, and soul interlocking with soul. Holt could no more contain his ravenous cravings than he could fly to the moon. He was a prisoner of his own lusty passion and Shiloh was a captive of her own uninhibited desires.

Holt felt himself being swept up into the vortex of a storm. The churning clouds of passion gobbled him alive. A tormented groan bubbled in his throat when Shiloh matched his fierce ardor and whispered his name and her affection for him. Incredible sensations pelleted his body like wind-driven rain. His pulse thundered like hailstones on a tin roof, and the intensity of the cloudburst swelled to gigantic proportions.

And then it came, that mystical moment that blew the clouds around and left time dangling in space. Holt clung to Shiloh for dear life as the wonder plummeted upon him, numbing him to everything but the quintessence of pleasure that engulfed him. Shiloh's unique brand of lovemaking always left him asking just what the blazes he had been doing for the past decade. For damned sure it wasn't what he had been doing with this inventive sorceress. She made passion a sweet, spellbinding dream.

God, how was he going to forget what they had shared when she had emblazoned these memories on his mind, body, and soul? He would always remember the feel of her delicious curves and swells molded to his, never forget the taste of kisses that were like cherry wine. Her smile would be the sun and the twinkle in her eyes would be the starlight. She would fill up his world with living memories that would never fade away. . . .

"I love you, Reuben," Shiloh whispered against the pulsing vein in his neck. "Never forget that in the years to come. . . ."

Holt soundly cursed himself for being such a deceitful cad. She was killing his conscience and preying on his emotions. This sultry beauty was making his job impossible. But what was even more impossible was the fact that he found himself returning her confession when he hadn't meant to. He had closed his eyes and forgot about the vow he had made after Anna died. The carefully protected words bubbled up from deep inside him—words he hadn't realized were there. His soul was telling him something that his mind had just now figured out and he had been too stubborn to admit to himself and to Shiloh.

"And I love you," he murmured huskily. "Even if this love wasn't meant to be. . . ."

A tear slid from the corner of her eye as he sank down beside her, cuddling her against his muscular frame. He still thought annulment was the answer, it seemed. And maybe they couldn't face the world together since they were different in so many respects. But in this secluded universe of dreams they would always be soul mates.

Shiloh ached, but it was comforting to know that Reuben did share her affection even if he wasn't sure he could deal with it on a day-to-day basis. Shiloh found solace in the fact that he, like she, would pause to reminisce on these few short weeks when they had discovered a rare, complicated attraction that no one, even themselves, could understand.

Perhaps this love of theirs had no place in either of their lives, but Shiloh would always remember the man who was trapped beneath his cumbersome shell. This warm, endearing personality may never take control of the awkward Reuben Gilcrest. Yet, deep down inside, where it really counted, there was a man who left the rest of the male population sorely lacking. And Shiloh had come to know him for a time. She was a better woman having experienced the warmth of his unselfish love. It wasn't much consolation, but it was infinitely better than never knowing that such wondrous love did exist, even if it was short-lived. Like a butterfly whose time was measured in days, so was this love she felt for Reuben. Together they had soared on velvet wings. Each of them had emerged from their confining cocoons to explore the wide horizon. And for that short span of time, they had found their special place in the sun. . . .

A scowl twisted Walter's lips when he pulled back the curtain surrounding his berth to see Shiloh's shapely legs protruding from the gap in the drapes that encircled Reuben's bunk. Disgruntled, he watched the tangled-haired beauty press a hasty kiss to her husband's lips before she sashayed toward the dressing room.

Faint amusement danced in Holt's eyes as he grabbed the wire-rimmed glasses and plunked them on the bridge of his nose. After rising to full stature, he winked at the dumbstruck Walter. "Train berths provide most comfortable accommodations, don't they, Mr. Jameson?" he commented as he loped down the aisle with Dog trotting dutifully behind him.

Walter swore under his breath. He felt as if he had slept on a bed of nails while Reuben had obviously enjoyed the finer pleasures in life. Damn, what in heaven's name did that vivacious goddess see in that four-eyed toad? The next thing Walter knew, that sexy little witch would turn her clumsy frog of a husband into a dashing prince! Why would a bungling oaf like Reuben intrigue Shiloh so? Walter couldn't begin to imagine.

While the passengers had slept in their berths, the iron serpent had slithered in and around the Ozark Mountains of southern Missouri to arrive at its destination. When the congregation stepped from the train, Shiloh glanced around the rowdy town of Primrose that had sprung up in eager anticipation of the railroad. It was a tough little town that gave no credence to its gentle name. Hard-looking characters prowled the streets and leaned negligently against the supporting posts that braced the covered boardwalks. A dozen saloons lined the dirt streets, and long before the noon hour, piano music and women's giggles wafted through the open doors of the taverns.

Just down the avenue from the train depot was the Rosebud Hotel which housed many of the men who worked on the road gang. And even farther down the street was the office where the newly appointed sheriff and his deputy made headquarters while doing their difficult duty of keeping the peace.

The community was flooded with immigrants, a few hardworking settlers, scores of scalawags, and several riffraff that could barely fit the distasteful category of ruffians. They were, in Shiloh's estimation, the lowest forms of life on the planet. Reuben must have shared her opinion, she thought, because he protectively curled his arm around her when a mob of thugs swaggered past to give Shiloh the once-over thrice.

"As if staking your claim on Shiloh would make any difference," Walter sniffed sarcastically. His mocking gaze ran the full length of Reuben's torso, one that was devoid of a holster and pistols. He tapped the Colt that was draped on his hip and displayed a smug smile. "If your wife needs protection, you wouldn't be able to provide it. These rowdy characters have respect for nothing except a blazing pistol. The Colt .45 is practically the only law Primrose knows."

Shiloh turned up her dainty nose and fell into step beside her father, who had also strapped on his holster for protection. While Shiloh was immersed in conversation with Victor, Holt wandered off to scout the town. When the congregation plodded down the street to confer with the rail foreman at the Rosebud Hotel, Shiloh glanced bemusedly around her. Where the devil was Reuben? Lord, she hoped he hadn't gotten himself in trouble already! He was unarmed, and he probably couldn't handle a pistol even if he owned one. She prayed that his guardian angel was watching over him wherever he was. As much as she loved him, he did lack experience in the area of self-defense, and Primrose was not a good place to be if one didn't know how to defend oneself.

"Come along, honey," Victor encouraged his reluctant daughter. "We are supposed to meet Brian King as soon as possible."

"But Reuben is . . ." she tried to protest.

Victor expelled an impatient sniff. "I'm sure Reuben can take care of himself if need be. He'll catch up with us later."

While Victor propelled Shiloh down the street, remaining between her and the throng of riffraff that loitered on the boardwalk, Shiloh's eyes strayed over her shoulder. She wasn't sure Reuben could take care of himself at all, and she was destined to fret over him until he appeared in the hotel lobby.

Even Shiloh had enough sense to stash a pistol in her purse for protection when venturing to one of these newly established towns along the railroad right-of-way. Reuben, on the other hand, was a gentleman from the East who rarely had to worry about being mugged by rapscallions who preyed like vultures on defenseless newcomers. . . . Or at least the Reuben she knew was incapable of defending himself. She didn't have a clue that Holt had written the book on confronting local toughs and bullies. If Shiloh had known the truth about Reuben Gilcrest, she wouldn't have fretted over his safety in Primrose. In fact, she would have been so furious by his deceptive ploy that she would have whipped her pistol from her purse and shot him herself!

Lucky for him she didn't know.

Chapter 17

The moment Holt veered into the alley, he heard uproarious laughter echoing from the garbage cans that sat beside the back door of the restaurant. Holt didn't flinch when Garret's brawny frame emerged from his hiding place.

"What in God's name are you wearing?" he snickered as his gaze flooded over Holt's ill-fitting garments and oversize spectacles.

Holt struck a dignified pose. "It is impolite to mock my apparel, sir," he countered in Reuben's mild-mannered tone.

Glancing cautiously to the right and left, Garret lumbered around the trash cans. Although he would have preferred to poke more fun at Holt's getup, he concentrated on the business at hand. "Did you receive my letter?"

Holt frowned. "What letter?"

"The one from your aunt Mildred," he prompted him.

"It must have arrived after we left Springfield," Holt speculated. "Have you dug up any valuable information?"

Garret nodded as he and the frumpy dandy ambled

245

deeper into the alley. "Your hunch was right. Walter Jameson appears to be the mastermind who has been buying up stock that is listed in other small-time investors' names."

"Tell me something I don't already know," Holt grumbled impatiently. "I swiped his wallet last week and there was a list of investors whom I contacted to confirm my suspicions. They told me what I wanted to know." A thoughtful frown puckered his dark brow. "But there was also an unsigned note that requested a private meeting here in Primrose that has me concerned. I think there is more to Walter's embezzling than I first suspected."

"From what I learned from the track foreman, Walter has been promoting the railroad and also buying up all the real estate along the right-of-way for himself and Max Fletcher—all under assumed names, of course."

"And he has also been writing checks from the company's funds to pay expenses," Holt declared bitterly. "The ledger notarized a bank draft written to pay the tracklaying employees' wages. When I divided the average salary of all the workers on the payroll, the amount was twice what you indicated you were being paid to lay track."

"The road workers deserve twice what they're getting," Garret complained, massaging his aching back. "Big as I am, it's still damned hard work!"

"You have been doing the back-breaking work and Walter has been skimming profits from the payroll fund," Holt snorted derisively. "But Walter has framed Victor McBride to take the blame for extortion. Every entry in the company ledger has been approved with Victor's initials. Victor's only crime was being a little too trusting of his second in command."

"Well, isn't Walter the clever one," Garret sniffed

caustically. "He plans to set Victor up and then scurry away with the real estate and undetermined amounts of cash when the company collapses."

Holt nodded. "That leaves us with a problem. All accusations are going to point to Victor McBride when I disclose the contents of the business ledgers to Pinkerton. J. W. Baxter will insist that the company's accounts be frozen and he will have enough evidence to take McBride to court. A formal investigation will bankrupt the company."

Garret knew his long-time friend extremely well. There was something Holt hadn't said, but he was thinking it. Garret could see Holt thinking. "What's on your mind?" he demanded to know.

"I can't prove my speculation and do the legwork required while Reuben Gilcrest is still alive," he said meaningfully. "There are too many complications now."

"Like what?" Garret queried curiously.

"Like my marriage to Shiloh McBride, for one," he grumbled, and then waited for Garret to explode in laughter.

"Shiloh married Reuben?" Garret hooted in between guffaws. "You're kidding." His laughing black eyes flickered down the uncomplimentary garments that detracted from Holt's muscular physique. "How in heaven's name did you manage that?" His amusement died a quick death when he realized he had lost the bet he had made against Holt. Suddenly it wasn't so funny. Now he had to not only tolerate the shaggy black mutt that constantly followed Holt, but he had to go out of his way to be nice to the mongrel. Damn. . . .

"Why we got married isn't important," Holt dismissed with a shrug. "The point is I need you to round up the other agents and stage my demise. And, in case you hadn't noticed, McBride is hauling the payroll car

247

in front of his personal cars. There's a helluva lot of money to be had, and it seems to me that the destruction of the track and supplies by raiders was a mite too conveniently planned around the regular monthly arrival of the payroll car."

A wry smile claimed Garret's leathery features. "I noticed and I came to the same conclusion. The other detectives have already been contacted. They are in Mt. Vernon, ready and awaiting your signal."

Holt smiled gratefully. "You're a good man, Garret."

Garret drew himself up into an arrogant stance and winked playfully. "Of course I am. That's why I have all those commendations for miraculously capturing offenders of justice and toting them off to jail. Some folks call it a supernatural gift. I call it Holt Cantrell."

He knew his fame was the direct result of Holt's imaginative undercover work and shrewd calculations. Garret thought it was a shame that he got all the glory and Holt took all the life-threatening risks. But they would have accomplished nothing these past few years without this effective partnership. The arrangement worked superbly. But neither of them had become detectives for the glory, only for the gratification of a job well done and seeing another criminal off the highways and city streets.

After Holt revealed his plans to Garret, he ambled back into the street. He stopped so quickly on the boardwalk that even Dog couldn't anticipate the abrupt halt. The mutt slammed into Holt's leg and glanced up at his master, who was frozen to the spot.

The ghosts of Holt's troubled past leapt up in front of him when a scraggly miscreant passed him on the street. Although Holt had never seen Kirby Thorn face-to-face, he had thoroughly interrogated the citizens who had witnessed several of his bold robberies and malicious raids. According to the descriptions Holt had been given, Kirby was a cross between Blackbeard the Pirate and Attila the Hun. Kirby was as tall as Holt and packed with muscle. His long, scraggly hair lay in tangles of chestnut brown. There was a cynical slant to his thin lips, a cold look in his gray eyes, and a distinguishing scar on the left side of his cheek. The thick beard that hugged his pointed jaws partially covered the unsightly scar, but Holt swore he would have recognized that bastard anywhere.

Boiling hatred spurted through Holt's veins. He had waited more than two years to confront Kirby Thorn, and here he was without a weapon—except for the bowie knife he always carried in his boot.

When Kirby swaggered into the nearby saloon, Holt stared murderously after him. If Kirby Thorn was in Primrose and so was McBride's payroll car . . . Holt compressed his lips in a grim line when he recalled the note he had seen in Walter's wallet. When Holt put two and two together and came up with more than ten thousand dollars that happened to be stacked in the payroll car, he swore under his breath.

Damn that Walter Jameson, Holt fumed. Unless he missed his guess, and he doubted that he had, Walter had gone looking for a band of thieves to do his dirty work for him. And as luck would have it, Kirby Thorn and his brigand of ruffians had come out of hibernation to their familiar stomping grounds in Missouri. McBride and his payroll car were ripe for the picking. And even though the pay car was built to withstand attack, Kirby Thorn was a master thief. Holt would bet his life that Kirby had every intention of making his strike and Walter Jameson had given that vicious bastard all the information he needed to do so.

Holt always made it a habit to learn all he could

about his quarry before he tracked him down. And he had gone to considerable effort to determine what made Kirby Thorn tick. Kirby had all the charm of a starved rattlesnake, and Holt was painfully aware of Kirby's vile sexual habits, his addiction to whiskey, and his ferocious temper. During raids he was known to carry off everything that wasn't nailed down and pry loose a few things that were. Kirby came from the school that believed in prowling around the vicinity he intended to terrorize so he would be familiar with the area and prepared in case of emergency. While robbing the payroll train, he would undoubtedly lay siege to the Primrose bank and steal every cent in it. That was the way Kirby's mind worked.

Frustrated, Holt forced himself to lumber toward the hotel where McBride was meeting with Brian King and the other company associates. As for Holt, he was itching to grab a pistol and shoot Kirby down in cold blood. After all, Kirby had done that very thing a dozen times. He deserved to die in the same heartless way he lived.

Suddenly Holt found the situation more complicated than he had imagined. He was not only dealing with the haughty, sly Walter Jameson, but he would inevitably clash with Kirby Thorn. Holt wasn't letting that bastard out of his sight!

The fact that Shiloh was underfoot scared the hell out of Holt. He knew how ruthless and abusive Kirby was with women. If Kirby had a chance to get his hands on that gorgeous minx . . .

Holt shook off the unnerving thought. Somehow he had to insure that Shiloh caught the train back to Springfield. Hopefully, Reuben's staged death would accomplish that task. It had to! If anything happened to Shiloh . . .

"Where have you been?" Shiloh asked the instant Holt clomped through the door.

Holt forced a smile and pushed the contrary glasses back in place with his forefinger. It was damned near impossible to act nonchalant when he was a mass of fury seeking release on its source—Kirby Thorn. "I thought I would have a look around town while the railroad potentates were conversing with the track foreman," he said casually.

"Looking around at what?" she queried, frowning bemusedly. "This is a rough town, Reuben. You could get yourself . . ."

Holt's dark brow climbed to a challenging angle when Shiloh refused to finish her comment. "Get myself into trouble because I don't know how to defend myself?" he speculated.

Shiloh didn't want to tread on his feelings, but yes, that was exactly what she was thinking. "Well, you must admit you don't carry a pistol," she hedged.

"Neither do you," Reuben parried.

To prove him wrong, Shiloh opened her purse to direct his attention to the derringer she carried. On cue, Holt's green eyes widened in alarm.

"You could get yourself hurt with that thing!" he croaked.

Before Shiloh could assure him that her father had taught her to defend herself with a pistol and knife, Victor veered around the corner to announce they were riding the rails to the place where the raiders had destroyed the supply car and track.

Shiloh made it a point to latch on to Reuben's arm when Walter appeared in the hotel lobby. She had every intention of rubbing his nose in the fact that she found Reuben far more appealing than her father's right-hand man.

After the procession paraded down the street to climb into their personal rail car, Walter clutched Shiloh's arm to detain her. "I have just one question," he grumbled after her husband tripped up the steps and disappeared inside. "What's he got that I haven't got?"

Shiloh pried his fingers from her sleeve one at a time. It was obvious that Walter was immune to frostbite, otherwise he would have turned into a chunk of ice.

"Class, Walter," she told him frigidly. "Reuben's got class."

Walter blinked in disbelief. In his estimation, he could run circles around the clumsy Reuben Gilcrest. The man was a joke!

"And the most pathetic thing of all is that you aren't smart enough to know a real man when you see one," Shiloh sniped.

When she spun on her heel to ascend the steps, Walter manacled her arm, cutting off circulation. His features took on a diabolical expression that did his striking good looks no justice. "One day soon I'm going to finish what I started that afternoon in the meadow," he growled. "You don't know what a man is because you've never really had one. It's time you realized you have been settling for less than I can give. . . ." His voice trailed off when a movement on the platform of the rail car caught his attention.

Holt was not in a particularly good mood anyway. Seeing Kirby Thorn had turned his disposition black as pitch, and Walter was darkening it more than it already was. The speculation that Walter was in cahoots with Kirby Thorn and his gang of butchers further tested Holt's temper. It was safe to say that Holt Cantrell was in a murderous frame of mind. Hearing Walter spout threats at Shiloh had Holt itching to shed his disguise and deal swiftly and severely with this blond-haired snake. If Holt could have stepped out of character for just five minutes, he would have felt ten times better. Walter was getting on Holt's nerves—ones that had already been stretched until they were dangerously close to snapping.

"Please step inside, Shiloh," Reuben requested in his soft-spoken voice that disguised his irritation.

Warily, Shiloh's gaze bounced back and forth between Reuben's well-schooled expression and Walter's menacing sneer. "I . . ."

"Please, Shiloh," he repeated without taking his eyes off his antagonist.

Reluctantly, she obeyed, but she walked on eggshells across the threshold that led to her father's private car. She feared Walter would make mincemeat of Reuben. If she had known how capable Reuben really was, she would have had nothing to worry about. But she didn't know, so she did fret over his safety.

A mocking grin curled Walter's lips as he eyed the harmless dandy on the platform. "What do you intend to do, Reuben? Strike me with your whiplash tongue because I propositioned your wife?"

The shrill whistle of the train shattered the brittle silence, and a fleecy white puff of steam shot down the track beside the engine and fuel car.

"You remind me very much of the wolf in sheep's clothing," Holt declared in a strangely calm voice.

Walter's hazel eyes narrowed momentarily, and then he threw back his head and laughed. "What do you intend to do, yellow belly? Kill me with analogies?"

The train groaned against its rails, slowly gaining momentum. When Walter attempted to pull himself up the step before he was left behind, Holt blocked his path. His retaliation was so quick and effective that Walter was totally unprepared. He had sprung up to grasp the railing, but Holt's hand swished through the air, knocking Walter's fingers just a scant two inches sideways. Instead of hoisting himself onto the bottom step to plow over Holt, Walter was left to clutch air. The movement of the train caused him to miss the step, and his back slammed against the railing. He spun around like a top. With a pained grunt Walter landed in an unceremonious heap. Cursing a blue streak, he collected his scattered dignity and rolled to his feet to latch on to the car that was coupled behind McBride's elaborate parlor on wheels.

Holt was far from satisfied. He had to settle for merely skinning Walter's knees when he itched to punch that swindling schemer black and blue again. But Holt had to bide his time. If Walter suspected he was being watched and that Holt knew about his underhanded methods of extortion, the scoundrel would bolt and run before all the evidence had been gathered. Walter's time was coming, and Holt had often been forced to be methodic and patient during his assignments. But there were so many factors involved in this particular investigation, he mused as he clambered inside to scrunch down on the sofa. Now he had Kirby Thorn looming in the background like a black cloud, and he also had Shiloh to stew about while he homed in on Walter Jameson.

Good God, how he wished he could have convinced Shiloh to remain in Springfield, where she belonged. It would have been so much simpler and she wouldn't constantly be around to tempt him. Holt was honestly and truly in love with this spirited minx, he realized when her silver-blue eyes lifted questioningly to him, wondering what he had done to Walter—if anything.

In the midst of the passion they had shared the previous night, Holt had told her he loved her. And one

254

look into her enchanting face and animated features made him vividly aware that he meant exactly what he had said. Damn, he had tried so hard to remain emotionally unattached to this saucy beauty. He knew they could have no future together. When Reuben Gilcrest perished, he had to sever all ties with Shiloh and with Springfield. She would go back to her mansion on the hill and he would concentrate his efforts on Kirby Thorn. But he would always remember those secluded moments when this sweet, compelling witch drew out the man who was locked beneath a dozen disguises. And those precious moments would sparkle in her memory like diamonds.

"Well? Are you going to tell me what happened?" Shiloh prodded when Holt volunteered no explanation.

Walter stamped through the door at the rear of the car to glare mutinously at Holt. Shiloh frowned puzzledly. The rip in the knee of Walter's breeches and the stains on his sleeves caused demons of curiosity to dance in her head. What had Reuben done to him and how had he managed with so little experience in the art of self-defense?

"What did you do to him?" she wanted to know that very second so she could applaud Walter's defeat at the hands of the man that varmint had insulted nonstop.

"Nothing," Holt replied modestly. "He merely missed the step when the train rolled down the track."

Disappointment clouded her brow. She had hoped Reuben had doubled his fist, stuffed it in Walter's face, and knocked him off his feet. Her spiteful thoughts trailed off when her husband slipped his hand into hers—a gesture that caught her by surprise. Reuben had never been so demonstrative with his affection.

"I want you to promise me something, Shiloh." From behind the wire-rimmed spectacles, Holt's green eyes drilled into her in a way they never had before. "I want you to take the train to Springfield tomorrow. I fear you are right about this town. It is not a safe place for a lady, especially one whose husband is not known to be an ample protector."

"I'm not leaving you," Shiloh said in a tone that indicated nothing was going to change her mind.

"I have asked very little of you," he reminded her, striving for a level tone.

Shiloh could be stubborn and contrary, and arguing with her always made her defensive. Holt preyed on her vulnerability to Reuben for lack of a more effective technique of dealing with her. But Holt still had his work cut out for him. Shiloh was very much her own woman, and he found himself in the middle of a debate whether he wanted to be there or not.

"And I have demanded very little from you," she parried. "I thought perhaps after last night . . ."

"It is because of last night that I don't want you here," he explained gently. Holt shoved his glasses back to the bridge of his nose and heaved a heavy sigh. "I have to know you are safe."

"I'm not going and that's that," she told him bluntly.

Holt rolled his eyes heavenward, requesting divine patience. Good God, what he didn't need was this rambunctious sprite underfoot in case pandemonium broke loose in Primrose, and chances were it would.

"There will be no more debate on this issue," he insisted in a tone that struck a chord of finality.

"Good, then it's settled," Shiloh announced with a nod.

"I'm glad you agree."

"I do."

Holt glared at her. He had the uneasy feeling she wasn't agreeing to the same thing he had agreed to.

And he was absolutely right. Shiloh had no intention of budging from her stand.

Well, damn, now he would have to make arrangements to insure she was out of the way. That meant another secretive conference with Garret. And just when was he to squeeze in a discreet meeting? Holt didn't know, but he had better think of something quickly or Shiloh could wind up in Kirby Thorn's clutches.

That unsettling thought hounded Holt throughout the day while Victor McBride and his associates inspected what was left of the broken track and demolished supplies. After Holt noticed the way the rails and equipment had been sabotaged, he knew who was responsible for the incident. The destruction of the tracks had Kirby Thorn's signature all over it. Kirby and his gorillas had ripped out their fair share of Union track during the war. Kirby, bastard though he was, was very good at sabotage.

While Holt was preoccupied with thoughts of Kirby, Victor sent one of his men with instructions to telegraph the nearest warehouse to order another carload of supplies as replacement. With the road gang working in shifts around the clock and hiring local citizens to do menial labor, they might be able to get back on schedule.

Victor McBride was fighting time. J. W. Baxter's railroad was laying track across Kansas and the crews were making excellent progress over rolling plains while Victor was flirting with disaster. To insure that catastrophe didn't strike again. Victor put Walter in charge of hiring men to stand watch over the incoming supplies. In Holt's opinion that was like sending the fox out to guard the geese. Walter would round up men who'd cause more problems than they could possibly solve. In fact, Holt was certain it was Walter's intention to bankrupt the railroad, and Victor was opening wide the door of opportunity for him. But Holt needed proof of his speculations and he intended to get it one way or another. Once he had shed his confining disguise of Reuben Gilcrest, he planned to do just that!

Chapter 18

Shiloh very nearly fell over when Reuben announced to the congregation of men who were huddled around the conference table that he and his wife were spending the night at the hotel. Reuben wanted to be alone with her? That was a switch! Shiloh stared frog-eyed at her bashful husband, who curled his fingers around her elbow to propel her down the aisle and onto the platform of the train. She ignored the fact that Reuben tripped off the steps and stumbled over his feet twice during their walk to the hotel. He wasn't surefooted, but when they were abed . . .

A warm blush crept up her throat to stain her cheeks. It was sinful of her to be so preoccupied with thoughts of passion when her father's company faced a crisis. But when she peered up at Reuben, the world shriveled to fill only the space he occupied. His best qualities of tenderness came to life while he was in a prone position and, shamelessly, she could think of very little else.

Each time she surveyed his wide spectacles, the crooked part in his waxed hair, and his unflattering clothes, she still couldn't believe she had fallen in love with Reuben. But she was definitely attracted to his potential. With Reuben she had been able to proceed at her own pace without being attacked by another human octopus like Walter Jameson. She was touched by this special man who was like no one she had ever known. Her affection for Reuben testified that there was nothing sensible about love. It had more to do with feeling than thinking, and that was just the way love was.

Her wandering thoughts scattered in all directions when Reuben closed the door behind him. He strode across the dark hotel room, pulling her with him. She heard the clink as he folded his glasses and dropped them on the nightstand. She held her breath when she heard the rustle of his clothing. With the moonbeams dancing in the open window, she watched Reuben strip to the waist, displaying the massive expanse of his chest and his lean, muscled belly.

When Dog trotted across the room, Holt ordered him back to the door. With his tail tucked between his legs, the mutt slinked back in the direction he had come to hunker down on the floor.

But still Reuben said nothing to Shiloh, and she was left standing in the middle of the room, wondering whether to appear overanxious and disrobe or wait for Reuben to reach for her. His unusual mood baffled her. He had been remote and distant all afternoon and evening. She wasn't sure if he was brooding because she had refused to comply with his request to return to Springfield or if . . .

"Come here, Shiloh," he requested huskily.

Shiloh recognized that tone of voice. It was low and thick with desire. So he was thinking what she was thinking! Thank God. She was beginning to think she was the only one around here who was entertaining an idea other than climbing in bed to sleep. Passion was still so new and wondrous to her that she had difficulty keeping the memories of their special moments together tucked in the back of her mind. They came pouring out at the most unexpected moments.

With an accommodating smile she sailed across the room and leapt into his arms. Without the least bit of reserve Shiloh planted a passionate kiss on his grinning lips. "For a while there, I thought your only reason for renting this room was to get a good night's sleep without Walter heckling you."

A shudder ricocheted through Holt's body when Shiloh came so eagerly into his arms. It still amazed him that the ice maiden of Springfield could be so free and giving with her affection. This rambunctious beauty had a heart as wide as the whole outdoors, and she gave unselfishly of herself. Holt may have been two different men, but she was definitely two different women. She had shown herself to be determined and defensive when approached by men whose forwardness offended her. She preferred to be in command, and men who had not recognized that quirk in her personality always found themselves in a power struggle when they utilized the typical approach employed while courting ordinary women. But there was nothing ordinary about this saucy blonde! She was independent, hot-tempered, and high-spirited.

But the time had come for Shiloh to learn to accept a man's amorous advances without becoming defensive and belligerent. And when Reuben Gilcrest was gone, Shiloh would learn to respond to another man's romantic intentions without feeling threatened by him. After all, there weren't many Reubens in this world. If Shiloh went looking for another one, she would be in for a long, futile search. There were a helluva lot more Walter Jamesons swarming around—men who thought they were doing women favors by offering them passion. Most men didn't expect to have to tread so carefully with a woman. That's why they ran amok in the pursuit of this feisty beauty. Shiloh needed to understand that Reuben had been very sensitive to her needs and aware of her apprehensions. She would not find that same kind of consideration in the men who came and went from her life after Reuben was taken from her.

Holt had in mind to give Shiloh subtle instructions as well as satisfy his burning needs—needs that bordered on desperation when he realized this was the last night he would spend in her silky arms. He had brought her here to say good-bye in his own discreet way, to give her hope for a future with a man who could offer her as much love and devotion as she truly deserved. For this night he would enjoy all the tomorrows they would never share. He would attempt to compensate for all the times he had unintentionally hurt her and for the grief he was forced to put her through when Reuben was strategically removed from her life.

When Shiloh planted another kiss on his lips, Holt pulled her arms from his neck and clasped her hands in his. "Tonight I am taking my husbandly rights," he told her gently but firmly.

Through the shafts of silver beams and slanting moonshadows he detected the confused expression on her face and smiled down at her. "This time, Shiloh . . ." His head tilted as it came steadily toward hers, courting her with promises of the pleasure to come. "This time I intend to be more of a man than I have been with you in the past. . . ."

What kind of crazy talk was that, she wondered as she automatically melted beneath his steamy kiss.

"In the past I have held my feelings in check for fear you were not prepared to accept all of them," he continued as he worked the lacings on the back of her gown. "You trusted me before. I ask you to believe in me now. . . ."

His mouth came down hard on hers, taking quick possession, displaying the intense hunger he had purposely controlled in the past. Shiloh's conditioned response was to jerk away. When she did, Holt pulled her full-length against him, letting her feel the full extent of his arousal.

Again his lips slanted across hers, devouring her with unprecedented impatience, stripping the breath from her lungs. Shiloh reminded herself that Reuben wouldn't hurt her. He wouldn't harm a fly. He wanted only to prove to himself that he was every bit the man Walter Jameson thought he himself was. That was what this was all about, she decided. Reuben was trying to exert his masculine power over her—testing his wings, so to speak.

When his hands slid beneath her gaping neckline to recklessly tug her garments out of his way, she permitted him to be rougher with her than he had ever been before. There was something intriguing about this sensual wild man who suddenly emerged from Reuben's inhibited shell. Shiloh couldn't take offense to his ravishing kisses and bold caresses. She was flattered by his impatience for her because it had been so long in coming. He was finally taking the initiative, bolstering his male pride and strengthening his self-confidence with women.

Shiloh thought she preferred to be in command, to set the pace, but she found Reuben's impetuous ardor wildly exciting. He made her feel incredibly feminine and desirable—as if she were the sole reason he had so little control over his male instincts. His kisses and caresses had become more masterful than they had been when they had made love in the past. The times when she had practically asked him to seduce her, she amended.

"You have a delicious body, Shiloh," Holt rasped as

he peeled away the skimpy chemise and hindering petticoats. "You make a man want you in wild, uncontrollable ways." His lips sensitized her skin, skimming over the slope of her shoulder to tease the throbbing tips of her breasts. "I don't want to be patient and gentle tonight. I want to devour you because you arouse savage instincts within me. . . ."

A tiny moan bubbled in her throat when his fingertips and lips took familiar possession. It seemed he had suddenly acquired another set of hands and they knew exactly where and how to touch to send her temperature soaring ten degrees. His hot, greedy kisses roamed everywhere—tantalizing, teasing, exciting her to the limits of sanity.

Sweet mercy! She never dreamed the mild-mannered Reuben was capable of such fervent emotion. Even the previous night, when their hunger for each other overwhelmed them, he hadn't been so zealous, so demonstrative. But then, Shiloh reminded herself, they had been forced to be quiet for fear of rousing the men who slept in the surrounding berths. Tonight there was only the two of them, and this unexpected ardor made it impossible for Shiloh to contain the soft moans of pleasure that insisted upon erupting from her kiss-swollen lips.

Reuben had blossomed into the most skillful lover imaginable. Shiloh didn't fear him, even though his breathless impatience reminded her of other men who had tried to possess her when she wanted nothing to do with them. But she wanted everything to do with Reuben, and that made all the difference. She responded to his adventurous caresses, his sizzling kisses that burned brands on her quaking skin.

Her heart was pounding like a sledgehammer, and breathing was practically impossible. His obvious hunger for her increased her craving for him. She longed to return the budding pleasure his touch aroused. And touch him she did, assuring him that she was willing to explore this new dimension of passion.

When he knelt on the bed and tumbled her onto the sheets, Shiloh never gave a thought to objecting to his playful manner. Tonight he was more like a powerful lion than a gentle lamb. But Shiloh didn't mind. She approved of this new facet of his lovemaking. He had come to life and she reveled in the changes that had overcome him. . . .

Shiloh's heart stopped beating when he twisted to spread fiery kisses and flaming caresses over every inch of her pliant flesh. He dared more than he had in the past, and her inhibitions came rushing back. When his warm draft of breath fluttered over her thigh, Shiloh stilled him, unsure of what he intended. But Holt caught her hand and pressed it to his chest, silently commanding her to let him do as he pleased without halting him from showering her with affection.

Hot flames seared into the core of her being as his kisses and caresses became more intimate and daring. Tidal waves of sensations toppled over her, towing her into the dark depths of passion—passion that was so wild and uninhibited that Shiloh felt herself losing her grasp on the last thread of sanity. He was doing the most incredible things to her body, making her want him madly. He teased her with his hands and lips, denying her and yet exciting her until she begged him to take her, pleaded with him to end this sweet, electrifying torment.

Shiloh wondered if she could ever instill such monstrous cravings within him. She wondered if he had any idea how devastating his caresses were. Loving him made her so vulnerable, so trusting, so responsive. She had granted him every whim, letting him do with her what he wanted. But he wasn't simply taking for his own satisfaction. Reuben was giving ineffable pleasure. Perhaps it was her fault he was just now exploring his ardent nature. She felt as if she had long deprived him of the rights to which he had referred and now she reveled in the magical ways they made love.

"Reuben . . . please . . ." Shiloh gasped as another wave of ecstasy drenched her writhing body.

"In time . . ." he murmured against her trembling flesh. "When you whimper my name and swear you'll die, I'll come to you."

She was sure she had nearly died twice already in tormented splendor. How could she possibly want him more than she did now? The answer to that question came in a slow, burning fire that sparked in the pit of her belly and spread through each tingling nerve ending. His name sprang from her lips in a gasping plea, and Shiloh trembled as if she had been besieged by an earthquake.

Her thick lashes swept up to see his shadowed face poised above hers. In the moonlight she spied a different man from the one she thought she knew. His raven hair was in disarray, and beams of light reflected off those fathomless emerald pools. He looked faintly predatory hovering over her—like a panther preparing to devour his prey. And yet, beneath that hungry, intense stare was the tender emotion she had always known and had come to love.

"I need you . . . I love you . . ." she whispered raggedly.

"How much?" he growled as his wayward hand slid across her breasts and then swirled over her abdomen. "Enough that you don't care if there is a tomorrow? Enough that I am all you need to make you feel whole and alive? Am I your reason for being, every breath you take?"

Fierce shudders pelleted through her as his intimate

fondling ignited a dozen more sizzling fires. Shiloh groaned in unholy torment. It couldn't be happening again! But it was. She was swamped by yet another indescribable feeling of infinite pleasure—a sensation so wild and fierce that she feared she would go mad if Reuben didn't appease this gigantic need that burned through her.

She had better say yes and quickly, Holt thought in anguish. His body was about to go up in flames. Pleasing and arousing her, teaching her all the ways a man could satisfy a woman, had taken its toll on his self-control. The immense sense of pleasure he received from teaching her the intimate delights of passion had very nearly devastated him. He wanted to press his taut body to hers, to gobble her alive. But he longed for their last night together to be the one she would remember long after he was gone. When he came to her, he wanted her to be so hungry for him that she was unafraid of the rough, forceful tides of desire that rumbled against his dam of self-restraint. He didn't want to be gentle. He wanted to ravish her and have her accept him for all that he was, all that she thought Reuben was *not*.

"Answer me," he demanded in a harsh tone that rattled with barely constrained emotion.

Rapturous torments riveted through her as she struggled to inhale enough air to speak. Why was he torturing her like this? Didn't he know he had filled her world to overflowing, that he was her sun and moon? Wasn't her wild response to his brazen fondling proof enough that she wanted him desperately? She couldn't want him more than she did now.

"You breathe life and love into me," she choked. "Without you I'm half, not whole. . . ."

With agile grace his body glided upon hers, knowing she offered complete and total surrender. Without any gentlemanly reserve Holt buckled to the intense needs that swelled and then burst upon him. Passion had never been so wild or satisfying. Impulsively, he lifted her to him, seeking ultimate depths of intimacy, letting go with his heart, his body, and his soul. The rough urgency of desire pulsated through him, and he marveled at Shiloh's responses. She welcomed him, reveled in the storm of emotions they had created in each other. She learned there was more than tender loving, more than carefully controlled passion. What they shared as they made this intimate journey across the heavens was indeed a turbulent cloudburst of splendor.

Their hearts thundered in frantic rhythm. Like lightning bolts, passion sizzled between them. Shiloh clung to him as the world spun furiously around her, threatening to pull her in every direction at once. And when his muscular body shuddered upon hers, she at last found sublime release from the maelstrom of sensations that had tormented her.

For what seemed forever, Shiloh drifted on the fringe of reality, marveling at the emotions Reuben had displayed. He had proved himself more than man enough to satisfy a half-dozen women, and Shiloh had discovered that allowing a man to succumb to his basic instincts was far more pleasurable than she had imagined. Yes, he had been rough and demanding of her at times, but she didn't feel less of a woman because he had become more of a man. What a dynamic man he was when he removed those oversize spectacles and shed those loose-fitting clothes. The Reuben she had met this evening would leave any woman's head spinning from his breathtaking brand of passion.

He trailed soft, whispering kisses along her shoulder, and Shiloh expelled a weary sigh. Absently, her hand drifted over the muscled planes of his back, awed by the power and strength that lay in repose.

"A man can't always be gentle," Holt murmured hoarsely, his voice still thick with the aftereffects of all-consuming passion. "You make a man forget everything except wanting you with every part of his being. Don't begrudge him the fierce feelings for you. . . ."

Shiloh reached up to comb her fingers through the tousled raven hair that tumbled across his forehead. "You make me forget to be wary of such recklessness in love," she confided.

"Remember it always," he requested as he speared his hand through the glorious silver-blond tendrils that cascaded across the sheet. "Some women bring out a man's ardent needs, Shiloh. It's that way with you. Sometimes even a gentleman has difficulty remembering that he is a gentleman. You make him very vulnerable and unable to control himself when you are in his arms."

"And sometimes a woman doesn't want a man to be quite such a gentleman," she added with an impish smile that caused his heart to melt all over his ribs. "You have taught me that, Reuben. And so much more . . ."

Holt could leave her now, though most reluctantly, knowing she fully understood what he had subtly tried to tell her when he communicated his unrestrained passion. There would always be men who would try to take what this much-sought-after heiress didn't wish to give. But when the right man did come along, she wouldn't condemn him for buckling to his own hungry desires. She could be, and would be, a man's equal in the throes of unbridled passion. Shiloh had learned the pleasure of both tender and uncontrollable urgency. There was a time for both in love, and she could accept both, knowing she had nothing to fear when she found a man who fulfilled all her dreams.

When Holt felt Shiloh drift off to sleep, he inched away to rise from the bed. His gaze flooded over her curvaceous form, marveling at the lingering emotions that refused to fade, even after the loving was over. When he walked out of this nymph's life, he would be leaving part of himself behind. Shiloh's innocence had touched something deep inside him. Her warm, unselfish responses had fulfilled his own elusive dreams.

If he ever had visions of settling down again, he would have wanted it to be with this pert beauty who was so full of spirit. But he and Shiloh could never enjoy a future together, Holt reminded himself sensibly. If he let himself become sentimental, he would no longer be capable of accomplishing his assignment for Pinkerton and satisfying his long-harbored grudge against Kirby Thorn. It was his daredevil deeds that got things done. Without that reckless daring he would be incapable, overly cautious, and inefficient.

Silently, he gathered his clothes and dressed on his way to the door. When he let himself and Dog out, he paused to stare across the moonlit room. A faint smile hovered on his lips when the sweet memories engulfed him. The man who truly won Shiloh's wild heart would be a lucky man indeed. Of course, he knew Shiloh didn't really love Reuben Gilcrest. The clumsy bumpkin was her first experience with passion, and she had allowed herself to be caught up in the romantic expectations of turning her frog of a husband into a dynamic prince. But in time she would realize Reuben had been only a challenge to her, a man not fully deserving of her love.

Shiloh would reflect on her brief marriage as a learning experience that prepared her for her future. She was a full-fledged woman now, and someday her real Prince Charming would come along. Now Shiloh

270

was mature and experienced. Holt didn't want her to search for another Reuben to replace the husband she was about to lose. She needed to look ahead to the next phase of her life instead of substituting another man for the mild-mannered, soft-spoken Reuben.

Still lost in thought, Holt ambled down the hall to quietly rap on Garret's door. While Shiloh drifted through rapturous dreams, reliving the precious memories, Holt confronted the Goliath of a man who was grinning from ear to ear. Garret didn't have to be a soothsayer to determine what Holt had been doing.

"You and the missus getting along all right, are you?" he drawled, his gaze racing over the haphazardly buttoned shirt and saggy breeches. "Marriage seems to agree with you, Mr. Gilcrest."

Holt flashed his partner a silencing glare. "My marriage is off limits to discussion," he snapped.

"My, aren't we sensitive all of a sudden," Garret observed with a taunting snicker.

"No, we are not!" Holt all but shouted, and then cursed himself for letting Garret's gibes get under his skin.

For a long moment Garret stared meditatively at his friend. "Well, I'll be damned, you're in love with her," he realized with a start. He knew Holt well. In a matter of seconds he could tell that his friend hadn't flitted through another shallow affair as he had in the past. Holt wasn't walking from Shiloh's life, relieved that the charade was over and done. The black scowl that puckered Holt's handsome features lent testimony to that!

"I said we are not discussing my marriage," Holt muttered through clenched teeth, struggling to keep his voice down.

In pretended sympathy Garret reached down to pat Dog's dome-shaped head. "Looks like you have a rival, ol' buddy. From now on you'll have to share your master's affection."

"That is enough!" Holt exploded. "There's been a change in plans. I want you to send a telegram to Pinkerton and get him down here as quick as you can." Glittering green eyes turned to cold emerald chips. "He's here in Primrose."

The words dropped like stones. Garret didn't have to ask who *he* was. Garret knew instantly. His preoccupation with Holt's love life immediately evaporated. He could see that Holt was troubled and concerned about Kirby Thorn's appearance in Primrose. And Garret didn't bother asking if Holt was certain he saw whom he thought he saw. Holt wouldn't have said so unless he had made a positive identification.

Holt retrieved one of Garret's cigars and puffed steadily on it while they shared a few drinks and discussed their change of plans. When Holt was satisfied that every minute of the following day was arranged to spring his trap, he tiptoed back to his room.

Again desperation overcame him when he stared down at the goddess who slept in his bed. Even after he and Shiloh had explored every realm of passion, a fire still raged in his blood. Holt felt like loving her again— for all the times in the future when he'd reach out, knowing she wouldn't be there. When he killed off Reuben Gilcrest, he would break all ties with his acquaintances in Springfield. He couldn't go back. And even if he could, there would be no delicate way to explain to Shiloh. She wouldn't understand and she would most certainly take offense to being played as his pawn.

Shiloh would hate him, he mused as he shucked his clothes. He couldn't blame her. Thank God she would never know the truth. . . .

His thoughts focused on the velvety flesh beneath his roving fingertips, and desire flared up as it always did when he touched this luscious beauty. Tonight was the end of his dream, and he intended to enjoy all the pleasures that would be no more than sweet memories after the events of the following day unfolded. But for the duration of the night Shiloh was all that mattered. . . .

Chapter 19

Decked out in Reuben's loose-fitting garb, hair parted as crookedly as ever, and Dog following obediently behind him, Holt escorted Shiloh down the street of Primrose. He could tell by the stares they received from passersby that the citizens of this rowdy, upstart community were having a good laugh at his expense. The leers Shiloh drew as she strolled beside him testified to the fact that every man they passed was silently fantasizing about her.

Although Holt's facial expression suggested he was calmly indifferent, he felt his nerves grow taut when Kirby Thorn swaggered from the restaurant to prop himself negligently against the supporting beam. Purposely, Holt pulled his plug hat down low on his forehead and glanced away. He had no intention of becoming a familiar face to that bastard, not yet anyway. But one day soon Holt's image would be the last thing Kirby Thorn ever saw.

Kirby was far too interested in the lady to pay much attention to her escort. His beady gray eyes made a long, thorough sweep of Shiloh's curvaceous figure and bewitching face.

From behind them Holt heard Kirby's comments

and felt Shiloh go rigid with irritation. "Ignore him," he instructed her.

Shiloh tried. But in their jaunt to the train depot she had already been undressed by one too many pairs of eyes. The fact that Reuben had received insulting stares along the way compounded her frustration and set a match to her volatile temper. When the long-haired scalawag mumbled a second time, Shiloh wheeled around despite Reuben's quiet request to turn the other cheek.

Silver-blue eyes flashed in the morning sun. Defiantly, she met Kirby's suggestive grin—one that displayed the wide space between his two front teeth. Shiloh spitefully wished she could knock out every last one of them when the man ogled her again.

"You can do better than your stilt-legged dandy, honey," he drawled in taunt.

Shiloh knew Reuben wasn't a violent man. In fact, all that saved him from Walter Jameson's punishing blows the previous day was that Walter had missed the step when the train rolled on its way. And since Reuben believed that resorting to pistols and fistfights was beneath a man's dignity, he refused to pick up gauntlets that were flung at his feet. Shiloh, however, was quick to temper and defensive of the man she loved—no matter what the rest of the world thought of his cloddish appearances.

"There are no better men than my husband," Shiloh spat out poisonously. "Why would I want to settle for a serpent when I already have a prince?"

Kirby liked this minx's fiery spirit. Anna had been a sassy little beauty, too, and he had taken pleasure in fighting his way through her defenses. That is, until she had ignited his temper with one too many escape attempts. Kirby was like a lion toying with a mouse. He had been content to play with his prey until she bit into his notorious temper. Then he had struck out to level a blow from which his quarry could never rise again.

A lusty smile cut into Kirby's craggy features, making the scar on his cheek wrinkle like an accordion. "A prince?" he scoffed, his ridiculing gaze flooding over Holt's back. "Your husband looks more like a joke to me, honey."

When Shiloh tried to lunge at the disgusting excuse of a man, Holt's hand snaked out to drag her back to his side. "Don't provoke him," he warned as he propelled her down the boardwalk against her wishes.

Kirby's mocking laughter nipped at their heels, but Holt refused to allow Shiloh to spend another minute flirting with disaster. She attracted trouble because she was so lovely and so full of undaunted spirit. She would probably take on Satan himself if he dared to cross her. And in Holt's opinion, Kirby was the devil incarnate. Holt would have delighted in facing Kirby in a showdown—right here, right now. But not as Reuben Gilcrest, and certainly not with Shiloh standing in the line of fire. When Kirby got his just reward, he was going to know who confronted him and why. Anna's death would be properly avenged at the proper time, Holt consoled himself.

Under Reuben's calm coaxing Shiloh settled her ruffled feathers back in place and proceeded to the train station. Walter Jameson took one look at the murderous expression that was stamped on Shiloh's pretty face and decided to keep his mouth shut for a change, even if he did derive wicked pleasure in poking fun at the awkward gentleman of whom Shiloh had become so protective.

Walter still couldn't believe this vivacious beauty could have saddled herself with this spineless dandy. What a bewildering mismatch they were! Shiloh was the epitome of poise and grace—a princess in her own right. Reuben was the picture of unstylish uncoordination—a frog with oversize spectacles and long legs that were constantly tripping him up.

While Walter was silently mocking him, Holt clamped a hold on his composure and assisted Shiloh up the steps into the luxurious passenger car. Victor had telegraphed the nearest warehouse in the area and had ordered a special train to deliver the necessary equipment to the road gang. He and Walter had hired on locals to assist in getting the company back on schedule, and Victor had promised his employees a bonus if they met the deadline set for them.

With the box car that was loaded with new equipment and supplies coupled between the fuel and payroll cars, Victor and his entourage chugged down the track. But they were only an hour out of Primrose when the train whistle screamed and the brakes screeched, hurtling dignitaries and rail workers hither and yon.

"Argh!" Walter grunted when he was catapulted from his chair and knocked flat by the flying body that sprawled on top of him.

To Walter's chagrin he swiveled his head around to see Reuben plastered against him. Reuben crawled onto all fours, making certain he had gouged and jabbed Walter with a few well-aimed elbows and knees to his softer spots. Although Reuben apologized for making Walter his landing mat, he wasn't the least bit sorry.

Walter had no time to reprimand the clumsy oaf because a volley of bullets resounded in the muggy morning air. Thundering hooves mingled with barking pistols, and the inhabitants of the passenger car crawled to the windows to see what was going on. The train sat on an incline that wound around the side of the Ozarks. It was impossible to determine what was transpiring ahead of them since their private car was bringing up the rear of the train. Bellowing voices and pistols echoed around them, and the clamor of feet outside the car had Victor and his associates muttering a raft of curses.

Walter was more shocked by this unexplained interruption than anyone. From the sound of things, the train was being held up, but it wasn't supposed to be terrorized for two more days! He had intended to be long gone before the payroll car was robbed. What the blazes was going on here? He had specifically stated his demands to Kirby Thorn and he expected to have his requests followed to the letter.

Before the private train arrived the gang of outlaws had pried the spikes from the tracks and constructed a blockade from a nearby thicket of trees. When the engineer rounded the bend, he spied the obstacle in his path not a moment too soon. He had barely managed to stamp on the brake before the locomotive plunged into the obstruction. While the engineer was recovering, masked desperadoes swarmed from the thickets and underbrush to discourage any of the passengers and workmen from grabbing the weapons that had gone flying when the engineer brought the train to a screeching halt.

The bandits uncoupled the payroll and McBride's private cars, setting them free. The coach in which the company's dignitaries were riding picked up momentum as it rolled back down the hill, wobbling as it went. Six pairs of wide eyes swung from one startled face to another as the private car flew back in the direction it had come.

Walter scrambled to his feet and swallowed with a gulp when the car creaked across the wooden bridge that spanned the creek and finally came to a halt.

Cursing rapidly, Victor pushed his way to the back door of the car and craned his neck around the corner to see four bandits, armed to the teeth, galloping toward the front of the bridge.

While the other passengers huddled around the platform at the rear of the car, Victor's urgent gaze swung to his son-in-law. "Get Shiloh out of here," he commanded.

"But, Papa . . ." Shiloh tried to protest, only to be cut off by Victor's gruff growl.

The urgency of his request was punctuated by the sound of feet stampeding over the top of the three cars that sat squarely in the middle of the bridge. In an attempt to comply with Victor's command, Holt clutched Shiloh's arm and pried her loose from the rail. Shiloh involuntarily ducked away from the echoing footsteps and the pistols that barked directly above them.

When Holt cautiously stepped to the narrow space left on the bridge beside the train, Shiloh's wild-eyed gaze flew down to the rippling water that lay twenty-five feet below.

"Can you swim?" Holt asked, plastering himself to the side of the train, dodging bullets.

"Yes," Shiloh chirped. "But I'm afraid of heights."

"This is a fine time to tell me," Holt muttered as he glanced up to monitor the progress of the thieves who were crawling all over the top of the train.

"Well, it never came up before," she grumbled, clinging to her father for support.

"Get her out of here, Reuben. Now!" Victor snapped in frustration. "We're running out of time." Unclenching Shiloh's fists from the lapels of his jacket, Victor thrust his daughter toward the steps and at Holt, who was balancing on one foot to outstretch his hand.

Shiloh panicked. There were very few things that

frightened her. Danger she could bravely face. Darkness didn't unnerve her. But staring down from the looming heights, especailly while bandits were pouring over the top of the railroad car, terrified her. The train took up so much room on the bridge that there was barely enough space for Holt to place his foot on the supporting beams. And just where was she supposed to step?

"Go on, dammit," Victor growled, giving Shiloh an impatient shove down the steps.

Her foot caught on the hem of her skirt. Desperately, she tried to clutch at Holt, but all she succeeded in doing was knocking him completely off balance. With a startled yelp Holt flapped his arms like a windmill but nothing helped. As he toppled backward, Shiloh latched on to his belt and found herself dragged through the air. While Holt accidentally executed a backward swan dive, she screamed bloody murder as they plunged into the river. Loyal to the end, Dog wound around the four pairs of legs on the platform and leapt off the step, refusing to allow his master to go anywhere without him.

Holding on to Holt's belt did Shiloh no good whatsoever. His oversize breeches did not fit snugly enough around the waist to keep them where they belonged. When Shiloh clung fiercely to his trousers, they immediately gave way. Shiloh dropped a quick three feet in the air. Her bloodcurdling scream pierced the air once again. Holt squawked when his breeches sagged on his hips, and Shiloh frantically clamped her arms around the knees of his baggy trousers as they nose-dived into the river.

If the situation hadn't been so tense on the platform of the railroad car, Walter might have laughed at this latest display of Reuben's extraordinary art of bungling. But Walter had the daylights scared out of him.

He didn't have time to snicker while Shiloh held on to Reuben's drooping breeches as if they were her lifeline—ones that were inching downward to reveal her husband's striped underwear. As the twosome plunged into the water below, Shiloh was left holding Reuben's breeches, but he was no longer in them.

Gasping for breath, Shiloh bobbed to the surface, still clutching Reuben's trousers. A half second later Holt resurfaced beside her, clinging to the spectacles he had braced against his face when he hit water. His raven hair clung to the sides of his head, and water dribbled down his glasses and cheeks in a steady stream. Holt reached up to clean his spectacles with a wet sleeve, but Dog popped to the surface to shake himself dry and splattered his master's glasses all over again.

"Are you all right?" Holt croaked in concern. Shiloh looked like a drowned rat. Her breath was coming in gulping snorts and her eyes were as round as dinner plates.

Shiloh was alive but visibly unnerved by her plunge. Her silver-blond hair hung around her like a mop and her stained gown clung to her like a second skin—its soggy weight pulling down on her like an anchor.

Since she felt she had swallowed half the water in the river and couldn't speak, Shiloh nodded in answer to his question. With trembling hands she thrust Reuben's breeches at him.

Holt curled an arm around her waist before she sank into the depths. With Dog swimming on the other side to assist Shiloh from the water, the threesome aimed themselves toward the cover of the massive beams of the bridge. Hurriedly, Holt wrestled into the wet trousers. When Shiloh finally found her tongue to speak, Holt touched his index finger to her lips and gestured toward the railroad car above them. Together they huddled beneath the bridge to eavesdrop on the conversation between the outlaw leader and Victor McBride.

"Open the payroll car, McBride," the masked bandit demanded, pointing his Colt at Victor's inflated chest.

"That money is meant for my employees and, by God, they shall have it!" Victor boomed.

Walter used Victor as a shield of defense. For all his bragging, Walter was very much a coward when it came to matching his skills with a pistol against an accomplished gunslinger. As for Max and Elijah, they had slunk back inside the private car to take cover under the sofas. Walter wished he would have had the good sense to follow Max and Elijah instead of confronting the four desperadoes who held them at gunpoint. Victor's bravura was going to get both of them killed!

"Give them the money!" Walter chirped in Victor's ear.

"I will not!" Victor blared.

"We can always blow up the train and you along with it," the gigantic bandit snarled from behind the bandanna that covered his face.

"Then fetch your blasting powder," Victor challenged him. "It won't do you any good. You'll blow the gold and silver to kingdom come and it will scatter up and down the riverbed. Before you can dredge it up, there will be a posse on your heels."

Walter gulped over the lump in his throat and stared at the ominous creature that loomed over them. He had the feeling he had met this man before. Somewhere . . . His imposing size and stature made him stand out in a crowd. . . .

Suddenly it hit Walter like a ton of bricks. This burly

gorilla had been working on the road crew when Walter made his rounds of inspection. The sneaky brute had obviously been planning this holdup for a month! Kirby Thorn was going to be furious when he discovered the payroll car he had been invited to rob was about to be picked clean. Damn, of all the rotten luck!

The oversize desperado scowled under his breath at Victor's defiance. After a moment he reached out a brawny arm and yanked Victor to him. With a quick snap of his wrist he wheeled Victor around and rammed the barrel of his pistol at his captive's throat. Glittering brown eyes focused on Walter, who had plastered himself against the outer wall of the car, wishing the platform would open up and he could drop out of sight.

"You open the door to the payroll car, Jameson, or I'll kill him," the bandit threatened in a vicious growl.

"I don't have the key and neither does McBride," Walter croaked. "It's at the hotel in the paymaster's charge. . . ."

"Then you damned well better fetch it or you'll never see McBride alive again," he vowed hatefully. "You've got until dusk to ride to Primrose and bring back the key." The huge desperado cocked the trigger and aimed it at Walter's sunken chest. "And if you don't come back, Jameson . . . I'll come and get you. . . ."

The threat hung in the air, permitting Walter to form his own speculations about what his life would be worth if this burly ape got hold of him.

Although Victor resisted, he was dragged off the platform and hoisted atop the train. The other bandits, who had confiscated every last weapon from the guards and employees, waited at the end of the bridge for their leader's return. Leaving only one mount at Walter's disposal, the band of desperadoes thundered off with Victor in tow.

Holt pulled Shiloh back against him when the procession of bandits splashed along the water's edge, searching for a shallow spot to ford the river. When they were no more than a stone's throw away, Shiloh wiggled free and charged after the bandits who had taken her father captive.

"Good God, what are you doing?" Holt crowed as he clambered to his feet, shoving his contrary spectacles back in place. "They'll see you!"

"I'm going to follow my father," Shiloh muttered, pulling up her hindering skirts so she could dash up the embankment.

"You'll get yourself killed," Holt assured her, tripping along in her wake.

"I have to try!" Shiloh flared.

"Of course you do." Holt sighed deflatedly. "I would have expected nothing less from you."

Holt had anticipated Shiloh's bold daring. Even though the odds were surely against her, that didn't stop her from her valiant crusade of retrieving her father. Shiloh may have been afraid of heights, but she feared very little else, not even a swarm of desperadoes. Determined of purpose, Shiloh scurried in and out of the trees, always keeping the gang of thieves in her sights, resolving to follow them to the ends of the earth if need be.

Chapter 20

For what seemed forever, Shiloh trudged along, clinging to the timber, keeping her gaze fixed on the ten men walking their horses. She refused to lose sight of the desperadoes who had kidnapped her father and were planning to hold him until they got their greedy hands on the gold in the payroll car.

When the bandits dismounted at the farm that was tucked in the Ozark hills, Shiloh crouched behind the brush to survey the situation. All she had was the derringer in her purse and a fierce will to save her father from disaster. And Reuben had nothing with which to battle a pack of bandits. Dammit all, she was so frustrated she wanted to pull out her hair.

"I think it wise to walk back to town and round up a posse now that we know where the gang is holed up," Reuben advised her.

Shiloh glared at him. "By the time we get to Primrose it will be dark and the men will have ridden back to determine if Walter was able to retrieve the key to the payroll car."

"Then what do you suggest?" he grumbled in question.

"We have to find a way to distract them while one

287

of us sneaks inside to rescue Papa," Shiloh instantly decided.

Holt stared at her in horror. "There are ten of them, in case you can't count," he sniffed sarcastically.

"Then *you* do the sneaking and *I'll* do the distracting," Shiloh volunteered courageously.

"Oh, no," Reuben protested. "I'll not have you becoming those scoundrels' object of lust! *I'll* do the distracting while *you* do the sneaking."

Holt unfolded his tall frame and glanced pensively around him. Once he had decided on his plan of action, he crept toward the house with Dog trotting dutifully behind him.

"What are you going to do?" Shiloh wanted to know.

"I'll fetch three horses for us and frighten off the rest of them," he explained in a whisper.

Shiloh vaulted to her feet and scurried along behind him. "You don't ride very well. Do you suppose you will be able to stay atop a horse while we are riding for our lives?"

A faint smile brimmed his lips as he stared at the house that was nestled in the pines and cedars. "I'll stick to my horse like glue if need be," he assured her. "Don't you worry about me. You just take care of yourself."

Her hand curled around his elbow, detaining him. "Please be careful, Reuben. I don't want anything to happen to you or Papa. I love both of you very much."

Holt tipped her smudged face to his, touched by the sincerity in her tone and her expression. "In case something does go wrong . . ." His lips whispered over hers in the slightest breath of a kiss. "Never forget that because of you, I have become a new man. And I love you. . . ."

Shiloh threw her arms around his neck and kissed him with enough heat to melt an iceberg. Her frustration and anxiety had transformed into instant passion that conveyed both her fear and her love. This was one time she wished Reuben were more capable of defending himself. He could get himself killed if he made one false move, and so could she. If anything happened, she would never forgive herself for forcing Reuben to do something he wasn't accustomed to doing. He was a far cry from the civilized society of Chicago and terribly far out of his element. But Victor's life was at stake, and he was all the family she had left. She couldn't bear the thought of losing her father.

Victor had battled Confederates and commanded a cavalry of troops throughout the war. He had assumed the task of building a railroad to connect the vast area between Missouri and Texas. She couldn't allow her father to perish in the backwoods of the Ozarks before he was allowed to enjoy his dream. There was no guarantee that these bandits would free Victor when they had the gold and silver. Absolutely no guarantee at all, she reminded herself bleakly.

For a long, breathless moment, Holt forgot about Victor and the ten men in the farmhouse. His body instinctively reacted to the feel of Shiloh's shapely contours molded familiarly to his. This was good-bye, and he intended to savor the intoxicating taste of her, to commit every tantalizing sensation aroused by her kiss to memory. And knowing this would be the last time he'd ever hold this vivacious sprite in his arms made each second as priceless as twenty-four-karat gold.

God, he was going to miss this silver-blue-eyed imp. He had awakened each morning and had fallen asleep each night with Shiloh lying by his side. But all good things must come to an end, one way or another, Holt reminded himself gloomily. Reuben Gilcrest would go out in a blaze of glory, and Shiloh would go back where she belonged—to her luxurious mansion in Springfield.

Reluctantly, Holt dragged his lips from her stirring kiss and set her away from him. After he wiped off the glasses that had steamed up after their passionate embrace, Holt mustered a tender smile. Affectionately, he brushed the smudges from Shiloh's creamy cheek and then did an about-face to march into battle. All that detracted from his bold advance toward the enemy's stronghold was the fact that he tripped over a fallen log and had to scramble to maintain his balance. When he noticed Dog treading behind him, he gestured toward Shiloh.

"Stay with her, Dog," he commanded sternly.

Dog almost always did what his master demanded. He didn't always like it, but he did it. But nobody had told Dog what was going on, and he didn't understand why he couldn't follow his master now. For a moment the shaggy mongrel peered at Holt, waiting for him to reconsider the request.

"Stay with Shiloh," Holt repeated in a firm voice.

Ducking his broad head, Dog lumbered back to sink down at Shiloh's heels. While Holt tromped toward the herd of horses that were tethered in the trees beside the house, Shiloh circled behind the quaint cottage, wondering if the inhabitants of the farm also found themselves hostages.

After Holt led three horses in the direction they had come from and hobbled them, he crept back to the rest of the herd. With a loud yelp and a sound whack on the horses' rumps, Holt sent the steeds galloping off in all directions at once.

The stage was set and Holt prepared himself to play out his role as Reuben Gilcrest. He glanced back to see Shiloh and Dog scrunched down beneath the back window, waiting the opportunity to rescue Victor. With regret Holt shut the door on the past few weeks he had spent with the saucy blonde who had come to mean far more to him than she should have. With grim resignation he walked forward to meet his destiny. . . .

The sound of thundering horses caught the attention of the men who waited inside the farmhouse. Shiloh wasn't sure what Reuben intended to do, but she did see from her lookout point at the back window the masked desperadoes file out of the front door. She could also see her father tied to a chair in the bedroom of the cottage. The instant the desperadoes paraded outside, Shiloh sprang into action. Quick as a wink, she pushed open the window and threw her leg over the sill.

Time was of the essence. She didn't dare leave Reuben holding the bag too long while she retrieved her father. While she darted apprehensive glances at the open front door, her fingers flew over the knotted rope that restrained Victor.

When she heard the outlaw leader's bellowing voice, her heart catapulted to her throat. With fiend-ridden haste she freed her father and slid back out the window, where Dog waited with a wagging tail. When Victor had exited and closed the window behind him, they scampered through the trees to await Reuben's arrival.

From their hiding place in the underbrush, Shiloh and Victor could see Reuben standing defiantly in front of the desperadoes. A muted curse erupted from Shiloh's lips. What the devil did Reuben think he was doing? He was the one who couldn't count! she thought in frustrated fear. The odds were ten to one and Reuben had no pistol with which to defend himself. If he thought he could reason with that mob of masked hoodlums, he was insane! Dammit all, that was not what Shiloh meant by distracting the desperadoes. This was suicide!

Shiloh tried to bolt forward, but her father restrained her. "There's nothing you can do for him without thrusting yourself into harm's way," Victor muttered as Shiloh fell off balance and kerplopped in the brush.

In anguish Shiloh listened to the conversation she had never intended to have while she was doing the sneaking and Reuben was doing the distracting.

"What the hell are you supposed to be?" the gorilla of a man asked Holt with an intimidating smirk.

Holt drew himself up to proud stature and stared at the desperado through his wire-rimmed spectacles. "I have come to parley with you," he announced.

Shiloh rolled her eyes in disbelief. Reuben's fall into the river had obviously warped his brain. He didn't know what he was doing!

"Parley?" the bandit parroted with a taunting snort. "We ain't a bunch of Indians, city slicker."

"But you are without your horses and without a means of collecting the gold from the payroll car."

The second time Shiloh tried to leap to Reuben's defense, Victor grabbed her wrist and jerked her back to the ground. "Sit still, girl," he growled. "You'll get all of us killed!"

In two lumbering strides the huge bandit stomped up to Holt, who courageously stood his ground. Cocking a sinewy arm, he knocked Holt clean off his feet and sent him skidding across the grass. The boisterous laughter of his cohorts rang in the air as Reuben's wire-rimmed glasses went flying and Holt bounced across the ground like a rubber ball.

Shiloh grimaced, knowing the powerful blow must have rattled Reuben's teeth, if not knocked every last one of them out of his mouth!

"That's the only parleying you'll get from me, dude!"

the outlaw guffawed as Holt scraped himself off the ground. "Now, get the hell out of here before I decide to string you up by your scrawny neck."

"I will make a better hostage than Victor McBride," Holt bartered out of the side of his mouth that wasn't swollen after being smashed by a meaty fist. "Victor is determined to see that his employees receive their wages. But I can wire for money from my bank in Chicago—paper money that will be easier to carry than gold."

"Well, what do you think, men?" the desperado questioned his rough-looking companions. "Shall we take the gold or this tenderfoot's paper money?"

"Gold!" was the unanimous decision.

Low, threatening laughter rumbled in the bandit's massive chest. With a flair for the dramatic, he drew his dagger and flashed its razor-sharp edge in the sunlight. "I don't much like your prissy clothes, dude," he mocked scornfully. "And I never did have much use for highfalutin dandies like you."

Holt retreated a step when the desperado taunted him with the stiletto. "I'll see that you get twice as much money as you'll find in the payroll car," Holt baited.

"Gold at our fingertips is worth more than a fistful of dollars in some bank in Chicago," the outlaw sneered. "You ran off our horses, tenderfoot, and you're gonna pay for that."

Holt tried to remove himself from the path of the brawny giant who charged like an enraged rhinoceros. But Reuben's lack of coordination and agility caused him to stumble, and he fell back with a decisive thud. Before he could roll to his feet, the bandit grabbed him by the nape of the neck and threateningly raised the dagger.

Victor clamped his hand over Shiloh's mouth when she shrieked in horror. From where she sat it looked as

293

if the murdering brute had stabbed Reuben in the ribs. Suddenly the rest of the desperadoes descended on Reuben like a pack of starving wolves. Shiloh felt her father tugging on her arm, demanding that she mount her steed. But Shiloh was frozen to the spot, her mind screaming at the horrible implication of what was happening to Reuben. He had bravely sacrificed his life in an attempt to save Victor, and it had been all Shiloh's fault! Her and her bright ideas! She had gotten Reuben killed just as surely as if she had stabbed him with the knife.

Glancing over her shoulder, Shiloh saw two of the ruthless murderers dragging Reuben's lifeless body into the underbrush. She knew it would be only a matter of minutes before the hoodlums discovered Victor had escaped. The moment they gathered their scattered horses they would be breathing down Victor's and Shiloh's necks.

"I'm sorry," Victor murmured as they zigzagged through the maze of trees. His sympathetic gaze focused on the stream of tears that boiled down Shiloh's ashen cheeks. "You really did love Reuben, didn't you, honey?"

Too distressed and bereaved to speak for fear she would burst into hysterical sobs, Shiloh nodded. Memories hounded her every step of the way. She could see Reuben leaning against the mansion door the first day she had met him. Him, with his oversize bowler that mashed down his ears and the mustache and goatee that sat crookedly on his face. Him, with that uneven part in his midnight-black hair and those big spectacles that made him look like a frog. Reuben—so awkward and shy around women. Reuben—the man who had just begun to realize his potential. He had come into his own in the darkness, introducing Shiloh to the meaning of passion, exploring the realm of warm, tender emotion between a man and woman. He was a lamb with the heart and courage of a lion. He had proved himself capable of boundless love and passion in both its gentle and ardent forms. He had taught her to look deeply within a man to find those qualities that mattered most—respect for others, compassion, loyalty, self-sacrificing . . .

Shiloh broke down and cried her eyes out. No one could ever replace Reuben, even if the rest of the world scorned their marriage as a ridiculous mismatch. In his own quiet, mild-mannered way he had put all other men to shame, and Shiloh had lost the only man she had ever truly loved.

While Victor led the way back to the bridge and took command of coupling the cars and repairing the track, Shiloh ambled around in a daze, trying to cope with her tragic loss, battling her severe feelings of guilt. Her name should be scribbled on Reuben's certificate under cause of death, she mused dispiritedly. She had brought Reuben to this lowly end. It was her fault he had been trapped into wedlock and her fault that he had perished after three weeks of matrimony. It didn't matter that she had known Reuben for only two months. She would never forget him. She would cherish each tender memory and allow him to live on in her heart until the end of time.

Swallowing over agonized gulps of tears, Shiloh inhaled a steadying breath. Somehow she was going to find a way to right this wrong! The men who murdered Reuben would follow him to his grave. She would see to that!

Part III

I hate and love—wherefore I cannot tell,
But by my tortures know that fact too well!

Catullus

Chapter 21

Holt shucked the baggy garments and shrugged on his well-worn buckskins that fit his muscular body like a glove. He hated himself for what he had been forced to do to Shiloh, but there was no other way to insure the life of Reuben Gilcrest was over. Holt would have preferred not to allow Shiloh to witness Reuben's brutal death. But if she hadn't, she might not have given up hope that he was still alive. The last thing he wanted was to have her snooping around in search of a body Holt would still be using. Holt felt terribly guilty about deceiving Shiloh, but he had made a solemn vow when Anna died that he would avenge her senseless death. He still had a job to do here in Primrose, and he had every intention of completing his assignment and settling his score with Kirby Thorn.

Odd, Holt couldn't remember another time when killing off one of his aliases played such havoc with his conscience and emotions. The whole affair left a bad taste in his mouth. He had deceived Shiloh from the onset, seeing her as an amusing challenge and conquering her cynicism against all men in general. But he hadn't counted on falling in love with the woman. His affection for her had sneaked up on him while he wasn't looking. Too late he had found himself wanting more than a fleeting affair.

"Dammit all . . ." he swore, unconsciously resorting to Shiloh's favorite expression. Still grumbling, he shaved off the lopsided mustache and goatee Reuben had worn. His tender mouth and jaw objected to being grazed with a sharp blade, and he spouted another curse.

"What's wrong?" Garret questioned. Leisurely, he ambled into the bedroom to plunk down on the edge of the bed.

"You didn't have to hit me so hard," Holt muttered resentfully. "You damned near knocked out my teeth."

"You said to make it look convincing," Garret reminded him glibly. "Besides, you had it coming for marrying McBride's daughter and then leaving her a grieving widow."

"What the hell was I supposed to do?" Holt scowled, wiping the lather from his face. "I couldn't very well invite her to become a member of my new outlaw gang, now, could I?"

Garret's buffalo-size shoulders lifted and dropped in a shrug. "Maybe not, but that was a rotten way to treat her. Even though she isn't my wife, I feel bad about the hell I put her through by making her watch that gruesome scene."

"I've got my own nagging conscience to contend with," Holt growled grouchily. "I don't need to be burdened with yours too!"

When Garret unfolded his gigantic frame, the bed creaked. "Now, what are we going to do since we sent Victor and Shiloh running for their lives?" he mumbled in question.

"We wait," Holt informed him. "I had intended to ride to Kansas after Reuben's death to check on my speculations. But with Kirby Thorn prowling around

300

the area, I'm not taking any chances of losing him. I've waited two years to get my hands on him."

Holt's green eyes took on a murderous glitter that would have shocked Shiloh if she could have witnessed the transformation in the mild-mannered man she had known as Reuben Gilcrest. For a time Holt had projected the image of a calm, meek gentleman, but Holt Cantrell could change like a chameleon.

The garments he now wore accentuated his whipcord muscles and the broad expanse of his chest. The lean contours and steel-honed planes of his body were complimented by the trim-fitting buckskins. The fringe that dangled from his sleeves and breeches called attention to his fluid movements. Two "peacemakers" hung on his lean hips, and he had discarded the pointed boots for the scuffed pair that suited his rugged lifestyle. The transformation was complete. There was a ruthless glint in Holt's eye now—the reflection of his long-harbored vendetta against Kirby Thorn. Holt had laid Reuben to rest and he had two scores to settle. He had waited an eternity to focus his attention on both of them.

"Tonight I'm going to Primrose to have a private conversation with Walter Jameson," he announced as he strode out the door. "With any luck at all, he'll tell me what I need to know to entrap Kirby Thorn. Unless I miss my guess, Walter hired Kirby to do his dirty work for him."

Garret wasn't surprised by the rumbling bitterness in Holt's voice. He knew Holt would be a happier man after he had avenged Anna's death as well as his father's. This quaint cottage in the Ozarks was the home in which Holt had grown up as a child. Jonas Cantrell had taught his son a respect for the land and a love for right and justice. Holt had been content to farm this homestead until war broke out. He had gone off to fight for what he believed in, unaware that border raiders were still cutting a wide path of destruction through Missouri and Kansas—a path too close to home.

Holt's sharp wit and phenomenal skills had earned him several quick promotions in the army. He and Garret had been given a score of difficult assignments in espionage, and they had earned the recognition of Allan Pinkerton, who requested their assistance in secret service for the Union. But when Holt returned to find that Anna and Jonas had become victims of Thorn's vicious raids, bitterness and regret had become his constant shadow.

Holt had always been handy with a pistol, but he had practiced religiously after the massacre. In each target he had seen Kirby Thorn's face, and Garret knew his longtime friend would never rest until he had sent that vicious murderer to hell.

Now the vengeance Holt had carried with him for over two years ached for release. Kirby Thorn had returned to his favorite haunt, and Holt wanted him. Garret could see the change in Holt as he moved swiftly down the hall of the house that was haunted with ghosts of the past. Holt had made several changes in the family farm since the disaster, changes that made it possible for the servants and hired hands to escape in case of raids like the one that had taken Anna's and Jonas's life.

The cottage sat on the slope of the hill, nestled among the trees. On the hillside below was the huge barn that was constructed of rock and timber. Beside it sat the servants' quarters. With Garret's help, Holt had dug a tunnel that led from the secret passage in the cellar to the loft of the barn. A man could disappear from the house and materialize in the stables without stepping outside to confront unwanted visitors. It was through the underground passage that Holt came and went between his investigative assignments. But when he walked the halls of his home, a black cloud hung over him—a cloud of Kirby Thorn's making.

The fact that Holt's mood deteriorated the moment he stepped from his disguise to resume his true identity was compounded by his frustrations in bidding Shiloh farewell. Holt heaved a sigh and attempted to regain his composure. Perhaps when this was over and he had his revenge on Kirby Thorn, he could garb himself in a disguise and wander through Springfield—just to see how Shiloh was faring. He shouldn't bother, he told himself sensibly. She would forget Reuben soon enough, Holt reckoned. Other men would come along to distract her. But Holt doubted he would forget that sassy minx, not for a long time to come.

For the first time in two years he felt something besides the fierce driving force that compelled him to avenge Anna's death and to rid the world of every Kirby Thorn he encountered. In so many ways Shiloh reminded him of Anna. Shiloh's dazzling beauty and high spirit had intrigued Holt from the instant he laid eyes on her. She was everything Anna would have been if Kirby Thorn hadn't turned her days and nights into a living nightmare that ended in her untimely death.

But what was the use of tormenting himself with the bittersweet memories of Anna and the memories he had made with Shiloh? Holt asked himself crossly. He had only one true purpose in life—to hunt down Kirby Thorn and take an eye for an eye. Kirby Thorn had so many murders to his credit, and Holt would be doing the world a great favor when he put an end to the robberies, raids, and massacres. . . .

"Do you want me to come with you?" Garret's quiet voice filtered through Holt's deliberations.

"No," he mumbled as he stuffed his boot in the

stirrup and gazed up to see the first star of the evening twinkling in the dusky sky. The silver-blue light reminded him of a diamond—a symbol of a distant dream that he had enjoyed for a short space in his life.

Garret frowned at Holt's grim mood. "I could—"

"No." Holt abruptly cut him off. "I'm the one who has an ax to grind with Walter Jameson. The man is a slow learner, but he is going to learn his lesson tonight. And when I finish with him, I'm going to exact my revenge on Thorn." Touching his heels to the steed's flank, Holt galloped into the darkness.

Garret expelled a heavy sigh. He certainly hoped Holt lived to enjoy his victory over Kirby Thorn. If something went wrong, Garret would feel obligated to take up the crusade for his friend and confidant. Garret had been exceptionally fond of Anna himself. But even if this was Holt's private war, Garret vowed to be there to provide reinforcements if needed. Yet, when it came down to the final confrontation, Garret knew Holt wanted that murdering bastard all to himself. And Garret would grant Holt's wish. He had to. Holt had made Garret swear on a stack of Bibles that he wouldn't interfere when Holt and Kirby finally came face-to-face in a fight to the death.

Walter peeled off his clothes and plopped down on the bed. He had rented a room at the hotel, as Max and Elijah had after the hair-raising incident that had ended in disaster. Walter had ridden hell-for-leather to retrieve the key from the paymaster. By the time he hotfooted it back to the site of the train holdup, Victor had returned and had thrown himself into the task of organizing crews and repairing track. Although Walter wasn't terribly grieved to hear Reuben Gilcrest had perished in his courageous stand to save Victor's life, he was shaken by the complications he hadn't counted on.

Now there were two rival gangs of thieves near Primrose who coveted the gold and silver that were locked in the payroll car. Victor had set a precedent with his defiance, and he wouldn't hand over the money that was to be paid to his employees even at the risk of his own life. Victor was a tough old bird who had come through the war with flying colors and who continued his bravura in his conflicts with highwaymen and setbacks in the progress of his railroad.

Walter grimaced when another thought skipped through his mind. When he first sought out Kirby Thorn—or, rather, when Kirby had attempted to rob him the day he rode into Primrose—Walter had offered the renegade a carload of gold in exchange for his life. Kirby had accepted the exchange. But Walter hadn't anticipated Victor's bravery or the possibility of competition in robbing the payroll car.

Lord, he hoped Kirby Thorn got his hands on the gold first! If not, Walter expected that ruthless scalawag to come gunning for him. Walter didn't usually do business with such deadly vermin. But he had been forced into it this time. And it was all Shiloh's fault, Walter mused resentfully. He wouldn't have resorted to extortion and fraud if Shiloh had been receptive to his advances. He would have been content to marry McBride's daughter and remain loyal to the company if that high-strung minx hadn't . . .

"Get up!"

Walter nearly leapt out of his skin when a harsh voice and a sharp-edged knife materialized out of nowhere. The blade pricked his throat and the gruff voice echoed in his ears, causing flashbacks of another night that had caused him considerable distress to dart through his mind.

Suddenly Walter couldn't breathe. At first he was

plagued with the horrible feeling that Kirby Thorn had pounced on him, but the silhouette reminded him more of the mysterious man who had attacked him in Springfield. God! What a day this had been!

"I said get up," the low voice demanded, emphasizing the command with another prick of his knife.

Walter still couldn't see the face of the man who lurked in the darkness. But it didn't matter. When a specter with a stiletto in his hand demanded a man to rise, he rose.

"Put 'em on, Jameson," Holt ordered brusquely as he tossed the clothes in Walter's face.

In spite of the fact that his fingers had suddenly become all thumbs, Walter did as he was told. Although he hoped he would wake up any second to find himself in the arms of a nightmare, he realized that what he thought was happening really was happening. He was being abducted by an apparition who reminded him of Shiloh's guardian angel, one who possessed fists of steel.

Walter had just set foot in the alley when a fist clenched the collar of his shirt and he was roughly slammed back against the wall. Not again, Walter thought. The last time he had been thrown against the wall he had been beaten black and blue.

The scant moonlight refused to reveal Walter's assailant. The broad-brimmed hat shaded the man's features. His scraggly beard, mustache, and long, wiry hair concealed his face. The cut of his clothes reminded him of Kirby Thorn's usual attire. Whoever this man was, he was notched from the same hard scrap of wood, Walter decided.

"I want some answers, Jameson," Holt snarled. His voice was punctuation in itself, even though the sharp blade added extra incentive for Walter to sing like a bird. "Who are you working for?"

Walter's eyes popped. "McBride," he insisted breathlessly.

Low, threatening laughter rumbled through Holt's chest. With lightning speed he doubled his fist and mashed Walter's belly against his spine. "You've been siphoning money from McBride's expense funds and buying up rights-of-way from men you persuaded to buy stock in name only," he accused.

Walter struggled to inhale a breath. He had no intention of confessing anything to anyone. And who the hell was this man anyway? How did he know about Walter's underhanded activities in McBride's company?

Another beefy fist made mincemeat of Walter's midsection. When Walter's knees folded beneath him, Holt grabbed him by the hair and slammed his skull against the wall.

"You had McBride sign his approval to all your transactions that you insisted were legal. Then you framed him, in the event someone detected discrepancies in the accounts," Holt growled.

"Yes," Walter croaked when Holt slammed his head back a second time.

"And you are the one who arranged the raid on the railroad supply train to undermine the company's race to the border, aren't you?" he snarled into Walter's peaked face.

Walter grimaced when a fist plowed into his ribs, knocking his knees out from under him again. A groan dribbled from his lips when Holt yanked him upright, jamming splinters from the rough wall into his back. "Yes," he chirped.

"Who instructed you to bankrupt McBride?" Holt sneered in question. When the answer was not quick in coming, Holt backhanded his captive, causing a trickle of blood to slide off Walter's lip.

"J. W. Baxter," Walter breathed in defeat. "He

bribed me to break McBride's company and frame Victor for scandal." The words tripped off his tongue in rapid succession. "When the company goes bankrupt and they lose the race, J.W. intends to take it over. The stock I bought was partly for him. We will have control over all the contracts I signed for McBride and J.W. will have the monopoly on the trade routes to the north and east of Texas."

Holt had arrived at that conclusion after he speculated that Walter was responsible for the destruction of the supply train. It had seemed too convenient that the raid on equipment had come just before the payroll car was to arrive in the area. To substantiate his theory, Holt had intended to check to see if there were accounts in Walter's name in the Kansas bank where Baxter kept his company funds.

When all evidence had first pointed to McBride, Holt thought the case looked all too cut and dried. When he searched deeper he suspected Walter, Max, or Elijah of sabotaging the company and framing Victor. But the other two large investors were only along for the ride—satisfying their dreams of fame and fortune in the railroad business. It was Walter who was working for McBride's rival company, insuring that Baxter did win the contracts through Indian territory.

Since Kirby Thorn had arrived on the scene, Holt refused to ride to Kansas to verify his speculations. Instead, he had chosen to confront Walter and pry the information directly from him. There was no time for lengthy trips while Kirby was on the prowl. Holt was eager to tie up all loose ends in the McBride case and focus his full attention on Kirby Thorn. God, he had waited a long time to clash with Kirby!

"When is Thorn planning to take the payroll?" Holt snapped impatiently.

Damnation! How did this man, whoever the hell he

was, know so much about Walter's business? And worse, what was going to become of Walter? He had made several thousand dollars and stood to gain even more profit when J. W. Baxter took control of McBride's company. But from the look of things, Walter wouldn't live long enough to spend the pile of cash he had gathered while he undermined McBride. Victor had delegated authority to Walter and it had been easy to take advantage of an honest, trusting man. . . .

"Answer me, damn your soul," Holt snapped, backhanding Walter to gain his full attention.

"Day after tomorrow at high noon—while the road gang and guards are taking their meal," Walter peeped.

Holt had obtained the answers he had come to get. But he wasn't satisfied. For almost two months he had tolerated Walter's snide remarks and his blatant pursuit of Shiloh. Walter had been warned to clamp down on his tongue, but he had continued to make life miserable for Shiloh and Reuben. Now Walter would pay full penance.

When Holt stuffed his knife back into his boot, Walter slumped in relief. It seemed he was not about to be carved into bite-size pieces after all. . . . But Walter's relief was short-lived. Holt loomed menacingly over Walter. He looked as ominous and threatening as a thunderstorm that was about to unleash its full fury.

"This one's for Reuben Gilcrest," Holt muttered angrily. "Since he is no longer around to deal with you, I'm doing it for him."

Holt cocked a sinewy arm and hit his wide-eyed victim as hard as he could. There was enough force behind the blow to fell a grizzly bear. Flesh cracked against flesh, and Walter's head snapped back against the wall. With a dull moan Walter pitched forward and Holt scooped the lifeless weight over his shoulder.

Carrying Walter's unconscious body, Holt moved through the alley in swift, precise strides. Determined of purpose, he marched toward the sheriff's office.

When the door banged against the wall, the dozing deputy jerked his feet off the edge of the desk and fumbled for his pistol. With his heart beating in triple time, Daniel Kroeker watched the mysterious stranger tote his victim through the outer office and into the cells as if he owned the place. When Holt had locked Walter up, he swaggered back to the desk to toss the bewildered deputy the ring of keys.

"Don't let anything happen to Mr. Jameson," Holt instructed as he paused to light his cigarillo from the flaming lantern. Penetrating green eyes drilled into Deputy Kroeker, who blinked like a disturbed owl. "He's the feast I intend to serve to Victor McBride."

A muddled frown clouded the deputy's brow. He didn't have the faintest notion what this rugged-looking renegade meant, but he didn't think it wise to debate the issue just now. The black mustache and beard that Holt had pasted on his face to conceal his identity gave him a dark, foreboding appearance. His confident manner shouted things about his personality, things the deputy was apprehensive about testing while he was at a disadvantage.

Daniel wasn't exactly sure what sort of individual he was dealing with. The brawny man certainly hadn't offered his name and occupation before he strode back to the cells to deposit Walter's unconscious body. Apparently, this scoundrel had spent enough time in similar jails to know his way around this one. He could have been a hired gunslinger or manhunter or even a fugitive from the law.

Since the sheriff had taken prisoners to Mt. Vernon

to meet the circuit judge, Daniel Kroeker had been left to keep a lid on this rowdy town. The appearance of this unkempt stranger had Daniel rattled. But, eager to perform his duties, Daniel sank down in his chair after Holt walked out. Pensively, he thumbed through the wanted posters that had piled up over the past few months. He came across the poster Holt had purposely drawn up on himself while he was hunting Kirby Thorn's ex-partner, Bob Henson.

Being new at the job, Deputy Kroeker didn't know that the man in the poster—Tom Morris—was supposedly dead. Nobody had informed him, and the town of Primrose had come into existence only around the time Holt was infiltrating the Henson gang. And Holt had been so eager to meet with Pinkerton after his assignment that he had neglected to send notice that Tom Morris was no longer wanted for murder and theft since he was not among the living.

It was an unfortunate oversight on Holt's part. He didn't usually make such mistakes. But his intense need to sniff our Kirby had made him careless. And when he encountered the distracting Shiloh McBride, he hadn't given the wanted posters on Tom Morris another thought.

And that was a damned shame because Deputy Kroeker came across the old poster that had been sent to Primrose. While Holt was making his way back to his home in the foothills of the Ozarks, Daniel Kroeker was nailing up the poster for all the world to see. And that was the very last thing Holt expected when he stuffed a booted foot in the stirrup and thundered off into the night.

Chapter 22

Although Victor's associates had deemed it safer to take rooms at the hotel, Victor had parked his private cars at the end of the track, where his employees were feverishly working around the clock to lay the rails. Torches blazed in the night while the road gang and their newly hired workers hurriedly replaced the damaged track. The enticement of the lavishly painted payroll car that sat behind the fuel car provided incentive when weariness plagued the crew.

Victor had forgone the comfort of his accommodations to pace back and forth, overseeing the task of laying the rails. Shiloh had demanded that her father pull some of his men from their tasks to form a posse for the purpose of rounding up the murderers who had ruthlessly taken Reuben's life. Victor, although he was sympathetic to his daughter's loss, could not spare the manpower when his company's future was at stake. But Shiloh, who had risked life and limb and had cost Reuben his life in order to save Victor, refused to give up her crusade. She couldn't bring Reuben back, but she fully intended that his killers hang for their despicable crime.

Deputizing herself as a one-woman posse, Shiloh

scrounged up a set of clothes from one young man who had signed on to work for her father. After paying the pint-size man an extravagant price for his extra set of garb, Shiloh wormed into the homespun clothes and ordered Dog to follow behind her. Mounted on a steed Reuben had confiscated from the gang of outlaws, Shiloh set out on her mission. It was her hope that sometime during the night Victor would realize she was missing and he would come looking for her.

Since Victor refused to lend her manpower to storm the cottage, Shiloh planned to force her father into action. In her estimation, laying rails to defeat the rival railroad company was not nearly as important as avenging Reuben's death. In most instances, Victor was compassionate and responsive to his daughter's needs. But he was now working against a deadline, and the threat of being outrun by J. W. Baxter hounded his every step.

Well, perhaps her daring scheme would cause Victor to lose the race to the border of Indian territory, she mused as she weaved through the maze of trees that encircled the hills. But she couldn't sit around twiddling her thumbs while Reuben's murderers were holed up at the nearby farm, making their plans to strike the payroll car a second time. She would see every last one of those blackhearted scoundrels swinging from trees if it was the last thing she ever did.

Determinedly, Shiloh picked her way along the route she had taken to and from the cottage in the foothills. Dog proved to be a useful bloodhound who trotted ahead of her as if he knew exactly where they were going.

The closer Shiloh came to the cottage, the more apprehensive she became. She found herself reliving the nightmare that had occurred earlier in the day, but she wasn't frightened for herself. After losing Reuben,

Shiloh was uncaring what happened to her. Her dreams had turned to dust and her perspective was blurred by grief and frustration and guilt. She was motivated by the fierce need for revenge. The turmoil of emotions left her with a devil-may-care attitude. She believed there was no risk too great when it came to getting those ten murderers to the gallows. Besides, all she had to do was stand as a posted sentinel until her father arrived. And Victor would come, Shiloh assured herself. When? She wasn't certain about that. Victor was preoccupied with his tasks, and it might be hours before he realized she was gone. But he would come, just as she had come to rescue him.

Cautiously, Shiloh crept around to the site where she had seen the gorilla of a man brutally stab Reuben. When this ordeal was over, Shiloh vowed to recover Reuben's body and see to it that he had a dignified burial, one that compensated for his violent death. . . .

Shiloh grumbled at the unpleasant thought of informing Reuben's poor aunt Mildred in Chicago of her nephew's untimely demise. The woman would be beside herself, just as Shiloh was.

A curious frown knit Shiloh's brow when an object sparkled up at her. Inching from the underbrush, Shiloh sought out the twinkle in the grass. The reflection of moonlight had come from Reuben's discarded glasses. Reverently, Shiloh knelt down to pluck up the wire-rimmed spectacles that Reuben had always shoved so endearingly onto the bridge of his nose.

Reuben. . . . The intriguing combination of courage, patience, and gentleness. The remarkable man who had helped her overcome her cynicism toward men. He had taught her the wondrous sharing of passion embroidered with tenderness and ardent desire that could sweep her into a tempest of reckless urgency. He

315

had come to mean all things to her, and now he had been stripped from her arms. . . .

Fighting back the sentimental tears, Shiloh set the spectacles on her nose to see the world as Reuben had seen it. A muddled frown puckered her brow. Reuben had given the impression that he couldn't see without his spectacles. But when Shiloh tried them on, she could see clearly through them. They were plain glass, she realized as she glanced up at the full moon. If Reuben had a vision problem, these spectacles wouldn't have helped him. Maybe that was why he kept tripping over his feet. . . .

A startled gasp erupted from Shiloh's lips when a pair of burly arms clamped around her like a beaver trap. Struggle as she may, she couldn't hurl herself away from the mountain of a man who held her fast.

"What are you doing here, kid?" Garret demanded gruffly.

Garret had ambled down to the barn to await Holt's return. After half an hour Garret gave up and wandered back up the hill to the house, wondering if Holt intended to return that night at all. He hadn't said one way or another—only that he was riding to Primrose.

When Garret heard the quiet whinny of an unidentified horse, he had gone to investigate. While he was frowning at the riderless steed that had been tethered in the trees, he spied what he thought was a thin lad wandering around the clearing in front of the cottage. Employing the tactic of sneaking that he had perfected and refined during his espionage missions and his assignments for Pinkerton, Garret had silently circled behind the boy. His dark eyes narrowed on the lad who was garbed in tattered clothes and was wearing a wide-brimmed hat that was almost as big as he was.

Garret knew Holt would have a fit if he returned

316

from town to find an unexpected guest prowling the night. But the kid was here, and here the snoopy brat would have to stay until the group of detectives had homed in on Kirby Thorn. . . .

His thoughts dispersed when the body in his arms wormed and squirmed for release. A discomforted groan bubbled from Garret's lips when the daring brat kicked him in the shins and gouged him with an elbow in the belly. Now, that made Garret mad!

"Hold still," he growled, but his command was flagrantly disobeyed. "I said hold . . . ouch!"

A loud yelp erupted from his lips when Shiloh sank her teeth into his forearm. Instinctively, he shrank away from the vicious bite. His captive hurled herself forward in a dead run. With a snarl Garret launched himself at the escaped captive and caught her in midstride.

Shiloh swore a boulder had avalanched upon her when she crashed to the ground with Garret's massive body on top of her. She had been squished flat, and the last bit of air gushed from her lips, leaving her muttering curses in the grass. Dammit all, this was not what she intended! She had planned to stand watch over the outlaw gang until her father came to rescue her. She had not expected to become a hostage! Maybe this hadn't been such a good idea after all. . . .

Suddenly Shiloh was jerked off the ground and held in midair. Her arms and legs flew in every direction at once, trying to level a blow on the Goliath who had captured her.

"When I say hold still, I mean hold still, kid!" Garret roared, hoping to scare the living daylights out of the unwelcome visitor.

When Garret shook Shiloh like a wolf shaking the life from its prey, her hat toppled from her head and silver-blond hair cascaded down her back. Garret was so shocked, he let go of Shiloh as if he had been handling live coals. Unprepared to be unloosed so quickly, Shiloh dropped to her knees, jarred by the sound shaking she had received.

"Holy hell!" Garret croaked like a waterlogged bullfrog.

Shiloh vaulted to her feet to dash away, but Garret, whose paralyzed body had begun to function, snaked out a hand to grab her trailing blond hair. Employing the silky tendrils as a rope, Garret towed her back into his arms. Carrying her kicking and screaming, Garret marched toward the cottage.

A wry smile pursed his lips, imagining Holt's reaction to seeing his widow sitting in his parlor. It seemed Holt had underestimated his spirited young wife, Garret thought in amusement. Shiloh had returned to the scene of the crime to avenge Reuben's tragic death. And damn if Holt wasn't going to have his hands full when this daring little imp realized she had been taken for the ride of her life!

Garret shuddered to think of all the names this proud beauty would be calling Holt Cantrell when he returned from Primrose—very much alive and well. If Shiloh was as high-strung and saucy as Allan Pinkerton claimed her to be, Holt could expect to be condemned to the fiery inferno of hell by this audacious young thing. Shiloh McBride would realize she had been played for a fool. And no matter what was between Shiloh and Reuben, she wasn't going to appreciate learning that her not-so-dead husband was living a new life with a new disguise.

For a half second Garret debated about setting Shiloh free and shooing her on her way. But he figured that if she was courageous enough to return to the cottage this time, she would do it again. And maybe next time would be an inopportune moment. Now Holt would have time to deal with his outraged wife—or, rather, the widow of one of Holt's aliases, Garret quickly amended. Later Holt might not have the time to sit Shiloh down and attempt to explain. Not that it would do him one bit of good, Garret thought to himself. Shiloh would be fit to be tied, that was certain.

Well, no matter what was about to happen, it wasn't Garret's problem, he thought mischievously. Holt was the one who arrogantly announced when he accepted this assignment that he could find his way around the sassy Shiloh McBride. Holt had cleverly tied up most of the loose ends in the McBride investigation, but one still dangled—Shiloh McBride Gilcrest.

It served Holt right, Garret decided as he stuffed Shiloh into the chair, rammed a gag in her mouth, and tied her up with so much rope that she resembled a mummy. Holt had waded in over his head and he had fallen in love with this spitfire. Not that Holt's affection would count for much when Shiloh learned the truth. Lord, she was going to be positively furious! She would undoubtedly hate Holt for the rest of her life. Holt had saved her father from bankruptcy and scandal, but Garret doubted Shiloh would thank him. Unless Garret missed his guess, Shiloh was going to be seeing red when the truth came swaggering through the front door and she and Holt met head-on.

Giving way to that particular thought, Garret picked up Shiloh—chair and all—and positioned her directly in front of the door. Then he pulled the spectacles from his pocket and set them on the bridge of Shiloh's nose—just where they had been when Garret spotted her in the clearing beside the cottage. Now Shiloh truly would be the first thing Holt saw when he strolled in. Sporting a devilish grin, Garret pivoted on his heel and veered off into the quarters where he and Holt planned to sleep. Garret would have delighted in waiting to hear

Holt talk himself out of this predicament, but he had the feeling this was one conversation between "widow" and "deceased" that no one else needed to hear.

Tiredly, Holt swung from the saddle and led his winded mount into the barn that had been built into the hillside. After he unsaddled his steed, he stopped by the servants' quarters to speak with the foreman who managed the farm while Holt was involved in his various assignments. When Holt ambled up the hill toward the cottage, Dog came bounding toward him. The mongrel's tail wagged so excitedly, he very nearly knocked his master over.

"What are you doing back here?" Holt questioned as Dog reared up on his hind legs to place his huge paws on Holt's shoulders. "I told you to stay with Shiloh."

Dog whined in response to being chastised and then plunked down on all fours to run circles around Holt. Since Dog was familiar with the surroundings, Holt assumed he had wandered away from the train to locate his master. Well, Holt was glad Dog hadn't obeyed him this time. They had been together through thick and thin. Holt could use Dog's silent companionship just now. Holt had been arguing with his conscience since the moment he walked out of Shiloh's life, and even though he had satisfied his vendetta and his curiosity about Walter Jameson's involvement, and had stashed the swindler in jail for safekeeping, his thoughts were hounded by a pair of sparkling silver-blue eyes and a dazzling smile that rivaled the radiance of the sun.

What a long, lonely night this was going to be, Holt mused glumly as his feet took him to the cottage. For more than three weeks he had slept by Shiloh's side. He had restrained himself from making love to her a dozen times, but the times they had shared passion had more than compensated for the times they hadn't.

He wondered if Shiloh would allow another man to take his place after a proper period of mourning. He had hoped to subtly send her back into the world after their last night together at the hotel. He had tried to assure her that a man in the throes of hungry passion could not always be gentle. He wanted Shiloh to get on with her life and to improve her perspective of men. But the thought of another man lying in her arms stabbed him like a knife. Good God, he missed that high-spirited minx, and they hadn't even been separated for a full day!

It was a little late to be possessive of her, Holt scolded himself. He had known from the beginning that his unplanned marriage to Shiloh would be short-lived. He shouldn't have let himself care for her. But, dammit, he had. Now he was left to troll through a sea of warm, arousing memories that inflamed the night, wishing things could have worked out differently.

If they had met at another time and place— Holt chided himself for playing the "what-if" game. If they had met elsewhere, Shiloh would have rejected any amorous advances he made because he wouldn't have been portraying the meek, bashful Reuben Gilcrest. He would have been himself, and Shiloh would have immediately erected her walls of defense. But the personality of Reuben Gilcrest had been specifically created to suit his assignment, and that was what had made all the difference in his relationship with Shiloh.

No, he would never have known the pleasures of Shiloh's responsive arms and explosive kisses, Holt reminded himself as he paused to light his cheroot. Their interlude in paradise was like the blooming of a delicate rose. Its lifespan was sweet and beautiful but short—a few splendorous weeks.

Holt blew several smoke rings into the still night air. It was over, he told himself firmly. Shiloh had brought a glimmer of light into his gloomy life—one that was plagued with a long-harbored vengeance. In the future, Holt would look back through the window of time to reminisce about his sojourn in paradise, to wander through each cherished memory. But his time with Shiloh had come and gone. He simply had to settle for being allowed to know that beauty as no other man had. She had touched the deep well of emotions that he had encased in stone since Anna's death.

Holt breezed through the front door. When he spied the obstacle that blocked his path, he bit into the end of his cigar. "Son of a bitch!" he yelped as if he had been stabbed. Murderous silver-blue eyes riveted on him—eyes that carried a death wish—a real one! The oath tumbled off his lips in a long-drawn-out groan. "Son . . . of . . . a . . . bitch. . . ."

In each critical moment in his life, Holt wound up muttering that same curse. And this was a particularly critical moment. Holt had sworn when Victor McBride burst into his daughter's room to find Reuben and Shiloh in the clench. That moment had been awkward, but this was infinitely worse! Holt was so shocked and dismayed to see Shiloh tied in the chair that had been placed right smack dab in front of the door that he cursed a third time and then wished with all his heart that the floor would open up so he could crawl into it.

Curse that Garret's warped sense of humor! If this was his idea of a joke, Holt didn't find it the least bit amusing. What Holt didn't need was the woman he loved glaring flaming arrows at him and silently comdemning his soul to the worst tortures of the damned.

Chapter 23

Shiloh's silver-blue eyes blazed behind the round spectacles Garret had mischievously planted on her face. She would have recognized the deep resonance of Reuben's voice and that startled oath anywhere. Even if Shiloh hadn't recognized the man beneath the thick beard and mustache, seeing Dog trailing merrily behind him was a dead giveaway. She took one look at his bright emerald eyes and a wave of unparalleled fury burst upon her.

Angrily, her gaze flooded over the trim-fitting garments that accentuated his swarthy physique—the one Reuben had purposely disguised with his baggy garb. He looked long and lean and imposing—nothing like her Reuben. Gone was the bowler that smashed down his ears, replaced by a stained Stetson. Gone was the wrinkled linen shirt and full trousers, replaced by rugged buckskins that clung sensuously to this deceitful bastard's muscular torso. Two Colts dangled beside his hips, the well-worn holster they occupied giving the impression that he did not carry them for decoration. The pistols and his rough appearance indicated his line of work. Shiloh silently seethed at the implications that shouted at her.

Poor Aunt Mildred? Ha! There was no sweet spinster aunt in Chicago to mourn Reuben Gilcrest's death. There was no shy, lovable Reuben! It was all a shrewd scheme, arranged to catch Shiloh off guard. . . .

Her thoughts flew back to the two nights in Springfield when she had caught Reuben prowling around the house at midnight. She recalled feeling the paper in the pocket of his nightshirt. When she had quizzed him about it, he had shrugged her off. And when she discovered him scribbling notes from the company's ledger, he had become angry with her for spying on him. Just what had this scoundrel been doing? Digging into her father's files to plan a robbery and familiarize himself with the workings of the company?

Damn this bastard to hell and back, she fumed, cursing into the bandanna Garret had stuffed in her mouth. It had all been a clever charade to rob the railroad payroll—an inside job accomplished by a master thief who had preyed on her sympathy and her naivete.

Ah, the hearty laughs Reuben must have had at her expense! This cunning mastermind had used her as his gambit to get his foot in the door and then he set about to bleed the McBride Railroad Company dry. He had arranged for his band of hoodlums to destroy the track and then he had attempted a robbery that would not implicate him in the crime. To top off his ingenious scheme, he had staged his death at the hands of his own men. Then this sly snake had slithered back to his den to shed the deceptive skin of the clumsy Reuben Gilcrest.

Mutinous fury pulsated through Shiloh's veins. She was seeing the world through a red haze—red walls, red Dog, red Reuben Gilcrest, or whoever the hell he really was! As much as Shiloh thought she had loved Reuben, she now hated him twice as much. It was one thing for a woman to make a complete ass of herself, but it was an entirely different matter when a low-down, good-for-nothing weasel did it for her. Hell had no wrath like the woman fooled and betrayed. Shiloh had never been so angry and humiliated in all her life. She had been deceived by her own desires. This sly thief had stolen her innocence, pretending she was his first lover just as he had been hers. And when she thought of all the sympathy and emotion, all the milk of human kindness she had wasted on this rapscallion, it curdled her stomach.

What a laugh he'd had, she mused venomously. She was such a naive fool that she didn't know what an experienced lover really was, and Reuben made sure she was none the wiser! No wonder Reuben had known how to make a woman respond so ardently to his touch. He wasn't blessed with a unique gift. He had simply perfected the art of lying and loving into a science. He had probably slept with enough females to populate the North American continent, damn his contemptible soul! And Shiloh, the defensive ignoramus who had never trusted a man any farther than she could throw him, had closed her eyes, opened her heart, and fallen into this clever tarantula's web. He had preyed on her emotions and forced her to live his lie. He had manipulated her and she had let her guard down, trusted him, believed in him! Dammit all, how could she have been such an idiot?

Everything he had said and done had been premeditated. He had hornswoggled her into seeing in Reuben Gilcrest only what she wanted to see. He had hoodwinked her by saying the things she wanted and expected to hear. But Reuben was a figment of her imagination. She had buckled beneath those lying lips and she despised the lingering taste of his poisonous kisses. She detested every tender emotion this vile vermin had evoked from her.

There was no lower life form on the planet. Reuben, or whoever this sneaky bastard was, was the personification of deceit. Shiloh hated him, loathed the memories they had made. Her skin crawled at the thought of having him touch her and make love to her as if she were the only woman in his life. She had grieved for a chameleon who changed colors to suit his surroundings. The love she thought she felt for Reuben wasn't there at all, and it never had been because there was no Reuben Gilcrest. He had been a mirage and she had been hallucinating!

Shiloh swore, then and there, that she would never love again. First she had been taken in by Lance Draper's eloquent lines of flattery, his pretended affection. And last, but hardly least, she had been conned by the most competent con man ever to walk the face of the earth. Love was only a boggled state of mind which, like a brief lapse of sanity, would pass if one had enough patience to let it. Love was a bitter illusion and Shiloh was through fantasizing!

Holt grimaced as he watched the multitude of resentful emotions chase each other across Shiloh's animated features. He knew she was positively furious with him and that she had arrived at the conclusion that he was a criminal of the worst sort. At this very moment she was silently wishing God would hurl down a lightning bolt and fry him to a crisp.

Holt wasn't stupid. He knew Shiloh was never going to forgive him for deceiving her. Hell, she wouldn't even listen if he tried to explain. He had squashed her pride and broken her faith in him. Now, instead of harboring affection for the departed Reuben Gilcrest, Shiloh was cursing his soul for all eternity and trying to forget he ever existed.

Garret had purposely deposited this shapely baggage in front of the door for Holt to handle. And Garret was probably snickering into his pillow right now. Holt cursed the hand of fate that had led Shiloh back to the cottage. He cursed his longtime friend who had played this exasperating prank on him.

And that damned Dog, he muttered, glaring at his loyal companion who was still thumping his tail against the doorjamb. Dog was probably responsible for seeing to it that this daring minx found her way in the dark of night.

Well, there was no sense in wasting his breath elaborating on why he'd done what he'd done, he reckoned. Shiloh wouldn't believe anything he said ever again. He hadn't wanted her to live out the rest of her life despising the ground he walked on, but it looked as if she would. Shiloh would carry a grudge and she would become more cynical than she ever was. Once a man fell from her good graces, she tossed the ladder after him. There was no way to climb back up from the pit of disappointment and disgrace to beg her forgiveness.

There was only one sensible thing to do—let her believe what she thought was true. Shiloh had undoubtedly deduced that he was the leader of this gang of desperadoes, so he would allow her to labor under that erroneous notion. Even if he boasted that he had saved her father from being framed for crimes he hadn't committed and had spared him from financial ruin, Shiloh wouldn't be grateful. There was no excuse for deceiving her, for stealing her innocence and leaving her to grieve her husband's death. He was as guilty as sin.

He had severely damaged her pride, and Shiloh McBride possessed oodles of stubborn pride. His only recourse was to ransom her back to her father for the gold in the payroll car—the same gold Kirby Thorn couldn't wait to get his greedy hands on. Later, the Pinkertons would recover the stolen money for McBride—after Kirby Thorn met his violent end.

For a long moment Holt stood wondering what to do with this fuming firebrand. He couldn't very well leave her tied in a chair for the duration of the night. Although he was going to allow Shiloh to believe the worst about him, he couldn't be cruel to her. Muttering over this unexpected predicament, Holt stomped across the room and stalked down the hall to the bedroom where Garret had settled down to sleep.

Garret found himself roughly nudged awake. His eyes fluttered open to see Holt's shadowed silhouette towering over him. A wry grin spread across his lips as he propped himself up on an elbow.

"Surprise," he drawled with a mocking smile that displayed his pearly teeth in the moonlight.

"Damn you," Holt growled at him.

Garret swung his long legs over the edge of the bed, intending to pull on his breeches. Before he could get up, Holt doubled a fist and knocked him down. Garret shook off the blow, knowing he had it coming and that Holt was only letting off steam. "Thanks," he snorted, exercising his stinging jaw. "I'm sure you thought I deserved that."

"What you deserve is to be stretched out on a torture rack," Holt muttered acrimoniously.

"Well, hell, I didn't know what to do with your widow," Garret said in self-defense as he cautiously unfolded himself from the edge of the bed, wondering if he would become the recipient of another punch in the jaw. "She sneaked back up here and she was snooping around. If I sent her running, stubborn and persistent

328

as she is, she would only have come back."

When Holt and Garret stepped into the hall, the lantern light glowed against Garret's bare chest and arms. Holt frowned at the flesh wound on Garret's forearm.

"What happened?" he murmured in question.

"That little wildcat bit me," Garret reported. "You should see my shins. They're purple."

If Holt hadn't been in such a snit, he might have laughed at the thought of Shiloh tearing into this burly ape. That bold she-devil had no fear of man or beast, and Garret was both. Casting the thought aside, Holt cut directly to the heart of the matter.

"I want you to take a ransom note to Victor. We'll exchange Shiloh for the payroll."

Garret gaped at Holt as if he had grapevines sprouting form his ears. "What?" he squeaked in disbelief.

"You heard me," Holt muttered crankily.

"But I thought we were going to—"

"We'll let Kirby Thorn come to us for the gold," Holt interrupted. "Using the secret passage to the barn, we can sneak from the house to surround him. I want Thorn to remember the last time he camped out at this cottage. The night he—" Holt's voice cracked with bitter hatred.

Garret said no more. He could tell Holt had been swamped by tormenting memories. "I'll fetch my shirt and see to your errand," he murmured, reversing direction.

Shiloh watched with boiling rage as Holt, Garret, and Dog filed past her as if she were a stick of furniture. When Holt and his devoted mutt returned, she flashed her captor a glower that needed no translation. If looks could kill, Holt knew he would, at this point, be pushing up daisies and Shiloh would spitefully stamp them back into the ground.

In silence Holt peeled off his wig, mustache, and beard and set them aside. This done, he unstrapped Shiloh from her wooden throne, but he had more sense than to cut her loose or remove her gag. Scooping her up in his arms, he strode over to place her on the sofa. She lay there like a corpse—her hands bound in front of her, her ankles secured. She was so rigid with fury that Holt wondered if she would permit herself to sleep. Judging by the mutinous expression that was stamped on her elegant features, she had every intention of staying awake all night to feed on her hatred for him.

Heaving a sigh, Holt shucked his shirt and boots and stretched out beside her. Impulsively, he leaned over to press a kiss to her flaming cheek, but she jerked away to stare at the back of the couch.

"I know you despise me and you have every right to. . . ."

He had certainly gotten that right! Shiloh hated no one the way she hated this lying serpent.

Holt curled his hand beneath her chin, forcing her to meet his level gaze. "But I did love you and I still do."

He knew better than to voice that confession, but the words tripped off his tongue of their own accord. He may as well have made his declaration to the wall. Shiloh was not the least bit receptive. She knew he was playing her emotions to his advantage, trying to draw tenderness from the bittersweet memories. But Shiloh knew he was lying to her now, just as he had for the past two months. Holt had proven himself unworthy of her affection, and Shiloh sorely regretted sharing it with him. She had wasted too much time and emotion on this bastard already. All he would ever get from her now was loathing disdain.

Love? He didn't love her and he never had, she mused resentfully. He loved money and he spilled

330

cunning lies to acquire it. All that motivated this miserable varmint was playing other people for fools and then robbing them blind.

His hand glided up her thigh to swirl across her belly. Shiloh winced, refusing to buckle to the memories and sensations of the past. He had once been able to make her soul sing, but it was humming an entirely different tune now. His touch was repulsive and it sickened her to think she had ever surrendered to this lying, thieving charlatan. He was a man of many faces and personalities, and she hated them every one. His masterful caresses sought to rekindle the flame that had once burned so brightly in her heart. But he had tainted every memory and had destroyed what little faith she had in men in general and him in particular.

Shiloh couldn't think of enough horrible things to say about this man. But she would try if he ever removed her gag! She would let him have it with both barrels. She had such a long string of curses and insults to hurl at him that it would take a full day to vocalize them all. Damn him!

Holt died a thousand agonizing deaths when he felt Shiloh tense instead of relax beneath his touch. He had taken something rare and beautiful and poisoned it. Shiloh was living proof why a man in his profession couldn't allow himself to become emotionally involved. The moment Reuben stepped from the grave, Holt had hurt the one person he loved most in this world—the one woman who wished he would have remained dead instead of returning to put her through such turmoil. The precious memories they had made had evolved into torment, and he had transformed Shiloh's dreams into nightmares.

Resigning himself to a battle lost, Holt leaned over to snuff the lantern, shading the room in darkness. Although Shiloh didn't want his touch and would have

331

fought to prevent it if her hands and feet hadn't been bound, Holt cuddled up against her. He laid his head against her rigid shoulder and closed his eyes, knowing he had enjoyed better days.

Back at the sheriff's office, Deputy Kroeker was making amends. Daniel had hung the wanted poster for the man he presumed to be Tom Morris—the deadly ruffian whose long list of crimes had earned him a huge reward.

If that vermin ever showed his face around Primrose again, Deputy Daniel Kroeker would be ready and waiting. And as for the battered man in the jail cell, Daniel had set him free. He was not about to hold anyone in custody because a wanted killer said so!

Tom Morris was not only a vicious rapscallion but he was also crazy as a loon, Daniel decided. There were not many wanted gunslingers who had the audacity to march into jail and drop off an unconscious body. Daniel didn't have a clue what Morris had meant about serving the man to Victor McBride. He supposed the outlaw thought name-dropping would stifle any questions. But Daniel wasn't that gullible. He was eager to make a name for himself as a lawman, and hopefully he would one day have his own town. But he wasn't scoring any points with the Pinkerton Detective Agency, that was certain. Daniel had managed to put the life of one of Pinkerton's most valuable agents in jeopardy.

Daniel did, however, accomplish a small amount of good while he burned the midnight oil. When he was thumbing through the stack of old and recent wanted posters he had noticed another familiar face—the one belonging to Kirby Thorn. After making his rounds the past few days, Daniel had a run-in with the beady-eyed hoodlum whose description reminded him of the drawing on the poster. There was a definite resemblance between the sketch and Kirby Thorn, whose facial scar was now partially concealed by the growth of a beard. Two days earlier Daniel had broken up a fight in one of the saloons. Kirby had been accused of cheating at cards. Daniel hadn't taken prisoners, but he had warned both men to keep their pistols in their holsters and all their cards on the table.

Kirby, who had been biding his time until all arrangements for the robbery could be made, had replaced his Colt in his holster and reminded himself to clamp down on his notorious temper. He had far more to gain than poker winnings when he robbed the bank and McBride's payroll car.

Daniel Kroeker sorely wished that all the competent men who were presently laying track for McBride were available for a posse. The deputy was handcuffed. Without reinforcements he couldn't sniff out Tom Morris or Kirby Thorn. And that was the reason Daniel Kroeker was still a lowly deputy. His skills as a lawman needed polish, and even he knew better than to bite off more than he could chew. He would have to wait for the opportune moment to arrest Tom Morris and Kirby Thorn—a moment when he'd have plenty of assistance!

Stuffing his belongings into his satchel with both hands, Walter Jameson prepared to make a speedy exit from Primrose. He didn't want to be around when the mysterious man who had punched him senseless and beat information out of him returned to point an accusing finger. Neither did he wish to be in pistol range of Kirby Thorn. Walter had seen Kirby's wanted poster on the deputy's desk when he was released from jail. If the law official had recognized Kirby, that was Kirby's problem and Walter's good fortune. He was heading for higher ground before all hell broke loose in Primrose. There were other railroad companies in the West that might be eager for an enthusiastic promoter. Walter had all the necessary qualifications. Let J. W. Baxter battle against Victor McBride. Walter didn't give a whit about either of them. His only concern was saving his own hide. Walter intended to be long gone before anyone realized he was missing.

With the haste of a man pursued by a passel of demons, Walter confiscated a horse and pointed himself toward parts unknown. Since the long arm of the law didn't extend into Indian territory, Walter decided to cut a straight swath through the protective boundaries where the white man's law didn't reach. Riding hell-for-leather, Walter galloped off into the night, thankful he had escaped with his life.

Chapter 24

The day dawned bleak and dreary, matching Holt's cloudy mood. He hadn't slept well. His ribs were tender. Although Shiloh had been unable to claw him to shreds, she had jabbed him with her elbow every chance she got. Before she turned him into a human punching bag, Holt had folded his tall frame into a chair and had as a result awakened with a crook in his neck.

Before Holt allowed the other detectives to wander into the parlor, he had gathered them in the kitchen. He quietly explained what Shiloh was doing at the cottage and informed them of his change of plans. Resuming their roles as desperadoes, the agents filed outside after breakfast, giving Holt time alone with Shiloh.

Bolstering his courage, Holt prepared Shiloh a breakfast tray and ambled back to the parlor. He knew he would have to remove her gag to feed her, and he dreaded unleashing her deadly tongue. She was going to call him every name in the book.

"I brought you food before we take you back to your father to exchange for the gold," he announced as he strode up in front of the wild-haired beauty whose flashing silver-blue eyes burned holes in his buckskin shirt.

Knowing he was going to be on the receiving end of some unpleasant words, Holt reluctantly removed her gag and braced himself for the entourage of insults. One look at Shiloh indicated that she had rolled out the heavy artillery and was preparing to blast away at him. And blast away she did the instant her tongue was free.

"You miserable son of a bitch! I hate you! I loathe you! You are the scum of the earth. I pray that God will bring down his wrath on his most obvious sinner. Words cannot describe the repulsion and disgust I feel when I am forced to tolerate your presence. I swear by all that's holy that I will watch you die a slow, agonizing death. And this time I'll make certain you are truly dead before I—"

Holt stuffed a fork into her mouth to shut her up, but Shiloh spit food on him and spewed curses like a hissing geyser. Again Holt crammed food into her mouth and again she spit at him.

"Eat this stuff," he growled, growing madder by the minute.

"No, I make it a policy never to eat when I'm furious," she hurled at him.

"It's probably just as well," Holt grunted sarcastically. "As often as you get mad, you would weigh two hundred pounds if you did."

"I hate you," she sputtered in outrage, straining against her confining ropes.

"So you have said."

"You lied and cheated and deceived, damn your wicked soul. I confided in you, trusted in you, and you repaid me by stealing my innocence and letting me believe you were as cautious of women as I was of men. I thought Lance Draper was a heartless creature, but you make him look like a saint." Her breasts heaved with indignation and her lips curled in a contemptuous sneer. "You made me want you and now I feel filthy

336

and poisoned because of your kiss and your touch."

Tears of humiliation sprang to her eyes, and Shiloh fought them back. She wasn't a crier. In fact, because of her strong constitutional makeup she rarely succumbed to sobs. There were some women who could dampen two handkerchiefs during crucial situations, but Shiloh wasn't one of them. Yet, Holt's deceitful betrayal had made her extremely vulnerable to her chaotic emotions. Despite her attempt to blink them away, salty tears scalded her flushed cheeks.

"I thought I knew you, but I realize I never knew you at all. You are probably in the habit of robbing banks and sleeping with a different woman every day," she yelled nastily at him.

"I don't rob banks every day," he said with a smirk.

The fact that he said nothing about dallying with a different woman every day put her temper on a rolling boil. Holt decided this was not a good time to tease Shiloh. The glare she flung at him was meant to maim and mutilate. Holt felt compelled to confess there had been no other females in his life since the day he met Shiloh.

"And as far as different women are concerned . . ."

"I don't want to know!" Shiloh growled. "I don't want to hear another pack of your lies."

Despite her attempt to hold another flood of tears in check, they trickled down her cheeks in a steady stream. "You were my first time, Reuben," she sobbed in gulping breaths. "And I thought I was yours. I hate you more for that than all the other lies you fed me to worm your way into my good graces."

"I never said it was the first time," Holt argued as he forced her to take a bite of food.

Still Shiloh refused to eat. "But you didn't deny what I thought to be true," she accused him in a furious tone. "I would have slept with Walter Jameson a dozen times before I ever lowered myself to accepting your touch if I had known of your cunning. At least Walter was open with his lust while you tricked me into trying to seduce you!"

Holt stared straight into her eyes, which was difficult to do when she glared so hatefully at him. "Shiloh, you were the first time in my life I *wished* it were the first time," he told her honestly.

"Liar!" Shiloh snarled at him. He wasn't going to soothe her bruised pride with that malarkey. "I was your tool, the device you used to get where you wanted to be so you could set up this raid and prey on my unsuspecting father like a bloodsucking leech."

It was with deep regret that Holt peered into her puckered features, ones that were livid with animosity. He was watching his precious memories go up in flames, and there wasn't a damned thing he could do about it. Her harsh words succeeded in making him feel two inches tall.

Holt let her rave on because she was entitled to it. And for the next five minutes he sat before her like a victim of a firing squad, letting her lambaste him with the tongue-lashing he so richly deserved. But enough was enough. Finally, Holt rammed the fork into her mouth.

"Eat this," he demanded gruffly. "Pretend it's my heart. You've chewed me up one side and down the other. Now try something with a little more nourishment," he urged. "You'll need your strength if you're going to rant and rail for another hour."

Begrudgingly, Shiloh munched on the ham and eggs, but she continued to glare poisonously at him. Dammit all, why had he forsaken her? Why had he betrayed her faith in him? And dammit all, why did he have to be so strikingly attractive? Why did she look at this vile man and feel the unwanted eruption of those tender memories that lay buried in their shallow graves?

338

Shiloh couldn't forgive him. She was too raw on the inside, too hurt by his clever ploy. She would get over loving him, she promised herself fiercely. But she would never get over hating him for what he had done. All she had to show for her wasted love was a broken heart and shattered pride.

A rueful smile hovered on Holt's lips as he fed Shiloh her breakfast. "I knew from the beginning I would wind up hurting you. At first it was a challenging game, I'll admit. I had heard of your reputation with men and I wanted to bring you down a notch. But when I got to know you, everything changed."

His emerald eyes slid over her baggy garments, knowing full well what lay beneath them, wanting her despite her hatred for him. "I kept my distance from you because of my respect for you. But when you touched me I—"

"Don't!" Shiloh grumbled between bites. "I don't want to remember."

"And I don't want to forget," he murmured softly.

Holt set the tray aside and bent down to untie her ankles while she warily watched him. Gently, he drew her to her feet. Holt slipped her tied wrists over his head to rest on his shoulders. Holding her cynical gaze, he slid his arm around her waist, drawing her rigid body to his. Tenderly, he cupped her face, wondering if she would take a chunk out of his lips when he tried to kiss her as he ached to. Despite the risk, Holt took possession of her mouth with a skillful kiss.

Shiloh pretended she was kissing a pillar of cold stone. She refused to let herself respond, refused to feel anything but repulsion for this man of a thousand faces.

When Holt realized Shiloh wasn't receptive to his embrace, he lifted his head to grace her with a humble smile—the kind Reuben wore so well. "I'm not asking for your forgiveness," he whispered as he traced her heart-shaped lips. "But for the moment I want you, more than anything, to forget the present and dwell on the past. . . ."

Shiloh was all set to reject him a second time. But her hopes of resisting were dashed when he employed Reuben's soft, husky tone of voice. Her traitorous body stirred to the feel of his muscular contours molded familiarly to hers. She could feel his desire for her. The burning ache in the core of her being began to channel through every nerve and muscle. Shiloh hated herself for buckling beneath her desires. This renegade, this master of disguise, was everything she detested. And yet, ironically, he was everything she wanted . . . or at least he had been before her handsome prince turned out to be a snake.

Holt deepened the kiss when he felt Shiloh's body surrender to his touch. Lord, her luscious curves and swells felt so good against him. It reminded him of the intimate moments they had shared before he shattered her dreams. His caresses flowed over her tantalizing contours, adoring the feel of her shapely body beneath his hands. Discontent with the hindering garments, Holt slid his fingertips beneath her shirt to make arousing contact with her bare flesh. He felt her wince, but she quickly lost the battle of mind over body, just as he had so often in the past.

Holt loosed the buttons of her shirt to taste the soft texture of her skin. His moist lips skimmed over the throbbing peaks of her breasts to tease them with his teeth and tongue. Shiloh's quiet moan encouraged him to continue his fondling. He did want her for all the right reasons, even if she refused to believe it.

After untying her wrists, he drew her palms under his shirt. "I need your touch," he said in a hoarsely disturbed whisper. "Please, Shiloh, just once more . . .

for Reuben's sake. . . ."

The moment her fingertips brushed against his flesh, her resistance folded up its tent and shamelessly slinked away. Shiloh had no defenses left to battle her wanton desires. Holt's soft, coaxing voice reminded her of the man she had known and loved. His masterful touch triggered the memories of secluded splendor. The old familiar feelings were there, and passion was still new and wondrous. The fact that this horrible man knew just how to make her respond when she hadn't meant to tore her composure to shreds.

When his adventurous caresses trailed across her ribs to dive beneath the band of her breeches, Shiloh felt her knees turn to jelly. His hand slid over the curve of her derriere, pressing her intimately against him. Shiloh gasped for much-needed air, but he stole the breath from her lungs, leaving her suspended in a trance from which she suddenly didn't care if she ever awakened.

As Holt deftly stripped away her garments, Shiloh welcomed the cool air against her seared flesh. But nothing seemed to ease the white-hot flames of passion. She was compelled to return his brazen caresses, to unearth the powerful package of masculinity, to taste him, to remember what was impossible to forget. . . .

A tormented groan rumbled in Holt's throat when Shiloh's warm lips feathered across his chest to investigate each nipple. He suffered oxygen deprivation when her kisses trailed lower, skitting across his skin like the velvet-soft wings of a butterfly. She showered every masculine inch of his exposed flesh with dewy kisses and swirling caresses. Her body glided provocatively against his, and Holt drew her down to the carpet before his legs folded and he fell into a crumpled heap.

His marveling gaze swept over her ivory skin. He

couldn't remember seeing another woman so perfectly formed, so utterly exquisite. She was every man's dream, and Holt wanted her desperately. She could breathe life into him, leaving him burning on a maddening flame of desire.

"I need you," he whispered as his knee slid between her thighs, longing for more intimate contact. "You make the world go away and I never want it to come back. . . ."

Shiloh's misty lashes fluttered up to see the ruggedly handsome face poised above hers. She was every kind of fool for wanting this desperado when he had thoroughly humiliated her. She was a hostage held for ransom. He had turned her every way but loose and still she craved what he could offer. She had become a slave to his sometimes gentle, sometimes savage brand of passion.

Reuben had taught her everything she knew about love—its hopes, its betrayal, its ecstasy and agony. And as much as she hated to admit it, there was a Reuben Gilcrest lurking deep inside this cunning renegade. The man who had hidden behind both foppish clothes and rugged buckskins was still there. He had been no illusion. And although she could never claim this magnificently built man as her own, they truly had found their place in the sun—a private place where identities didn't exist.

Then as now they were only a man and a woman who gave and shared their hearts and spirits, who communicated their deep feelings for each other in physical language that needed no translation. They had no future and they would always be worlds apart, but there was something fierce and compelling between them that defied the lies, the deceit, and the betrayal. Shiloh wasn't sure what it was that lured her to this frustrating man. He tempted her and that was all there was to it. There was such a fine line between love and hate, she realized. She kept tripping back and forth over it as her senses took flight and she reveled in the pleasures that Reuben had always been able to arouse in her.

When he came to her, feeding the billowing flames, Shiloh marveled at the emotions that consumed her. They were one beating, breathing essence, an entity unto each other. They were like two different parts of a living puzzle that made no sense at all until they were flesh to flesh, soul to soul. . . .

Hot, bubbling sensations unfurled inside her, fueling the already raging fire. Shiloh arched to meet his driving thrusts, impatient to appease the intense cravings. She longed to forget her anger and humiliation. She yearned to soar in motionless flight with the Reuben she had known and had come to love.

Shiloh could feel herself held aloft like a bird on outstretched wings riding the wind. And then, slowly but steadily, a hazy cloud of rapture drifted over her and she let go with her heart, body, and soul. She was pulled down into the depths of ecstasy, drenched by ineffable pleasure. Her body shuddered in sweet, satisfying release.

Holt crushed her to him as if he never meant to let go. His body and mind were numbed with unrivaled pleasure. He longed to hold Shiloh, to revel in the sublime moment that pursued and captured time. But all too soon the haze evaporated and reality returned to torment him.

Realizing he was probably squishing this petite pixie flat, Holt eased down beside her. A smile hovered on his lips as he combed his fingers through the shiny tendrils that danced with sunbeams. He just wanted to lie and caress her with his gaze, to remember each delirious moment of splendor. All too soon he would have to gather his discarded clothes and tote this lovely minx back to her father.

Perhaps Shiloh would always hate him for what he had done to her, but she still cared for him, even if she refused to admit it to him or herself. Pride would not permit her to confess that they aroused something in each other that even the deceptive lies and impossible situations couldn't smother. Although that thought was comforting, it did little to lift Holt's sunken spirits. He had again become Shiloh's lover but not her friend. He could see the shadow of resentment clouding her eyes when the loving was over.

"Know this, sweet nymph," he whispered as he bent to graze her kiss-swollen lips. "You brought out the best man in me that I could possibly be. Reuben lived and thrived because of you, and I am a much better man because you allowed me to realize my potential."

When Shiloh looked as if she were about to contest his confession, he silenced her with a deep, penetrating kiss. "It was you who brought Reuben to life," he murmured against her cheek. "And in a way, it was the first time for him—a rare, unique time that can never be duplicated. I can't change what is to come, Shiloh, but don't take the precious memories away from me. . . ."

Shiloh tried to blink back the infuriating tears that came so easily when this man trifled with her emotions. Only he could make her cry. Only he had the power to hurt her.

"Words," she choked out. "All words to cast a different light on the lies. No matter how you phrase it, the outcome is still the same. You are a powerful magician who brings Reuben back to life when he can accomplish your purpose for you. You made my body respond with your black magic, but in my heart I still loathe you. You betrayed me and, now that I know the

344

truth, you have forced me to betray myself in your arms."

"Forced?" Holt parroted in frustration. "Now who's lying to whom?" His tone conveyed his anger with her remark. "I don't recall forcing you to do anything. You were a willing participant, not a helpless victim."

His sharp voice caused Shiloh to fling herself away from him. Hurriedly, she pulled on her clothes, refusing to glance back at him for fear of confronting his mocking smile. "You are a devil. . . ." Shiloh would have called him by name, but she didn't have the faintest idea what it was. "Who are you anyway?"

"What difference does it make now?" Holt grumbled as he yanked on his breeches and boots.

"Absolutely none," she said coldly. "But I would at least like to know whom I hate."

"The name is Holt Cantrell," he informed her woodenly.

"Your real name or one of your aliases?" she sniped.

"It's the one I was born with," he muttered.

"I'm surprised you still remember it since you have undoubtedly gone through so many names and personalities the past three decades," Shiloh flung at him.

Holt shackled her wrists and Shiloh glowered at him while he replaced the rope. He was willing to free her while he seduced her, but when the loving was over, it was business as usual. His callousness set a match to Shiloh's explosive temper.

"You can't possibly know how much I hate you," she growled contemptuously.

"Don't I?" One dark brow elevated as he hurriedly buttoned her into her shirt. "You have certainly told me in a hundred different ways."

"I could go on forever listing your disgusting flaws."

"What a pity we are pressed for time," he snorted in a

345

sarcastic tone.

Swiftly, Holt pasted on his mustache and beard that gave him a foreboding appearance. In long, swift strides he returned to shepherd Shiloh toward the door. "Come along, wife. I'm officially returning you to your father."

"I am not your wife. My husband is dead," she insisted, staring venomously at the man of a thousand faces.

It amazed her how easily Holt could change his appearance and personality when he slipped from one masquerade to another. The man was a skillful magician, she'd give him that. She despised him, but she begrudgingly had to admit that he played the most convincing roles. Holt had wasted his talents as a criminal. He definitely belonged in the theater.

Holt compressed his lips, refusing to debate the issue of his marriage. He had no intention of venturing to the stable to meet the congregation of detectives while he was in the middle of a shouting match with Shiloh. They had both said more than they should have on a variety of subjects.

Holt glanced skyward, noting the clouds that hung low over the wooded Ozark hills. The distant rumble of thunder echoed around them. Grumbling at the inclement weather and the billowing storm between him and Shiloh, Holt propelled her down the hill to the barn.

It was over, really over this time, Holt mused disparagingly. Shiloh couldn't wait to put a world between herself and her captor. And she would be itching to put his neck in a noose the moment she could arrange it. The murderous glare in her silver-blue eyes assured him of that. Knowing how vindictive she was, Holt wondered if she would hire Pinkerton to hunt him down. Now, that would be a ticklish situation, Holt

346

thought to himself. Allan Pinkerton would have one helluva time explaining why he couldn't put Holt Cantrell on the gallows when one of his clients demanded it.

The thick gray clouds swallowed the sun, flinging crisscrossed shadows through the canopy of trees that lined the hillside. Another grumble of thunder rolled across the sky as the sun peeked out and then disappeared completely.

After Shiloh was upon her steed, she flung Holt a smug smile. "You are a fool if you think my father will exchange me for the payroll. He already refused to open the pay car the first time you and your brigand threatened him."

"Ah, but you are wrong, ma'am," Garret contradicted her before Holt could respond. "I took the ransom note to your father last night. He intends to hand over the gold the moment he sees we have returned you to him safe and sound."

Shiloh gnashed her teeth and silently fumed. The thought of having Holt Cantrell sashay off with the payroll money galled her no end. She would prefer to meet with disaster than to have this miserable blackguard's scheme meet with success.

Giving way to that spiteful thought, Shiloh gouged her heels into her mount's flanks, sending him lunging into his swiftest pace. She wasn't certain she could outrun this band of thieves, but she was determined to try. Maybe she couldn't change the outcome of this exchange of her life for the railroad payroll, but she damned sure wasn't going to make things easy for Holt!

A wordless scowl erupted on Holt's lips when Shiloh unexpectedly took off like a house afire. Rolling his eyes, he glanced at Garret, who was grinning from ear to ear.

"She's your wife. *You* go after her," Garret insisted. "She already took a chunk out of my arm and punctured my shins."

Bounding into the saddle, Holt galloped off in fast pursuit. He threaded through the maze of trees, cursing Shiloh's daring. If she broke her lovely neck during her escape attempt, he would never forgive himself. Good God, that woman never accepted fate for what it was. She persisted in taking matters into her own hands regardless of the odds or consequences. Holt wasn't sure if she was unusually courageous or just plain stupid. She took terrible risks. Blast it, sometimes this wild-haired hellion reminded him so much of himself it was scary!

As the thunder exploded overhead, Shiloh spared one hasty glance over her shoulder while she zigzagged back and forth beneath the low-hanging limbs. It was one glance too many. A pained squawk gushed from her lips when a branch rammed against her shoulder and scraped her off the saddle. Shiloh braced her arms in front of her as the ground flew up at her with incredible speed. But she still landed with a bone-jarring thud. Determined to escape, Shiloh bounded to her feet and sprinted away. Her heart thudded furiously when she heard the ominous pounding of hooves behind her and the foreboding creak of leather.

Like a vulture swooping down on its prey, Holt leaned out from the saddle. One steely arm hooked around Shiloh's waist as he whizzed by. A frightened yelp bubbled in her throat when her head snapped backward and her body was launched off the ground. Shiloh emitted a pained grunt when she found herself tossed over Holt's lap like a feed sack. And to further frustrate her, he whacked her on the derriere as if she were a misbehaving child.

"Good God, woman, don't you know when to quit?" Holt growled, bringing his steed to a skidding halt. When her body rolled toward the horse's neck, Holt clamped a hand around her to insure she didn't tumble to the ground.

"I'll never quit as long as I live and breathe," Shiloh spat at him. "Mark my words, Holt Cantrell, I'll see you hang for all your crimes."

"I'm beginning to think it might be worth it," he muttered crossly. "At least then you will be out of my life!"

"No, *you* will be out of *mine*," she corrected him. "You will be dead . . . which is exactly what you deserve, and I intend to insure you don't keep popping in and out of your grave by constructing a building on top of you!"

A gust of wind whizzed past Holt's face as he reined his steed in the direction her runaway mount had gone. While Shiloh jostled uncomfortably, Holt stared down at her shapely backside. Good God, what a feisty little vixen she was. He was just beginning to know her as other men did. He could understand why Shiloh tormented all the males in the world and why they longed to tame her. She was the spitting image of her father's fierce determination and her mother's southern-bred beauty. Victor had scratched and clawed to insure that he won the race to the border, and Shiloh fought tooth and nail to maintain her independence. Her fighting spirit demanded Holt's respect even if he was mad as hell at her for risking her life to escape him.

When Shiloh had slammed against the tree branch and toppled from her steed, Holt feared she had broken several bones. It never bothered him to confront life-threatening situations, but it scared the hell out of him when Shiloh did. Lord, this minx truly was a handful and he was just now discovering how much! He hadn't known exactly how defiant and daring she was until he got completely crosswise of her. Life had been so much simpler when he portrayed the foppish Reuben Gilcrest. At least then Shiloh had respected his good qualities. Now she hated every square inch of him.

It was on the tip of Holt's tongue to confess the truth. Shiloh would still despise him for tricking her, but at least she might understand why he had employed his charade to infiltrate the company. Then perhaps she wouldn't be so dead set on her crusade to hunt him down and watch him swing from the nearest tree.

A dribble of rain fell from the sky as Holt eased up beside Shiloh's steed. Impulsively, he decided to explain himself as best he could, hoping to mellow Shiloh's hatred for him. "Shiloh, I'm not what you think I am," Holt declared as he reached out to grasp her steed's trailing reins.

Her head jerked up from her folded position over the back of his horse. Her eyes sparked hatred. "You are everything I thought you were and worse!" she spluttered.

While his steed shifted uneasily with the squirming Shiloh on his back, Holt plucked her up and then deposited her in her own saddle. Keeping a tight grasp on her reins, Holt leaned over to tie Shiloh's wrists to the pommel. He had no intention of allowing her to leap off her horse and tear through the timbers again.

"Walter was swindling money from company funds under J. W. Baxter's orders," he informed her as he led her back to the other men. "He is also the one who planned the raid on the supply train. I had him locked away in jail for safekeeping."

A muddled frown knit her brow. That made no sense, she mused as she stared at Holt's broad back. "If you exposed Walter as an extortioner, why are you planning to rob the payroll car?" she wanted to know that very instant.

"Because I want Kirby Thorn," Holt muttered bitterly. He hadn't meant resentment to seep into his voice. But the mere mention of the man's name always left a bitter taste in Holt's mouth.

"Who in Hades is Kirby Thorn?" Shiloh quizzed him bewilderedly.

"The man who raped and murdered Anna. . . ."

The tone in which Holt spoke Anna's name threw Shiloh for a loop. She still didn't have a clue what was going on, but she could decipher Holt's affection for the woman in the tone of his voice. Was Anna his wife or lover? Knowing there had been other women in Holt's life cut her to the quick. It hurt to know this man of many faces had used her body for sexual pleasure, but it nearly killed her to realize she had become a substitute for a ghost from Holt's past.

Holt's last comment shut Shiloh up like a clam. She knew more than she wanted to. Each time Holt imparted bits and pieces of information, Shiloh found herself to be a bigger fool than she was the previous moment.

Tormented beyond words, Shiloh allowed herself to be led back to the clump of men who waited on the riverbank. In grim procession the group scaled the steep incline beside the bridge and trotted down the tracks. Mutely, Shiloh sat in the saddle, listening to the clank of sledgehammers driving spikes, staring at her father's personal train and the bright-colored payroll car. Suddenly she didn't care much about anything. She only wanted her ordeal to be over so she could find a private place to fall apart. She kept hearing Holt's quiet words and they confused her. She didn't know what to believe or how she truly felt about him.

A steady drizzle dampened Shiloh's clothes and her mood. Her troubled gaze swung to the man who sat so tall and confident in the saddle. Behind the disguise of a beard, mustache, and wig was a man she knew better than anyone else in the world and yet she didn't know him at all. He was a liar and a thief, a master of charade. And yet he was the most responsive and tender lover imaginable. How she longed to recapture those few precious weeks with Reuben. If only he had been what he seemed! Shiloh could have been content to spend the rest of her life with him, even if he did stumble around like a clumsy dandy. She hadn't cared about his outward appearance, only the gentle, loving man who dwelt inside that mysterious shell. . . .

The touch of Holt's hand brought Shiloh back to the present. Her thick lashes swept up to see the rugged renegade beside her. Holt died a little inside when he peered into those captivating silver-blue eyes that dominated her pixielike face. What a beauty this nymph was, even in her boyish garb. He had never grown tired of feasting on her exquisite features, watching the sparkling radiance in her eyes when she smiled. She had been like a breath of spring in the middle of a gloomy winter night.

Holt was going to miss this high-spirited imp just as he had missed Anna when she was taken from him. But it was time Holt converged all thought and energy into setting his trap for Kirby Thorn. Two years had come and gone and Holt had a vow to keep. Kirby was long overdue in paying penance for his violence and murdering sprees during and after the war. He was an outlaw of the worst sort—a man who had no regard for human life. He was Lucifer in the flesh, and Holt wanted Kirby's long reign of terror put to an end.

Forcing a faint smile, Holt reached up to trace the

soft curve of Shiloh's lips. "This is where we say good-bye, Shiloh," he murmured. "My men will make the exchange."

"Ah, yes, how could I have forgotten that you're supposed to be dead," Shiloh sniffed sarcastically. "What a pity my father can't thank you for exposing Walter before you rob his payroll car."

There was no time for lengthy debate, only for hasty good-byes. Holt leaned out to plant a swift kiss on her unresponsive lips. Shiloh winced at the unfamiliar feel of his beard, but she was addicted to the intoxicating taste of his kiss. As he raised his shaggy head, Shiloh fought down the unwanted tingles his touch aroused and stared straight ahead.

When Garret grabbed the reins to lead Shiloh away, Holt stared unblinkingly at her rigid back. God, how he wished he were Reuben Gilcrest! He could have endured all the ridicule and mocking taunts if he were allowed to enfold Shiloh in his arms every night for the rest of his life. It would have been worth it. Shiloh was worth any price a man had to pay to earn her love.

Heaving a dispirited sigh, Holt watched Garret lead the sassy blonde out of his life once and for all. Now that Reuben Gilcrest was dead, Shiloh had intended to bury all affection for him. Holt had destroyed the special bond between them. Their love was no more than a fading memory. . . .

Chapter 25

Garret reined in his steed in front of Victor McBride, who stood poised on the platform of the payroll car, awaiting his daughter's return. Victor had cursed Shiloh soundly for charging off to avenge Reuben's death. But when it came down to it, nothing and no one meant more to him than his high-spirited daughter. His dreams for the railroad were dim shadows in comparison to the bright spot Shiloh was in his life. She had suffered enough. Victor wanted her safe and protected by his side, even if she was prone to impulsive wild-goose chases over hill and dale that got her into serious trouble.

Seeing Shiloh straddled on her steed, garbed in men's clothes, reminded Victor of her younger days, when, bent on proving her independence, she had taken to scampering off in garments more befitting a boy. That had been the rebellious phase of her life, he reflected. Shiloh had cast off the yoke of overprotectiveness and had wound up jilted by a silver-tongued adventurer who wanted to marry her for her fortune while her father was off battling the Confederates. Victor hadn't been there to console her, and he had returned from battle to find a very cynical young woman who compensated for having her heart broken by hiding behind a wall of fierce defense.

And then along came Reuben Gilcrest, a man who appeared to have absolutely nothing in common with the rambunctious but skeptical Shiloh. She had come to trust in men again, to believe in the existence of love. Then suddenly Reuben was gone and Shiloh was left to mourn, to avenge her loss.

It would have been easier on Victor if he could have lived Shiloh's life for her. He was accustomed to being in command. But Shiloh had grown very strong-willed while he was leading troops into battle. She had been knocked down and stepped on and Victor cringed, wondering what sort of invisible scars she would suffer after the incidents she had endured the past two days. He wanted more for his daughter, but life was never quite so kind as to allow men and women to enjoy their every whim.

"Are you all right?" Victor asked Shiloh when the huge masked man drew her steed up beside the payroll car.

"I'm fine," she muttered in a tone that indicated she was nothing of the kind. She was hurt and angry and confused.

While Garret and Victor prepared to make the exchange, Holt waited in the skirting of trees that lined the track. He was laboring under the delusion that his plans were neatly unfolding. He was unaware that Kirby Thorn had become suspicious when he sought out Walter Jameson and found the varmint had vanished into thin air. And he was downright furious when he spied his wanted poster hanging outside the sheriff's office.

Kirby smelled a rat. His experience in guerrilla warfare as a Confederate raider and his hit-and-run attacks along the Missouri and Kansas border the previous two years had made him a seasoned and very flexible outlaw. Since he was unable to locate Walter, Kirby had ridden back to his hideout to round up his men. Employing their technique of sneaking through the underbrush without being detected, Kirby and his brigands had gone to scout the position of the payroll car the day before he intended to rob it. To his delight, Victor McBride was perched on the platform, prepared to dole out the gold. The congregation of masked men who had somehow managed to convince the president of the company to hand over the gold were waiting to fill their saddlebags.

Sporting a devilish smile, Kirby crouched in the brush, waiting until the gold was stacked on the platform of the payroll car. The instant the canvas sacks of coins were carried outside, Kirby issued the order to strike. Armed to the teeth, Kirby and his desperadoes sprang into action. Thunder shook the countryside and all hell broke loose! Like a swarm of angry hornets, the bandits descended from the wooded hills to surprise Pinkerton's agents disguised as thieves.

"Get down!" Garret barked when a bullet whizzed past Shiloh's shoulder, missing her by scant inches.

But Shiloh had nowhere to go and no way to get there. Her hands were still strapped to the saddle horn. The best she could do was plaster herself to her prancing steed and pray there were no oncoming bullets with her name on them.

The railroad track suddenly became the site of a skirmish that was reminiscent of the battles fought between the Union and Confederate border gangs that ravaged Missouri during the war. Pistols barked in the air and men scattered like buckshot to defend themselves from the unexpected attack of Thorn's marauders.

Kirby Thorn set his sights on the sacks of gold that

had been stacked on the back platform of the payroll car. Sliding to the side of his steed, using the wide-eyed animal for protection, Kirby blasted his way to the coupling between the payroll and fuel cars. With his men providing cover for him, Kirby unlatched the cars. When half the train rolled backward, Pinkerton's men were forced to dive for cover.

Although Garret tried to grab Shiloh's dangling reins with his free hand, the skittish horse bolted forward under gunfire. As the cars gained momentum on their downhill roll, Shiloh's steed rushed toward safety. But as fate would have it, Kirby had just bounded back to the saddle when Shiloh galloped toward him. He didn't know who the young woman in men's clothes was, but he recognized the enchanting face of the sassy wench he had met in Primrose.

Kirby had never been a man to turn down a pretty woman when she practically landed in his lap. Women were his weakness. When Shiloh's steed swerved beside him, Kirby thrust out an arm to latch on to her. But instead of depositing her on his lap, Kirby was yanked sideways because her wrists were tied to the pommel.

It was obvious that Kirby's second language was profanity. He erupted in sizzling oaths and curses when he was ripped from his saddle. Kirby clawed to grab hold of Shiloh's steed. Agilely, he hopped on behind Shiloh, employing her as his protective armor.

Wheeling the frightened steed around with a fierce jerk, Kirby aimed himself toward the wobbling cars that rocked down the hill. Racing along the back side of the cars, Kirby snatched up two sacks of gold. He had wanted it all, but he feared he would be forced to settle for less when his men found themselves confronted with sharpshooters who displayed amazing abilities with weapons.

When the other bandits saw Kirby scoop up the

unattended sacks of gold, they circled to utilize the same tactic. Some of the desperadoes were successful in their feats. Some weren't. The Pinkertons picked off three men like flies when they appeared in the opening between the railroad cars. But the three men who met with success followed their leader, who rode on the opposite side of the rolling cars for protection from the blazing rifles of Pinkerton's men.

Holt's heart had stopped dead still in his chest when he saw Kirby swing up behind Shiloh. "Son of a bitch," he growled when Kirby took off with Shiloh like a bolt of lightning.

He didn't give a damn if anyone recognized him. He was driven by the terrifying fear that Shiloh would wind up like Anna. Holt leapt into his saddle in a single bound. Like a bat out of hell, Holt charged from his hiding place in the trees to cut off Kirby before he escaped.

The instant Kirby spied the daring rider approaching from his flank, he plastered himself against Shiloh. With his pistol blazing, Kirby fired at Holt, and he swore he would have hit his challenger between the eyes if Shiloh hadn't bucked like a wild bronc, causing the shot to go astray. Shiloh had spitefully vowed to see Holt stabbed, shot, poisoned, and hanged for what he had done to her. But the thought of this scraggly hoodlum stealing her thunder was too much. If anyone was going to blow Holt Cantrell out of the saddle, it was going to be her, not some despicable bandit who reeked of whiskey and perspiration. And as much as Shiloh hated to admit it, her deeply embedded feelings for Holt refused to allow her to sit idly by to watch him die. She had seen him perish once already, and she was not about to endure that anguish again.

Cursing in foul profanity that burned Shiloh's ears, Kirby headed for the cover of the bridge and plunged down the slippery slope. One of his men was not fortunate enough to follow suit. Although Holt had been unable to bury a bullet in Kirby's cold heart without shooting through Shiloh, he had picked off one of the desperadoes.

Giving chase, Holt fired again, hoping to make Kirby's departing back his target. But Kirby was no fool. He curled himself around Shiloh like the snake he was, leaving only his rump as a target. As the three horses skidded down the slick embankment, Holt bellowed at Garret, who had mounted his steed the moment he saw his friend give frantic chase to Kirby and his captive.

While the other Pinkerton agents chased down the two men who had given up their attempt to retrieve the gold and had scattered into the hills, Garret thundered after Holt.

Frantically, Kirby glanced behind him, searching for a means of escape. He was familiar with the area and he knew exactly where to find the farm where he had holed up two years earlier. It was at the Cantrell cottage that he and Bob Henson had battled for the rights to a sassy beauty. After the confrontation the gang had split up. Kirby and half the men had ridden off to Texas. But Kirby remembered all too well the quaint cottage in the Ozark foothills. The farm was perfectly located on the side of a slope that allowed its inhabitants to keep a close lookout on activities. Since he didn't have time to circle back to his new hideout three miles away, he headed for the Cantrell homestead.

Nothing suited Holt better than to entrap Kirby at the cottage. But there was one gigantic hitch—Shiloh. Murdering fury pelleted Holt as he dodged the maze of trees that lined the trail to his family's homestead. The last thing he intended was that Kirby take Shiloh captive. Kirby wouldn't use her as a hostage in exchange for the rest of the gold, not before he molested her the way he had molested Anna. Kirby Thorn was unpredictable in many instances. He had quickly changed his mind about robbing the payroll car because the moment was ripe. But in some ways Kirby was easy to second-guess. He was a ruthless, lusty man who took what he wanted and then discarded women when he tired of them or when they pushed him to the end of his short, violent temper. During the war Kirby had acquired a taste for killing. He thrived on violence, and his disregard for others' lives made him a most formidable foe. He had no loyalty to anyone, and he had been known to kill his own men if they dared to cross him. His ex-partner Bob Henson had come dangerously close to losing his life at Kirby's hands.

The firm tug on Holt's arm jostled him from his thoughts. Garret refused to loose Holt's arm until he had reined the mount to a halt. When Holt jerked to a stop, he glared into Garret's broad face.

"You're letting the past influence your thinking," Garret growled. "Don't drive Kirby past the cabin. If you're breathing down his neck, he might keep right on riding."

Holt knew Garret was right. He was allowing his emotions to do his thinking for him, and he was overeager to remove Shiloh from Kirby's clutches. But, dammit, Kirby had Shiloh, and it scared the hell out of Holt! How was he supposed to think straight under those unnerving conditions?

"Let Kirby tuck himself into the cottage, thinking he lost us," Garret advised. "You already warned the farm-hands to head for cover if someone like Kirby showed up. They will be safely tucked away. And if you wait for the rest of the men to catch up with us, we will outnumber them three to one. Tonight, while they're sleeping, we can converge on them."

"Tonight?" Holt snorted incredulously. "By tonight Kirby will have raped Shiloh once or twice and then he'll kill her because she's too damned feisty for her own good! You saw how she attempted to escape even when she was surrounded by a throng of our men! She's got more daring than I do, for crying out loud!"

Garret fell silent. His head swiveled on his wide shoulders, wishing the other detectives would magically appear. "I still don't think it's a good idea to move in so soon," he mumbled. "They'll be as jumpy as grasshoppers."

Cold green eyes riveted on Garret's somber face. "Have you got a better idea that will insure Shiloh lives to greet another sunrise?"

"Well, no, not right offhand," Garret grumbled sourly. "It would have been a helluva lot better if you had infiltrated Kirby's gang. I'd feel more confident if you were on the inside, like you usually are."

Holt stared bleakly at the hill on which the cottage sat. "So would I, Garret, so would I. . . ."

The picture forming in Holt's mind drove him mad with frustration. For two years he had lived for this confrontation, had dreamed about it. But now he was considering setting Kirby free to spare Shiloh's life. If Holt thought Kirby would allow him to exchange places with Shiloh, he would have made the offer. But knowing what a lusty beast Kirby was, Holt expected to be shot on the spot for making the suggestion. Inevitably, Shiloh would be forced to endure that outlaw's ruthless molestation.

In torment Holt surveyed the scant rays of sunshine that spilled down from the sky after the thunderstorm rolled northeast to drench Primrose. Only a distant rumble of thunder broke the stilted silence. With his mouth set in a grim line, Holt nudged his steed toward the two-story barn that was built into the hillside.

"What are you going to do?" Garret called after him.

"I'm going after Shiloh," Holt informed him matter-of-factly.

Garret rolled his eyes heavenward, requesting divine assistance in this critical situation. Lord, he and Holt needed all the help they could get! "You'll get yourself killed, sure as hell," he muttered bitterly.

"Maybe," Holt agreed. "But I can't wait until dark. Shiloh may not last that long."

"And I'll be planning a double funeral," Garret exploded in frustration.

"You ride back to round up the men," Holt threw over his shoulder. "If you open fire, maybe you can distract the bandits while I sneak in through the tunnel."

"Give me an hour," Garret pleaded, spinning his steed around.

"A lot can happen in an hour, Garret," Holt snorted derisively.

"All right, dammit, then give me thirty minutes to get back here," Garret insisted before he thundered down the hill as fast as his horse could gallop on the slick grass without slamming into a tree.

Clinging to the cover of the timber, Holt approached the barn with his faithful dog trailing along behind him. Swinging down, he strode through the stalls and climbed the ladder to the loft. Behind the shocks of straw was an inconspicuous door that led into the tunnel he and Garret had dug from the barn to the cellar of the cottage. Holt had devised the idea after seeing a similar tunnel employed as a hideout for a gang of thieves who operated in Indian territory. The tunnel had eventually cost the bandits their lives. Pinkerton's agents had kept surveillance on the area and noticed the gang entering and disappearing into thin air. A careful search had led to the door in the back of a storage building that sat a good distance from the cabin. The outlaws were eventually trapped in their own tunnel, smoked out, and picked off one at a time.

Plunking down on the straw, Holt bided his time until Garret returned with the detectives. He hadn't meant to intertwine the McBride assignment with his relentless search for Kirby Thorn, but Walter had entangled them and Shiloh had been caught in the middle. Holt closed his eyes and cursed vehemently. He never should have taken the McBride assignment in the first place. All he had succeeded in doing was hurting Shiloh, not to mention the risk of getting her raped and killed by one of the country's most ruthless renegades. Holt should have gone in search of Kirby Thorn, no matter how much time the manhunt consumed, no matter what Pinkerton thought of the idea.

While Holt sat there, stewing and brooding, he sent a prayer heavenward, offering himself in Shiloh's stead. If anybody had to die, it should be him. Holt was good at it. After all, he had himself killed a dozen times the past few years. Holt wasn't a pessimist. He was a realist. The chances of both Shiloh and him coming out of this alive were odds that even the most daring gambler wouldn't take. There were three outlaws holed up at the cottage and none of them would bat an eyelash at committing another murder. It was second nature to them. One false move on Holt's part and he and Shiloh would both be trying on a pair of wings at the pearly gates!

"Son of a bitch," Holt scowled as he checked his timepiece. Thirty minutes an eternity when Shiloh's life was at stake. . . .

364

Chapter 26

Shiloh jerked away after Kirby had slung her around like a rag doll. She recognized the scalawag who had taken her captive, but she didn't really care who the blazes he was. No one was going to manhandle her! Her temper had been sorely put upon the past two days. She had lost it thrice and hadn't bothered to find it. This ruffian's rough handling put her in another snit.

A life-threatening quirk of Shiloh's character was her tendency to become angry when being scared was the safer, more natural reaction. She did not appreciate being cornered by the man who had leered at her in Primrose and who had abducted her. Her independent nature protested being pushed and shoved around as if she were a stupid mule.

"Get your hands off me," Shiloh spewed, slapping at Kirby's stubby hand, one that rested on her derriere.

Her abrupt command earned her a hand across the cheek. Stumbling backward, Shiloh landed on the same sofa where Holt had forced her to sleep by his side the previous night. She would have traded this abusive bastard for that green-eyed, lying sneak any day. At least Holt had never physically attacked her when she lost her temper.

A furious squawk erupted from her lips when Kirby lunged on top of her, pressing his perspiring body intimately between her thighs. Shiloh scratched and clawed with every ounce of strength to discourage him from raping her, but Kirby was a persistent cuss.

"Damn!" Kirby yelped when Shiloh peeled the hide off his face with her nails and bit a hole in his shoulder. "You're a feisty little bitch, ain't you?" His devilish smile revealed the space between his two front teeth. "You probably ain't accustomed to having a real man on top of you after sleeping with that dandy of a husband."

"Hey, Kirby," one of the bandits called from the kitchen. "There's enough food to keep us for a week."

Shiloh froze when she discovered who had captured her. Sweet mercy! This was the man Holt was trailing—the man who had murdered Anna. Shiloh swallowed with an apprehensive gulp. Now she was more afraid than angry!

The instant Kirby climbed to his feet, Shiloh vaulted off the couch and shot toward the door like a discharged cannonball. Before she could fly to freedom, Kirby mashed her into the door through which she tried to escape. Roughly, he grabbed her around the waist and jerked her off the floor. Shiloh fought valiantly for release but Kirby clamped on to her, forbidding her from escaping him.

"I had the same trouble with the fiery little minx who used to live in this house," Kirby growled in her ear. "If you don't watch your step, woman, you'll wind up dead, just like Anna did. . . ."

"Better dead than repulsed by filthy scum like you," Shiloh hissed like a disturbed cat.

Kirby's vicious temper exploded. He doubled his fist and punched Shiloh in the jaw. A dull moan tripped off her bleeding lips when the punishing blow knocked her off her feet. Swearing profusely, Kirby jerked Shiloh's unconscious body into his arms and carried her into the bedroom. A wicked grin puckered his homely features as he tossed her on the bed and proceeded to tie her hands and feet to the bedposts. This sassy vixen had issued him a challenge. She would endure his touch, he promised himself as his gray eyes raked her shapely figure. And she would be fully awake when he took her again and again. Chuckling diabolically to himself, Kirby reversed direction to the kitchen to round up some food before he helped himself to this tantalizing morsel of femininity for dessert.

A throbbing headache plowed through Shiloh's skull when she climbed from the depths of unconsciousness. Her swollen jaw complained when she tried to lick the dried blood from her lips. Bitter hatred coursed through her veins when she realized she had been strapped spread-eagle to the bed. The click of boot heels in the hall caused her to flinch in gloomy anticipation of what Kirby Thorn planned for her. But when he appeared at the door, Shiloh pretended to be unconscious.

Unfortunately for her, Kirby had checked on her once already and he was not a patient man when it came to satisfying his lusts. "Wake up, bitch!" he demanded, shaking her shoulders.

Well, so much for pretending not to be awake, Shiloh mused dispiritedly. Now she had to pretend to be dead, pretend she felt nothing—not the humiliation, the pain, degradation—nothing. Kirby may rape her, but she would not permit him to break her spirit. And if she died, she would do so knowing that Holt Cantrell would hunt Kirby down and put a bullet through his black heart for murdering Anna. . . .

The rending of cloth forced Shiloh to accept the harsh reality of what was about to happen. Her body tensed when Kirby loomed over her to tear away the chemise beneath her ripped shirt. Shiloh couldn't contain the bloodcurdling scream that erupted from her lips when Kirby tore her undergarment down the middle, leaving it gaping between her breasts.

"Now, little wildcat," Kirby chuckled victoriously. "You're gonna have a real man." His words dropped like stones in the silence as he unbuckled his holsters and raked her with his beady gray eyes.

Holt scuttled through the dark passageway with Dog tagging along behind him. Quietly, he lifted the trapdoor in the cellar and eased to his feet. With the silence of a stalking tiger, he climbed the steps to reach the ground floor. Holt pricked his ears to the voices of the bandits who were lounging in his parlor. Shiloh's piercing scream broke the silence and cut through the air like shattering glass. Holt whipped out his pistol, prepared to shoot anything that crossed his line of vision.

Shots rang out around the cottage, and Holt heard the two men in the parlor curse a blue streak as they dived for cover. Swiftly, he moved down the hall to the bedroom from whence Shiloh's frightened shriek had come.

Kirby was prepared to drop his breeches when he heard the explosion of rifles. Growling in disgust, he wheeled around. His gray eyes widened in disbelief when Holt's massive frame filled the doorway. Where the hell had this man come from? And who was he?

Holt's murderous glare flicked first to Shiloh's bruised face and torn garments. His skin crawled with disgust and hatred for the man who had put such fear in this courageous woman's eyes. The shaken expression on her face tore at Holt's heart. Still holding Kirby at gunpoint, Holt cautiously reached into his boot to retrieve his knife. With a quick flick of his wrist Holt sliced the rope tied to Shiloh's right hand. After he tossed her the knife to cut herself free, he focused absolute attention on Kirby, who was glancing in every direction at once, mentally planning his escape.

Gunning Kirby down after two years didn't seem satisfaction enough. Holt would prefer to tear this murdering bastard apart with his bare hands. Yielding to that temptation, Holt laid his pistol on the bed beside Shiloh.

Icy green eyes drilled into Kirby, who prepared himself for hand-to-hand combat. But he wasn't expecting a vicious blow that instantly sent pain plowing through his soft underbelly. Stumbling back to catch his balance, Kirby dodged the next oncoming punch and kicked like a mule. To his chagrin, Holt caught his foot and flipped him into a tangled heap. Weaving a tapestry of obscenities that hung over the room like a cloud, Kirby rolled away. But as agile as he was, he was no match for Holt's lightning-quick attack. Holt sprang on him like a hungry cougar devouring his prey. For what seemed an eternity, Kirby was hammered by meaty fists that split flesh and cracked bone. Blindly, Kirby shoved at his overpowering foe, but Holt was intent on beating his victim to a bloody pulp, intent on avenging every horrifying moment Anna and Shiloh had suffered.

While Shiloh cut herself loose, she stole glances at the two men who were rolling and tumbling around on the floor, emitting malicious growls and snarls. Never in her life had she expected Holt to be so proficient with his fists. He had portrayed the clumsy Reuben Gilcrest for so long that Shiloh was shocked by this phenomenal display of combat. Holt was so light on his feet that Kirby couldn't land a solid blow. And when Holt reared back to strike, she swore she heard Kirby's teeth rattling in his head. Never in all her life had she seen anyone so skillful with his fists and feet. Holt's entire body had become a lethal weapon. He was vindictive fury personified, and Kirby had become a mushy punching bag.

"Kirby! Get out here!" one of the desperadoes roared. "We've got trouble."

But Kirby didn't come. He had his own trouble in the bedroom. Frantic, he kicked Holt in the groin, causing him to double over momentarily. While Holt gasped for breath, Kirby reached into his right boot for his dagger. The blade swished through the air and Holt shot sideways to escape being slashed to shreds. Cautiously, he circled his foe, waiting for the perfect moment to strike. Shiloh, who had freed herself, crouched on her knees on the bed and clutched Holt's pistol. How she itched to pull the trigger and blow Kirby to smithereens. But she couldn't risk hitting Holt. He was as eager to have his revenge on Kirby as Shiloh was, and his constant movement made it impossible to get off a clear shot at Kirby.

"Who the hell are you?" Kirby sneered out the side of his mouth that wasn't swollen twice its normal size.

"Cantrell," Holt growled between clenched teeth.

Kirby's eyes widened when the name struck a chord of memory. With the dagger from his left boot poised like a sword, he lunged at Holt, knowing his competent challenger had a personal vendetta against him. It was kill or be killed.

A muted groan erupted from Kirby's puffy lips when Holt kicked the hand that held the dagger. As the knife clanked to the floor, footsteps resounded in the hall.

"Dammit, Kirby, I said get out here! There's a whole

passel of bushwhackers surrounding the house. . . ."

"Dog!" Holt barked as the desperado barged through the bedroom door.

Shiloh would never have believed the mongrel who had appeared as good-natured as Reuben Gilcrest could turn into such a vicious, snarling beast. Dog's tail was usually swaying in a permanent wag. But when Holt issued his sharp command, the huge mutt laid back his ears and sprang through the air. His lips curled to reveal the long, deadly fangs. His threatening growl was enough to make the hair stand up on the back of Shiloh's neck. The mutt sank his teeth into the bandit's arm, instantly drawing blood. With a terrified yelp the outlaw shrank back, but Dog wasn't letting go until his master gave him the command. He tore gashes in the desperado's arm, pouncing again and again until the man lay sprawled on the floor, screaming bloody murder.

Shiloh's wild-eyed gaze bounced back and forth between Dog and Holt, wishing she could vent some of her frustration. This fight was hers as well as Holt's, and she wanted to inflict a few blows on Kirby Thorn while he still had his wits about him so he'd remember who had hit him. But Holt was pulverizing Kirby, punishing him with blow after blow.

Shiloh got her chance to aid in the battle when the third bandit darted into the room with his pistol poised in front of him. With her heart pounding in her throat, she squeezed the trigger. The bandit pitched forward before he could shoot Dog loose from his cohort.

When Shiloh glanced back at Holt, he had straddled Kirby on the floor. As Kirby grasped the discarded dagger, Holt clamped on to his wrist. Two pair of murderous eyes locked as both men matched their strength. The knife that was aimed at Holt's belly slowly turned toward Kirby's heaving chest.

371

"You murdering bastard, this is for Anna. . . ." Holt snarled as rage spurted through his body, giving him superhuman strength.

The blade plunged into Kirby's chest and Shiloh glanced the other way, sickened by the dead bodies that were strewn around the room. The moment Dog had downed his foe he went for the throat while Holt went for the heart. Shakily, Shiloh dropped the pistol she had used to kill the third desperado. With a horrified cry Shiloh bounded off the bed and into Holt's outstretched arms, bleeding tears on his tattered shirt.

Through the foggy mist she glanced up to see half of Holt's mustache and beard dangling from the side of his cheek. "Your face is falling off," she informed him between sniffles.

Her trembling hand rose to press the disguise back into place, but the distraction didn't aid in reconstructing her shattered composure. Suddenly she burst out in hysterical sobs. Shiloh realized that she had never really had anything to cry about until the past two days. Her emotions had been torn asunder and the tears leaked through the cracks in her self-control.

Lovingly, Holt cradled Shiloh in his arms. He hadn't wanted her to see the bloodbath or be a party to it, but there had been no choice. Now, at long last, he could bury the ghosts that haunted this cottage. The deaths had been avenged and Shiloh was safe.

For several moments Holt held Shiloh close and let her have her cry. She certainly deserved one after all she had been through. The tautness ebbed from his own rigid body when he reminded himself that the long, tormenting wait was over. His crusade had put an end to Kirby Thorn's killing spree. Never again would that menacing renegade strike fear in the hearts of Missouri citizens or leave a smoldering path of destruction behind him. Now Shiloh was safe and Kirby was on his way to hell.

Holt closed his eyes and drew Shiloh as close as he could without squeezing the stuffing out of her. Tenderly, his lips grazed her forehead, whispering consolation while she spilled an unbelievable river of tears. Good God, he never dreamed this petite minx had so much water in her! He had never seen her cry until the previous day, and suddenly she had become an eternal spring.

"Shh . . . shh . . . it's over now," he murmured against her bruised cheek. "You can go home, where you belong. I will never hurt you again, Shiloh." He bent his raven head to press a kiss to her quivering lips. "You can forget me and this entire nightmare. But don't ever forget how much Reuben loved you. . . . I swear to God he did. . . ."

Shiloh wilted beneath the most incredible kiss ever bestowed upon her. Holt had kissed her dozens of times, but never quite as reverently as he did just then. She could feel him breathing life back into her, reviving the strength that had been depleted during her terrifying ordeal. He touched her and the memories came back to life, refueling her spirit. Behind her closed eyes she could see rainbows and sparkling mountain springs. Holt's masculine fragrance filled her senses, and she breathed him, tasted him, touched him. His stirring embrace triggered the sweet splendor from another lifetime, and Shiloh let herself drift in the memories of time past.

And for an immeasurable moment Shiloh forgot everything except the hypnotic spell this mysterious man had cast upon her. She was left suspended in a fog of pleasure that healed her cuts and bruises and smoothed the wrinkles from her troubled soul. . . .

Chapter 27

It had all happened so quickly and Shiloh wasn't sure how. One moment she was nestled in Holt's protective arms, feeling his sensuous lips move expertly over hers. The next instant she found herself standing alone. The faint aroma of smoke had filled her nostrils and she fled the house. Shiloh had glanced bewilderedly around her, but Holt and his devoted mongrel had vanished into thin air, just as he had appeared to save her from Kirby's degrading assault.

Dazed, she stared at the rolling smoke and leaping flames while she clutched her torn garments over her breasts. She would have thought the recent rain would have prevented the cottage from blazing like a torch, but the brittle lumber crackled beneath the holocaust of fire that consumed it. In confused astonishment Shiloh watched the inching fingers of flame crawl up the roof of the quaint cottage, engulfing it. She kept expecting Holt to make a mad dash from the house any second. But he never came. The men who had provided gunfire from the circle of trees were nowhere to be seen. Shiloh was left alone to watch the cottage with its shattered windows and bullet-notched walls tumble beneath the intense heat and dancing flames. Shiloh wasn't sure how or where the fire started. Her mind had been fogged by the terrifying incident. She could only speculate that a stray bullet had ignited it or one of the bandits had knocked over a lantern. Whatever the cause, the cottage was being consumed by fire and nothing could save it.

Shiloh had no idea how and when Holt had exited from the smoke-filled house, but she refused to believe he had perished with the three men who had met their match in Holt Cantrell. Holt was an escape artist who died and returned from the grave at will. He was around here somewhere, waiting to slip into another disguise to do only God knew what. . . .

"Shiloh!" Victor's rumbling voice conveyed his concern. Bounding from his steed, Victor rushed to his daughter, crushing her in his arms. "Oh, baby, I was so worried about you!" he said breathlessly.

"I'm fine, Papa," she assured him as he mashed her nose against his shoulder.

"When that scoundrel made off with you I was afraid . . ." Victor didn't complete the thought. He wasn't sure Shiloh had managed to escape unscathed this time. Her ripped garments and bruised face indicated she had been abused. To what extent, Victor didn't know.

"Nothing happened," she insisted. "Reuben found me before I was . . . oh, Papa!" Shiloh choked on a sob.

Victor didn't seem shocked by her announcement that Reuben had miraculously returned from the dead. That made Shiloh a mite suspicious. Wiping away the tears, Shiloh peered up into Victor's somber expression.

"You knew all along, didn't you?" she accused him harshly. "Are you going to tell me what the devil is really going on around here or must I force it out of you?"

When Shiloh pushed away from him as if he were as deceitful as Reuben Gilcrest, Victor refused to meet his daughter's agitated glare.

"Now, before you get mad . . ."

"Get mad?" Shiloh muttered peevishly. "I'm already mad! My own father has kept me in the dark! I thought you and I had no secrets."

Victor placed his hands on Shiloh's rigid shoulders and finally met her fuming glare. "I couldn't tell you what was going on, honey. It is difficult to trap a rat if the whole world knows what's coming."

Shiloh was growing madder by the minute. "Dammit all, I want to know what was happening when I didn't know anything out of the ordinary was happening," she demanded tartly. "And don't you dare leave out even one little detail!"

Curling his arm around her shoulders, he led her away from the blaze that engulfed the home in the Ozark hills. "The truth is, I met Holt Cantrell, Garret Robertson . . . he's the burly giant who kidnapped me," he informed Shiloh, and then grimaced when she spewed several unladylike curses.

When she finished muttering oaths, Victor continued. "As I was saying, we met during the war. Holt and Garret were involved in espionage missions and became legendary for their ability to walk back and forth between Union and Confederate lines, providing us with valuable information. Their unique talent earned them Pinkerton's recognition."

"Pinkerton?" Shiloh's silver-blue eyes riveted on Victor's weary features. "Are you referring to the Pinkerton Detective Agency? The man I met in St. Louis?" she chirped incredulously.

Victor nodded. "Holt and Garret had been working for Pinkerton since the middle of the war. A dozen times Holt brought me valuable information about

Confederate plans of attack and the location of their strongholds. Holt's exceptional techniques and bold daring have made him one of Pinkerton's most sought-after detectives. He usually takes on the most difficult assignments and names his own price."

He paused to assist Shiloh onto her steed, trying to ignore the accusing glances she was bestowing on him for refusing to take her into his confidence. "When J. W. Baxter accused me of cheating and scheming to win the race to the border, he hired the Pinkertons to investigate. Baxter also requested that Pinkerton send his best detective."

A wry smile pursed Victor's lips as he pulled into the saddle. "But thank God Allan Pinkerton and Holt considered me to be an honest man. Because of our friendship during the war, Holt came to see me before he slipped into his disguise of Reuben Gilcrest. He informed me of Baxter's accusations. I told him he had free rein to do what needed to be done because I had nothing to hide."

When Shiloh's temper was in full bloom, anger burst out all over. She was irate that her own father hadn't taken her into his confidence. "So I was the only one who didn't know what was going on!" she spurned resentfully.

Victor diplomatically rephrased Shiloh's remark. "No, I was the only one in the company who knew what was going on." His sapphire-blue eyes focused on his daughter's condemning frown. "I wanted you to accept Reuben into our home without fearing that I was shoving another prospective husband at you. But I don't think I was to blame for what happened between the two of you."

Shiloh pretended to be distracted by the clump of trees through which they rode. The subject of being found abed with Reuben/Holt was a sensitive one, especially since she knew he had deceived her.

"But I openly admit I would have been satisfied to have Holt Cantrell as my son-in-law. I am quite fond of the man. And under the circumstances I had no recourse but to insist on marriage. I only wish—" Victor squelched his whim and sighed disappointedly. "Well, we both know a man like Holt cannot look back on his past. It is an occupational hazard that he must close all doors behind him when he moves from one assignment to another."

Victor ducked beneath a low-hanging branch. "To make a long story short, I have been informed that Walter was guilty of siphoning funds and framing me. But I was shocked when Holt dug so deep to discover that Walter was actually working for J. W. Baxter, who intended to sabotage and bankrupt the company so he could take us over."

Shiloh blinked at the news. It seemed Holt Cantrell was indeed an exceptional detective. She supposed she should thank him for saving her father's reputation and sparing him embarrassment and financial ruin. But she was still humiliated to think she had been a pawn in his clever ploy, not to mention that he had lied to her on a number of occasions.

"The whole incident surrounding my kidnapping was carefully planned, Shiloh," Victor declared. "Holt wanted to strike fear in Walter, hoping he would think his scheme to have the payroll stolen by another gang of hoodlums had gone awry. Holt needed to shed his disguise so he could confront Walter and force a confession out of him. The men who kidnapped me and supposedly killed Reuben Gilcrest are Pinkerton's men, every last one of them."

Shiloh was thoroughly bewildered and frustrated. She had been hoodwinked so many times, it made her head spin. And to top it all off, Holt let her believe he was the leader of an outlaw gang whose intent it was to rob the train. Sweet mercy, she had said some horrible things to Holt, and all he had been trying to do was save an old army friend from disaster. She couldn't forgive him for stealing her innocence and allowing her to think he was something he wasn't, but she did owe him a great deal for sparing her family scandal and ruin.

"There is something you must understand, honey," Victor said gently. "Changing personalities and disguises is part of Holt's life. There is no better agent in Pinkerton's band than Holt Cantrell. He accepts dangerous assignments and receives none of the glory for his efforts. Garret is the one who has to take all the praise, the man who appears to possess all the legendary talents of sniffing out criminals and bringing them to justice. But the truth is Holt is the clever force that moves mountains in the world of law enforcement. There are some folks who are suspicious of strangers asking questions. They are leery of offering information because of a fear for their own personal safety. For that reason it is often necessary for Holt to go undercover to succeed in his assignments."

Victor reached out to clutch Shiloh's hand, imploring her to meet his solemn gaze. "Holt had no intention of hurting you. I know that and you should too . . . if you will look past your anger to consider why he had to handle the situation the way he did. Holt endured the taunts while he played the role of Reuben Gilcrest because his ultimate goal was more important than having to endure Walter and Felicia poking fun at his foppish clothes and seeming lack of coordination. It was all part of his job—one he does exceptionally well. Holt Cantrell is what myths and legends are made of."

Shiloh stared into her father's eyes, reading his sincere wish that she would accept what he was trying not to say. He was subtly informing her that her marriage was over. At the moment Shiloh wasn't certain how she felt about the man who was the recipient of her father's glowing accolades. Holt Cantrell might well be the best detective on Pinkerton's force, but he had broken her heart and trounced on her pride. As much as she admired what Holt had done, she was still bitter about his treatment of her, still wary of his confessions of love.

What difference did it make if that green-eyed rogue did or didn't love her? she asked herself glumly. She would never see him again. He would be off to another assignment, never to return. In a month he would probably forget she even existed. And if Shiloh knew what was good for her, she would bury all the emotions Holt had aroused in her. What she felt for Holt Cantrell alias Reuben Gilcrest was part of another lifetime. She had to slam the door on the past and look toward the future, she told herself sensibly.

By the time the McBrides reached their private quarters on the train, Shiloh had made up her mind to wipe every memory of the midnight-haired detective out of her thoughts. She would forget all the hateful remarks she had made to him and the deceptive lies he had fed her. She was now a widow and she would behave like one.

Shiloh sighed heavily as she washed and changed into her stylish clothes. She had gotten over hating Holt for betraying her, but she wondered if she would ever get over loving him. Despite her lectures to herself, Holt Cantrell was a difficult man to forget. It was going to take some time, Shiloh knew. But only a fool would cling to memories that would only depress and torment her. . . .

"Would you like to see Holt one last time before he leaves?" Victor asked, studying Shiloh's rueful expression.

A frown puckered her brows as she busied herself by sweeping the long silver-blond strands into a bun on her head. "I don't think it would be such a good idea," she murmured.

"I thought perhaps you would like to retract some of the horrible things you said to him," Victor suggested with a wry smile. Garret had informed him of Shiloh's temper tantrum when she discovered Reuben Gilcrest had returned from the grave. "And it wouldn't hurt to thank him for a job well done, despite your personal conflicts with him."

Still Shiloh didn't respond. She simply stared at her father's reflection in the mirror and held the hairbrush in her hand tighter.

"Holt is presently on his way to retrieve Walter from jail and hand him over to Allan Pinkerton, who is due to arrive in Primrose tomorrow," Victor reported. "And by the first of next week, J. W. Baxter will be the one Garret Robertson arrests for sabotaging our company and disregarding government regulations for the railroad." He paused and then heaved a heavy sigh. "This is your last chance to tell Holt good-bye, honey. Later, you may wish you had and it will be too late to change your mind."

Shiloh wasn't sure she wanted to put her emotions through the meat grinder again. But she did owe Holt some sort of apology and gratitude for what he had done for her father. Finally she nodded, although reluctantly, to Victor's suggestion.

"I'm glad," Victor said with a wide smile. "Both of you will feel much better if you can part on a friendly note, at least I know I will. I'll have Garret send Holt a message that you would like to speak to him once more before he packs up and leaves."

*   *   *

But Holt didn't return that night. Shiloh began to fret over his disappearance. Had Holt decided to avoid meeting her again? She had been terribly rough on him, Shiloh reminded herself. Maybe he simply wanted to dwell on his memories of Anna.

Holt must have loved Anna deeply, Shiloh mused as she paced the confines of the elaborate parlor on wheels. Shiloh had probably been no more than a substitute for the wife or lover Holt had lost. He may have felt something for Shiloh, even love perhaps, but she would never mean as much to him as his first true love.

Disappointed that Holt didn't show up, Shiloh wandered outside while the railroad crew labored to lay their tracks while torchlights blazed in the night. The skipping shadow beside the sleeper car caught Shiloh's attention. Her heart leapt into double time when she spied the figure.

"Holt!" Shiloh scurried around the corner and into his arms without reminding herself to display any reserve. She hadn't intended to fly at him like a homing pigeon, but the instinct had become as natural to her as breathing.

Unfortunately, it wasn't Holt who clung to the shadows. Shiloh had accidentally flown into Garret Robertson's arms to plant a juicy kiss on his lips!

"Why, thank you, ma'am," Garret chuckled. "I wasn't expecting such a friendly greeting."

The darkness concealed the blush of embarrassment that stained her cheeks. "Where's Holt?" she asked, backing a respectable distance away.

"I don't rightly know, ma'am," he mumbled in concern. "Holt went to Primrose, but I haven't seen or heard from him." Garret bowed his head, unable to endure Shiloh's probing stare. "I suppose your father told you why Holt and I were here and what has been going on."

"He did," she assured him.

"I want to apologize for frightening and upsetting you. We never mean for innocent people to get involved in one of our assignments. But sometimes . . ." Garret expelled a long sigh. "Sometimes the good have to suffer to apprehend the wicked. But you should know that you were one of the lucky ones. The elderly couple whose home Kirby Thorn turned into his hideout for the past few weeks wasn't so fortunate. We buried them this afternoon. . . ."

Shiloh winced at the distressing news. She was indeed fortunate that Holt had arrived when he did to save her from imminent disaster. She would have become another of Kirby Thorn's victims.

"Holt was supposed to confer with your father before he handed Walter Jameson over to Pinkerton. Please tell the colonel I'll be in touch when I find out what the devil is keeping Holt."

Shiloh smiled graciously when the brawny giant tipped his hat to her and strode off into the darkness. But when she was alone, concern clouded her brow. What could be keeping Holt? Even his confidant didn't know what had become of him. And it was certain the only one who knew what was keeping Holt was Dog. That shaggy black-haired mongrel was always one step behind his master.

Still stewing, Shiloh walked off to relay Garret's message to her father. And it was well into the night before sleep found its way into her troubled thoughts. Shiloh did want to see Holt again, to assure him that she no longer despised him for his cunning charade, to hold him just once more before he walked out of her life forever. Good God, she missed him already, and he wasn't even gone! Or was he?

*   *   *

384

A soft, persistent nudge brought Shiloh from her restless sleep. Jerking back, Shiloh stared at the hand that had invaded her curtained berth in the sleeping car. Shiloh peeked through the drape, certain this time it was Holt who had come to wake her. And again she was disappointed. Garret's looming figure was framed by the moonlight that skipped through the open window. A grim frown was plastered on his rugged features.

"Come with me," he whispered urgently. "There is something you need to see. This time you're going to have Holt exactly where you want him. . . ."

Shiloh was baffled by Garret's words, but she quickly responded. When he lifted his arms, Shiloh leaned out to him. Once he had effortlessly set her to the floor, she padded into the dressing room to change into her clothes. Without riddling him with questions, she followed Garret's long, swift strides into the darkness from which he had come.

Chapter 28

Holt had stared at the distant curls of smoke that swirled above the cedars and pines. A melancholy smile had curved his lips while he reflected on the good times he'd had in the cottage on the hill and tried to forget the bad times. It had been a purely impulsive response on his part to set the house aflame. But he was glad he had burned it down. Holt had trod among the ghosts in that house for more than two years. He had no desire to return to the room where Shiloh had barely escaped rape, where three men had lain dead. All the sentiment that had once drawn him back to the family homestead was gone, destroyed by Kirby Thorn's evil deeds.

Someday Holt would rebuild, using the stone cellar that led into the secret passageway. But his new home on the hillside would be of his design, one that didn't remind him of the cottage of his childhood days and the tormenting massacre.

Holt hadn't waited for Shiloh to come to her senses and then fling herself from his arms. He knew she would eventually remind herself how much she despised him and that his arms were the last place she wanted to be. Besides, they had said good-bye twice already. Shiloh wanted him out of her life and he intended to do her the greatest favor a man could do for a woman who hated him—make a hasty exit.

Lost to a turmoil of memories, Holt had pointed himself toward Primrose to wrap up the loose ends of the McBride assignment. He intended to let Colonel McBride chew Walter out before he turned the sneaky sidewinder over to Allan Pinkerton, who was due to arrive in Primrose the following afternoon. Garret would be appointed to ride to Kansas and place Baxter under arrest.

The moment Holt entered Primrose, he aimed himself toward the sheriff's office. But to his shock and disgust, Deputy Kroeker met him at the door with a sawed-off shotgun. Holt had been in too much of a rush to notice the wanted poster for Tom Morris hanging outside the office.

"You are under arrest, Mr. Morris," Deputy Kroeker announced with a decided air of authority.

"Good God," Holt muttered. Cautiously, he raised his arms above his head as the deputy directed.

A victorious smile pursed Daniel's lips as he indicated the adjoining room that was lined with cells. "I set Walter Jameson free. Now you are going to occupy his cell until the gallows are constructed for Primrose's first hanging. You, Mr. Morris, are going to become an example for the other thugs who have been hanging around my town and are thinking they can swagger down the streets of Primrose without reprisal. You and your kind are giving *my* town a bad name and I will not tolerate it."

Daniel paused to listen to the rap of hammers and whining saws that were, at this very moment, erecting gallows at the west end of town.

Holt swore two blue streaks. Blast it, he had come to town to wrap up this case, not open another can of worms! *Jeezus,* this was just what he needed—an overeager deputy who had designated Primrose as *his* town.

"Your timing is poor, Mr. Morris," Daniel mocked as he nudged his captive toward the cell. "There was a battle between two rival gangs who had their sights set on the railroad payroll. You wouldn't happen to know anything about the incident, would you?"

"Of course not," Holt lied through gritted teeth. "I spent the whole day doing chores for my dear spinster aunt Mildred."

"I'll just bet you did." Daniel smirked sarcastically. "A man who is followed by a reputation like yours finds other activities to occupy his time—like robbing pay cars. But I intend to make it known that Primrose will not be a den for fugitives from justice or easy pickings for outlaw gangs. This is going to be a peaceful, law-abiding town, Mr. Morris. It's a shame you won't be around to see what a fine town Primrose turns out to be."

With a wordless scowl Holt plopped down on his cot to stare at the barred window. Hell's bells, he could get himself hanged because he neglected to send out notices that declared Tom Morris had died four months earlier. How could he have forgotten that detail? He had been too occupied with plans of hunting Kirby Thorn down.

"I'll fetch you some supper," Daniel announced before easing the door shut behind him.

Holt listened with abject frustration while the carpenters hammered away on the gallows. Just his luck that he had run headlong into an eager-beaver deputy who was trying to make a name for himself in the annals of law enforcement. Kroeker was undoubtedly bucking for promotion and recognition, and Holt Cantrell, alias Tom Morris, was about to become his ticket to fame. Damn. No, double damn, Holt thought after giving his predicament second consideration. It was bad enough that alias Tom Morris was scheduled to die a second time for his long list of offenses, but the worst of it was that Walter Jameson was running around loose. Now that scoundrel would have to be rounded up and only God knew where he had gone!

By dawn the following morning Holt was in the sourest mood imaginable. Rattling his tin cup against the bars, he summoned Deputy Kroeker. "You've made a mistake," he declared, unsure of what else to do except plead mistaken identity. "I'm not Tom Morris. Maybe I look like him, but that sure as hell isn't who I am!"

"I made no mistake. You did," Daniel snorted derisively. "You thought you could waltz in here to use my jail for your own purposes. But I found your wanted poster after you left the other night. I've been waiting for your return and you are going to be swinging before too long."

Holt's gaze flooded past the stocky deputy to see Garret and Allan Pinkerton standing in the outer office. Thank God, salvation! Pinkerton would devise a way to get him out of there, Holt comforted himself.

"Those two men can identify me," Holt insisted with great conviction. "I know both of them. Just ask them and they will tell you I'm not this Tom Morris character you're looking for."

Daniel glanced back at the visitors and frowned. Neither of them had made mention of the fact that an acquaintance of theirs was occupying a cell in jail.

"Gentlemen, could you step in here for a moment, please," he requested. "My prisoner claims you know each other."

Shock registered on Holt's weary features when Shiloh and Victor filed into the back room behind Allan and Garret. Shiloh had her hand curled possessively around Garret's arm, as if they were as chummy as two people could get. Shiloh had bitten a chunk out of Garret's arms and beaten his shins black and blue. Two days later she was leaning on him for support. What the hell was going on around here?

Holt was growing more exasperated by the second. The way the foursome was staring at him left him feeling like a circus freak. No one said a word. They all just stood staring back at him.

"Tell this overly ambitious deputy who I am," Holt demanded impatiently. "I've already lost enough sleep lying on that hard cot."

Allan gave him the once-over twice and thoughtfully brushed his hand over his beard. "I'm sorry, Deputy, but I don't recall ever seeing this man before in my life," he declared.

"Me neither," Garret chimed in with a deadpan expression.

Holt looked as if someone had punched him in the midsection. He stared frog-eyed at the men he had long called his friends. If this was their idea of a prank, it wasn't a damned bit funny, at least not from where Holt was standing. What the sweet loving hell were they trying to do? Help get him hanged? Good God, with friends like these, a man didn't need enemies!

Shiloh pushed her way through the men to stand directly in front of the cell. "Mr. Morris looks like one of the men who tried to rob my father's payroll car," she testified, studying Holt closely. "In fact, he looks exactly like the man who murdered my poor dear husband, Reuben." At this point Shiloh fished a kerchief from her purse and spilled a few crocodile tears into it. "This man is dressed in clothes similar to my husband's murderer. I'm sure he is the same man."

"I do believe you're right," Victor added with a nod of his head. "The sooner this man is hanged, the better off Primrose will be!"

Holt clenched the bars so hard his knuckles turned white. He wove a tapestry of obscenities such as he never had before. It seemed his so-called friends had decided to let him swing since they couldn't figure out how to spring him from jail. Damn, a jailbreak would have been a nice touch!

This was probably all Shiloh's doing, Holt silently seethed as he glared poison arrows at the weepy blonde. Shiloh had sworn she would make Holt pay for deceiving her. Victor, who worshiped the ground his daughter walked on, would see to it that Holt suffered for taking advantage of her. Garret, who was a sucker for a pretty face, had undoubtedly been coerced into siding with Shiloh because he felt so guilty about the ordeals she had suffered at Holt's hands. Even though Garret was big and burly, he was a soft touch for a woman, especially when she was in tears.

But Allan Pinkerton's denial was the one that really got Holt's goat. Holt had nearly gotten himself killed a score of times because Allan needed a difficult job done. Was this the thanks Holt got for all the years of dedicated service? Good God, he would be greeting St. Peter before he knew it!

"Now, don't you worry, Mrs. Gilcrest," Daniel soothed Shiloh, who was spilling a flood of tears into her handkerchief and wailing like a banshee. "Your husband's killer will pay his penance tomorrow."

"Tomorrow?" Holt parroted in disbelief. "What the hell happened to a fair trial and sentencing? You're a one-man vigilante committee!"

"I told you that you were going to be a shining

example of what happens to renegades who think they can overrun my town," Deputy Kroeker snapped back at his prisoner. "You are a menace to society, and your endless list of crimes is testimony enough for prosecution. We don't need a judge to sentence you."

"Is this your idea of justice?" Holt snorted disdainfully. "It sounds like your personal version of the Spanish Inquisition. Good God, I'm surprised you aren't planning to burn me at the stake! In case you have forgotten, you were sworn to uphold the law, not break it."

"I intend to put the fear of God in your kind, Mr. Morris," Daniel insisted. "You weren't concerned about justice when you were robbing banks and killing innocent bystanders in cold blood!"

When Shiloh wailed all the louder, Deputy Kroeker shuffled the congregation into the outer room and locked the door behind him. After Shiloh and Victor signed a complaint against Tom Morris, the foursome ambled back to the street, where Dog was still patiently but futilely waiting his master's return.

"Do you think Holt is worried?" Victor questioned Allan as they strolled down the boardwalk.

"He should be," Allan sniffed in annoyance. "It serves him right for not paying attention to details. He should have posted a notice after he finished with the Tom Morris alias. And he should have seen the wanted poster hanging outside the office before he blundered inside."

Shiloh broke into an impish smile. "While he is sitting there frying in his own grease, I hope he repents for deceiving me."

"And I hope he thinks twice before he sets up another trap in which he barely escapes with his life. He's given me several heart seizures the past few years with

393

his wild daring. Lord, you wouldn't believe some of the stunts that man has pulled," Garret grumbled resentfully.

"I could have shot him when I found him in—" Victor clamped down on his tongue. He decided it best not to embarrass his daughter by referring to the night he had burst in on her and Holt. And, dammit, just whose daughter did Holt think he was dallying with anyway? She wasn't some trollop whose profession it was to ease a man's lusts. Holt deserved to mildew in jail.

"But all the same, I would hate to lose Holt," Allan remarked with a regretful sigh. Veering to the right, the group entered the telegraph office so Allan could send a message to his roving agents in Wyoming and Kansas, requesting an extensive search for the missing Walter Jameson. "Holt is one of the finest agents I've ever had. Garret would be handicapped without Holt."

All three men paused at the door to peer down at Shiloh, who had enjoyed the most satisfaction in seeing Holt sitting in jail, awaiting a hanging at noon tomorrow.

"It's up to you, Shiloh," Allan told her solemnly. "I can pull a few strings, but it will take some time and Holt doesn't have much of it with Deputy Kroeker ruling the roost in the marshal's absence. But no matter what I do, it will jeopardize any future assignments Holt might take in this part of Missouri." His deepset eyes riveted on Shiloh's enchanting features. "It seems, my dear, that what happens to Holt Cantrell is entirely up to you. My hands are virtually tied in this instance."

As the foursome ambled to the restaurant to dine on steak, Holt stared at his meager rations of rancid stew and biscuits that were hard enough to break windowpanes. He had the inescapable feeling that Pinkerton was operating under the policy they had been forced to employ during the war—if you get caught, we don't know you. And Holt had definitely been caught by a careless oversight and an eager-beaver deputy. Damn. . . .

Holt felt deserted by those whom he had called his friends, and frustrated by that silver-blue-eyed blonde who was having her revenge for the torment he had put her through.

Well, Holt sincerely hoped Shiloh was delighted that he was spending his last few hours locked up in this tiny cubicle, listening to the banging of hammers! She had vowed to see Holt hang and, sure enough, she was going to get her way! Holt was scheduled for a public execution.

"Son of a bitch," Holt muttered before he set his cold stew aside. He, like Shiloh, refused to eat when he was angry. And right now he was about as irritated as one man could get.

Chapter 29

Deputy Kroeker's eyes widened in surprise. The pretty blond widow who had pointed an accusing finger at her husband's killer earlier that evening swept into his office with a Bible clutched to her bosom.

Shiloh drew herself up before the puzzled deputy. "As a good Christian, I feel it is my responsibility to see to it that Mr. Morris begs forgiveness for his many sins before he faces his Judgment Day," she declared piously. "I would like a few moments with the prisoner."

"It's a waste of time, Mrs. Gilcrest," Daniel sighed. "The man already has one foot in hell."

"Nonetheless, he has the right to ask for divine forgiveness and to have comforting words from the Good Book read to him on the eve of his hanging," Shiloh contested. "Since this new town does not yet have a pastor to tend its wayward flock, I feel it is my duty to allow Mr. Morris to pray for his wicked soul."

Since Shiloh had a very determined look about her, Deputy Kroeker escorted her into the back room. The moment Shiloh breezed in with her Bible, Holt frowned warily. He didn't pay her the courtesy of rising to his feet. He merely lay on his cot with his linked fingers cushioning his head, and his feet leisurely crossed at the ankles.

"What do you want?" he questioned her impolitely.

Shiloh couldn't see his eyes. The brim of his Stetson shaded the upper portion of his face. Holt looked very much like the ruffian he portrayed with his thick mustache, beard, and scraggly wig.

"I have come to hear you repent for taking Reuben away from me," she told him bluntly. "Your soul faces eternity in hell's inferno and you should plead for salvation."

"I'm not in the mood for a confession," Holt grunted in an unreceptive tone.

"Since your hours are numbered, Mr. Morris, I should think you would be extremely concerned about the hereafter. This is your first and last chance to pray for deliverance." Shiloh glanced back at Deputy Kroeker, who was hovering indecisively in the doorway. "Please grant us some privacy, sir. Perhaps Mr. Morris would be more comfortable meditating without an audience."

Hesitantly, Daniel backed away, closing the door behind him. He still didn't think this was a good idea, but it was difficult to tell the curvaceous beauty no when she was bent on saving this sinner's damnable soul. More power to her, Daniel finally decided. He ambled back to his desk and plunked down in his chair to thumb through the new wanted posters he had received that afternoon.

When the door creaked shut, Holt studied Shiloh's shapely figure. With pantherlike grace he unfolded himself from the cot to loom behind his bars.

"Just what the hell is going on?" he questioned gruffly.

"You are going to be hanged tomorrow, Mr. Morris. That is what is going on," she informed him flatly. Her gaze darted toward the closed door to insure Daniel wasn't eavesdropping on the conversation. "How does it feel to be abandoned, forsaken, and betrayed?" A mocking smile hovered on her heart-shaped lips, a smile that grew wider when Holt muttered a colorful string of curses.

"I don't like it worth a damn, thank you very much," he growled resentfully. "You have made your point, curse your ornery hide!"

"It seems you have a great deal of repenting to do," Shiloh noted as another black scowl swallowed his ruggedly handsome features. "Now you have added cursing to your list of sins."

Holt expelled a defeated sigh. "All right, Shiloh, you win. If you want to hear me beg forgiveness, I will." He tilted his head, peering at her from beneath the shadowy brim of his hat. "I'm sorry I deceived you. It was a rotten trick and you didn't deserve to be my gambit."

Shiloh set the Bible aside. Her eyes flooded over Holt's swarthy physique, still amazed this was the same man who had portrayed the bungling Reuben Gilcrest. It was little wonder Allan Pinkerton didn't want to lose Holt. He was a master detective who could plant himself in any situation in any disguise and behave as if he had been born into any number of contrasting roles. And despite all the heartache and humiliation she had suffered because of his crusade for justice, she still hadn't gotten over loving this man of multiple personalities.

"The truth is, I didn't come here to hear your apology," she murmured, her silver-blue eyes locking with emerald green. "All I want is your love. . . ."

Of all the things Holt expected this spiteful minx to say, that wasn't even on the list! He gaped at her as if she were a creature from outer space. "You want me to say I love you so you can gloat while I'm swinging from the gallows?" he crowed incredulously. "Lady, you're nuts!"

"You have said you loved me once or twice," she reminded him in a much calmer tone than he had employed. "Was that another of your deceitful lies?"

Damn, he was going to his grave loving this high-spirited sprite. What would it hurt to repeat his confession? She could gloat to her heart's content. Why should he care? After all, he wouldn't be around to see her smirks because he wouldn't be around—period!

Holt grasped the bars that separated them and stared Shiloh squarely in the eye. Good God, she looked delicious enough to eat. The pink satin gown was adorned with rows of dainty lace that enhanced her delicate form and features. Her silver-blond hair had been swept atop her head, and provocative curls dangled around her forehead and temples. In spite of the lies and misconceptions, one thought rang true, Holt realized as he drank in her exceptional beauty. He did love this feisty hellion with all his heart, even if she was seeing to it that his neck was stretched out like a giraffe's.

The belligerence in his green eyes faded when the sweet memories of the past converged on him. When Holt stood on the gallows the following day he would preoccupy himself with thoughts of Shiloh, relive those warm, tender moments he had spent in her arms.

"I do love you," he assured her huskily. "And it is for that which I beg forgiveness. That was my only downfall. I'm trapped like a fly in a black widow's web. I'll go on loving you until the end of time, Shiloh."

Shiloh moved closer. "Do you truly mean that, Holt?" she queried as her tapered finger traced his lips. "Don't lie to me now even if you think it will change things. It won't, you know. Your fate still awaits you."

400

The feel of her hands playing on his lips was sweet torment. She was so temptingly close, so utterly desirable. Holt doubted anyone had ever attempted to make love with iron bars between them, but he would have liked to try. He ached to be as close as two people could get, just once more, before he sacrificed his life so that she could have her final revenge on him.

"I meant what I said, now and before, even when you didn't believe me, even when you swore Reuben said only the things you wanted to hear."

Shiloh pressed close to the bars, slipping her hands around his waist, feeling the whipcord muscles that lined his back. "I want to hear Holt Cantrell say the words and mean them—not Reuben Gilcrest or Tom Morris or whoever else you have been these past five years. I want to hear the confession from the man behind the many disguises."

Holt's body caught fire and burned each place her hands touched. It wasn't going to be easy to kiss her through the bars, but he was eager to try. He was going out with the taste of this witch angel's kiss on his lips even if it was the kiss of death. He wanted to remember the feel of her curvaceous contours molded familiarly to him just one more time, because he would never be this close to her again—at least not in this lifetime.

The silence was ablaze with tension. The fire that raged between them was almost hot enough to melt the iron bars and grant Holt freedom. He devoured her as if she were offering him a feast after years of starvation. As if they possessed a will of their own, his hands glided over her hips, pressing her intimately against him, allowing her to feel his burning desire for her.

When Shiloh's wandering caresses slid down to his buttocks, Holt groaned in unholy torment. Flames spread over his flesh, and passion threatened to burn out of control. Holt was desperate for her touch, her answering kiss. This sassy beauty had unleashed every emotion—even the ones he had carefully held in check while he flitted from one charade to another.

Never in five years of investigation had he allowed himself to become so emotionally attached. He had remained remote and unfeeling, completing his assignments and walking away without looking back. But then along came this saucy blonde with the mysterious silver-blue eyes. She had made Holt want more from life than solving crimes and fluttering from one masquerade to another. It was important that he remain footloose and fancy-free because he never stayed in one place long enough to develop a strong, lasting relationship with a woman. But Shiloh had delved deep inside him to touch the man beneath the disguises in ways no other woman had been able.

"When you're gone, always remember that I love you, that I will go on loving you," Shiloh murmured against his sensuous lips. "I have gotten over despising you, but I will never forget the feelings that your touch and your memories arouse. . . ."

Her wobbling voice and sincere confession tore at Holt's soul. He kissed her again with such intense longing that his body shuddered in frustrated desire. Damn these bars! He could die a happy man if he could make wild sweet love to this enchanting goddess before his execution. . . .

Like a bolt out of the blue Shiloh wheeled around, flattening her back against the bars. Before Holt could question her abrupt maneuver, Shiloh clamped her hand over his. She positioned his left arm diagonally across her shoulder and laid his hand intimately on her breast. Shiloh curled his right arm tightly around her waist. And to his stupefied astonishment, she let out a bellow that could have raised the dead.

"Deputy Kroeker!" she yelled for all she was worth. *"Help!"*

Daniel yanked his feet off the edge of his desk, snatched up his sawed-off shotgun, and burst through the door like a charging rhinoceros. His eyes were as wide as saucers when he spied Shiloh mashed against the bars and the scraggly villain's hands clamped around her like an octopus.

In the few seconds it took for Daniel to barge into the room, Holt realized what Shiloh was doing and why. She intended to become his hostage, offering him the opportunity to escape with his life. That was what she meant when she asked him to remember she loved him when he went away. She was giving him a fighting chance to avoid the hangman's noose.

"Get the keys, Deputy, or I'll break her neck!" Holt growled in an ominous tone. To emphasize the threat, Holt curled his hand around Shiloh's throat. She reacted by squealing like a stuck pig. *"Now,* Deputy!"

Daniel couldn't conjure up a single counterthreat to dissuade this vicious criminal from wringing Shiloh's lovely neck. The man had been condemned to hang, and he certainly had nothing to lose. Desperation made him daring.

With his heart rattling against his ribs, Daniel scurried back to the desk to fetch the key to the cell.

"Open it nice and easy," Holt instructed the deputy. "If you make one foolish move, this she-devil is as good as dead."

Daniel heard and he believed. The menacing sneer on Holt's woolly face would have sent a mountain lion cowering in its den. The scoundrel's hands were all over the stunning beauty, and she looked so terrified that he feared she would die of fright.

"Let the lady go," Daniel pleaded as he swung open the door to the cell.

Ignoring the plea, Holt let loose with one hand. "Give me the shotgun and then toss your pistols on the cot," he demanded impatiently.

Daniel stared at his deadly weapon, wondering if the varmint intended to turn the shotgun on him. Then he glanced over at Shiloh, whose bewitching features were frozen in a most convincing expression of horror. The lady should have been reading *her* last rites, not Tom Morris's, Daniel thought gloomily. This malicious murderer probably had it in mind to kill her when he had no more use of her.

Begrudgingly, Daniel did as he was ordered. But the moment Holt took control of the shotgun, he stepped from the cell to latch on to Shiloh once again. Dragging her backward, Holt entered the front office. The instant he and Shiloh disappeared outside, Daniel raced back to retrieve his pistols. When he dashed to the front door he hollered for assistance in his buglelike voice.

Lanterns illuminated the streets, revealing the route the escaped prisoner and his hostage had taken. After Daniel expelled his cry of alarm, a flood of humanity poured from the saloons and restaurants. Helplessly, Daniel and the other bystanders watched the convict propel his captive toward the wagon that sat in front of the dry goods store.

To Daniel's amazement, Garret Robertson, the giant of a man who had been introduced to him as one of McBride's employees, charged from the restaurant with two Colts clutched in his fists.

"Morris!" Garret boomed, his voice vibrating off the wooden buildings that lined the street. "What kind of lily-livered coward hides behind a woman's skirts?"

With jaw gaping, Deputy Kroeker viewed a convincing but repetitive performance that was staged to suit this particular situation. But the deputy didn't know that. He was only one of the many eyewitnesses who wasn't seeing exactly what he thought he was seeing, only what Garret and Holt wanted him to think he saw.

As for Allan Pinkerton, he stood back and watched with amused glee. He had never been on hand when his best two agents staged a showdown. And judging by the expression on the faces of the bystanders, they were waiting with bated breath to determine which man, if either, would emerge from this daring confrontation alive.

Garret's taunt caused Holt to smile wryly to himself. He had been here a dozen times before—not in this town or this exact situation, but he knew his role nonetheless. Shiloh had been the only one who could have aided him in his escape. It would never have been convincing if one of the three men had blundered into the arms of Deputy Kroeker's prisoner. But Shiloh had given the performance of her life to spare him from this overeager deputy who seemed determined to put Primrose on the map.

"Thanks, love," Holt murmured in Shiloh's ear before he thrust her away from him and wheeled to face the gorilla of a man who had challenged him to a gunfight.

Since Holt hadn't roughly shoved her aside, Shiloh made the scene more dramatic by flinging herself to the ground. A scream gushed from her lips as she skidded in the dirt. Her ear-splitting screech was followed by the bark of Garret's Colts which was preceded by a moment of absolute silence.

Holt staggered back as if he had been struck by a bullet. The shotgun exploded, scattering the dirt beside his feet. With a muted growl he collapsed in a lifeless heap. While the other Pinkerton agents held back the crowd, Allan, Garret, and Victor scurried forward to determine the condition of the escaped prisoner.

Victor pressed his boot heel against Holt's shoulder, rolling him to his back. "Dead," he pronounced with an air of authority.

Before Deputy Kroeker could rush upon the scene, Garret slung Holt's limp body over his shoulder and tossed him facedown in the wagon. When Daniel scuttled up to the back of the wagon, Victor wedged his way between the "deceased" and the deputy.

"I'll see to it that Mr. Morris is buried," he volunteered.

"That won't be necessary," Daniel replied. "I'll—"

Shiloh's wail interrupted the deputy. She sailed into her father's arms like a ship seeking port in a storm. On cue, Garret hopped onto the seat of the wagon and popped the reins over the steeds' rumps, sending them clattering down the street.

While Victor discussed the incident with Deputy Kroeker, Shiloh inched her head away from her father's shoulder to watch the wagon disappear into the night. Silently, she whispered her final good-bye to Holt Cantrell.

Since the moment Victor had explained to her why Holt had passed himself off as Reuben Gilcrest, Shiloh knew that green-eyed rake would never be hers to keep. Holt liked living on the edge, testing his abilities to their very limits. Danger and life-threatening challenges were his shadow and his reason for being. He was not the kind of man a woman could hold on to forever. It would be like trying to hitch a ride on a cloud. Her solace came in knowing that Holt did love her in his own way. He had taught her all she knew about passion and made her believe in love, even if it wasn't the kind that could last forever, even if it wasn't as strong as the affection he felt for Anna. . . .

When Shiloh pivoted to offer Deputy Kroeker her rendition of what had happened in the cell room, the tears that shimmered in her eyes were very real. She felt as if part of her had died when Holt was taken from her life. She cried for all the wasted moments when she could have been in his arms, expressing this all-consuming love she felt for him. She cried for all the empty tomorrows that lay ahead of her.

Shiloh would never know where that raven-haired devil was or what he was doing or even what he looked like when he was garbed in another of his disguises. But she would remember how it felt to be held in Holt's sinewy arms. She would recall the joy she had discovered when they were swirling in the tempest of ardent passion. And when she paused to wish upon a star some dark, lonely night, she would pray that Holt paused occasionally to remember her, because she was never going to be able to forget him. . . .

Garret was too busy gloating over his most recent grandstand play to notice the "corpse" in the back of the wagon had drawn his legs beneath him to crawl toward the seat. When Holt tapped him on the shoulder, Garret swiveled his head around. To his surprise, a beefy fist plowed into his jaw, causing stars to twinkle before his eyes. The fierce blow knocked him sideways and Garret kerplopped into the wagon bed. While Holt jerked the horses to a halt, Garret braced himself up on one elbow and massaged his pulsating jaw.

"What the hell did you do that for?" he mumbled out of the side of his mouth that Holt hadn't clobbered.

"That's the thanks you get for letting me mildew in jail for two damned days," Holt scowled crossly.

Garret scraped himself off the wagon bed to peer at Holt. "You're sure in a sour mood for a man who barely escaped a hanging," he mocked. "A simple thank-you would have been nice."

"Consider yourself thanked," Holt grumbled, his

tone nowhere near sincere.

Garret glanced over his shoulder at the distant lights of Primrose. He knew why Holt was in such a huff. He was already missing that feisty bundle of femininity and he hadn't been away from her for more than ten minutes.

In all the years Garret had worked on assignment with Holt, he had never seen him get so attached to a woman. And there had been plenty of them along the way, Garret reflected. For the past two years Anna's hauntingly lovely image had clouded Holt's mind and his thinking. Now there was a new face to torment his dreams. Holt was going to be hell to live with, Garret predicted glumly. When a man found himself married to a pretty little spitfire like Shiloh McBride, even for a couple of months, he would have an agonizing time getting over her. . . .

Garret's thoughts dispersed when he heard the patter of paws and heavy panting behind him. And sure enough, there was Dog, eager to catch up with his master. In a single bound Dog leapt onto the back of the wagon. Using Garret's lap as a springboard, Dog hopped to the seat to greet Holt with a slobbery lick on the cheek. A muted growl tumbled from Garret's lips as Dog's wagging tail slapped him in the face.

"Move over, mutt," Garret snapped as he swung a muscled leg over the back of the seat and plopped down beside the mongrel.

"Be nice to him," Holt bit off testily. "From now on you are going to treat Dog with the courtesy and respect he deserves. You lost the bet, remember?"

"No, my friend, I think perhaps you came away the loser this time," Garret contradicted him in a quiet tone.

Taking up the reins, Garret aimed the wagon toward the stable on Holt's property where Pinkerton and the other agents had left the survivors of Kirby Thorn's gang tied in knots. While Garret drove the rockety wagon, Holt stared off into the distance, mulling over his friend's remark. Garret was right, Holt mused dismally. He had lost something very near and dear to him. Shiloh. . . .

He smiled as he absently patted Dog's broad head. In the black velvet sky Holt stared at the stars that sparkled like diamonds. Their mystical brilliance reminded him of the unusual color of Shiloh's eyes. The moonbeams reminded him of the glowing strands of silver-blond hair that framed her enchanting face. How tempting it was to sneak back to Primrose to seek Shiloh out, to take up where they left off in the jail.

Holt could almost feel her luscious body pressed to his, taste those responsive kisses that inflamed his soul and his passions. But if he returned to Primrose, he would still face the inevitable. He could return only to say good-bye, and they had said that enough already.

The McBride assignment was left unfinished. Walter Jameson was still running around loose, and J. W. Baxter had yet to be taken into custody for conspiring to undermine his rival's railroad company. And chances were Allan Pinkerton already had an assignment waiting him.

Holt expelled a frustrated sigh. He craved the challenge of his assignments. But his enthusiasm dimmed to the memories of the shapely blond hellion who had burrowed her way into his heart. He and Shiloh had created unforgettable memories in their private corner of the world. They had discovered something in each other that set off compelling reactions. But Holt couldn't expect such a lively sprite like Shiloh to sit and wait for him for months on end, never knowing where he was, or what he was doing, or when he would be back.

Theirs was a star-crossed attraction. Shiloh needed a man around to keep her out of trouble. With her stunning good looks and fiery spirit she constantly attracted men. Perhaps one day the right man for her would come along to provide her with all the love and companionship she needed to make her happy. Holt could only hope that in the years to come, Shiloh would gaze through the window of time and reminisce about the few months of adventure and passion they had shared. He wanted to be the secret smile that pursed her heart-shaped lips when no one else was around, the warm tingle that forbidden memories aroused.

It was for damned certain that he would reopen the door to the past and stroll through those sweet dreams they had shared. . . .

Good God, he hated being so sensible! A woman like Shiloh—his equal—came around only once in a lifetime. Unfortunately, he and Shiloh couldn't find common ground to build a future. She couldn't fit into his life and he wouldn't be content in hers.

"Do you know what Anna would say if she were here?" Garret remarked, yanking Holt from his contemplations.

"Yeah, she'd say you always talked too much and you still do," Holt muttered crankily.

Garret overlooked the gibe. For years now Holt had insisted there was a motor hooked to Garret's tongue, one that was not regulated by an off switch in his brain. But Garret had something to say and he was determined to say it.

"Anna would have wanted you to put the past in its proper perspective. She would have wanted you to be happy and to live your life to its fullest for the both of you."

"I'm happy," Holt growled in a tone that indicated he was nothing of the kind.

Garret observed the menacing scowl that was stamped on Holt's shadowed face. "You don't look all that happy to me."

"Well, what the hell do you want me to do, jump for joy?" he snorted sarcastically. "This is how I look when I'm deliriously happy. I'm sorry you don't approve."

"I still think you are making a grave mistake," Garret declared with great conviction.

"And I still think you talk too much," Holt groused as he snatched the reins from Garret's big hands. "Is that as fast as this wagon will go? I can't wait to shake the dust of Primrose off my heels."

"Running isn't going to help," Garret prophesized, bracing his hands on the seat while Holt thundered off with fiend-ridden haste. "You can't outrun that pretty little lady's memory, Holt. She matters too much to you, and you know it."

"When are you going to stop babbling?" Holt flared.

"When are you going to start listening?" Garret countered.

Dog sat perched between the men, his gaze bouncing from one frowning face to the other. Tiring of the verbal sparring match, Dog hopped into the wagon bed to catch a nap. But it was impossible to sleep when Holt and Garret were blaring at each other as if they were both stone deaf!

Part IV

Love that flew so lightly to my heart,
Why are thy wings so feeble to depart?
                                    Meleager

Chapter 30

Springfield, Missouri
February 1868

An icy wind pelleted Shiloh as she and Kevin Shales exited from the theater. Shiloh had accepted Kevin's invitation for no other reason than to battle boredom. For the past few months she had moped around the brick mansion without her usual zest and panache. Victor had suggested a dozen times that she find something to occupy her. Since Victor had been busy on his private train, overseeing the laying of rails through Indian territory, he had little time to devote to his daughter. Shiloh no longer traveled by his side, but preferred to remain in the solitude of their estate.

Each time Victor returned from his jaunts, Shiloh looked more miserable than the time before. Nothing had brightened her moods and nothing appeased her finicky appetite. She prowled around the house like a lost spirit searching direction. Victor had attempted to console and reassure Shiloh, but her disposition had become as sour as a lemon.

"The traveling troupe presented a marvelous performance, don't you think?" Kevin commented as he assisted Shiloh down the steps.

"What? . . . Oh, yes," Shiloh murmured distractedly. The truth was she had been so absorbed in her own thoughts that she barely noticed there was a theatrical performance going on.

Her long lashes fluttered up to assess the spectacles that were perched on her companion's pug nose. Odd, she mused pensively. She just realized that all the dates she had accepted of late, as well as marriage proposals she had promised to consider, came from tall, lanky men who wore glasses. It seemed she had been subconsciously searching for another mild-mannered Reuben Gilcrest. But they were all meager substitutes for the man who haunted her thoughts.

Shiloh awakened each morning to the vision of a rakish smile and sparkling green eyes that were embedded in craggy, bronzed features. And as the day progressed, she felt decidedly worse than she did when Holt's image first greeted her. Her spirits had nose-dived to rock bottom. Her appetite was nonexistent, and she had the energy of a snail. After dozing off from time to time during the day, she was wide awake at night.

Victor and Marcella complained that she paced around the mansion like a specter, but only the evening hours brought minimal relief for Shiloh. She would stare at the stars and remember when she felt whole and alive. In short, Shiloh felt and acted like a ghoul, and Victor and Marcella constantly reminded her of that fact. But what was a woman supposed to do when she was . . . ?

Her thoughts came to a screeching halt when a stoop-shouldered old man hobbled toward her. A mop of gray hair protruded from the rim of his derby hat and his face was hidden behind a full beard and mustache. Thick spectacles bridged the elderly gentleman's nose and an intricately carved cane propped up his slumped body.

"Shiloh McBride?" the old man questioned in a nasal voice.

Shiloh scrutinized the silver beard and mustache. Her heart hung in her chest like a rock when sparkling emerald eyes peered back at her. Her mouth opened and shut like the damper on a chimney, but no words formed on her lips. She was too thunderstruck to speak.

"You probably don't remember me, my dear," he said with a hoarse laugh. "I'm an old friend of your father's. You and I met a long time ago, a lifetime ago, it seems."

Kevin pushed himself in front of Shiloh like a shield. "Sir, I think perhaps it would be proper for you to pay a call to the McBrides at a more reasonable hour," he suggested tactfully. "Mr. McBride is due back in Springfield tomorrow. Perhaps you would be granted an audience with Victor and his daughter in the evening."

When the young man attempted to steer Shiloh around the hunchbacked obstruction, she refused to budge from her spot. "It's all right, Kevin," she assured her overprotective escort. "I remember my father's colleague."

For a long moment Shiloh stared past the wire-rimmed spectacles into those fathomless green eyes. The man looked as old as she felt—nine years older than God, to be exact. But beneath the disguise, Shiloh knew there was a powerhouse of dynamic masculinity. All the tender memories erupted inside Shiloh, and a mist immediately clouded her eyes. Lately, Shiloh burst into sobs when anyone looked at her the wrong way. Suddenly she was swallowing with great gulps and a river of tears was boiling down her cheeks.

417

The old man wrapped his arm around her quaking shoulders before the lanky young man could console her. "I hope I have not upset you, my dear Shiloh. I have good news for your father, and I was most eager to convey it. The housekeeper suggested I might find you here, so I took the liberty of seeking you out, even though the hour is late."

"Sir, I think it best . . ." Kevin tried to protest.

Holt was doing his damnedest to control his black temper. He did not appreciate this spindly-legged dandy hovering around Shiloh like a mother hen. And one look into Shiloh's pale, drawn features cut Holt to shreds. He knew he was responsible for her lack of spirit, just as she was responsible for making him feel as old and irascible as he looked. The past few months hadn't been kind to Holt either. He had chased all over the country in search of the elusive Walter Jameson, spending more hours in the saddle than in a comfortable bed, and he had been so distracted by thoughts of Shiloh that he had made one or two careless slips that had nearly cost him his life.

"Sir, I demand that you take your hands off the lady," Kevin blustered when Holt's comforting pat began to resemble a caress.

"Oh, shut up, sonny," Holt crowed irritably. "You're beginning to get on my nerves."

Forced to display what little bravura he possessed, Kevin clamped a hand on the old buzzard's shoulder and pried him away from Shiloh, who couldn't stop crying.

"Argh!" Kevin squawked when the old man's cane rammed his shins.

"Get lost, Junior," Holt growled as he shepherded Shiloh toward his waiting brougham. "I'll see the Widow Gilcrest home."

"But . . ." Kevin contested. His voice trailed off

when the old coot brandished the cane in his face. Meekly, Kevin watched Shiloh disappear inside the carriage. The vehicle sped off down the street under the charge of the gorilla of a man who sat atop the coach beside the shaggy dog, whipping the reins over four slapping black horses.

Apprehensively, Shiloh watched Holt peel off his disguise. Nothing would have pleased her more than to fling herself into his arms. But she feared Holt had gotten over her long before she got over him. She knew she couldn't compete with his adventurous life and the lingering memories of Anna. Shiloh had forced herself to be content knowing Holt had loved her once.

"Dammit, you should have told me," Holt grumbled as he yanked off his hat and wig.

"Told you *what?*" Shiloh gaped at him through a mist of never-ending tears.

"You know *what?*" he muttered crankily.

Suddenly her sagging spirits inflated. This was not the type of reception Shiloh had anticipated. But if Holt wanted to pick a fight with her, she was game. Silver-blue eyes flashed like lightning and her chest swelled with an angry breath. How dare he swagger back into her life to interrupt her date and demand that Kevin get lost! He had no right, no right at all!

"If you are referring to the *what* to which I presume you are referring, it is none of your concern," she spouted through the infuriating tears that still hadn't let up. Frustrated, Shiloh wiped the back of her hand over her damp cheek. "And how did you find out anyway? I didn't tell a soul!"

"I'm a detective," he reminded her with an intimidating smirk. Good God, why did she have to keep bleeding tears? He hated it when Shiloh cried. It was so unlike her. She had never been a gushy, sentimental female who sprang a leak at the drop of a hat. "It's my

419

business to know who, where, how, what, and why. But I would like to know when!"

The lantern in the enclosed coach reflected the defiance in her misty eyes. "You're such a whiz at investigation, you figure out when," Shiloh snapped back at him. "And what are you doing here anyway? If you have news for my father, you could have sent him a telegram or letter . . . that is, if you know how to write," she tacked on nastily.

Holt almost hated this sassy minx for making him realize how human he really was. He had been to hell and back the past few months and all because of her. He hadn't been able to look at another woman without seeing Shiloh's bewitching face, and he hadn't been able to touch one either. Her memory had ruined his sex life. Holt had rattled off all the consoling platitudes, assuring himself that time would heal the aching, that there was life after Shiloh. But this wasn't living. This was existing in an unemotional vacuum. All he felt these days was frustration, and now he was taking out his exasperation on its true source.

Shiloh dug into her purse to fetch her handkerchief and mopped her cheeks. "I think it best if you wait until tomorrow to speak with my father. I will make it a point to be gone when you arrive."

Holt expelled a harsh sigh. "Dammit all, this isn't the way I envisioned our encounter. You look like hell!"

Shiloh jerked straight up in the seat after being slapped with the insult. "You don't look so good yourself." And he didn't. His eyes boasted dark circles. His shaggy raven hair jutted out in all directions after being crammed beneath his wig. "No one asked you to interrupt my date with Kevin. Good God," she grumbled, unconsciously resorting to his favorite expression. "I would have preferred that you didn't come back at all. I was satisfied remembering the way

420

we once were."

"Is that why you were gallivanting around town with that four-eyed toad who has the same nervous habit of shoving his spectacles back to the bridge of his nose with his forefinger? Now, isn't that a coincidence?" Holt snorted caustically. "Are you searching for another Reuben Gilcrest?" He didn't give her the opportunity to respond. He ranted on. "It certainly looks that way to me."

Out of control, Shiloh emblazoned her handprint on his cheek. She didn't want to hear her secret whims voiced, especially not by Holt. Hell's bells, he could have babbled all night without saying that.

"Get out right this minute!" Shiloh spewed, her cheeks flushed with fury.

"You get out," Holt flared. "This is my coach!"

Garret Robertson, who was in control of the brougham, couldn't help but overhear the shouting match inside. For months he had endured Holt's thunderous moods. Holt had chewed on him as a between-meal snack. Nothing pleased him these days. He was as ill-tempered as a wounded lion.

Finally, Holt had returned to Springfield after Garret threatened to bind, gag, and tote the sourpuss there himself. But instead of telling Shiloh how he felt, Holt was picking fights with her. The stubborn fool, Garret muttered to himself. Whom did Holt think he was kidding? And Shiloh wasn't behaving one damned bit better, Garret noted. If she could stop being angry long enough to read between the lines, she would realize Holt was only saying he loved her in his own tormented way.

Sporting an ornery grin, Garret jerked on the reins to turn a short corner, hoping to throw the occupants of the carriage into each other's arms. It was time to take drastic measures. Shiloh and Holt were getting nowhere fast, and somebody needed to play Cupid. Garret deputized himself as the mythical matchmaker.

A startled yelp erupted from Shiloh's lips when she was hurtled into Holt's lap. The feel of his powerful thighs beneath her hips triggered sensations from another lifetime—sensations that had lain dormant for four months since his departure from Primrose.

Garret's mischievous prank did the trick. The instant Holt found Shiloh in his arms, all the fight went out of him. Good God, why had he dragged her into an argument in the first place? This was where he wanted her—the same place he had wanted her since she gave him his freedom. She had set him free, but the strings to his heart had stretched only so far before he flew back to her like a damned boomerang.

There was no getting around it. Life after this silver-blue-eyed firebrand was a scant few inches from hell. He couldn't work. He couldn't sleep. And Garret had declared Holt was absolutely impossible to live with. Even Dog had taken a wide berth around him lately because Holt was doing more snapping and growling than the animal!

The plumed bonnet that sat atop Shiloh's silver-blond curls toppled to the seat. Strands of sun and moonbeams streamed across Holt's elbow. Reverently, he limned her exquisite features and combed his fingers through the silky tendrils. A tidal wave of memories splashed over him, and he forgot what they were quibbling about.

"Good God, you're lovely," he breathed in appreciation. "I tried, but I couldn't forget you, sweet witch. You cast a potent spell. . . ."

His sensuous lips grazed hers, worshiping what he had long dreamed of possessing as his own. His hand glided beneath the hem of her blue satin gown to feel the satiny texture of her skin.

A choked sob bubbled in Shiloh's throat when his tantalizing touch sent a fleet of goose bumps cruising over her skin. "Why did you have to come back to stir up the memories all over again?"

"For this," he murmured hoarsely. "I came back for this. . . ."

His mouth slanted over hers, savoring and devouring her at the same moment. Boldly, his fingertips swirled over her leg to trace the star-shaped birthmark above her knee. Higher still, his caresses roamed to tease and arouse her until she gasped with awakened desire. Her body burst into instant flame as he deftly removed the hampering undergarments to rediscover every inch of her quivering skin.

A path of scalding kisses descended down her cheek and collarbone to seek out the rigid peaks of her breasts. His tongue swirled and flicked at the throbbing buds while he tantalized her with his masterful caresses. The world slid out from under Shiloh and she felt herself falling back into the well of forbidden memories.

Shiloh knew he had walked back into her life and that he intended to make love to her, here and now, before he left her again. But she wasn't putting up a fuss. There was no sense fighting the hot, bubbling feelings that unfurled inside her. Loving Holt and wanting him had become second nature to her. Shiloh longed to return his touch—kiss for kiss, caress for caress. She wasted no time in sliding her hand beneath his jacket and shirt to make arousing contact with the rippling muscles of his belly and chest. He was warm flesh and blood—the personification of her elusive dreams. Touching him was pleasure in itself, and yet it created monstrous new cravings that spurted through her bloodstream, demanding appeasement.

With a tormented groan Holt laid Shiloh upon the

seat and shoved her gown out of his way. He shouldn't take her like this, he scolded himself while his pounding heart threatened to beat him to death. Gentleness had flown out the window the instant she dared to return his brazen caresses. Like a flash of lightning, passion sizzled through him, burning reason and logic to a crisp. Urgency overwhelmed him, and Holt surrendered to his need to relive the unparalleled moments of splendor he had discovered in her arms.

Bracing himself above her, Holt slid between her thighs. His eyes locked with those wide pools of silver blue and he plummeted into their dazzling depths. It was a wild, impatient coming together in a most awkward position on the narrow seat. But neither of them noticed their cramped quarters, not when passion burst like a volcanic eruption. They were aware of nothing but each other, engulfed by emotions that overshadowed all else.

Holt could feel the molten flames channeling through him. He couldn't control the fiery cadence of their lovemaking. He had become an instinctive creature who was driven by his ungovernable passions. He wanted to lose himself in ecstasy, to spread his wings and soar like an eagle.

This was where he had wanted to be for the past four months. Even while he assured himself Shiloh was better off without him, the feelings for her never faded. Well, maybe she was better off, but he damned sure wasn't. Loving her was what he needed more than life itself. No price seemed too great to pay if it meant he could go on holding this luscious enchantress in his arms, he could glide past the stars and encircle the sun. . . .

His brain broke down when a holocaust of fire consumed him. His body shuddered convulsively as the tumultuous sensations collapsed upon him, stripping away what was left of his sanity.

For an eternity Holt waited for the numbing ecstasy to ebb. But Shiloh had absorbed his strength. Moving was out of the question. He had no reflexes left, no energy whatsoever. He had boiled down to the consistency of strawberry jam, and he didn't care if he dripped into puddles.

"I've missed you terribly, damn you," Shiloh sobbed against his shoulder, hating herself for saying so and disgusted that these infernal tears kept clouding her eyes.

A rakish grin quirked his lips as he raised his ruffled raven head. "And you are impossible to forget, damn your gorgeous, high-spirited hide!" he countered.

A sigh escaped Shiloh's kiss-swollen lips. Absently, she rearranged the wavy black hair that lay across his forehead. "I tried letting go, Holt. It didn't work. What are we going to do about this . . . thing between us?"

"Since I am going to be a father, I think we should get married," he murmured. Affectionately, he re-routed the incessant stream of tears that dribbled down the side of her face.

"I married you once already," she replied with a muffled sniff. "But you just wandered off and got yourself killed. And what will our child think when his father comes to visit him only every three or four months? He won't call the stranger who breezes in and out of his life his father. He'll call you *the wind.*"

Holt expelled a frustrated breath. He had returned because this magical pixie drew him like metal to a magnet. But nothing had changed. Shiloh didn't fit into his life-style and he wasn't meant for hers. Holt had constantly kept tabs on Shiloh through Victor. He had received a telegram while he was in Laramie that knocked him for a loop. Victor indicated that Shiloh, who had no appetite because of morning sickness and who now cried over little or nothing, needed some direction in her life. Holt had read the note and promptly sat down before he fell down. He had come running back the moment he wrapped up his most recent assignment in Wyoming.

All his intense feelings for this sassy blonde hadn't changed one whit, but, unfortunately, neither had the situation. He was miserable without Shiloh, but accepting Victor's offer to take a position in the railroad was distasteful. Victor had dedicated his life to connecting the East and South with rails, and Holt wanted all the Kirby Thorns in the world behind bars or swinging from ropes.

Loving Shiloh demanded extreme sacrifices, ones Holt wasn't sure he could make and still be content. And he couldn't expect Shiloh to do all the giving either. She would become restless. With her beauty and spirit there would always be an endless rabble of men around who were chomping at the bit to take Holt's place. Damn, again they had reached a stalemate. He couldn't live without this lively beauty, but she couldn't live with him, not when he rambled about like tumbleweed, changing personalities as most men change shirts.

The rap on the carriage door sent Holt scrambling to fasten himself into his clothes and assist Shiloh back into hers. "Just a min—"

Garret opened the door. An ornery grin pursed his lips when he peeked inside to see Shiloh's silver-blond hair in tangles, her bonnet mashed on the seat, and her lips swollen from Holt's ravishing kisses. And Holt looked every bit as ruffled. His hair appeared to have been styled in a cyclone and the buttons on his shirt were incorrectly fastened in his haste to dress.

Camouflaging his snicker behind an artificial cough,

Garret greeted the young lady. "Good evening, Shiloh. I trust the ride home was satisfactory."

"It is good to see you again, Garret," Shiloh peeped self-consciously. Mustering what was left of her dignity, Shiloh accepted Garret's proffered hand and stepped gracefully from the coach. "Thank you for delivering me home."

She pirouetted around to see Holt staring pensively at her. She was so frustrated she wanted to scream. How she loved this man! And how impossible it would be for them to enjoy a life together. Why couldn't she have fallen hopelessly in love with a man who could put down roots? It would have made her life so much simpler!

"Good night, Holt," she mumbled before spinning on her heel and zooming up the steps to the mansion.

An exasperated frown puckered Garret's leathery features. This is not what he had anticipated. Because of Holt's inability to forget this stunning minx, he had become as testy as a disturbed rhinoceros. If Holt thought a quick rendezvous in a brougham was enough to ease his frustration, then he was a fool and Garret proceeded to tell him so.

"You are making another critical mistake," Garret lectured. "You can't keep popping in and out of Shiloh's life. If you can't give her up, then stay with her."

"And do what?" Holt exploded. "Become Victor's shadow?"

"Open a clothing store," Garret suggested flippantly. "With all the garments you've utilized for your disguises, you have enough inventory to start a business."

Holt was not amused by the taunt. He was frustrated as hell. He loved Shiloh and none of the pep talks to himself had helped him forget how much she meant to him. And yet, he had made a commitment to his profession. Holt couldn't have it both ways and he knew it. But knowing it and accepting it were two entirely separate matters. Not having Shiloh in his arms each time he ached for her was making him crazy. . . .

Garret's hand latched on to Holt's arm, catapulting him from the coach. "You'd better make a decision," he growled. "That is one unhappy lady, and you are one miserable man. If you want to know what I think . . ."

"I don't want to know," Holt bit off brusquely.

Garret told him anyway. "I think you should find her a good, honest, dependable husband to raise your child. Select a man who can love her for the woman she is without stifling her spirit. Shiloh needs a man who will love her and love her often. Find a man who will raise your child as he sees fit. He can instruct your child in all the things you won't be around to teach him, and your son can call him father."

A wry smile hovered on Garret's lips when Holt's face puckered in a distasteful scowl. "And every night Shiloh can cuddle up in her husband's arms and enjoy the pleasure you could give her only three or four times a year. There will be no other children, not yours anyway," he added to intensify the gloomy picture he was purposely painting for Holt's benefit. "But what the hell? You are still trying to rid the world of every criminal on the continent, as if you were the only man appointed to uphold justice. And when you're too old to chase cross-country on horseback, you can retire to that nice cottage you had rebuilt near Primrose and sit in your rocking chair all by yourself. . . ."

"Don't you ever shut up?" Holt grumbled, soured by Garret's depressing speculations on the future.

"Not until I'm finished saying what I want to say, I don't," Garret insisted, certain his reverse psychology had cracked Holt's composure. "For you, dying has been the easy part. Living has been the tough part. You've been trying to live to avenge Anna for almost three years now. But she's gone, Holt. You have to let her memory go. She wouldn't have wanted you to continue this reckless crusade. And you wouldn't have wanted her to kill herself time and time again as some sort of symbolic punishment for being forced to go on living if you had been the one to perish instead of her."

Holt raised his tormented gaze to meet Garret's perceptive stare. "That is what I have been doing, isn't it?" he realized with a start.

Garret nodded enthusiastically. "When we began working together during the war, the technique was an ingenious tactic of removing yourself after you infiltrated enemy lines. But after Anna died, you began to flirt with disaster more and more. You challenged death. When you arranged to have me shoot you in a showdown, it was as if you were dying for Anna, over and over again, to punish yourself for not being there when she needed you."

His brown eyes locked with Holt's. "And what about Shiloh? Are you going to be there for her when she needs you or are you going to begin killing yourself for her now that she carries your child? Isn't it about time you quit dying a little at a time and begin living for yourself?" Garret's breath came out in a weary sigh. "As for me, I'm tired of thundering all over the country in fast pursuit. You can find someone else to shoot you down from here on out. I want to put down roots and get on with the next phase of my life."

With that Garret climbed back atop the coach and clattered down the street with Dog perched beside him. As sour as Holt had been of late, even his devoted mongrel didn't want to be around him.

For a moment Holt stared after the departing

brougham and then glanced at the light in the second story window of the McBride mansion. The lantern beamed like a beacon in the night, splattering a path of light on the lawn below. Indecision furrowed his brow. It would be all too easy to go to her on impulse, but it wasn't the sensible thing to do while his emotions were shooting up and down like a teeter-totter.

Stuffing his hands deep into his pockets, Holt kicked at a clump of dry grass beneath his feet. He was so immersed in thought, he was oblivious to the chilly breeze that whipped through his coat. His footsteps echoed on the brick walkway as he ambled off into the night. Pensively, he mulled over what Garret had said. It seemed there was a time and a season for everything, a time for every purpose. Holt needed to decide what his purpose was. He needed to determine what mattered most to him—Shiloh or his profession. He cared deeply about both of them, and giving either one of them up was going to be pure and simple hell. . . .

Chapter 31

Tormented by Holt's sudden appearance in Springfield, Shiloh tossed in bed, begging for sleep. But even counting sheep didn't help. Shiloh was still wide awake after counting thousands of flocks. Muttering, she flung her legs over the edge of the bed to pace like a caged tiger. If she had any sense at all, she would select a suitable husband and accept her life for what it was—a mess.

There were plenty of men in Springfield who were eager to marry a wealthy widow and accept her child if her fortune was part of the bargain. There were scads of marriages based on mergers instead of love. If she wed, Holt would no longer flit in and out of her life to haunt her. She would be safe within the institutional walls of wedlock. Kevin Shales was as good a prospect as any, Shiloh mused indifferently. She didn't have to love him, she only had to tolerate his boring presence in her life.

For months now Shiloh had ambled around as if she had lost her best friend. It was time she took control of her life again and ceased lamenting over a love that could never be. Holt was off limits to her. That was as obvious as a wart on the end of one's nose. If she kept hoping and praying for a miracle, she would only wish her life away.

When Holt returned the following day to confer with her father, she would march herself to Kevin's law office and accept his proposal. Then Holt would know that she was letting him off the hook as father of her child. When he left Springfield, there would be no reason for him to come back. She would sever all ties with him forevermore.

Inhaling a deep breath, Shiloh resolved to give her child first consideration from this day forward. She couldn't have Holt, but she had his child—a child who was the symbol of an ill-fated love. She could cherish their child in all the ways she could never love Holt. That raven-haired, green-eyed rogue was a part of her that no one could take away, a dream that could never mingle with reality.

Shiloh flinched when an unseen hand snaked around her waist. Before she could twist around, another hand clamped over her mouth. Blast it, why did Holt have to sneak up on her after she had made her decision about her future? She didn't want to see him just now.

Shiloh was granted her wish and she cursed herself for making it. For it was not the elusive Holt Cantrell who had crept into the house. Shock settled on Shiloh's features when Walter Jameson spun her around to tie a rag over her mouth and bind her hands behind her. Dammit all, what the devil was he doing here? She had assumed that Holt had returned to assure her father that Walter had been apprehended. Apparently, that was not the "good news" to which he had referred.

A pained groan erupted from beneath her gag when Walter jabbed her in the ribs with his pistol. Roughly, he shackled her arm and propelled her down the hall toward the back entrance. The cold blast of air sent a shiver ricocheting through Shiloh. In Walter's haste to abscond with his captive, Shiloh was left to fend off the icy February wind in her flannel gown, robe, and slippers.

Walter glanced nervously around him as he whisked Shiloh into his waiting coach. The past months had been hellish for Walter. He was a desperate man who had been hounded by poverty and frustration. He had tried to wedge his way into several railroad companies, but the Pinkerton Detective Agency had sent out an all-points bulletin on him. At McBride's insistence, no doubt, he thought bitterly. The only employment Walter had been able to obtain was laying tracks, and he detested being on the bottom of the totem pole after he had been perched at the top.

When he spotted the burly giant, Garret Robertson, in Laramie, Walter had high-tailed it back in the direction he had come. Surely no one would dream he would return to Missouri. This was the last place anyone would think of looking for him.

Walter now carried a personal vendetta against the McBrides. Because of Victor, Walter's scheme had somehow exploded in his face. Because of Shiloh's rejection, Walter had taken J. W. Baxter's bribe to sabotage the rival company and eventually wound up a fugitive. Since the McBrides were to blame for the upheaval in his life, Walter was determined to make them pay.

He knew the railroad magnate kept cash in his safe and that he paid his employees once a month. And it was that time of the month. By ransoming Shiloh, Walter could acquire enough money to get himself out of the country. England was known to be laying railroad lines all across the countryside, as well as instigating passenger and freight lines in Australia and Africa. If Walter could sail to England with a sizable amount of money, he could invest and devise a takeover. He would become far wealthier than the McBrides ever hoped to be, and they would sorely regret crossing him!

A triumphant smile hovered on Walter's lips as he shoved Shiloh into the coach and sped off into the night. McBride would gladly dole out the cash for Shiloh's ransom. Victor's only weakness was Shiloh. He adored his misfit of a daughter. By this time tomorrow Walter would have a first class ticket on the train bound for the East Coast. In a week he would set sail for England to begin his new life. . . .

A yelp erupted from his lips when Shiloh gouged him in the groin. Walter didn't have time to plan his future. He had a full-fledged fight on his hands! Shiloh had suddenly attacked him with her feet and knees. The pistol clanked against the floor of the carriage, and Walter was forced to ward off her jabs while he hung on to the reins and groped for his pistol.

The moment Walter doubled over to retrieve his weapon, Shiloh's slippered foot connected with his chin, snapping his head backward. As always, Shiloh became angry rather than frightened when she was threatened, and she considered all injustices toward her a personal insult and challenge. She was not about to be dragged around like a rag doll again. Shiloh was not about to be manipulated by this blond-haired serpent. If he intended to ransom her, he would earn every penny of his ill-gotten gains, Shiloh vowed stormily.

She had seen Walter toss a note on her unoccupied bed before he whisked her out of the house. She didn't have to be a genius to determine what Walter wanted from her. He had tried to swindle her father's railroad company out of a fortune. Since extortion failed, it seemed he was resorting to kidnapping.

Even though Shiloh was pounding Walter with her heels, he managed to grasp his pistol. Pushing back onto the seat, Walter jammed his weapon against Shiloh's hip. "Sit up!" he snarled at her.

Flashing him a glare that was as hot as the hinges on hell's door, Shiloh eased back onto the carriage seat.

"In case you think it matters whether you are dead or alive, it doesn't," Walter growled in a vicious tone that was meant to scare the living daylights out of her.

But Shiloh didn't scare easily after her terrifying ordeal with Kirby Thorn. Nothing could have been worse than that. Whatever Walter had in mind for her was child's play in comparison, she reckoned.

"Victor is going to pay to get you back, and he won't know until it's too late that you perished." To prove his point, Walter cocked the trigger and held the pistol against her ribs. "We can end it here and now if that is your wish. Victor will never know what became of you unless he seines the river for your remains."

Shiloh stared at the shiny barrel of the Colt and cursed her fate. She would have risked her own life to thwart Walter's plans, but not her unborn child's. She recalled hearing Reuben Gilcrest once say that every dog had his day. It seemed Walter had postponed his again. More was the pity that the blundering deputy in Primrose hadn't allowed Walter to rot in jail.

Disgruntled by the unexpected turn of events, Shiloh decided against attempting to escape. She wished she had invited Holt to accompany her into the house. If he had been around, Walter would have met with disaster. Holt would, at this very moment, be doing what he did best—dealing with criminals who were a menace to society. . . .

That thought solidifed Shiloh's vow to marry Kevin Shales. That is, if she escaped with her life, she added. Society needed all the Holt Cantrells it could get to fight the battles that ordinary citizens were incapable of handling. She had been selfish to think she could ever have Holt all to herself. He was destined for greater things besides being her one and only love. He was a shrewd, talented man among men, and he was better off thinking she didn't want him in her life anymore. Holt could go his own way at last and she could get on with her life, knowing she had made the right decision for both of them. At least she would have his child to love. That was enough. It had to be enough because that was all she could ever hope to have.

Tiredly, Victor trudged into the house. He had ordered his private train to head for Springfield the moment the last stretch of track was laid over the bridge that spanned the Arkansas River in Indian territory the previous afternoon. He had boarded his luxurious coach and headed home to meet with Allan Pinkerton once again. It was time he arranged for security agents to guard his trains. Since the line had infiltrated deep into Indian territory, there had been a rash of holdups by several bands of outlaws who had robbed passengers of coins and jewelry. Victor had no intention of losing business because of raiders. It was his desire to keep his passengers and trade goods safe from desperadoes. What he needed was a full-time force of detectives riding on board the trains, and Pinkerton had agreed to supply them.

Victor glanced up when Marcella sailed down the steps, her face white. Before he could inquire as to the reason for her distress, Marcella thrust the ransom note at him. A burst of rapid curses erupted from Victor's lips. After he read the instructions, he ripped the note to shreds and let it fall around him like snowflakes.

Damn, who had dared to take Shiloh hostage this time? She had endured enough of these tactics during the complicated ordeal in Primrose. Shiloh was having

436

enough difficulty coping with her pregnancy and the loss of the man she loved without being ransomed.

Still muttering under his breath, Victor stamped into his office to retrieve the money from his safe. The fifteen thousand dollars demanded by the extortioner was on hand, ready to be converted into gold and silver for the payroll car's monthly trek. While Victor was counting out the ransom money and cursing the man or men who had kidnapped Shiloh, Pinkerton strolled inside, bookended by Garret and a stove-up old man with gray hair, a beard, and Dog at his heels.

Victor's frustrated gaze landed on the man behind the disguise. "If you were hoping to avoid seeing my daughter, you needn't have bothered with a charade. Shiloh isn't here! She's been kidnapped!" His voice had grown higher and wilder by the second. By the time he finished relating the news, he was practically yelling at Holt as if the crisis were all his fault.

"When?" Holt demanded to know.

"How the hell do I know when!" Victor blustered in exasperation. "I just got back and Marcella handed me the note she found on Shiloh's bed this morning."

"Where's the message?" Holt asked in concern.

"I tore it to smithereens," Victor grumbled.

Swearing profusely, Holt pivoted on his heel and stormed into the hall, where Victor indicated he had left the scattered pieces of paper. When Holt had put the bits together, it took only an instant to recognize the elaborate handwriting. He had seen dozens of Walter's embellishments in the ledgers while he was investigating the McBride company.

Good God, the last place Holt expected to find Walter was in Springfield! He and Garret had been given a lead that Walter had migrated to Wyoming. After wrapping up another assignment with vigilante cattlemen, they'd raced off to Laramie. But before they could track Walter down he was gone. J. W. Baxter

437

had been easy to entrap since he didn't have a clue that his scheme had been exposed. But Walter had bounded from one town to another like a jackrabbit, afraid of his own shadow.

"Don't give him the money," Holt advised. "It's Jameson."

"What?" Victor crowed incredulously. "Why not? And what is Walter doing in town?"

Holt managed a semblance of a smile. "Jameson is extracting money from you, it would seem," he replied.

Victor vaulted to his feet to flash Holt a venomous glare. "Don't pay him?" he parroted in a mocking tone. "I suppose that would suit you just fine, wouldn't it? Then Walter can dispose of Shiloh and your obligations as a father would no longer exist."

"Father?" Allan chirped, fixing his astonished gaze on Holt's concealed face.

Holt scowled when three pairs of condemning eyes focused on him. "My feelings for Shiloh have no bearing on the proper method of dealing with Jameson. He isn't a bloodthirsty killer, only a desperate swindler. He had his chance to employ his pistol the day we staged the train robbery near Primrose. But according to Garret, Walter huddled behind Victor for protection. I'm willing to bet he never shot anything in his life."

"Are you willing to bet Shiloh's life on that?" Victor growled sarcastically. "This is all your fault, you know. If you hadn't toyed with my daughter in the first place, she wouldn't be suffering bouts with morning sickness and listless depression. And if you hadn't been so all-fired eager to trap Kirby Thorn, Walter would still be in custody."

Holt permitted Victor to vent his frustration. Victor was visibly shaken by Shiloh's disappearance, and he was looking to lay the blame wherever he could, just to blow off steam. Holt hated the fact that Victor was also right on every count. If not for him, Shiloh would not be with child, and she would not have gotten mixed up in his feud with Kirby Thorn. But all things considered, Shiloh had been in worse hands. And if Victor could gain control of his emotions, he would realize he could capture Walter as well as retrieve his daughter.

"No matter what you think of me, Victor, I love Shiloh," he admitted somberly. "I wouldn't have come back here after I received your telegram if I didn't. But there are ways of sniffing out Jameson without giving him what he wants."

"Like what?" Victor queried dubiously.

The fact that Holt had confessed his affection for Shiloh helped to ease Victor's torment. He had bled for Shiloh these past months, knowing how deeply she cared for this crafty master detective who looked more like Victor's grandfather than a seasoned secret agent. But Shiloh was all Victor had and he was unnerved by her kidnapping. She was the living memory of the woman he adored, the woman he had never been able to replace. During the years since Marjorie's death, Victor had never been unfaithful to her memory. Having never had children of his own, Holt couldn't possibly understand Victor's apprehension of watching his child, the symbol of his undying love for Marjorie, perish at the hands of her greedy abductor.

Holt's gaze fell to the mongrel who sat devotedly at his heels. "Dog has a nose like a bloodhound and plenty of experience in tracking," he reminded Victor. "You saw him in action during the war. He led you to a regiment of Confederates who intended to ambush your troops. Or have you forgotten?"

When Dog became the object of everyone's attention, his tail wagged enthusiastically. A faint smile found its way to the corner of Victor's taut mouth. He had seen this shaggy, oversize mutt in action many times. And Walter Jameson had no idea that Dog's killer instincts

439

could spring to life at Holt's command. Walter wouldn't be anticipating trouble from this seemingly mild-mannered creature whose tail thumping against the desk sounded like a drum.

Victor sank down on his haunches. "Come here, Dog."

The mutt pushed up on all fours and trotted over to the colonel with whom he and his master had served in years past.

"If you find my daughter for me, you are going to dine on steak." Fondly, he brushed his hand over Dog's broad head. "Extract a few pounds of flesh from Jameson's hide for me while you're at it."

Dog responded by lapping his long tongue over Victor's cheek, causing him to sputter distastefully.

"That's one habit I wish you'd break him of," Victor grumbled, wiping his face with his sleeve. "One of his wet kisses is enough to last a lifetime."

When Holt pivoted toward the door, Victor trailed along behind him. Holt came to a halt and Victor smashed into him in his need to locate Shiloh.

"Why don't you and Allan work out the details for your detective service," Holt calmly suggested. "Garret and I can handle this matter."

"But I—" Victor started to protest.

Allan snagged Victor's arm, directing him back to the desk. "Holt is right. We will only be in his way. After all, you have just elicited the service of the best two men I've got. Why don't we let them employ their polished skills."

It was a comforting thought to know the very best men were in pursuit of Shiloh, but Victor was still apprehensive. Shiloh could sometimes be a bit too courageous for her own good. If Victor had known Shiloh had already attempted to smash Walter flat, he would have suffered a heart seizure. But Allan kept him distracted by offering suggestions to set up the guard force, just as the Pinkerton Detective Agency had done for the Illinois Central Railroad and various banks that had been plagued with robberies.

When Dog was given the scent from Shiloh's discarded gown, Garret stared at the man behind the gray beard and wig. As the mutt trotted down the steps, Garret heaved a sigh. "I hope the hell you know what you are doing," he muttered, falling into step behind Holt.

"Your confidence in me is touching," Holt sniffed sarcastically. "Et tu, Brute?"

"This is the mother of your unborn child we are chasing, in case you have forgotten," Garret growled irritably.

"I haven't forgotten," Holt murmured as he quickened his step to keep up with Dog.

"Well, you couldn't prove it by me," he snorted. "You seem a little too calm and confident, even if you announced to Victor that Shiloh was the light of your life. Was that all part of your attempt to reassure him in his hour of frustration?"

As usual, Garret didn't know when to clamp his jaws shut. His tongue was running away with itself.

"You reminded me when Kirby rode off with Shiloh that I was letting sentiment distort my thinking. You were right. And now, if I don't keep my wits about me while everyone else wants to dash off like decapitated chickens, I face disaster," Holt replied, quickening his pace into a near run. "I want Shiloh alive just as much as Victor does."

"So you can do what?" Garret grunted breathlessly. "Kiss her good-bye again?"

Garret missed a step when a doubled-up fist sent him staggering backward. Holding his stinging jaw, he glared flaming arrows at the old buzzard who packed a tremendous wallop.

"That's the third time you've punched me lately. There better not be a fourth time or you're going to find out that I've been holding back every time we've staged fisticuffs."

Holt wheeled around to flash Garret a glare that would have stopped a stampede of horses dead still. He wagged a lean finger in Garret's crimson face. "Don't you ever again try to tell me I don't care what happens to Shiloh," he snarled, completely losing his composure. "She's all I've thought about for four months. I've been sleeping, eating, and breathing that little misfit. I have tried to trust my instincts about Walter Jameson just as I have every fugitive I've encountered the last few years. If you're getting too soft for this kind of work, go back and hold the colonel's hand!"

When Holt spun on his heel and shot off like a bullet, Garret grinned triumphantly. The sock in the jaw and that harsh tirade was what Garret needed to convince him that Holt was as concerned about Shiloh as Garret was.

That was one characteristic about Holt that Garret admired. He always knew how to handle himself in the face of the worst adversities. Holt could usually switch off his emotions in tense situations that demanded split-second decisions where life and death hung in the balance. Even in Shiloh's case, Holt had quickly but carefully weighed his options. He could read the men he pursued with amazing clarity. When it came to psychological warfare, no one was better than Holt Cantrell. He knew what he was doing. Garret was certain of it. Now, if only Garret could put his own apprehensions aside and concentrate on the problem at hand as well as Holt was!

Chapter 32

Bleakly, Shiloh stared at the walls of the abandoned shack that was situated on the outskirts of Springfield. Walter had been pacing, checking his timepiece every five minutes, waiting to snatch up his booty at the designated hour. She wondered if Holt had been informed of her disappearance. Knowing how adept Holt was comforted Shiloh greatly. If there was any chance of saving her, the fact that Pinkerton's master detective was in town tremendously tipped the scales in her favor.

Walter noticed that certain inner confidence about Shiloh, and it annoyed him no end. In all his dealings with this feisty hellion, he couldn't recall seeing her frightened of anything except height. This she-cat didn't scare easily.

"I don't know why you're looking so smug," Walter muttered, checking his timepiece for the umpteenth time.

"I have taken solace in the fact that Reuben will come back from his grave to haunt you," Shiloh declared with firm conviction.

Walter gaped at her confident smile. "Reuben couldn't defend himself while he was alive. He's probably afraid of his own ghost!" he snorted sarcastically.

No sooner was the mocking rejoinder out of Walter's mouth than an unidentified scratching sound rattled the door. Whipping out his pistol, Walter plastered himself against the wall to peek out the high, portholeshaped window. But his view did not allow him to see the creature who had sniffed out Shiloh and who was presently digging at the crack between the door and the threshold.

Walter's bumfuzzled gaze flew back to Shiloh, who sat strapped to her chair, wearing a haughty smile. She knew who could make such a racket and she well remembered how Dog had made short shrift of the desperado in Thorn's gang.

"Is no one there, Walter?" she taunted while Walter glanced in every direction at once. "Stranger things have happened, you know."

A wry smile pursed her lips as the scratching noise came again. Shiloh remembered Edgar Allan Poe's poem *The Raven*.

"'Tis the wind, and nothing more,'" she quoted.

"Shut up," Walter spat out.

But the scratching became louder at the sound of Shiloh's amused snicker. Shiloh could tell by the look on Walter's face that he was unhinged by the quotation and by the unexplainable sounds that filtered through the cracks around the door. Ah, the power of suggestion, she thought with a devilish grin. She had Walter believing in the revenge of ghosts.

"Shiloh . . ." The chilling wind carried the sound of her name through the drafty shack as if it had trumpeted from the other side of eternity.

Holt had crouched beneath the window on the opposite side of the shack while Dog dug at the door. When he overheard Shiloh's taunt he decided to play it for all it was worth.

"What was that?" Walter croaked, frog-eyed.

"'And the raven, never flitting, still is sitting, still is sitting . . .'"

"I told you to shut up," Walter growled. Nervously, he tugged at his cravat to relieve the sudden pressure in his chest and throat.

On cue, Shiloh's name again whispered in the wind, stronger than before. The familiar voice shocked Walter out of his boots. Suddenly he was pointing his pistol at every wall. He didn't believe in ghosts . . . or at least he hadn't until then.

Worriedly, Walter backed into the rear corner of the shack and aimed his pistol at the rattling door—in the event the portal did fly open on its own accord to reveal Reuben Gilcrest's ghost. Bullets probably wouldn't penetrate an avenging spirit, Walter mused shakily. But he didn't have a stake or silver cross or whatever one was supposed to utilize to send a ghoul back to his eternal resting place!

While Garret crouched beside the door and twisted the knob to add to the unsettling sound effects, Holt peeled off the gray beard and wig. Moving a good distance away from the door, Holt positioned himself in plain view. His glasses, hat, and baggy clothes closely resembled the disguise Reuben had worn.

When Holt gave the signal, Garret shoved open the door and shrank back. The gray sky and low-scraping clouds silhouetted Reuben's distant figure in the crisscrossed shadows cast by the canopy of trees beyond the shack. The scene was so eerie and convincing that Walter's overworked heart very nearly popped out of his chest. Reflexively, he fired at the looming figure in the distance. Under Holt's command, Dog pounced on the wild-eyed scoundrel who had raised his pistol to take a second aim at the disembodied spirit who loomed just out of his weapon's range.

A pained squawk erupted from Walter's lips when Dog, who appeared possessed by demon spirits, launched himself through the air to clamp his fangs on his victim's wrist. The pistol dropped from Walter's fist and he shielded his face from the once mild-mannered mongrel who suddenly had it in mind to shake the life out of him.

While Walter was fending off Dog, Garret's huge frame filled the doorway. "Dog, come here," he ordered sternly.

Immediately, Dog returned to his gentle nature and wagged his tail as he trotted back to Garret. Walter cradled his wounded arm against his chest as he huddled in the corner. Where the devil had this awesome giant come from? The man had the most remarkable habit of turning up everywhere! How did this powerful figure of a man always know where to find him, Walter wondered bewilderedly.

His stunned gaze flicked past the gigantic bulk of a man to stare at the space Reuben's ghost had occupied moments before. But there was nothing there. . . .

"Shiloh . . ." The haunting voice echoed in the wind as if it had vibrated through a long tunnel, and then faded into silence.

"There! Did you hear that?" Walter questioned Garret, as if to insure that his mind hadn't snapped.

Garret cocked a dark brow as he stalked forward with his Colt trained on his captive.

"Mr. Jameson seems to think he has been seeing and hearing ghosts," Shiloh announced with a sly smile.

"Shiloh heard and saw him too," Walter insisted as Garret hoisted him to his feet.

"I saw and heard nothing, Walter," she assured him

with a mischievous smile. "Twas the wind and nothing more. . . ."

Walter stared at the empty space outside the door in stupefied astonishment.

In mock sympathy Garret patted Walter's quaking shoulder. "I think your harrowing attempt to elude me the past few months has damaged your sanity, Mr. Jameson," he teased unmercifully.

A muddled frown knit Walter's brow as he peered at Reuben's shaggy black dog and then glanced at Garret, who was in the process of untying Shiloh. "Who the hell are you?" he demanded to know.

Garret broke into a wry smile. "I'm the long arm of the law, Mr. Jameson. One of Pinkerton's men . . ."

Dumbstruck, Walter allowed himself to be led from the shanty and deposited in Springfield's jail. And while he sat on his cot, he grappled with the eerie incident that had landed him behind bars. His tormented mind left him questioning what he had seen and heard, but for the life of him he couldn't explain what he thought had happened. He was relatively certain that Shiloh McBride Gilcrest had a guardian angel who had appeared in various forms over the past six months. Although Walter hadn't noticed any wings attached to Reuben's shadowy form, he swore Shiloh's deceased husband had been there in spirit. That was the only explanation, no matter how fantastic it sounded.

Shiloh emerged from the cabin in her robe and slippers, looking unruffled by her captivity. After the ordeal at Primrose, Walter's abduction was more of an inconvenience than a nightmare. Instead of rushing into Holt's arms when he stepped from the skirting of trees, she merely stuffed her hands into her pockets and rocked back on her heels.

447

There was something different about the way Shiloh was looking at him from beneath that fan of long, thick lashes that knocked the props out from under Holt. Her beauty, resilience, and inner strength had always amazed him. After all she had been through the past six months, it was a wonder she wasn't a basket case. But not Shiloh. She was made of sturdy stuff, and she was still the personification of strong-willed femininity. It wasn't entirely Shiloh's calm demeanor that baffled Holt. It was the quiet acceptance in her attitude toward him—a detachment that seemed to leave miles between them.

"What's wrong, Shiloh?" he inquired as he moved deliberately toward her.

"Nothing. Thank you for coming to my rescue." A melancholy smile curved her lips as she surveyed the clothes that reminded her of the Reuben she had met a lifetime ago. And yet, beneath that uncomplimentary garb was a unique, dynamic, and talented man. Shiloh never expected to get over loving Holt Cantrell, but she had finally accepted the limitations of her affection for him. He was like a splendorous dream she'd had once upon a time—a sweet, elusive dream that had no place in her life.

Emerald-green eyes raked her long, tangled hair and full robe. Why did he feel as if they were standing on opposite sides of an ocean? It was the most unnerving feeling, considering how strongly he felt about her. He had survived these long, lonely months, knowing this silver-blue-eyed vixen loved him. That was all that kept him going. And now she seemed so remote, so indifferent to him and her surroundings. Good God, it would kill him to lose her love!

"Shiloh, I—"

"Please take me home, Holt," she interrupted when he looked as if he were about to delve into a topic of conversation that would excavate the tender memories she had sensibly tucked away. "I'm sure Papa is worried about me."

As Shiloh ambled toward the coach Walter had left behind, Holt stared thoughtfully after her. "You don't love me anymore, do you?" His voice was low, his tone rustling with frustration.

Not love him? Shiloh sighed at the ridiculous question. No woman could love a man more than she loved this man. She loved him enough to give him up. What greater love could offer such a supreme sacrifice?

Slowly, she pivoted to face his pensive stare. "I have decided to accept Kevin Shales's marriage proposal," she declared. "You can go back to your life and I will live out mine. Kevin will provide me with a suitable mate and a respectable father for my child."

Holt felt as if someone had doubled a fist and clobbered him in the midsection. Although he managed to maintain his composure as he climbed into the carriage to drive Shiloh home, he was growing angrier by the minute.

Fickle woman! She had sworn she would love him forever when he left her in Primrose. Obviously *forever* didn't span as much time as he had assumed. Or had *she* said what she thought *he* wanted to hear for a change? Holt was a master at reading people's faces, but Shiloh had him stymied. She seemed to have as many personalities as he did. He had come to love the tender young woman who responded so ardently and unselfishly to Reuben Gilcrest. He had come to respect her proud defiance when she confronted the man she presumed to be the ruthless leader of an outlaw gang. And now, knowing him for who he was, she had become polite and respectful, but unbearably distant. She had calmly thanked him for rescuing her as if his technique were no great feat. That stung his pride.

Good God, what was he going to do about this woman? Holt grappled with that question all the way back to the McBride estate. He began to wonder if Shiloh had outgrown her need of him. She no longer seemed to want him for much of anything. It appeared her interest in him could be measured in months and that she now considered him a thing of the past.

Kevin Shales? Holt exhaled loudly. Blast it, how could Shiloh be satisfied with that splindly-legged goose? Kevin wasn't man enough for this rambunctious sprite. She was more woman than the average man could handle. And hell, Kevin was not even close to being average! If she married Kevin, he would be so henpecked that he would molt twice a year. He would have Shiloh's footprints on his back. And what in heaven's name could Kevin offer Holt's child besides financial security and a flimsy father figure? Holt shuddered to think how that overly diplomatic lawyer would raise a child—*Holt*'s child!

Shiloh hadn't set foot on the first step of the porch when Victor sailed out the door like a cyclone to scoop her into his arms. Fussing over her, Victor whisked his daughter through the door and upstairs to her room, where Marcella waited to cluck over her like a mother hen.

Allan raised a curious brow when Holt ambled inside with his wig and beard in hand. "Did you and Garret meet with difficulty?"

Holt shrugged a broad shoulder. "We managed well enough," he mumbled absently.

"Come sit down a moment," Allan requested. "I think you and I need to have a talk."

Holt didn't particularly want to talk to anyone at the moment. He wanted to brood and sulk. His spirits had taken a nose dive when Shiloh dismissed him from her life. His love for her had become a casualty of his time-consuming profession. But there was a place deep inside him that just couldn't quite let go of that mystical-eyed elf. Her nonchalance tore him apart, and he ached to recapture what they once had. He could feel himself losing her bit by agonizing bit, and it hurt like hell!

Gloomily, Holt scrunched into a chair, only half listening to Allan relate his conversation with Victor. Holt didn't give a tinker's damn what arrangements Victor had made with the Pinkerton agency. All Holt knew was that he wanted a moment of privacy with Shiloh and he wasn't likely to get one. She was no longer his wife, and he had no right to barge into her room as if he belonged there.

Kevin Shales? For God's sake, that was the most ridiculous decision Shiloh had ever made, Holt fumed silently. And he was going to tell her exactly what he thought of her decision if she ever emerged from her boudoir. Holt wasn't budging from his chair until he had said his piece.

Shiloh took great pains in dressing that evening. She wanted to look her best for her final encounter with Holt. When he walked out of her life forever, she wanted him to carry a picture that evoked fond memories. Dammit all, it was difficult to be self-sacrificing and noble, she mused dispiritedly. She was going to have to forget about the man she wanted most in the world. But Holt was not hers to keep, she reminded herself sensibly.

There were just some men that women were not meant to have. That raven-haired, emerald-eyed rogue was one of them. He would always put his dangerous

451

profession and the memory of Anna above Shiloh. She couldn't take a backseat to his occupation or to a lover whose memory refused to die. As much as she would have liked to try, it simply had to be all or nothing. Otherwise the love they had once shared would wither and die in bitter resentment. It was far, far better to say good-bye and go on loving Holt than to watch his affection for her fade day by day. Shiloh couldn't bear to be a party to destroying something so precious and dear as her memories and her love for Holt. There were instances when loving a man wasn't enough. Her relationship with Holt Cantrell was a shining example.

Resolutely, Shiloh drew herself up in front of the mirror while Marcella put the finishing touches on her coiffure. Her waistline wasn't as trim as it had once been, and her eyes lacked luster. But she would muster enough enthusiasm to endure the evening, she told herself determinedly. A rueful smile spread Shiloh's lips as she remembered the incident with Walter Jameson. He thought he had seen a specter hovering in the distance. And in a way he had. He had seen the ghost of Shiloh's living past—an apparition of gone-but-not-forgotten memories that would torment her all the rest of her days.

Inhaling a determined breath, Shiloh murmured a quiet thank-you to Marcella and mentally prepared herself for the performance of her life. She would be a gracious hostess to Garret, Allan, and Holt. And when she retired for the night, she could cry into her pillow and lament her loss. This was the way it had to be, Shiloh assured herself for the zillionth time. She was going to do what was practical and sensible for her as well as for Holt.

A lump constricted Holt's throat when Shiloh

breezed into the parlor with all the poise and feminine grace imaginable. Although she was pale and serene, she was still the most dazzling young woman Holt had ever seen.

His gaze wandered over the creamy swells of her breasts that were exposed by the scooped bodice of her lavender gown. Even though there was a hint that Shiloh was losing her maidenly figure to pregnancy, nothing could detract from her natural beauty. In the months to come she might become as awkward as Reuben had been, but she would still be gorgeous. Holt had no doubt of that!

A frown plowed Holt's brow while he watched Shiloh greet her other guests. She was putting him off until last, as if he were a tedious chore she dreaded attending to. In all his various associations with women, he had never felt so ill at ease with a female. Good God, he felt as Reuben Gilcrest had behaved! It was his vulnerability to this one particular female that caused him distress, he decided. It stung his male pride to know he didn't matter all that much to her these days. She had gotten over him, not physically perhaps, but emotionally. And when Shiloh clipped the silken threads that bound them together, Holt bled like a stuck pig.

Damn her indifference! He had left Primrose wrapped in a cocoon of her love. But knowing this fickle butterfly had given him his walking papers and showed him the door turned him as sour as curdled milk. Who did she think she was? This independent sprite couldn't just shove him aside after all they had been through. He had taught her the meaning of passion. They had created a child—their child, not her child. He had as much right to fatherhood as she had to motherhood.

Kevin Shales? Holt muttered under his breath. That

lanky oaf was not raising Holt Cantrell's child! And if Shiloh didn't think he would have a say in the matter, she thought wrong. . . .

"Mr. Cantrell, I wish to convey my gratitude for all you have done for me and my father," Shiloh commented as she extended her hand to him. "The glowing accolades Mr. Pinkerton has heaped upon you and Garret are richly deserved. We shall always be indebted to you."

Mr. Cantrell? She behaved as if they were total strangers, and that really got Holt's goat. He stared at her dainty hand as if she were offering him a slab of raw liver.

Now, Holt could have been gracious and diplomatic if he had wanted to. In fact, he could be anything he set his mind to. But he was in the foulest of moods, and he wasn't within shouting distance of cordial or tactful behavior.

"If you think for one minute that you are marrying that long-legged stork of a lawyer, you had better think again," he burst out of the blue.

Allan Pinkerton looked politely incredulous. Victor appeared thunderstruck and Garret simply grinned in amusement. He had wondered how long Holt was going to tolerate Shiloh's decision to marry someone else. Apparently, not long at all.

Shiloh retracted her hand and clenched it in the folds of her gown. The world suddenly narrowed on Holt's craggy features. How dare he blare out such a challenge in the midst of this social gathering!

"There is a time and place for such discussions, sir. This is neither, and I find your rudeness offensive. I have other guests to entertain, ones who display a good deal more courtesy than you. We are not having this debate because it is none of your business what I do." Dammit all, he was spoiling their last evening together, she fumed.

"The hell we aren't!" Holt exploded, despite the fact that his associates were eavesdropping on this confrontation.

Shiloh's body became as rigid as a flagpole. Flashing silver-blue eyes blazed down on him, matching the spark of rebellion in his gaze. "Your arrogance is equal only to your audacity."

"And nothing matches your stubborn defiance," Holt threw back in the same insulting tone. "My child is not going to be raised by a mealy-mouthed twirp!"

"Thank you for insulting me," Shiloh spumed, her voice growing louder by the second.

"I wasn't referring to you, you little fool," Holt growled.

"So now I'm a fool, am I?" The hair on the back of her neck stood up like an arched-back cat's. "Well, you are not God's gift to womankind," she sniffed distastefully. "You have a most annoying habit of pushing off your own weakness of character onto others. If the truth be known, you are a deceitful, arrogant jackass who has played so many conflicting roles that you can't even see yourself for what you really are! You are a multiple-faced actor whose bizarre talents should be exhibited on a stage!"

Garret bit back a snicker while Victor and Allan concealed their amusement behind their glasses of brandy. This was the spitfire Allan had met in St. Louis a few years earlier, the hellion Victor had sought to control during her difficult transition from adolescence to adulthood, the firebrand Garret had confronted at the cottage in the Ozarks. Shiloh could hold her own against any man in any situation. She was Holt's challenging match, and she parried each cutting insult with her rapier wit. The exchange of verbal blows was a source of delight to the three men who sat on the couch.

"A jackass?" Holt crowed indignantly. Like an agile cougar, he bounded to his feet to loom over the seething blonde who was suddenly her old fiery self again. "If I'm a jackass, you're a stubborn mule."

In Garret's, Victor's, and Allan's opinion, the two most obstinate creatures on the planet had just squared off and were staring each other down.

"My father has taught me never to argue with an idiotic fool for fear bystanders couldn't determine which one of us held the title. Good night, Mr. Cantrell."

Wheeling about, Shiloh made a beeline for the door. But Holt lunged and grasped her wrist before she could take flight.

"You are marrying *me*, not Kevin—the twirp—Shales," Holt declared in a tone that anticipated no argument.

"I have more respect for myself than to settle for the likes of you," Shiloh blared, struggling to unclamp his bone-crushing grip on her hand.

"You're not getting off that easily, minx," Holt snapped. His flaming gaze swung to Victor, whose shoulders were shaking in silent laughter. "Colonel, I request permission to marry your daughter and to take this troublesome misfit off your hands."

"Permission granted," Victor announced with a triumphant smile.

"No," Shiloh spewed adamantly.

"Yes," Holt blared at her.

"No!"

"Yes!" Holt threw up the hand that wasn't clamped on Shiloh's wrist. "Woman, you are driving me nuts!"

"Well, it wasn't a long drive," she sniped, eyes flashing. "You were already halfway there when I met you. And you have no right to call Kevin a twirp. Reuben was that and worse!"

Shiloh puffed up with so much agitation that her breasts heaved with each furious breath she inhaled. "I will decide whom I will marry. There will not be another shotgun wedding in this house," she tartly assured her father. "I was deceived by this multiple-faced character once. I was employed as his gambit for the benefit of all of you! I demand to take control of my own life and make my own decisions."

Her snapping silver-blue eyes seared over Holt, reacquainting him with her look of disgust. "Wild horses couldn't drag me to the altar to marry this man again. He never stays in one place long enough to put down roots. I will not have him gadding about all over creation while I'm left to do his laundry each time he makes a stop between hither and yon! And so long as he is bound to memories of his lover, I will not become a substitute for the woman he lost."

A muddled frown knit Holt's brow. His curious gaze flew to Garret, Allan, and then to Victor, who all looked as baffled by the remark as he was. "What the sweet loving hell are you babbling about?" he demanded to know.

For the past few minutes Shiloh had successfully warded off the tears that welled up in the backs of her eyes. Anger had held them in check. But inevitably, the emotions poured out. She had attempted to maintain her composure and cling to her noble convictions, but Holt's taunts were spoiling her disposition.

"Anna . . ." Shiloh choked out. "You and your obsessive need to avenge her death . . ."

Holt clamped his lips together and propelled Shiloh toward the door. Although she stubbornly set her feet, Holt uprooted her from her spot and dragged her into the hall.

"Where are you going?" Victor called after them.

"Somewhere we can be alone," Holt threw over

his shoulder.

"Not the bedroom!' Victor growled, bolting to his feet. "That's how all these complications got started in the first place."

Garret yanked Victor back down beside him. "They have been married once, and they are married still," he contended with a wry smile. "If you plan for your grandchild to know his natural father, I suggest you look the other way in this instance, Colonel."

Victor thought it over for a moment and decided Garret's point was well taken. It was a mite late for formality, he reckoned. There were times when the differences between a man and a woman needed to be settled in a bedroom—to remind them how much they truly meant to each other despite their conflicts. Shiloh had convinced herself to give Holt up. But it was time she remembered why she had come to care so deeply for Holt. Since the beginning there had been a magnetic bond between the two of them. Victor had watched it blossom and grow, wondering if Holt could make the commitment that Shiloh's all-consuming brand of love demanded.

A satisfied smile hovered on Victor's lips as he sipped his brandy. He had noticed the change Holt had undergone when he realized Shiloh was slipping away from him. Suddenly Holt was grasping to recapture what he was afraid he was about to lose forever.

The bond between his daughter and his friend was much too strong to sever, Victor assured himself. Holt would find a way to make things work. He always did. He hadn't earned the reputation as Pinkerton's best detective by bungling his assignments. . . .

"Did you decide to buy Baxter's railroad company?" Garret questioned, averting Victor's attention while Holt shuffled Shiloh up the staircase.

Victor nodded. "Allan has offered several helpful

suggestions for keeping both lines safe from highwaymen." A sly smile curved his lips as he focused his full attention on the burly giant. "I have a proposition for you, Garret, one I hope you will consider carefully."

Patiently, Garret listened to Victor explain his idea in detail. What else did he have to do while he was waiting for Holt and Shiloh to come to terms? He damned sure wasn't leaving until he knew if he was going to be best man at Holt's wedding!

Chapter 33

Holt refused to release his grasp on Shiloh until he had kicked the bedroom door shut with his boot heel. Then he placed himself in front of the exit like an ominous blockade. A lesser man would have slinked away when Shiloh's furious glare bombarded him like a volley of cannons. But Holt bravely stood his ground.

"Dammit all, get out of my room!" Shiloh boomed, stamping her foot while she rerouted the infuriating tears that fell down her cheeks. "We have nothing more to say to each other."

Inhaling a deep breath, Holt struggled to regain his temper. The time of reckoning had come. Both of their emotions had been stretched out of proportion. If he and Shiloh didn't resolve their problems tonight, this turmoil could drag on forever, just as it had for the past six months. After coming so close to losing Shiloh, Holt had realized just how much he did want a life with her. He wanted the chance to raise his child as he saw fit, not how Kevin Shales saw fit!

The fact that Shiloh was tormented by misconception troubled him. He had spoken of Anna only briefly. It hurt to reopen the seeping wounds of his past. But it was time Shiloh knew the agony he had suffered, the guilt, the deep regret, the special kind of love he reserved only for Anna.

"Please sit down," he requested, gesturing toward the tufted chair.

"You won't be staying long enough for me to require a chair," she bit off with a get-the-hell-out-of-here glower.

Since Shiloh refused to sit, Holt picked her up, stormed across the room, and planted her in her seat. Bracing his hands on the arms of the chair, Holt held her prisoner.

"While I was running a reconnaissance mission for your father and two other commanders in Georgia, I left my father to manage our farm alone. The borders of Missouri became a bloody battleground for both Union and Confederate guerrilla bands, as you well know. It was while I was on assignment that I received word of the raid on my family's farm."

A flicker of pain slashed through Holt's emerald-green eyes. When the tormented memories erupted inside him, Shiloh tensed.

"Kirby Thorn and his marauders ransacked the house and killed my father on sight. They took Anna as their whore, abusing her, making her life hell. I do not need to remind you of Kirby's abusive lust, since you came within a hairsbreadth of experiencing it yourself."

Shiloh's dewy lashes swept down while she stared at her clenched fists. Yes, she well remembered the horrors Kirby Thorn inflicted on her. It was a nightmare that had taken months to forget.

"Kirby and his partner fought over sole rights to Anna as if she were a piece of coveted property. It was Kirby who won the battle and took half the gang with him to Texas to squander the stolen riches he had obtained during his trail of terror and bloodletting along the Missouri border. Anna was dragged along

462

with him and then ruthlessly disposed of when she tested Kirby's notorious temper once too often."

Holt rose to full stature. A rueful smile touched his lips as he stared down at Shiloh. "Anna was so much like you—a rambunctious child at heart, the very breath of vivacious spirit and exquisite beauty. I doted over her the way your father dotes over you, wanting to protect her and yet marveling at her wild, free spirit. When she died at such a tender age, I swore vengeance on every man who rode with Kirby Thorn and Bob Henson. Over the past three years I have seen justice served to each one of those murdering bastards. I grieved for my father, but he had lived a long, full life and had made a success of the farm by reaping profits and acquiring hundreds of acres of meadows in the fertile valley of the Ozarks."

His eyes took on a faraway look that tugged at Shiloh's heartstrings. Heaving a sigh, Holt paced in front of her, forcing himself to continue. "But it was different with Anna. She had her whole life ahead of her, and I loved her in a way that I could love no other woman."

Shiloh swallowed the lump in her throat. It hurt to be subjected to this testimonial, even though her curiosity was eating her alive. "I understand," she murmured. And well she did too! She loved Holt with that same fierce sense of possessiveness. He was her whole world, even if she couldn't share it with him.

"No, I don't think you do," he contradicted her as he squatted down in front of her. "Anna was my kid sister," he told her quietly. "My mother died when Anna was four. Mother made me promise to protect and watch over my sister." Holt blinked, fighting for composure. "I did as my mother requested. Anna followed me around the way Dog does now. She worshiped the ground I walked on and I adored her. I had such dreams of her finding a man who would cherish her, who would allow her to spread her wings and fly. . . ." He inhaled a shuddering breath. "She was barely sixteen when Kirby got hold of her."

When Holt's voice cracked completely, Shiloh cupped her hands around his face to view the mist of sentiment in his eyes. She hadn't realized how well he had hidden his torment from the world until now. He was such a strong, vital man, but he was capable of great emotion. He had allowed her to see his vulnerability, and Shiloh was strangely touched by this rare moment. They had experienced every emotion in the wide spectrum—anger, joy, sorrow, and passion. When he allowed her to share his innermost thoughts, Shiloh felt closer to him than ever before.

"I'm so terribly sorry, Holt," she whispered with genuine sincerity. Her trembling lips skimmed his bronzed cheek, offering compassion.

"I don't want your sympathy," he murmured as he peered into those mystical eyes that shimmered like diamonds. "What I need is your love. I can't go on the way I have been, consoling myself with empty words, telling myself we're better off apart. Don't take your love away from me, Shiloh. I have survived on it the past four months. But I want to *thrive* on it. I want the chance to know our child, to be the same kind of loving, caring father that my father was to Anna and me."

A tender smile touched the corners of Shiloh's mouth. Reverently, she traced his distinct features, committing each one to memory. "You have my love, Holt. You always have and you always will. I will love this baby enough for both of us. And when your spirits fall and your duties frustrate you, all you need to do is close your eyes and listen to the silence. I will be there, whispering my love for you."

Holt vaulted to his feet and went back to his pacing. "That is the point, Shiloh. I see your face in every crowd. I reach out for you but you aren't there. You're here, and it's been hell without you," he growled bitterly.

Pivoting, he peered down into her enchanting face. "Do you have any idea what a lousy place Laramie, Wyoming, is when you aren't in it? Or Kansas City?" Holt expelled a derisive snort. "They are simply towns, places on a map that begin to look the same no matter whether they sit in the foothills or on rolling plains. Hell, even the sun doesn't shine as brightly when you aren't around! I feel like I'm walking under a black cloud all the damned time!"

"The nights are the longest," Shiloh added, calling upon her own anguishing experiences. "And the days blend into monotony."

With masculine grace Holt crossed the room to tower over the petite blonde. "If you've been miserable and I've been miserable, don't you think it's about time we did something about it? I'm not having a bit of fun and Garret says I make terrible company these days. He's refused to take another assignment with me."

"Marcella says I'm as cross as a baby deprived of naps," Shiloh tittered, but the faint smile on her face evaporated in an instant. "But you can't change what you are any more than I can change what I want and need, Holt. We are like two planets revolving around the sun, each on our own course and at our own pace. The ordeal with Walter only confirmed what I know to be true. You are too good at your job to give it up. This love of ours wasn't meant to be. You came back because you felt responsible for my child and you felt an obligation to my father and the long-standing friendship between you. But you and I just don't quite fit into each other's worlds."

465

"Then we'll make a world of our own—our own time and place," Holt declared as he drew Shiloh to her feet. His hands settled on her hips and his raven head came slowly toward hers. "I need you. . . ."

Shiloh turned her face away before Holt's skillful seduction chased away logic and firm resolve. "There is no fairyland, no Camelot. I tried to pretend there was with Reuben."

Holt gnashed his teeth and cursed Shiloh's infuriating stubbornness. Curling his hand beneath her delicate chin, he forced her to meet his level gaze. "Look me squarely in the eye and tell me you'd be happier if I walked out and never came back," he demanded.

"I can't," Shiloh admitted tremulously.

"All right then, look at me and tell me you are going to take Kevin Shales as your husband and lie beside him every night, accepting his caresses and assuring yourself it is better that way."

"I can if I must," Shiloh insisted.

"And when he touches you like this . . ." His masterful hands glided down her ribs, his thumbs brushing provocatively over the peaks of her breasts. "Will it be my face you see in the darkness? And when he holds you like so"—Holt drew her luscious body familiarly to his, feeling the spark of desire leap from him to her and back again—"will you be betraying your husband with another man, in spirit if not in body?"

Shiloh jerked away as if a wasp had stung her. Indeed, she felt stung! Holt made it sound as if she were already committing an unforgivable sin and she truly felt that she was. Unable to face his probing stare, Shiloh presented her back and focused on the wall.

"And what of me, Shiloh?" he whispered as he pulled her stiff back against his broad chest. Gently, he lifted her left arm, curling it back around his neck. His fingertips slid over the sensitive flesh of her arm, along her elbow, down the swell of her breast. He drew lazy circles on her belly that made her knees go weak. "Do you suppose I will reach out to some faceless female in some dusty town and touch her the way I'm touching you now? In my loneliness, will I caress her and pretend it is your delicious body beneath my fingertips? And when we make love, will I be loving you as I long to? Shall I tell her then that she was only the warm, unresisting body I utilized to compensate for the woman I really wanted? Or shall I deceive her into thinking she is the woman I need in my arms?"

"Stop it, Holt," she muttered through another flood of tears. "You are confusing me." Indescribable jealousy distorted her logic. Holt painted much too vivid a picture of his nights of passion with other lovers.

Holt flagrantly disregarded her command to stop. Instead, he reworked his subtle magic on her traitorous body, making her respond to his practiced touch. Nimble fingers unlaced her gown, leaving it drooping over her full breasts. A draft of warm kisses descended along the pulsating column of her throat, leaving fires burning in their wake.

"All the other women in my future will be you," he murmured as his hand slid beneath her gown and chemise to tease the throbbing crests. "And if I whisper my love for you to another woman in the mindless throes of passion, will you hear my whisper in the silence as well, Shiloh?"

Again her knees threatened to buckle beneath her. If not for Holt's supporting arm, she swore she would have dripped into puddles at his feet.

"What do you suggest we do about these fantasies we'll be having in the future?" she chirped, her voice ragged with unappeased desire.

467

Holt slid his right hand under her knees and lifted her into his arms. "I'm more concerned about the fantasy I'm having right now," he growled seductively. "Good God, Shiloh if you had any idea how much I want you, you would run for your life."

She had a good idea what he was feeling. If he felt as unbridled as she did, they were both in serious trouble. She was hounded by the insane urge to rip his clothes from his magnificent body and make a meal of him! He would be the one running for his life because Shiloh feared she would never be able to let him go. He aroused such primitive needs, such intense longings—ones that all the logic and common sense in the world couldn't shake.

Shiloh wasn't certain how they wound up unclothed and in bed. Her mind was in a whirl. All she knew was that they were there—kissing, touching, whispering their needs, sharing intimacies that no one could possibly understand but the two of them. And even in their urgency to rediscover each other there was an underlying gentleness in their impatience. Shiloh adored running her hands over his chest, investigating the lean, corded tendons of his back and the rock-hard muscles of his thighs.

Holt was the stuff women's dreams were made of, and she reveled in touching him as if he belonged to her and her alone. He was her sun. She drew energy from his potential strength. He was the moon that commanded the tides of passion to rush over her. He was the summer rain that quenched her parched lips and made the love she felt for him grow like a wild desert flower. He was all things to her—a part of her that time and determination had not been able to erase. Without him she was half, not whole. He had been away from her for months on end, but he could make these precious moments span forever before he left her alone again. . . .

When his flaming caresses spread over her quaking flesh like the rolling surf teasing the shore, Shiloh's mind turned to mush. His touch was magical—a spell from which she never wanted to wake. His sensuous lips tantalized and explored, weaving a silken tapestry of pleasure that caused her heart to thud furiously against her ribs. His tongue flicked at the dusky buds that begged his attention. His fingertips delved and swirled, pleasing her and driving her mad all in the same moment. The quiet whisper of love words flooded over her pliant flesh as Holt expressed his affection in the most inventive ways imaginable.

Shiloh moaned softly as wondrous sensations cascaded over her, drenching her with splendor. Holt could do what he wanted with her and she couldn't have objected to save her life. Her body possessed a will of its own. Helplessly, she responded to his love play. She needed more than his titillating kisses and caresses. She needed to feel his masculine body forged to hers, to hold him to her until the potent cravings had been appeased. She was prepared to sacrifice her last breath to feel his muscular flesh gliding intimately upon hers, to share the joy of letting her soul soar beyond the sun.

But still he didn't come to her, even when she begged him to take her to paradise and satisfy the empty ache that he alone could fulfill.

"Marry me, Shiloh," he murmured as he teased her with an erotic caress that left him so close and yet so frustrastingly far away.

"No," she managed to say before her vocal cords collapsed.

"Stubborn sprite, must I make you transform your *no* into a *yes?*" he whispered as his hands trailed lower to glide along her inner thigh.

"Just love me for now," Shiloh gulped as the mad-

469

dening tremors engulfed her.

"I have for six months," Holt breathed raggedly. Blast it, if she didn't consent . . . and quickly, he was going to be the one to buckle to this sweet torture. "I need your love, but I want you as my wife."

It wouldn't work, Shiloh told herself, battling the daze of rapture that fogged her senses. But he had bribed her with his magical brand of passion that demanded unconditional surrender. She could no longer resist, even if it was more sensible to reject his proposal.

"Yes," she murmured hoarsely.

Her supple body arched to meet his, wanting him with every part of her being, craving him like a mindless obsession. A tormented groan erupted from Holt's throat when he lowered himself to her. Quickly she absorbed his body and soul, appeasing his restless spirit. This silver-blue-eyed pixie was all he would ever need, even though he had tried to convince himself otherwise for four hellish months. If he had Shiloh, he held the world in the palm of his hand. . . .

Reality slipped from his grasp when unleashed passion crested upon him like a tidal wave. Holt felt the fierce undercurrent tugging at him. Swells of ineffable pleasure lifted him and then sent him plummeting into the sensual depths of desire. Sensations of ecstasy battered him like frothy waves crashing against a seashore. He gasped for breath, but there was no oxygen left in his lungs. And in that split-second when he was prepared to sacrifice his life in exchange for this all-consuming love that was engulfed by wild, maddening passion, he felt the hindering garments of the flesh fall away. Like a meteor blazing across the starlit heavens, he skyrocketed through time and space. Even while he lay in Shiloh's encircling arms, he felt as if he were arcing across the midnight sky. It was the sweet paradox of passion—the exquisite death in living.

His body shuddered, and numbing pleasure spilled over him. Holt crushed Shiloh to his palpitating chest and buried his face in the tangled mass of blond hair that cascaded over her shoulder. It amazed him that this spirited vixen could be such a passionate lover. But Shiloh could fulfill every fantasy when she gave herself up to the wild desires they ignited in each other.

In all the years of wandering, only one woman had the power to lure him back and make him beg to spend eternity with her. And even if Shiloh's mind was still plagued with doubts, Holt vowed to love her skepticism away until she believed she was the most important part of his life.

In the aftermath of love, Holt was still demonstrative in his affection. His light caresses fluttered over the tips of her breasts to glide down the faint swell of her abdomen. Shiloh was one of the great wonders of the world. She was absolutely exquisite. She was perfection. . . .

"So many times in the past I have longed to lie beside you, to touch you to my heart's content," he whispered.

Shiloh stretched beneath his feather-light caresses like a contented feline lounging in the sunshine. Eager to return the warm pleasure that channeled through her, Shiloh ran a tapered finger over the scar on his shoulder and followed the curve to his hip.

"If I marry you, you realize I may never let you past the bedroom door," she teased as her leg slid provocatively between his. "You may have gotten more than you bargained for. . . ."

"I think I'm getting exactly what I deserve," Holt chuckled, delighting in her playful banter.

One delicate brow arched as she regarded his rakish grin. "A mite cocky, aren't you?" she mocked.

The teasing smile slid off his lips and a solemn

471

expresson settled on his chiseled features. "I've never been in love before," he confessed. "When a man waits as long as I have for the right woman to come along, he deserves the very best." His lips grazed hers in a worshiping kiss. "You are that and so much more. I have all I want in you, Shiloh. You've become every breath I take. . . ."

"I'll keep telling myself that while you're flitting about to only God knows where," she replied, unable to prevent the resentment from infiltrating her voice.

"There aren't going to be any long months of separation,' he promised. "Pinkerton has requested that Garret and I set up an undercover headquarters at my farm in the Ozarks to monitor the train and bank robberies in Indian territory and Missouri. We will be in charge of training other detectives and tracking a few leads. If we are familiar faces in the area, we'll stand a better chance of sniffing out the locations of outlaw hideouts and prying information from citizens who wouldn't divulge any knowledge to strangers."

Shiloh blinked in surprise. "You would settle for a more sedate life after the adventures you've had?" she squeaked.

Holt nodded his tousled raven head. "Haven't you figured out yet that you mean more to me than my work?"

"I didn't think anyone or anything could matter that much to you," she said honestly.

A wry smile dangled on the corner of his sensuous mouth. "Then you have sorely underestimated your powers over me, little witch," he said huskily. "You make all the difference. . . ."

"I can have you whenever I want you?" she asked with a flirtatious smile.

"All you have to do is snap your fingers and I'll come running," he assured her before he bent to press a

472

passionate kiss on her inviting lips.

To test his generous promise, Shiloh snapped her fingers. And sure enough, Holt was willing and eager to convey his love in the midst of stormy passion. And Shiloh returned each heartfelt kiss and caress as the crescendo of desire built to a fervent pitch.

"I do love you," Holt murmured as he came to her again. "With every beat of my heart . . ."

"I love you madly," she assured him in a throaty whisper. "All I'll ever need is you. . . ."

Chapter 34

While Dog was dining on a thick, juicy steak, Victor checked his timepiece and glanced expectantly toward the hall. "How long does it take to decide whether or not there will be a wedding?" he questioned the room at large.

Garret took another sip of his drink and smiled mischievously to himself. "I'm sure Holt and Shiloh had dozens of plans to make."

Victor emitted a volcanic snort. He wasn't fooled for a minute. If Shiloh and Holt were discussing wedding plans, he would eat his hat, brim and all. It still rankled him that his daughter and Holt were lollygagging in the—

"Well, it's about time," Victor muttered when Holt and Shiloh appeared at the door.

Holt was still so distracted by the interlude that he couldn't take his eyes off the curvaceous blonde who had consented to be his wife. "We had a great many things to discuss, Colonel," he said, absorbed in the sight of twinkling silver-blue eyes.

"You mean you actually did get around to talking?" Victor grunted sarcastically.

Shiloh blushed up to the roots of her blond hair and

glanced away from her father's condescending glare. "Holt convinced me that your grandchild does need his father's constant attention as much as I do."

"Does that mean you and Garret are going to take command of the branch headquarters and arrange a guard force to patrol Victor's railroad line?" Allan questioned hopefully.

Holt nodded. "I have only one request, and that is that you see to it that Deputy Kroeker is reassigned. I don't want to risk any confrontations with him in Primrose."

"Done," Allan said with a satisfied smile. "You will save me several jaunts between Missouri and Illinois. And with the reports of the James gang terrorizing the countryside, I will have my best detectives maintain a surveillance on the trouble spots as well as train other agents for difficult assignments."

Setting his glass aside, Allan bade the McBrides good night and started toward the hotel. Garret filed out behind the detective chief. When Holt made no move to leave, Victor cast him the evil eye.

"You have yet to marry my daughter," he declared. "And knowing you as well as I do, I think you had better leave with Garret and Allan."

A roguish smile quirked Holt's lips as his appreciative gaze wandered over Shiloh's arresting figure. "Colonel, we still have a great deal left to discuss. And if you recall, I have already married Shiloh once. It seems to me that—"

Victor towed Holt toward the door. "Shiloh married Reuben Gilcrest," he clarified. "You have things to do. It will take you the rest of the evening to decide which disguise you will be wearing to the wedding. Good night, Holt."

Now, the last thing Holt wanted to do was to share a room with Garret after he and Shiloh had come to terms. Their private moments had fulfilled his wildest fantasies. Leaving Shiloh was going to force him to spend a long, frustrating night of wanting to be elsewhere.

"Good night, Holt." Shiloh stood directly behind her father, who stood directly between her and Holt. An impish smile curved her lips as she peered around her father's broad shoulder. "As quickly as time flies, it will be morning just like that—" She snapped her fingers to emphasize her point.

Holt caught the invitation in her sparkling eyes.

With his lips pursed in roguish amusement, he dropped into a courteous bow. "Very well, then, until tomorrow, Colonel . . . Shiloh."

To Victor's astonishment, Holt swaggered out the door without further protest. When he disappeared into the shadows, Victor heaved a sigh of relief. "I hope you know how pleased I truly am about the prospect of having Holt as my son-in-law," he announced as he looped his arm around Shiloh's shoulder to escort her upstairs.

Shiloh paused to give her father an affectionate hug. "I'm so happy, Papa, as happy as I have ever been. I love him. . . ."

"I know," Victor murmured.

Odd, he felt as if he were about to lose something precious and dear to him. It wasn't going to be the same anymore. For years Shiloh had been his little girl and he had been the only man in her life. Now she would become Holt's wife a second time and not a moment too soon! Shiloh had been miserable without him.

"Good night, baby. Sleep well." He sighed and then reluctantly let her go.

"I expect I will, Papa. I expect I will. . . ." A cryptic smile hovered on Shiloh's lips as she pirouetted around to sashay down the hall.

The moment Shiloh closed the bedroom door behind her, her gaze swept the shadows. And sure enough, Holt was there as he had promised to be each time she snapped her fingers. Without hesitation Shiloh dashed into his sinewy arms, marveling at the way she came alive each time she nestled in his loving embrace. She didn't bother inquiring how he had sneaked into her room so quickly. Sneaking was what this master detective did best . . . well, one of the many things he did better than anybody else, she amended as she surrendered to his explosive kisses and masterful caresses. No man could compete with Holt Cantrell in any arena. Although Holt was a man of a thousand faces, he had but one heart, and it belonged to Shiloh. And she intended to cherish the gift of Holt's love for the rest of her days.

While the two young lovers gave themselves up to the sweet, compelling fire that consumed their souls, Victor was lying abed, smiling secretively to himself. He wasn't an idiotic fool, after all. Holt Cantrell wouldn't let a little thing like a father's interference stand in the way of the woman he wanted. He had already set a precedent while portraying the role of Reuben Gilcrest. Holt hadn't been able to resist Shiloh then, nor could he now. But Victor couldn't very well come right out and invite Holt to spend the night with Shiloh. He had his image and the family's reputation to uphold. But he could turn his head the other way while Holt and Shiloh reaffirmed their affection for each other.

While Victor was speculating on how many grandchildren he would have, Shiloh and Holt were setting sail on the most intimate of journeys through time and space. *I love you* was embroidered in each tender caress

Holt bestowed on her and in each kiss Shiloh so eagerly returned. Their emotions had come full circle, and their love had withstood the test of time, trials, and torment. They had both earned their happiness and they reveled in a love so strong and yet so gentle that it would shine through eternity—like diamonds in the night.